"It's as bad as it gets. IN HER ~~PRESENCE~~ will have you sitting on the edge of your seat. You will be angry and sad while witnessing the abuse Maebelle and her children endure. My heart went out to the Poygoode family, and being the person that I am I wanted to help them. I wanted to find a way for them to escape. Can't think of a family that has it worse off than you? I introduce you to the Poygoodes."

Reviewed by Eraina B. Tinnin
of The RAWSISTAZ Reviewers
http://www.rawsistaz.com

"Here's a Suspenseful Novel Waiting For You. Nancy Weaver has written a powerful and compelling saga that covers many years on one man's family living in the southern part of the USA. The novel is inspired by real life events and is indeed a genuine SHOCKER. Be prepared to take deep breaths as you turn the pages of this gripping and riveting novel."

Reviewed by Emily Means-Willis
Literary reviewer: http://www.anutwistaflavah.com

"Nancy Weaver has proven to be a storyteller for the ages–a rising star on the scene of fiction writers. Her book brought tears to my eyes. It is an outstandingly, good down-home read. Every woman should read her book."

Delores Thornton, radio talk show host
http://www.artistfirst.com

"A masterpiece."
Irma Tyrus, Editor, NYC

"Selected Book of the month October 2004."
Souls on Wheels online bookstore

In Her Presence:
A HUSBAND'S DIRTY SECRET

In Her Presence:
A HUSBAND'S DIRTY SECRET

A Novel

By

Nancy Weaver

Time & Chance Publishing™
Staten Island, NY

Weaver

Library of Congress Card Number: 2003116574
ISBN: Soft Cover   0-9748274-0-1

Printed in the United States of America.

Published by Time & Chance Publishing™
149 Freedom Avenue, Staten Island, NY 10314.
www.timeandchancepublishing.com
Cover Design by Doing80.com

For additional information, please contact:
Time & Chance Publishing
P.O. Box 488, NY, NY 10116.

This is a work of fiction.   While as in all fiction, the
literary perceptions and insights are based on experience.
No reference to any real person living or dead is intended
or should be inferred.

All names, characters, places, and incidents either are
the product of the authors' imagination or are used
fictitiously, and any resemblance to any events, or locales
is entirely coincidental.

To order copies of this book, send your e-mail to:
E-mail: tandcpublishing@yahoo.com
Fan Mail: Gottlieb, P.O. Box 488, NY, NY 10116

Dedication

Dedicated to mothers, daughters and sons, whose lives have been shattered by the man you most loved and trusted. Like the Potter with the clay, your life can be made whole again.

Acknowledgements

I give thanks to God for giving me the gift of storytelling.

I offer my thanks to my editor, Irma Tyrus.

Much love to family and friends who keep cheering me on, especially to my aunt and uncle Bertha King and Andrew King; my friends Martha Illeghameba and Juanita Lyons—you've been very encouraging and supportive. Thanks to Tim Miller, author of *Without A Trace,* for all the guidance you gave me; and last, but not least, thanks to my former high school English/Literature teacher, Sarah Gordon-Chambliss, an excellent teacher and inspirational writer.

Most of all, I am infinitely grateful to my beloved husband, Kenneth, whose echo I always hear when I'm in limbo over a project that I'm working on; "You can do it, Nancy. I believe in you." I give thanks to my precious daughters La'Shima—and June, who kept asking me when are you going to let me read your manuscript, when are you going to publish it? I give thanks to my beloved son, Melason for believing in me, telling me to go for it. You are all my joy—my world.

Author's Remarks

The author has attempted to use as little profanity as possible so as not to turn off her audience. Yet, she wishes to lend depth to the characters lives and the hardship they faced, growing up in a rich, but, nevertheless, degenerate household.

A dangerous Pursuit

In the late 1950's amid segregation, Beulah Creek, Mississippi, is a barren place for a girl searching for the perfect husband. Maebelle Hawkins, a 5'4" dark-skinned beauty—divorced with mouths to feed—moves her children to Derriene Crossing, seeking for a perfect husband—a man with money, power, and prestige—her definition of the perfect husband.

Upon her arrival, a night out on the town is what she needs. She struts up in a Juke house, owned by Rufus Poygoode, a tall, handsome man, who is anything but a gentleman, who some folks say is one of the wealthiest landowners in Derriene Crossing, Mississippi. He is a man whose wedding vows are about as important to him as a half-hearted promise that he never intended to keep.

Maebelle's heart shivers when he asks her for a dance. It is love at first sight, but Rufus is a rare creature. When he first lays eyes on her, believing she is the daughter of the aunt who abused him, she awakens sleeping demons deep inside him. Before long, he would give her more than she dared to get.

"I don't trust Rufus," Leslie Wills said. "My brother Brandon has told me so many bad things about him. I know he doesn't like dark-skinned women. I'm not saying this to hurt you. I'm only telling you because we've been friends forever, and I care about you."

"Well, I wish you wouldn't always try to be such a good friend," Maebelle mumbles, ignoring her warnings.

Chapter 1

Maebelle thought it was romantic of Rufus to plan a surprise picnic for her on that warm Sunday afternoon. None of her past dates had ever done anything so touching for her. Rufus was her ideal man. He had money, land, good looks, and charm that could con a rattlesnake into submission.

However, something had gone seriously wrong at the picnic—for no apparent reason—at least not one that she could figure out. She only noticed a change in his disposition after the blood had drained from his face. Then, the next thing she knew, he was ordering her to get in the pickup.

Seated inside the pickup almost in tears, Maebelle watched Rufus through the windshield, as he quickly gathered up the picnic remains, packed them into the basket, and hurried back toward the pickup. She watched him as he placed the basket and blanket in back of the pickup; she watched him open the door and climb inside the pickup without ever lifting his eyes. During the entire drive, he never spoke a word. And she had been too afraid and too confused to attempt any communication.

Now, here she was, showered with dust, dumped like an old sack of potatoes in front of her friend, Leslie Wills' house, confused as ever, and scared as hell. She didn't want to lose Rufus. Even though they had only known each other for a few weeks, she was already in love with him.

"What happened?" she muttered.

Glaring at the ground, she went over everything that had happened between them, trying to figure out what had induced his frightening mood-swing and caused him to dump her like that.

Maebelle began at the point when they spread the blanket on the lush green grass and sat down next to each other. He made a remark about his wife, Charlotte,

1

being an outstanding chef, which she thought was inappropriate. Perhaps she'd over reacted, but they had gotten pass that. She watched the way he meticulously tore apart the biscuit and placed the breast of chicken inside. When their mouths weren't full, they engaged in amicable conversation.

Then out of the blue, he asked her if she were sure she had never heard her parents speak of some woman named Olga Berry. Of course, she had grown upset, and rightfully so, because he had asked her that question for the umpteenth time, and she had said no for the umpteenth time. What? Did he really think her answer would be any different today than it had been a week ago? Today she had given him an irritable, level look and had said "no" vehemently. He looked away, staring vacantly for a long moment. Then she saw him looking at her out the corner of his left eye, as if he still didn't believe her.

Maebelle remembered how Rufus washed down the biscuit sandwich with a cold drink. Then he reclined on the blanket, propping his head against a fallen log. He crossed his ankles, and looked before him at nothing in particular, that she could see. She thought he was avoiding her, so she approached him. Suddenly, Rufus grabbed her hand and pulled her down. She wrestled with him. She ended up sprawled on top of him. His hands pressed hard on her lower back. He pulled her closer to him. She tried not to face him. However, their eyes met, and she detected menacing anger. Was he the type to force himself on a woman, despite her resistance, she wondered?

She willed herself not to yield as she tried to release his grip. She wanted to avoid the mistakes of the past—giving herself freely to men before they barely knew each other. Suddenly, she found herself allowing him to indulge, as his strong fingers roamed freely, until they nearly touched her hot, moist garden. She did a safe thing as she pushed him back.

"Maybe he got upset because of that," she muttered.

"No! That can't be. I'm sure he's been rejected before."

An alarm went off in Maebelle's head. Thinking that maybe it was something about her breasts, he didn't like. During the next few minutes, she repeatedly asked herself, why didn't he like her, like she likes him?

She threw her hands in the air, stomped her right foot, and looked up at the sky. "I give up!" she exclaimed. She was anxious to understand him.

If the truth were told, Maebelle's breasts did rock Rufus' secret world and shifted his emotions into his murky past. He recalled seeing breasts like hers many years ago. They reminded him of his surrogate mother– Aunt Olga Berry's breasts. She and Maebelle had an unusually dark, broad ring circling their nipples—much larger than most women's breasts he'd seen—even their striking resemblance bore high cheekbones and smooth, velvety, black skin. To his surprise, as he began kissing her firmly, his arousal became limp. If he had decided to rape her, it didn't matter. He didn't have the means necessary.

Maebelle had no idea she was endangered. She fell for Rufus since the night she danced with him, at his wild juke house, as his party crowd watched them, right after he cut in on her dance with a guy name John Puntier, she had just met. Thereafter, she practically threw herself at him; and though he responded, that night actually marked the beginning of his suspicion that Maebelle was the daughter of his surrogate mother–Aunt Olga Berry.

Over the years, Rufus carried a grueling vendetta against his mother-Aunt Olga Berry. She had been cruel and sexually abusive. He often vowed the day would come when he would get even with Olga, or her daughters, if it were the last thing he did on earth. So when he first noticed Maebelle, and got to know her a bit more, she became his ideal target to pay back Olga.

3

Now, he was rushing to Dobbs County to see his confidant, Mr. Walker, nicknamed I Does, to ask him about Olga's estranged daughters.

****

It had been a while since Leslie heard the car door open and close. Not expecting anybody, she languidly headed towards the door. Peering through the screen, she saw Maebelle standing awkwardly by the side of the road, fanning dust out of her face. Leslie pushed opened the screen door and stepped onto the porch. "Maebelle?" Leslie cried.

Maebelle turned around, startled. "Oh, God," she said through clenched teeth, imaging an open ground swallowing her up. "How long has Leslie been standing there?" she wondered.

"Hi... nosy," Maebelle said lightheartedly. She tried blocking the bright sunlight from her eyes, while awaiting Leslie's reaction. Leslie stopped at the edge of the porch, watching the direction where Rufus' pickup was heading.

"Well, Hi," Leslie sighed, as her head wiggled momentarily. She was spontaneously sarcastic. "Are you coming in, or just standing out here, inhaling the dust the booty-man left behind?"

Maebelle hung her head in embarrassment. She subdued herself, as she slowly strode toward the house, knowing that Leslie was meddling in her business. "How long were you on your porch?" she asked.

"Long enough," Leslie said, shrugging her shoulders. Her hands were on her hips, as she focused on the dust ball left by Rufus' pickup. Giving Maebelle her full attention, Leslie pried. "Now, Maebelle, do you, or do you not know that man have a family? You've got no business messing with him, right?"

Though Maebelle wanted to tell Leslie to kiss her behind, she climbed her porch steps, preparing to sound less vulgar, yet bitter. "Mind your own damn business,

Leslie! Remember, I'm here to pick up my kids, not to hear your big mouth." Intuition told her to charm Leslie. "And before we start arguing, please let me say thank you for taking my children off my hands. Now, will you be kind enough to bring my little ones to their mother? Please tell them I'm here, because I can't hang around, I have so much work at home with six kids, you know."

Leslie's mouth fell open; her usually cool temper suddenly flared.

"Look!" she said, pointing a stiff, long, thin finger. "Let's you and I get something straight right now, Sister Love! Just because I take your children to church, something you ought to be doing yourself instead of running around with Charlotte's husband, don't you dare think I'm your baby-sitter! Now sit your behind down, because I have some choice words for you. You don't learn, do you? You've only recently moved here and already you're living wild. I thought you came here to make a change."

Maebelle shot her an angry glance. Plopping down on the ladder-back chair, looking up at Leslie, eyes blazing, Maebelle retorted, "You're always trying to act like you're my mother! My parents are dead! Neither of them left you in charge before they died. I'm grown, Leslie. I'm 28, dammit! You're only one year older!"

Maebelle paused momentarily. "Why don't you want me to have myself a man? Okay?"

Leslie didn't respond, knowing she could never talk sense into Maebelle's head.

"Child, he's got so much money!" Maebelle continued arrogantly with her hand on her right hip. "And he's so good looking! I never saw a black man with hazel eyes and red hair." A sinister smile crept on her lips. "Leslie, now really. You're just jealous," Maebelle said, not looking directly at Leslie. "You should start looking, too. Wills' been dead for over a year, right?"

Leslie pursed her lips, nodding in disbelief. In her opinion Maebelle was a rather indignant self-centered mother.

"The kids are eating lunch," Leslie said, changing the subject. Later, they'll go play ball. Are you hungry? I made collards, potato salad, and baked ham."

Maebelle rubbed a hand across her belly. "No thank you. I'm stuffed. I just returned from a picnic with Rufus."

Hearing her own words echo, she felt a ripple of sadness. It hurt to even say Rufus' name, knowing their relationship was becoming difficult. Pretentiously happy, she smiled at Leslie. "Guess what? I didn't lift a finger. Rufus planned the whole thing; brought all the food."

Leslie's brow arched in disapproval, as Maebelle planted a wicked smirk on her face, while staring at the long rows of young, tender cotton stalks.

"The food his wife cooked, right?" Leslie retorted.

With a few quips under her sleeve, Leslie brushed the back of her skirt with her hands before sitting down on the porch swing.

"It sure is nice out," Leslie said, yawning and stretching her arms above her head. Her eyes were moist. "You should come to church sometimes. Our sermons are good. That Reverend Weeks can preach!" She leaned forward with her face close to Maebelle's. "As a matter of fact, today he preached on what you're doing."

Maebelle grunted, looking away from Leslie. "I'm not interested in what some old-ass, jack-leg preacher has to say. The very things they preach against, they do. They're all up in these silly women houses eating the food from the children. They climb in bed with the women as soon as their husbands' backs are turned. You heard how old Reverend Douglas Diggs died in Dede Wells' saddle. No, child. Uh-uh, I'm no hypocrite. Besides, I'm young," she said happily, as though youth was without its consequences. "I'll serve the Lord when I'm too old to smell my own fart. Know what I mean?" She nonchalantly lifted a hand and bit off a jagged fingernail, and spat it on the floor. "I'm living my life as I see fit."

Then, Maebelle's temper suddenly flared out of control. She felt Leslie was antagonizing her. "Get the hell off my back! Stay out of my business! I don't need to hear this shit from you whenever I come here, Ms. Holy-Roller." Silence fell amongst the two friends.

Momentarily, Maebelle realized she hadn't really meant to fly off the handle, and that her angry reaction toward Leslie was a reflection of the anxiety she felt toward Rufus. She bet his attitude had to do with that Olga person, and his belief that she was related to her. She was sick of it, already. She always told him she didn't know any damn Olga Berry.

Leslie was startled by Maebelle's strange conduct. She sank back in the swing with her arms covering her chest, as she crossed her ankles. She started laughing.

"You know, girl, the devil got you thinking you've found yourself a prince in shining armor, never mind that the man is already married."

Leslie sat up straight. "I don't mean to be cruel," she continued. "Don't you notice the color of those women, the same women who sat around the bar hissing at you when you strutted up in that juke house a couple of weeks ago, like you were somebody special?"

Maebelle gave Leslie a baffled look, wondering how she could've known what occurred at the juke house.

"You know I don't hang out at anybody's juke houses," Leslie remarked, vociferously. "So don't look at me that way. John Puntier told my brother Brandon all about you, and Brandon told me. John is sweet on you, you know. At least that's what he told Brandon."

Leslie paused. "I heard that you and John were rather disgusting on the dance floor before Rufus cut in on you all. You know—why don't you take up with John? He's single, and he's good-looking. I mean, since you're so desperate for a husband. He's a nice man."

Maebelle didn't comment. Leslie's persistence continued. "Oh! And this is something you're probably not aware of. John told Brandon that when you appeared in the juke house, Rufus looked at you like he saw a ghost from hell! I'm telling you, girl, something isn't right about all this! You know, he's been asking a lot of questions about you, too. To be honest, you're not the right complexion for him. Everybody, except you, of course, knows the man likes women his own complexion. I'm telling you, girl, you'd better be careful."

In deep thought, Maebelle didn't answer. Leslie's remarks weighed heavily on her mind. She felt perturbed. Leslie quickly observed Maebelle's uneasiness.

"You and I have been friends since we were little girls, Maebelle. It's hard to see you headed for trouble, and don't warn you. I'm a real friend; you know that. I'm not saying things just to hurt you."

Maebelle sighed heavily. "You know, Leslie, sometimes I wish you wouldn't try to be such a good friend. You really get on my nerves."

Leslie reached out and put a hand on Maebelle's knee. "I can't help it. I've known you too long."

Feeling utter resentment for Leslie, Maebelle looked away. She crossed her knees so Leslie's hand would fall off her lap.

"Look, Maebelle," Leslie said, indifferent to Maebelle's actions. "I do sympathize with your being divorced with those two boys and four girls. I know you would like to re-marry. You said you couldn't find anybody in Beulah Creek, so you came here looking. You're aiming too high for the wrong man. Ever since I've known you, you've been careless. You'll see a man you want and go after him and think about the consequences later. I know what you're thinking. You're thinking that if you get Rufus to leave his wife and marry you, you'll be set for life—and he has the means to set you up. But he's no Jake Blakestone, Maebelle. You don't want that kind of man over your children, especially your girls! Those girls—Jinni and Jennifer—are blossoming like young magnolia trees in the springtime. Before you know anything, Rufus will be drawn to those girls like a bear to honey. Why don't you try patching things up with Jake?"

Maebelle held her head down. Fat chance that will ever happen, she thought. Knowing it was Jake who'd sued her for the divorce. There was a lapse in conversation.

Tilting her head to one side, Leslie looked Maebelle in the face. "You got your eyes on that man's money and land, don't you? Love has nothing to do with it, does it?

It does, Maebelle thought to herself. I love Rufus.

"You've come here and fallen in love overnight," Leslie stated sarcastically. You were always money-hungry! Its why you stole Jake from your oldest sister Pauline, and kept leading Jake into that barn, until you got your belly pumped up. Am I right?"

Maebelle's cold eyes fell upon Leslie. "You're doing all the talking, like I'm the child; and you're my mama, dredging up all my mistakes."

Leslie laughed. She decided to change the subject; but, of course, Maebelle wouldn't appreciate what she was about to say any better.

"It doesn't bother you that he's aping the white man with all that land he's got, does it? That's what he's doing, you know."

"No, it doesn't bother me!" Maebelle snapped. "Hell, no! Why should it? Like others, he has earned his way in life." She shot Leslie an indifferent glance.

"Well, I'll tell you something else about him you may not know," Leslie said. "He hates paying people what they're worth. He's mad that Charlotte won't spit out a bunch of babies for him so he can put them to work in the field. But I suppose you think you're willing to do what Charlotte got enough sense not to do. But should you do get him to marry you, which I doubt, it'll only be because of what he thinks he can get from you—a bunch of children just so he can work them like slaves. But, may God help you!"

Maebelle felt like putting a fist in Leslie's mouth. She didn't reply.

Leslie went on. Once she got started it was hard to stop her.

"I know you've seen all his other women hanging around the bar. But I tell you what. Not one of them is anxious to take him from his wife. You know why? They're scared of him. They see how he's trampling all over Charlotte. He won't even allow her to leave the farm. She probably hasn't been in to town since her granddaddy died. That's because Rufus' jealous; he doesn't want other men looking at her, if you ask me." She paused. "I'm telling you, he'll work your kids' fingers to the bone, and yours too. You won't become a queen like Charlotte, born into money, and never worked a day in her life."

Maebelle was seething. "Oh shut up! I'm not listening," she said, as her hands covered her ears.

Leslie just laughed. "Rufus has got all that land!" she cried. "And looking to get more! It's not honest money he's buying all that land with, you know? He's just like these white crackers profiting from other people's misery. Running that whorehouse, and making and selling illegal whiskey! He gets away with it because he's paying the white man off."

Maebelle turned around on her seat and faced Leslie. "It's a juke-house, where people dance, drink, and smoke! And what's wrong with him wanting to own a lot of land? You're one to talk. Look at you. That's why you married old Mr. Willie Wills. He's old enough to be your great-grandpa! God bless the dead." Maebelle chuckled because she really knew Willie was not that old when he married Leslie.

Leslie swallowed hard, sinking back in the swing, fixing Maebelle with an angry frown. "Maebelle, I'm so disappointed in you." Her voice shook. "Wills and I loved each other. Of course, he owned quite a bit of land, but he inherited most of it from his father; the rest . . . well, he got it honestly. He was a good family man! Nothing like that rascal you're chasing. Besides, you're a complete stranger to him. You think he's going to . . . Forget it," she said, throwing up her hands in exasperation. "You do what you want. You always have! He doesn't mean you any good. I know. I can feel it in my spirit." Rufus' greed irritated Leslie, not to mention how he used and abused women, and then left them. She couldn't stand him.

Enraged, Maebelle sprang to her feet, and got right up in Leslie's face, pointing a finger at her. "Now listen to me, Ms. Holier-than-Thou! I'm sick and tired of you always talking to me about your damn spirit!"

"Yuk!" Leslie frowned, lifting a hand and wiping the spit Maebelle sprayed on her top lip. She wanted to slap some sense into Maebelle's thick skull. Maebelle was now furious as she began to speak, pointing at Leslie.

"Get your finger out of my face!" Leslie ordered. "Who the hell do you think you are, putting your finger in my face like that? I've not once put mine in yours! Not once!" Maebelle withdrew her finger.

Maebelle was embarrassed, but determined. "Well, you know something? I feel things in my spirit, too. Guess what I'm feeling?" She cocked a thumb and pointed at her crotch. "I feel his *thang* in my...!" Maebelle quickly recanted, shocked by her lewd words.

Leslie scrambled to her feet and stood near Maebelle. "Ump! Don't tell me he's already been in it! I can't imagine that! And how does he show his appreciation? By putting dust in it!" She laughed as her head rolled back on her shoulders.

"Oh! And then he drove away and left you standing on the road like a complete fool! What else happened between you two?" Leslie sat down on the swing, crossed her ankles, waiting for Maebelle's reply.

"You know something?" Maebelle remarked. "Think what you want. I've had enough of you. I'm going home!"

11

"Go home!" Leslie retorted. "Just remember, Charlotte is an educated woman—unlike somebody else I know." She knew that remark struck Maebelle, but she was being honest. This was the only way she could get Maebelle to understand.

Maebelle stomped her feet. "Damn you, you yellow heffa! I cook for one of the richest white families in the county. I'm just as good as anybody! Don't talk about my not being educated. You yellow heffas all think you're somebody special. I look better than your butt, any day. I got nice hips, nice legs, and nice thighs. You're a tall, flat-booty, plain yellow piece of mess! Wasn't for your hair you'd be pitiful!"

Leslie quickly digested Maebelle's razor sharp words. Quivering, she realized she had set herself up for that one. Knowing she didn't have so-called fine features; nevertheless, she never considered herself ugly. No one had ever called her ugly. She felt like slapping Maebelle.

Nearly a minute passed before Leslie responded. "The truth is, you're not criticizing me, honey! You're criticizing God! He made us all! And another thing, we all taste delicious to the maggots. Black-skinned, yellow-skinned, white-skinned—my mother once said—it's all a delicious meal to the maggots." Maebelle refused to comment and nearly five minutes passed before either woman spoke.

Maebelle moved to the end of the porch. Toward the back of the house the children were playing ball. She hated to break up their game, but she'd had all she could take from Leslie. Right now, she wanted Leslie out of her life.

Leslie approached Maebelle again. Maebelle glanced out the side of her left eye at her.

"That Jennifer is as smart as a whip!" Leslie remarked, changing the subject. "Loves church! She told me she wants to be a school teacher when she grows up."

"I know," Maebelle replied. Her voice was flat.

"You know what?" Leslie quizzed, just to see if Maebelle had heard the part about church.

Maebelle faced Leslie. "I know she's smart, dammit! She took after her daddy, and not after me. Satisfied?"

Leslie shook her head, feeling slightly sorry for Maebelle for having removed herself from God and the church.

"What's the matter?" Leslie asked, hearing Maebelle's heavy sigh.

None of your business, Maebelle thought silently. She was, however, willing to give Leslie the benefit of the doubt.

"Oh, I'm just thinking about tomorrow." Maebelle lied. Nonetheless, she elaborated. "Monday is always the hardest day of the week for me. Sometimes I think the Klappers deliberately entertain their wild animal-friends every weekend, just to sit back and watch me work like a slave. I'm supposed to be the cook, you know. But whenever Thelma doesn't come in, which always seems to be a Monday, I must cook and clean. I'm so tired of cleaning up behind nasty-ass, rich, white folks. You've no idea. I got to remarry, Leslie. I know you don't like what I'm doing, but I'm tired of living this way. It's so hard trying to make ends meet by myself. Look at you. Wills did right by you and the boys. He was the perfect husband, as far as I'm concerned. I'm just another colored woman needing a nice husband."

Leslie looked away, abstractly. Yes. Wills did do right by us, she thought. Thank God. But sometimes I'm lonely for companionship, too, like I'm feeling now. But, I won't confess that to Maebelle. She placed a hand on Maebelle's shoulder.

"I think I know how you're feeling. I'm only warning you about Rufus because I care about you. My brother, Brandon, has told me so many bad things about him. He's no good. I don't trust him."

13

Nancy Weaver

Maebelle hunched her shoulder. "Yeah, well, I've heard enough." She walked away, calling her children. "Children! Come on. We have to leave now. I got things to do around the house!"

"So, what are you going to do, Maebelle? At least think about the things I've told you?"

Maebelle nodded. Again, she became angry. "You know, Leslie…! Forget it!"

"Well, just remember he's not a nice husband; otherwise, he wouldn't be cheating with you, never mind all those other women." Maebelle ignored her, as she stormed down the steps without saying good-bye.

"Our friendship is over," she shouted, turning back toward Leslie. "You hear me! I said it's over! You sound like a damn broken record! Every time I come over here, it's the same mess! Your mouth alone will drive a person crazy!"

"You'll be back," Leslie mumbled.

Leslie stood on the porch, watching Maebelle and her children walk down the gravel road. Maebelle was walking so fast she was nearly running.

Jennifer, Jackie, Jinni and Lynn walked with their arms entwined. They turned around and chorused good-bye. "Come get us next Sunday, please!"

"See you bright and early," Leslie called back. She resumed her joy, as she looked across the yard, watching her three young sons toss the ball to each other.

A warm, gentle afternoon, May, breeze fingered through her long, coarse black hair. Moments later, she went inside her house. She knew Maebelle didn't care what she had said about that 'ol dog, Rufus, but she did wonder why he was speeding.

****

Half way to Dobbs County, Rufus started wondering what the hell he was doing.

"I should've raped your ass!" Conveniently ignoring the fact that his glory pole had become useless. "Either I

14

trust my eyes or I don't." He guessed he didn't because he didn't turn the pickup around.

He started rationalizing the situation. He just needed to be certain, beyond any doubt, as to who Maebelle is. She had adamantly denied she'd ever heard of anyone by the name of Olga Berry. He knew she could've been lying. He had to be sure because he had plans for her. His mind shifted to I Does.

How Walker could ever let anybody nickname him I Does was beyond him. From Beulah Creek, Mississippi, to Dobbs County, Mississippi, everybody called him I Does. It was because whenever Walker spoke of himself, he was always saying, I does this, or I does that.

I Does was in his eighties. He had spent most of his life in Beulah Creek, but because of family connections, he knew people from far away and nearby.

When Rufus arrived in Dobbs County, one of I Does' neighbors informed him that I Does had passed away over the winter. Rufus felt devastated—not necessarily over I Does' death—but because he couldn't ask him about Maebelle, or her people. There was only one thing left to do: He'd return to Chancy, Louisiana, and face the demon that had abused him. Trick the witch, if he had to into telling him Maebelle was one of her estranged daughters. He wished Olga Berry hadn't given away her girls! Then it would be easy to know who Maebelle is. But, what would he say to Olga Berry when they were face to face? Well, he would tell her Maebelle had waltzed into his life, wait for her response. Once she acknowledged Maebelle was her daughter, he would tell her what he planned to do.

If vengeance isn't sweet, then it isn't vengeance, he thought. Having made up his mind to go to Chancy, Louisiana, he returned home to get his suitcase.

* * *

Later, he pulled into his yard. He rushed up the porch steps and entered the house. The house was quiet, except for the ticking clock, hanging on the living room wall. He had a feeling Charlotte wouldn't be home. Damn her, he thought.

He moved toward the kitchen and drew back the curtain. He felt rage when he saw Charlotte with his daughter, Sari, sitting on Mrs. Daisy's back porch. He withdrew his hand and spat out a few chosen curse words. Charlotte practically lived at Mrs. Daisy's house in his absence. For she had no other social contact, except for those rare occasions when John or Clarence would stop by the house on business. Rufus would call on her to bring them a soda pop or a glass of water. He would keep a close eye on them and her.

Annoyed, Rufus walked away from the window. He stopped and looked back at the curtains to see if they had fallen back neatly into place, conscious that Charlotte was a good housekeeper. He loved that about her. But he also believed that was partly the reason she had refused to bear more children. She was too in love with the house.

He spotted a pile of neatly folded paper bags on the kitchen table. He grabbed one of the bags, reached inside his shirt pocket and brought out a pencil. He scribbled a crude note on the bag: Why in hell can't you stay your skinny ass home sometimes? I have to go out of town. I would like to have had sex with my wife before I left. He stuck the pencil back in his shirt pocket and pushed the note aside.

Flustered, he pulled the chair out from the table and sat down. He hooked an arm over the back of the chair and drummed his fingers on the table, thinking hard about Maebelle and Olga Berry. He found it difficult going back and facing the woman who'd scarred him for the rest of his life. If it turned out Maebelle was, indeed, her estranged daughter, he vowed to use Maebelle to get back at her. He would live with Maebelle, sire children with both her and her four beautiful daughters, and get the field hands that he was dying to have.

I'm tired of paying out good money to other people to work my land, he thought to himself. But first I have to figure out a way to get Maebelle to get rid of her two boys. His mind shifted back to Charlotte.

He moved back toward the window and drew the curtain. A surge of jealousy rose inside him when he saw Sari seated at the old woman's feet. Although the old woman treated him courteously, his gut feelings were that deep down inside she didn't like him, which is probably why she won't sell me her land, he thought. Her dark brown eyes always seemed to hold some deep, dark secret. "Lord only knows what Charlotte's been saying about me." He took a breath, then turned and moved toward the bedroom.

He kept a packed suitcase for times he needed to go away on short notice. He took it off the closet shelf and moved through the living room onto the porch. He locked the door. Inside the pickup, he started the engine, and drove towards John's house.

He would talk to John concerning Tuesday night card game. When he got to John's house, his white Chevy pickup was not parked in the yard. With all that had happened, he had forgotten that today was Sunday, and that John went to church on Sundays. "Damn!" he muttered.

With dismay, he stepped on the gas and headed toward Clarence Allison's place. He dreaded seeing Clarence's wife, Claire, who didn't hide her contempt for him, although he never did anything to her. He guessed it was because Clarence ran his whisky business.

When Rufus reached the house, Clarence and Claire were in the garden putting down seedlings. Rufus laughed when he saw Claire. She always reminded him of a long-legged ostrich. "Sure looks like a Quaker to me," he muttered. He pulled into the yard and tooted his horn and left the engine idle.

Claire and Clarence straightened. "Oh no! What's he doing here?" Claire complained. "I hope he doesn't think he's coming to dinner."

"Hardly," Clarence replied. "I think the man knows you just might poison him."

Claire gazed at Clarence with her moody eyes. "Oh?"

"It's true, baby. You never speak back when the man speaks to you. He knows you don't like him."

Claire shrugged. "What's there to like? He's a whoremaster and a wife-beater. I think he hates women."

Clarence looked at her thoughtfully.

"Don't get me wrong. There is certainly no reason for you to like him." He handed her the bucket of seedlings. "Are you going to continue planting, or are you calling it a day?"

"I'm calling it a day!" she replied, then snatched the bucket from him.

Clarence smiled apologetically. "This shouldn't take long," he said, walking toward Rufus.

Claire hurried out the garden and up the front porch steps, fussing under her breath. She went inside the house, slamming the door hard behind her, to let Rufus know he wasn't welcomed.

Rufus stood outside his pickup, resting his right arm over the sill.

"Hey, man!" Clarence said. They pumped hands. "Everything all right?"

"Yeah, yeah," Rufus said, glancing at the house. "I didn't mean to take you and the Misses away from your gardening. She looks fed up."

Clarence glanced slightly at the house, scratched his head. "Oh, well, we were just about to call it a day, anyway. So what brings you by?"

"Well, I have to go down to Chancy, Louisiana . . ."

"Oh!" said Clarence, cutting him off. "You're not thinking about running whiskey way down there, are you?"

Rufus grinned, rubbing his forehead. "Nah, man. I'm not about to risk getting locked up in some strange city." He heard himself call Chancy, Louisiana, a strange city, and wondered why he had said it, knowing he grew up there. "No," he said. "We got plenty local business."

He changed the subject.

"You think you'll be seeing your cousin John any time soon? I went by his house, but he wasn't home."

"I'll see him tomorrow night, matter of fact. We're delivering whiskey to the juke house, right?"

Rufus snapped his finger. "That's right! I forgot. Well, let him know he should get the place ready for the card game on Tuesday night, in case I don't make it back on time. And tell him to check on my foreman, make sure he takes good care of my livestock."

Clarence slapped him on the shoulder good-naturedly. "Don't worry about a thing. I'll tell him. We'll look after everything. There's nothing to worry about."

Rufus noticed Claire peeking out from behind the curtain. Seeing Rufus looking at her, she jerked her head and moved away from the window. Rufus looked at Clarence and said, "Well, I'm going. Your wife just looked out the window until she saw me."

Clarence peered at his house. Trying to ignore her wrath, he told Rufus that Claire was waiting for him to eat dinner with her.

"Well, don't let me keep you," Rufus replied, as he opened the door and got in his pickup.

Clarence stood back, jingling the loose change in the deep part of his pocket.

Rufus put the pickup in gear and backed onto the gravel road. He straightened the wheels, then honked the horn, and drove in the general direction toward the highway.

Clarence waved good-bye. As he entered the house through the kitchen, the aroma of green-fried tomatoes made his mouth water. He pulled a chair out from the table and sat down.

19

Claire was still standing over the stove, stirring the green-fried tomatoes. "What did that old heathen want?" she asked, disdainfully.

"Oh, he wants me to give John a message about the card game that's coming up on Tuesday night, and to tell him to keep an eye on his foreman."

"Why couldn't he tell him himself?"

"John wasn't home, baby. Church service probably ran late, as usual."

Claire saw him frowning.

"What's the matter? Why are you frowning?"

Clarence stirred in his chair. "Oh, I don't know. I'm just thinking about Rufus, and the trip he's making to Chancy, Louisiana. I was just wondering if this trip has anything to do with that woman Rufus chased John away from. I told you about her, remember? I told you she hasn't long moved here. He's been asking unusual questions about her."

"What did you say her name was, again?" Claire asked. "And where is she from?"

Clarence extended his leg and crossed his ankles. "Her name's Maebelle Hawkins. She used to be married to a cat name Jake Blakestone. According to John, she comes from Beulah Creek. You know? John and I can't understand why Rufus has gone after her.

"Baby, I'm telling you! When that woman first strutted up in that juke house...!" He licked his lip. "Rufus looked at her like he saw a ghost straight from hell! Everybody saw that! A few minutes later he chased John away from her. He was real rude about it, too. He told John, 'Your break is over. Go back to serving drinks.' John was hot! I don't have to tell you about his temper. That 21-year old young stud was hot I tell you, by the way Rufus disrespected him. John and I still don't know what's going on between them two."

"Ump. I don't know what to make of it, either," Claire remarked.

Then Clarence suddenly burst out laughing. Claire stared at him.

"What's so funny?" she asked.

"Rufus' other women," Clarence replied. He uncrossed his ankles and sat up straight in his chair. "They were hissing like a pack of jealous pussycats when Maebelle come strutting up in the juke house, acting like she was somebody special done hit the town. One thing for sure, though, Derriene Crossing won't ever be the same. I'm telling you! Rufus has always stayed away from dark meat. But she's one fine looking babe, though. I suppose after he saw that she wasn't who he thought she was he went after her fast, right in front of his other women. ...And the way they danced together! Wow!"

Claire's brow shot up. She wondered if she should start feeling insecure with all the going-on Clarence was witnessing. So far, he gave her no reason to doubt the stability of their marriage. Nevertheless, she wished he would stay out of the juke houses.

"I tell you, Claire, his other women were just about yowling." He laughed. Claire found herself laughing with him until her side ached. Then, she sobered and said, "New stuff in town, huh?"

"I guess you could say that. But you and I both know that that's not the kind of stuff any of us ever thought Rufus would ever mess with. Everybody is suspicious. Women with my complexion never were his cup of tea. Rufus always liked the kind that looks like you."

Claire stood speechless. She wadded the dishrag and playfully threw it in his face. "Don't use me as an example for that 'ol creep!" she said mildly, as she put her arm around her husband's shoulder. "When will you stop running his whiskey business?"

Clarence grabbed Claire around her waist. "Soon, baby, soon. Just be patient with me a little bit longer," he replied, as he pressed his lips on hers.

Nancy Weaver

Chapter 2

Rufus arrived in Chancy, Louisiana, early Monday morning, bleary-eyed and totally exhausted. He drove slowly through the downtown area, equivalent to three city blocks, in search of a place to stay.

The town's century-old red brick courthouse supported by tall, white columns, stood tall and stately in the Public Square. Rufus stared warily at the solemn-faced strangers bustling on the sidewalks, en route to work. White men wearing dark pinstripe suits, toting brief cases, entered and exited the huge doors of the courthouse. A few people milled around outside. Yellow, purple, and white tulips circled the tree trunks lining the sidewalk. This old small town had barely changed over the past twenty- odd years, except for two new restaurants.

He crossed the railroad tracks into a part of town that was familiar. He relaxed a little, as he noticed that Mr. Wallace Simon's cafe was still standing. The old one-story structure held a trunk full of memories for Rufus. In one of the back rooms, Lucas Wilburn, nicknamed Lucky Fingers, had taught Rufus the art of a winning hand in card games and other vices, to survive in a world that white men claimed as their own.

Mixed emotions stirred throughout his weary body. In spite of everything he had been through, Rufus had beaten the odds. As a Negro, he educated himself, and found his niche in the so-called white man's America. He was a powerful Negro landowner now—with white men eating out of his back pocket.

To his left, a young Chinaman was pulling boxes of wares out of his store and lining them along the sidewalk.

Surprisingly, after all these years, Mr. Bartoe's Funeral Home was also still standing, leaning tired and worn. Rufus groaned upon recalling his once-upon-a-time fascination with corpses. Weird, he thought now, remembering as a youngster, with no money in his pocket, and nothing to do, how he would visit the funeral home and stare at the dead corpses. Back then he wondered if it was possible that the corpses would awaken, climb out of their caskets, and start life where they'd left off. He could still hear Mr. Bartoe speaking to him in what sounded like riddles back then. 'Wherever the tree falls, son, so shall it lie. Their work is finished whether it was good or bad. I've been in this business twenty years and none of 'em ever woke up and got up out of them caskets. If one of them ever does, I assure you, boy, I'll quit the undertaker business and get the hell on up outta here!' In retrospect, those were very lonely years for Rufus. Suddenly, a wave of panic engulfed him. He was having an anxiety attack, due to past memories. He inhaled and exhaled, trying to forget his youth.

He hung a right off Main Street, onto Florida Grove. Just ahead was Bee Henderson's two-story gray, wood-frame boardinghouse. She stood on the porch, wearing a white apron over her dress, and clutching a long-handled straw broom.

Rufus parked the pickup, killed the engine, and removed the key from the ignition. He opened the door and climbed out, dragging his suitcase with him, and sauntered toward the boardinghouse. She probably won't remember me, he thought—not that it was important. He preferred she didn't.

Bee Henderson had only seen him that once when he brought Ina Wilson, his first real girlfriend, who was his age, to the boardinghouse to rent a room. It was rumored that Bee rented rooms by the hour.

Coincidentally, Bee Henderson had stood on the front porch in the same manner back then. He was amazed that he could remember that so vividly. Back then Bee's hair fell loosely on her shoulders. Today, her gray hair was pinned up in a bun. Her baggy fitting sleeveless, gray dress did not conceal her fleshy elbows. She was a tall, big-boned woman, whose once beautiful skin had turned sallow. He thought he saw her glance at him, but wasn't sure since he was too far away. She beat the dust out of the broom and turned around and entered her boardinghouse.

Rufus was fifteen when Bee Henderson chased him with her broom handle. She watched him and Ina come sauntering up the sidewalk toward the boardinghouse, with his arm encircling her waist. She stopped sweeping and suspiciously watched the two youngsters reach her yard. Before he had a chance to request a room, she chased them away, telling them to go home pick up a book and get some knowledge into their thick heads. At the time he thought she was kind of mean. Today, he knew better. An education is a powerful tool for Negroes to have, he thought.

His mind shifted back to Ina, whom he always thought, had yielded to quickly to Bee. "She's right," Ina said. "I should be home studying. Let's just go!" He refused to give in that easily. Ina was young and pretty, a far cry from the women who always grabbed at his fly. Besides, he was anxious to pop her fresh, sweet cherry. He recalled feeling the fist-full of dollars in his pocket, and the thought of bribing Bee Henderson. Lucky Fingers had taught him money talked and bullshit walked. He figured his money would "talk" and Bee Henderson's bullshit would "walk."

When he pulled his wad of money from his dungarees, Bee Henderson's eyes had lit up like a Christmas tree. Then abruptly, she bore an expression of anger. Momentarily, she held her broom above her head, and warned them not to set foot on her steps. Ina gasped and stumbled over his foot, clinging to him as he grabbed her. He left from the front of the boardinghouse feeling like a wet dog. Yep, he thought. "Thanks to 'ol Bee, Ina held on to her virginity."

Not long afterward, Rufus left Chancy, Louisiana, drifting from one southern state to the next, trying to find

25

purpose. During that time, he learned more tricks and trades, like making bootleg whiskey; becoming a slick gambler; becoming a partner in a prostitution house disguised as a juke house; working in construction, and learning mechanics. Any situation he found himself in, he learned to master it, except for the pain from past scars that just wouldn't heal.

By 1936, his luck changed more so, when he landed in Derriene Crossing, Mississippi. Starting off as a hired hand on Charlie Hanson's farm, he fell in love with farming. He ended up buying old ailing Charlie's land for peanuts, so to speak. But 'ol Charlie was a shrewd, intelligent man, who always referred to his land as the family legacy, and would talk about the history of his family to anyone willing to listen.

The story was that Charlie's great-great-grandfather, a white man and a slave owner, fell in love with his wife's maid, after his wife died, leaving him childless. So fond of the kitchen maid, his great-great-grandfather took up housekeeping with her. She bore him seven illegitimate children—four boys and three girls. Being an only child with no other living relatives, Charlie's great-great-grandfather made the maid and the children his sole heirs. The land had since been passed on to his great-great-grandfather's four sons, then to the first-born males in the family.

Unfortunately, Charlie had no sons; nevertheless, he chose to keep the land in the family. Aware that Rufus needed a trophy to complement his new image, Charlie masterminded the marriage between Rufus and his granddaughter, Charlotte. Rufus fell in love with Charlotte's beauty just as the old man had imagined.

Suddenly, out of the sky an agitated blue jay swooped dangerously close to Rufus' head, snapping him back to the present. Rufus ducked and ran up the porch steps. He pulled opened the screen door and stepped inside the lobby. He moved toward the counter.

"Good morning." Bee greeted him cheerfully without a hint of recognition.

"Good morning. I'd like a room, please."

She pushed the register over to him.

He set down his suitcase and signed the register. He lifted the black leather wallet from his pocket, and pulled out a fifty-dollar bill and handed it to her. She took it, rubbed the bill between two fingers, and then held it up to the light.

Rufus cleared his throat.

"Just making sure its real," she remarked. She rang up the cash register, opened the drawer and placed the money inside and returned his change.

He returned the money to his wallet, and picked up his suitcase.

"You're in Room 1F," she said, handing him the key. "The last room, down the hall to your right. Breakfast is served at 6:30 a.m., lunch at noon, and supper at six o'clock."

He nodded, and went off to find his room. He felt glad she hadn't remembered him. He moved down the dimly lit hallway, unlocked the door and entered the small room, furnished in mahogany, smelling like fresh squeezed lemon. He felt exhausted and dragged himself toward the four-poster bed, covered in an embroidered yellow summer coverlet. Perched on the edge of the mattress, he wiped his tired face. Still studying the small room, he pulled the long-tail shirt from his dungarees, lifted the gun from the back of his pants waistband, and slid it under the pillow. Sprawled out on the length of the bed, seconds later he began snoring.

***

Rufus awoke at noon. The adrenaline started pumping in his veins. He was anxious to begin his mission. Pulling his gun from under the pillow, he secured it in back of his pants waistband, and tucked in his shirttail. He quickly finished dressing and hurried

27

down the dimly lit hallway toward the lobby. Bee was asleep behind the counter. Her head bobbed, and her lips were agape. "What a sight," he said silently, as he passed her.

When he reached his pickup, the gray-haired, old, gentleman coming up the sidewalk tipped his hat. Rufus nodded. As he fed the key into the ignition, his hand trembled. He felt nervous. He sank back against the driver's seat and started deep breathing.

My mission is too important to mess up, he thought. He had rehearsed what he would say to Olga, all the way to Chancy, Louisiana. Curling his lips into a crooked smile, he imagined Olga's reaction to revealing that he knew Maebelle's identity and what he planned to do to her. He regained his confidence, started the engine, and sped toward Highway Three.

***

Some time later, Rufus turned off the highway, onto a gravel road. After a few hundred yards, the road surrendered to dirt and deep ruts that caused him to drive at a reduced speed. He cursed profusely because of this inconvenience.

He looked disturbed at the dilapidated houses punctuating the fields. Some of them stood close to the road. Destitute faces of young, poor Black mothers sitting around on their porches, with their small nappy-headed children, made him recall the life of Negroes as he had once known it—dire poverty! He hated poverty! "To hell with the bumps and ruts," he told himself, speeding through the deep, winding curves.

A half hour later, he arrived at his destination. He was startled to see the old wooden shack Olga was living in, when he and his father left her, dark, desolate, and nothing more than a black hollow amidst tall weeds and overgrown Johnson grass. So, too, were the houses belonging to Mrs. Hattie Bell and her husband Mr. James Bell, and Dora Span, and others who once lived on that stretch of land.

It suddenly occurred to Rufus that Olga Berry might be dead. His heart sank. Although it was a warm, sunny, day, and the spring breeze rippled through the grass, he started shivering.

"Where's everybody!" he said dejectedly. "This can't be the end of my mission!"

He drove the pickup to the shoulder of the road and let the motor idle, as he got out and leaned against it with his right arm resting over the sill. Unpleasant thoughts rushed into his head.

He remembered the night he and his father left Olga and how disappointed he felt when they only moved next door with Dora Span. He thought about Dora, who further destroyed his innocence. She told him his good looks were a curse, and that no woman could resist wanting him. He could nearly taste her on his tongue. Wrenching, he hated his father, Jessie, for letting his women take advantage of him. He wondered if the old buzzard was still alive.

Nevertheless, a couple of laughable memories ensued, recalling how his crazy surrogate mother, Olga, used to run out of her house, down the steps, and pick up clods of dirt, throwing them at Dora because Dora had taken her family from her. Mrs. Hattie Bell always griped about having to live between the two devils. Much to her chagrin, Hattie always had to sweep dirt off her porch that Olga had thrown.

He remembered that hot, summer day when Mr. James Bell was on the porch starting to cut his watermelon. Suddenly, a clod of dirt whacked him upside the head. He dropped the watermelon on the floor, splattering it every which way. Mr. James Bell became furious, threatening to beat the living daylight out of Olga, calling her everything but a child of God.

Rufus began laughing, until those bad memories returned. He wanted to forget them. Looking around him, no matter how he tried to ignore them, his mind brimmed with many sad memories. So much that he didn't hear the twigs crackling under the old man's shoes approaching from behind him.

"Rufus? Is that you, young man?"

Rufus snapped his head around. Peering at the old man, his brows became knitted in skepticism. Who remembers me well enough to call my name? he wondered.

The old man came toward Rufus and extended his hand, and they shook.

"I'm Lester Berry," he said, withdrawing his hand, while stepping back.

"I didn't mean to shock you. It's just that I saw you standing here, and you look like someone I knew. If you're who I think you are, then I'm your uncle–your mother's brother, and Olga's brother, too."

Rufus stared at this tall, thin, old man clad in coveralls and a sleeveless gray T-shirt. My mother's brother and Olga's brother! he thought with disbelief. What a stark contrast between you and Olga—that is if you're telling the truth. Never having known his mother, Rufus could not determine if this old man resembled her. The sunlight reflecting in the old man's green eyes made them look striking against his sun-baked skin.

The old man slightly grinned. "Well, are you Rufus, or not?"

Rufus blinked. "Yes, sir. I'm—I'm Rufus."

"I don't blame you fer, fer staring at me like that. Here I am, coming out of nowhere, telling you I'm your uncle. I remembered you by, let's see, your red hair. You were knee-high-to a-duck the last time I saw you. But look at you now. You're nearly six foot four, ain't you? I'd been living out in Texas 'til my wife died a few years ago."

"But I--I thought all Olga's folks were dead!" Rufus blurted out. "Olga told me...."

Before Rufus could finish his sentence, he saw the excitement fade from the old man's eyes. The old man knew why Olga would say such a thing; he supposed she had had every right to, though. He turned sideways, looking abstractly at the horizon. Guilt gnawed at his heart. To be honest, he would have to agree with the way Olga felt about him. She really didn't have a family after their parents died, and especially after he went to Texas, after their sister Amber died. He never wrote Olga a letter.

Their mother was killed when they were small. That same year, their father died of alcoholism and a broken heart. The children were split among different families. The woman who took Olga treated her very poorly. Olga grew up in filth, abused by different stepfathers. Edward Hawkins and his wife Betty adopted Olga's twin sister, Gina. But, then, they upped and moved without saying a word. To this day, the old man hadn't a clue where Gina was or even if she was alive. The Boyd's, who were kind people, took in him and his sister Amber.

"Did I say something wrong?" Rufus inquired.

The old man lifted his eyes and flicked a glance at him, then looked away.

"No, son," he said facing Rufus. "I was just thinking. Seeing my sister's child, after all these years, is truly an act of God. I always wondered about you. You know you got your mother's eyes! She got hers from her great-grandfather! She didn't get his red hair, though." He paused. "I see you can hardly believe me. You probably think I'm--I'm just some old, lonely fool wanting to talk." He put up a hand. "Just hold on a second." He reached in his back pocket, pulled out a brown leather wallet, and handed it to Rufus.

Rufus took it.

"There's a picture of your mother Amber in there. I'm not going to tell you which picture is her; I'm going to let you figure it out by yourself."

Rufus felt his heart pounding inside his chest. Finally, he was going to get to see what his mother looked like. It sounded strange hearing the old man say his

31

mother's name without adding a curse word to the end of it the way he had grown accustomed to hearing Olga do.

"Well, go ahead! Open it! There's a long line of our ancestors in that wallet."

Rufus swallowed. He looked at the old man and his wallet, afraid of his own reaction, seeing his mother.

"Go ahead. Open it, son! Today, you'll discover your roots. It helps a man to know about his roots. Gives him a sense of belonging! We got three different bloodlines running through our veins, son: The Indian, the Negro, and the white man. Now of course, some people have a problem with white folks. But as I see it, we all come from Adam, made by the hand of the Almighty," he said, holding up a tight, proud fist. As Rufus arched his brow, the old man lowered his fist. "Maybe I'm too excited about this," he said.

Rufus slowly opened the wallet, first gazing at a handsome old couple's photo. The old man stared at him through his wire-rimmed glasses. Rufus' hands trembled, as the old man moved closer to him.

Pointing to the next photo, the old man continued. "They're your great-grandparents: Arthur Ross and Yucreta Ross. Arthur was half-white, and Yucreta was part Seminole and part Black, as you can probably see."

Rufus stared dumbfounded at the handsome couple, with a lost of words. He never knew anything about his people.

"You can't tell from the picture," remarked the old man. "But his hair is red, too, and his eyes are hazel. That's whom you take after. Now this is a picture of your grandmother and grandfather—my mama and papa. Mama's name was Ceedy; Papa's name was Claude Berry. He looks white, doesn't he? But he's a Black man— just like you and me."

Rufus looked at the old man, wondering what in the world happened to Olga—why did she have such a dark complexion?

The old man took note of Rufus' puzzled expression, and then stared at the ground. He lifted his eyes explaining, "Your er--your grandma was never faithful to your grandpa. She liked dark-skinned men. Married, single, divorced—it didn't matter. If they were dark, she loved them. I think she was cursed." He paused for a moment. "In the end one of them took her life from her, and left her body rotting in the cornfield."

Rufus stared at the old man, shaking his head in disbelief. He didn't comment, as the old man stood by silently, recalling his mother's sins that changed their family's lives forever.

Rufus turned the photo page. The smiling face of his young mother, Amber, made his heart jump, at their striking resemblance. He saw himself in her. They had the same pointed nose and sleepy eyes. He knew she was his mother. His heart pounded. He brought the wallet closer to his eyes, absorbing everything about her, including the turquoise Indian necklace around her neck, and her two long, thick braids draped over the front of her shoulders. She appeared to be smiling at him.

I'm sorry, Mama, he thought to himself. I don't know how I....

"Pretty, ain't she?" said the old man, breaking into his thoughts. "That's Amber, your mother. I guess I couldn't wait for you to figure it out for yourself."

Rufus fought back tears.

"She was the only one of us who took pride in being part Indian."

Overwhelmed by so many pent-up emotions, Rufus didn't hear a word the old man said, as he continued reminiscing.

"There were four of us children," said the old man. "I was the first born. Amber was second. We were close, I tell you! And Papa, he loved Amber so much that I think it affected Mama in the wrong way. That little girl got all of Daddy's affection. She always said things that kept us laughing all the time." Pausing, with his hands entwined behind his back, he held his head down, until other thoughts occurred.

"Then the twins came," he said. "Olga and Gina—identical at that, and blacker than mid-night down in one of them cypress swamps!" He shook his head sorrowfully.

"Well. Olga didn't like herself," he continued. "As a child, she was jealous of Amber. But Daddy, being who he was, he treated Olga and Gina just like they were his own flesh and blood. He was a good man. The only thing he did wrong was to stop Mama from taking pictures of them. Papa didn't want pictures of them on the walls, nor tucked away somewhere. You won't find a single picture of them inside that wallet. Other than that, he was good to them. He said they were innocent. He was a good man . . .."

"Olga told me I killed Mama!" Rufus blurted out.

"What! That's baloney!" The old man couldn't believe what he'd just heard.

Rufus closed the wallet and gave it back to the old man. The old man pushed the wallet inside his pants pocket. Placing a hand on Rufus' shoulder, he assured him, "Son, you didn't kill your mama. The midwife killed her. She had been drinking, and forgot and left afterbirth in Amber. That was how poor Amber died."

Rufus closed his eyes and turned away. Finally, the weight of the monkey he had carried around since he was a child fell off his shoulders.

The old man shook with rage.

"That dammed Olga!" he muttered. "She deserves a good old-fashioned ass-beatin'! There was no need for her to go that far!"

The two men stood shoulder to shoulder, followed by a long interval of silence. The old man realized Rufus was ready to leave, and wondered if he'd come to put a headstone on Jesse's grave.

"Did you come here to put a headstone on your daddy's grave? Because if you did, I can tell you which cemetery he's buried in."

Rufus was unaware of Jesse's death. He showed no emotions. But hell no! He hadn't come for that. I'm not putting shit on his grave, he thought to himself. The sucker never gave a damn about me. He was too busy lying up with Mama's sister. He let her ruin my childhood. Hell, no!

He looked at the old man, and answered him as calmly as he could. "I didn't know he was dead." He looked up at the blue sky, with memories of not seeing his father since he was thirteen.

As the old man studied Rufus, he made up his mind to ask him a touchy question.

"Son, this is a hard question, but did Jesse know what Olga was doing to you?"

He saw Rufus' jaws suddenly turn rigid.

Rufus sniffed. He kept his eyes lowered. How dare you pry into my private life, he thought, feeling appalled by the old man's question. However, quickly thinking things over, his attitude softened. He realized the old man was concerned.

However, Rufus didn't answer right away because he had a question to ask the old man. He lifted his eyes and turned and faced the old man.

"Did you know Papa was messing with Olga?"

Although, the old man had looked down, he didn't appear to be shocked. He'd heard every rumor there was about Olga since his return. He lifted his eyes, and looked Rufus straight in the eyes. "People told me." His voice was flat.

Rufus sniffed, rubbing a hand across his mouth. Finally, he answered the old man's question. "We never talked about it. But he knew."

The old man dropped his head.

"Well, I can tell you where he's buried if you're looking to put a headstone...."

"I'm not looking!"

The old man put up a refraining hand; he spoke kindly.

"I understand, son. Well, if it's any consolation to you, I heard that the undertaker and the gravediggers were the only ones who attended his funeral—and they didn't want to be there, but somebody had to put him in the ground!"

"Is Olga still alive?" Rufus inquired.

The old man was caught off guard by the question, and Rufus stared him straight in the eye, making it impossible for the old man to lie to him.

The old man ran a hand inside his pocket and brought it out again.

"She--she's in poor health."

Rufus breathed a long sigh of silent relief. He didn't care about her health, so long as she was alive.

"Where's she living?"

The old man's brows shot up in surprise, even though he expected that would be Rufus' next question. He deliberately answered Rufus' question with a question.

"Where's she living?" He hated to be the one to lead Rufus to Olga. No matter what she had done, she was still his sister.

"She probably won't remember you, you know. She's in such poor health." He turned away from Rufus, feeling his gaze burning into his face. Knowing his nephew wasn't going to let him wriggle out of not telling him where Olga lived, he told him a half-truth.

"She lives about a mile down the road—in the direction your pickup is facing."

"Can I give you a lift?" Rufus asked.

The old man flicked him a quick glance, detecting bitterness in Rufus' eyes. Rufus was his nephew, a stranger, and a bitter one, at that. "Nah, son. I'm-I'm going to go on and finish-finish my walk." His heart was beating fast.

Looking at him apprehensively, Rufus climbed inside the pickup and leaned his head slightly out the window.

"You sure you don't need a lift, Uncle?"

"No. Like I said, I need to finish my walk!"

Rufus put the pickup in gear and drove away in a hurry.

The old man changed his mind about finishing his walk. He felt his old ticker vibrating inside his chest. "That Negro is got Injun in him," he muttered. "He's bound to find you, Olga. Might even come back looking for me."

When the pickup was out of view, he cut a path down beside the empty shacks. He slowed down after reaching the clearing in the woods. Chester, his dog, met up with him wagging his tail. Chester's wet nose touched the old man's hand. They walked together toward his cabin. The old man felt faint; he needed to lie down.

***

Rufus soon realized that the old man had sent him on a wild-goose chase. All he kept coming across were abandoned, run-down shacks. After driving some five miles, he was agitated. Finally, he spotted a narrow road and turned onto it.

That part of the woods echoed with whining saws and blows from wood choppers' axes. He drove a few hundred yards and came upon several dilapidated houses, to his surprise were inhabited. His hope was restored as the adrenaline started pumping inside his veins again.

A short distance away, in the clearing, he saw three men splitting logs. A large, rusty old green truck was parked nearby. Lying on the ground was a brown and white mutt watching over them. He got up and started barking. The men stopped working and stared at the pickup. A short, stocky man turned his head slightly and spat tobacco juice on the ground. They talked amongst themselves for a while, and then they went back to splitting logs.

Rufus parked the pickup truck onto the shoulder of the road, letting the motor idle. He gazed at the houses, hoping to find Olga in one of them. He cast a stealthy glance at the men in the clearing, hoping none of them lived in any of the houses. He knew it would be dangerous if they thought he was up to no good.

As a small boy appeared in one of the windows, he cut off the engine and got out of the truck, leaving the key in the ignition. All the way to the house, he occasionally looked to see what the men in the clearing were doing. Luckily, they were hard at work, as the dog lay near the front of the pickup. Rufus became relaxed.

The child moved away from the window. Seconds later, the screen door screeched open, and a half-naked little boy stood in the doorway. He looked warily at the tall stranger walking across the sagging porch. The planks creaked with old age under Rufus' booted feet. The child backed away quickly and strained on his tiptoe to hitch the screen door.

Smart little fellow, Rufus thought. But he knew how to get the little boy to cooperate. He put his hand inside his pocket and brought out a stick of chewing gum. He bent over, with his free hand resting on his knee, speaking softly to the child. The boy's eyes were riveted on the yellow wrapping.

"Hi, son. Is your mama home?"

The little fellow didn't reply.

"Would you like this stick of gum?" Rufus asked impatiently.

The child nodded. Rufus straightened.

"Well, you're going to have to open the door so I can give it to you."

The child stepped forward and strained on his tiptoe and unhitched the latch.

Rufus grabbed the doorframe and pulled open the door. He handed the boy the gum and stepped inside the house. The sparsely furnished room smelled musty. Rufus tensed as he looked around for something familiar: a piece of furniture; a lamp; an old chair—anything recognizable.

The boy removed the yellow wrapper and dropped it on the floor, and chugged the gum into his mouth. He stared up at the tall stranger, following his line of vision around the room. The cracks between the planks were littered with breadcrumbs and slivers of threads and fabrics—and now the gum wrapper. Beneath the window, a newborn slept on an old faded quilt. Rufus recognized nothing!

Frightened by Rufus' actions, the little fellow darted out of the room. He went and tugged on his Big Mama's sleeve.

"Gannma! Gannma wake up! Wake up! Man in house!"

His Grandma woke up with a start. She grabbed the arms of the rocker and scooted to the edge of her seat.

"What! What! Who are you talking about, Chuck! What man!"

She wiped the spittle off the side of her mouth with the heel of her hand, and then rubbed her hand on her lap.

Chuck stood shivering, and laced his small fingers together. The wad of gum inside his cheek was now forgotten.

Rufus jumped when he heard the old woman scold the boy. He wasn't aware that the child had left the room. He cocked his head and listened intently. Her voice sounded old and nondescript. He moved cautiously toward the room where they were, and stood in the doorway. Unnoticed by either of them, Rufus stared at the old woman without knowing who she was.

I know this isn't Olga, he thought.

The old woman seated in the rocker wore dark glasses. Her woolly, white hair, a striking contrast to her black face, made her look ghastly. Her profile didn't fit the mental picture he had tucked away in his mind of his surrogate mother. Olga's hair had been black and coarse and long. And she had weighed much more than the woman seated in front of him.

"Damn you, Chuck! You ain't supposed to let anybody in the house!"

The old woman patted her foot around on the floor, frantically looking for her stray house-slipper.

"Where's my other slipper?" she asked in her high-pitched anger.

Chuck didn't answer, as he turned slightly, glancing nervously over his shoulder. He jumped off the floor when he saw the tall stranger standing in the doorway.

"Gannma! Gannma!" he screamed, moving toward her lap. "Man in room!"

He tried to climb onto the old woman's lap, but she shoved him away.

"Who's there?" the old woman cried angrily, exposing her dull teeth. The tall male figure hovering inside her doorway appeared fuzzy. Diabetes had severely damaged her eyesight.

Believing he chose the wrong house, causing such a ruckus, Rufus thought it wise to be careful and address the frightened woman as Aunt. Show her respect and perhaps calm her down, because the men in the clearing weren't far away. He cleared his throat, and approached her with his hands clasped in front of him. Chuck hid in back of the rocker shivering.

"Uh, hello, Auntie."

The old woman sank back cautiously in her chair. She cocked her head and wrinkled her nose in distaste.

"W—Who's calling me Auntie. I ain't nobody's aunt!" She stared up at him without recognition.

Rufus stared down at her ghastly face, thinking that if Olga was as half-cocked as this one, his trip was a total waste. He hoped not, because it would mean that she probably wouldn't even remember she ever had any daughters, let alone remember that she had given them away. She probably wouldn't remember him, either. The thought of such a thing distressed him.

The old woman sat with her head bowed, trying to remember if she had a nephew. She placed a slender, ropy finger against her nose. Her gray brows were tightly knitted. Twenty-four years had passed since she last saw him. And she had long since put him out of her mind. She gripped the arms of the rocker and scooted forward and gazed up at Rufus.

"Uhn-uhn!" she said shaking her head. "I--I don't have no nephew. You--you got the wrong house."

Her tone was softer, now. His compassionate greeting had worked.

"It's been a long time since I was down here," he told her. "I'm looking for an aunt that I haven't seen in a long time. Someone told me she lives in one of these houses, but they didn't say which one. I'll try next door."

He started to leave, but turned back. "Don't blame the little fellow. I let myself in. I was just so sure I had the right house."

She peered at his silhouette through the dark glasses.

"Well, thanks for telling me, 'cause I was fixin' to tear his ass up! W--what's your aunt's name? If she's living in one of these houses, I'll know her. And what's your name, son? You have to forgive me. I wouldn't have been so upset earlier if my sight were better. I'm wearing these dark glasses because the light bothers my eyes."

At the precise moment he stated his name, a hair-raising crash impacted out on the back porch that sent Rufus into a tailspin. He heard a man's angry voice and thought about the men inside the clearing. He would be in danger if they thought he was intruding.

Above the ruckus, the old woman had caught his name, and an alarm went off inside her head. Rufus! Sonofabitch! She had hated him and his father, Jesse, with a passion, for walking out on her. An extremely loud, shrilled cry erupted from her throat.

"You sonofabitch! I'll kill ya! Get out of my house!"

The small baby sleeping on the pallet beneath the window woke up screaming at the top of his lungs.

Rufus swung around and faced the old woman. Already seized by terror from the crash out on the back porch, Rufus' feet felt as though they were anchored to the floor. But he knew he had to escape this house; he couldn't let the men from the clearing find him here!

Enraged and furious, the old woman wielded her cane wildly.

Rufus ducked, pivoted, and fled the house, almost tripping on an old raggedly tennis shoe. Hitting the screen-door with his flat hand, he sent the door reeling back on its hinges. His mad dash down the porch steps sent the roosters and mother hens and their baby chicks scattering across the grassy yard cackling wildly. Like a deadly tornado, a ferocious, gleaming, black dog tore from beneath the front porch, snapping violently at his heels.

The old woman moved onto the porch spluttering vulgarity after vulgarity and shaking her cane wildly.

Rufus hurriedly climbed inside the pickup, slamming the door hard. He fumbled inside his pocket for the ignition key.

"Where's the damn key! Don't tell me I dropped it!"

He looked up and saw the old woman standing on the porch ranting and raving like a lunatic. She tossed her cane on the floor and gathered the hem of her gray duster in both hands. Pulling her skirt above her knees, she then spread her thighs, and gyrated her stiff pelvis.

"Is this what you come back here for?" she called.

"My, God! You're Olga!" Rufus cried mortified. He had thought she was peculiar. A fusion of anger and disbelief spiraled through him.

"Is this what you come back here looking for?" Olga screamed again, and spread her legs even wider until she nearly fell over backward.

Rufus felt ill. He felt hot tears sting his eyes.

He furtively glanced out the windshield, looking for the men in the clearing, but they weren't there. He thought for certain now, the man's voice he had heard belonged to one of them. He had to get out of here. He looked down and happened to see the key sticking out of the ignition. He quickly started the engine and stepped on the gas pedal.

His attention was drawn back to the porch. He saw the small boy move around opened-mouthed and awe-struck, watching Olga's flaccid skin flapping around her black, thin thighs. The boy pointed at Rufus as the pickup truck sped past the house.

Olga's grandson Melvin Poke rushed around to the front of the house. "What's going on? Who was that man?" he asked, staring at the fast moving pickup.

"It's nobody. Gone about your business. I told you not to put that corn on the porch!" she scolded.

Melvin waved a hand at her and turned and left, mumbling under his breath.

The dog chased the pickup as far as he could, as it rocked violently in and out of the deep trenches.

Angry tears stung Rufus' eyes. He berated himself for letting the chance of a lifetime slip through his fingers *"You damn Jackass! You're running like a stupid fool. You come all this way. And for what!"* He slammed the heel of his right hand against the steering wheel. For a second, crazy thoughts entered his mind. The old man went home and worked voodoo, he thought. I don't know one person that I'm scared of.

Rufus drove in and out of the winding curves at an insanely high speed. A handful of field hands, walking leisurely in the middle of the road, caused him to slam on the brakes. The pickup swerved violently, careening onto the right shoulder of the road.

The frightened field hands scurried out of the way in desperation. Upon recovery, they shouted obscenities and threats of bodily harm at Rufus. They threw huge chunks of dirt at the back of the pickup window. Rufus, hurriedly straightened the wheels, got back on the road, and drove like a maniac.

Thank God the windows didn't shatter, because Rufus was angry enough to kill.

****

Back at the boardinghouse, Rufus parked the pickup. Irritated, he climbed out of the pickup, slamming the door hard. He tromped toward the boardinghouse. Because he was furious, he, yanked opened the screen door, and stepped inside the lobby snorting fire. It helped that the lobby was empty because his mood was foul. He moved down the dimly lit hallway, toward his room. He entered the room, locked the door, and tossed the key on the bureau. As he hit the wall with his fist, he asked himself, "What the hell was I thinking to run away like a damn fool! What happened to me? Damn! I had the damn gun on me!"

Rufus held his head in his hands. He felt like screaming. He plopped down heavily on the edge of the mattress, and pounded his tight fist into the mattress. For a long moment, he sat hunched over, with his elbows on his knees and his chin in his hands. Tears ebbed down his face. He wiped his eyes with the heel of his hand. Cussing himself, he sat up; pulled the shirttail out of his dungarees, removed the gun, and slid it under the pillow. He had a reason to return to Olga's house, but common sense convinced him that he hadn't come to Chancy, Louisiana, to get arrested.

After he removed his boots, he stretched himself full length upon the bed and laced his fingers behind his head. Crossing his ankles, he stared up at the ceiling, trying to forget what happened in the past three hours. He failed miserably, as Olga wouldn't be shut out. He could still hear her laughing at him—her indignant words beat inside his head, like sleet against a windowpane: *"Is this what you come back here for?"* As a child, she abused him. As a man, she chased and humiliated him. Rufus hated Olga Berry.

Sighing heavily, he sat up, swinging his legs over the side of the mattress. Tears rolling down his cheeks again.

"Your daughter will pay for this!" he exclaimed. "I don't need you to tell me who she is! I know who she is! One way or the other, I'll get even with you! Do you hear me, Aunt Olga?"

He felt a bad headache coming on. He tried to lie down again, only to find himself cowering in the fetal position, staring out the window at the gilded sunset. The powder blue curtains lifted and fell in the gentle evening breeze. Between his troubled thoughts, sleep invaded his tortured soul.

****

The next day, Rufus woke up to the sound of choking lawn mowers and whining chainsaws. Mexican immigrants were hard at work cleaning up broken branches and fallen trees after last night's sudden thunderstorm. He looked at the clock on the bedside table and realized, to his surprise, he had slept for almost twelve hours.

The urgent call of nature forced him to get out of bed. He went to the bathroom and emptied his bladder. He decided that as long as he was up, he would get dressed and prepare to check out of the boardinghouse. Today, he would be going home.

As he somberly packed his suitcase, Olga's horrible words suddenly echoed in his head: *"Is this what you come back here for?"* Her taunting words were like salt poured into an open wound. It was difficult as it was to admit that his mission had failed. But, Maebelle—the woman whom he believed was Olga's daughter—would pay dearly for her mother's sins.

His growling stomach brought him back to the present. After a day and a half without eating, Rufus was starving. Gathering his personal belongings together, and taking one last look around the room, he made his way to the restaurant on the south side of the boardinghouse.

Entering the restaurant, he stopped and studied the sparse crowd of diners. He strode toward the booth at the back of the room. He cast a sly glance at the conspicuous, buxom, middle-age woman, seated in the booth near his. She gave him a short glance, then turned her attention elsewhere.

Rufus took his seat and slid the suitcase under the table. He picked up the flyer that was on the floor. It was an advertisement from a local psychic. He read the flyer slowly.

WANT TO KNOW WHAT'S IN YOUR FUTURE? THEN, COME SEE MOTHER HAZEL. PALM READING, TEA LEAVES, TAROT CARDS, AND CRYSTAL BALL.

Rufus placed the flyer inside his shirt pocket. He would pay Mother Hazel a visit after he'd finished his breakfast.

Starving, he scanned the laminated menu. Though not a breakfast food, collards, cooked with neck bones and okra appealed to him. He would have fried chicken—a leg and thigh—and buttered corn bread, as well.

Having decided on what to eat, minutes later, he spotted a pretty, young waitress across the room. His heart jumped, as he gaped at her. The resemblance of the young waitress and the image he recalled of his mother were strikingly similar: They had the same pointed nose, and sleepy eyes. And, she too wore her hair in two ponytails draped in front of her shoulders. She was incredibly beautiful.

His reverie broke when a disgruntled female customer called her. The waitress went over to the customer. They spoke briefly, and then she went toward the kitchen.

Waiting for the waitress to return, his unruly mind drifted back to yesterday's fiasco. Part of him still wanted to go back. But he knew Olga would never let him get that close to her again. He stared vacantly out the window at the manicured lawns across the street. The Mexican immigrants had done a thorough job of cleaning up the debris.

The young waitress reached his table. "Are you ready to order?" she asked.

His eyes rested for a second on the turquoise Indian necklace around her slender neck. The red stitching across her breast pocket read Madeline. It was an unusual name; one he hadn't heard before.

She started to feel uncomfortable under his strange gaze and stepped back.

"Why don't I come back later?" she said.

"No, I'm ready! I'll have this," he said, his index finger pointing to the selection he had chosen.

"...Anything to drink?"

"Ah, yeah. Dr. Pepper, please."

Then he said something he would later regret.

"You--you remind me of my mother, if you don't mind my saying so, Madeline."

Poor Madeline misunderstood him. She was baffled. Detecting pain and anger in his eyes, she backed away, turned on her heels, and left. His face was embittered. Madeline thought he was crazy. As she passed by, she cast a stealthy, confused glance at the buxom woman seated at the booth opposite Rufus.

The woman shrugged and returned the same confused look.

All the way to the kitchen, Madeline fussed under her breath.

"What does he mean I remind him of his mother? I'm only eighteen. He's old enough to be my father!"

Before she reached the kitchen, Rufus watched Madeline carefully, saw her flip her ponytails over her shoulder. Her soft black skirt moved fluidly with her every move.

"How could something so beautiful be so damn heartless? Damn women! They're all the same!" he mumbled.

47

Resting his elbows on the table, and lowering his head into his hands, troubling thoughts began resurfacing. He was unaware that Madeline had returned, until she accidentally set down the plate hard on the table. He jerked his elbow and nearly knocked over the glass. Madeline grabbed the glass and kept it from tumbling to the floor. She replaced it on the table. She lifted her eyes and met his cold steely gaze. Though nervous and confused, she forced a cheerful smile as she left his table.

On her way to another customer, Madeline stopped and whispered to the buxom woman. Rufus could hear bits and pieces of their conversation.

'...Crazy...telling me I remind him of his mother...weird!'

He picked up that the buxom woman was the girl's Aunt. Finished with their conversation, Madeline straightened and looked over her shoulder at Rufus. She went and waited on the other customer.

It took Rufus only a short while to devour the delicious meal. He was just that famished. When he finished eating, he retrieved the suitcase from under the table and fished deep inside the dark part of his pocket. He slapped down an insulting buffalo nickel.

"Take that for a tip, you little witch!" he murmured. He looked over his shoulder with icy hard eyes at the buxom woman, leaning forward trying to see what sort of tip he was leaving her niece. Their eyes held momentarily. His lips curled into a sinister smile. She averted her eyes from his icy stare, and quickly sank back on her seat.

Rufus made his way to the register and paid his bill. He then went to the front desk to turn in the key. Bee Henderson's back was turned. He cleared his throat.

She turned and looked at him cheerfully.

He handed her the key.

She took it, looking up at him.

"I hope you enjoyed your stay."

He glared at her without saying a word, then turned and headed for the door.

She shrugged her shoulders.

"Don't know what's wrong with you," she grumbled. Then a bell went off in her head. She remembered him. "Hey! Wait a minute!" she called, walking around in front of the counter.

Rufus stopped abruptly; he turned around noticeably irate. He was rushing. What did she want from him, now? He had paid in advance and had just now turned in the key.

"You know, I just remembered you!" she said excitedly. "You're that little 'ol red-headed boy I chased away from my boardinghouse—oh about twenty-odd years ago, ain't you? I knew you looked familiar. My memory is like an elephant." She came forward. "That's really nice of you to come all this ways to put a headstone on Jesse's grave."

She saw his jaws grow rigid.

He gripped the handle on the suitcase.

Nevertheless, she stood close in front of him.

"Well, don't look so upset. I'm not tryin' to mind your business or anything like that. I bet you were probably hopin' I wouldn't recognize you, now weren't you? And I nearly didn't."

His fuse got shorter by the seconds. He put up a refraining hand.

"Look, Mrs. Henderson---"

"Bee," she interrupted. "Call me Bee. You're a grown man now. Ain't no need to be---"

"I really can't stay and talk," he said, trying to calm his voice. "I have an appointment I have to get to."

Feeling insulted, Bee Henderson waved him off.

"Oh go on! I was going to tell you that your uncle lives here now. But you done got all nasty. Well, go on. Ain't nobody studin' you either. I wasn't trying to get into your lousy business."

Rufus was seething!

"Liar!" he said under his breath. "That's exactly what you were trying to do."

Leaving Bee behind, he bounded down the steps and hurried toward the pickup. After securing his suitcase onto the bench seat, he put the pickup in gear and drove in the direction of Twenty-Three Linden Walk. He was eager to learn about his future.

Ten minutes later, Rufus parked the pickup outside Mother Hazel's Victorian home. He crossed the street and rushed up the steps to the house. He brought the iron knocker down with an ominous thud against the rustic wooden door.

"It's open!" a voice called.

He pushed open the door and stepped inside. A thin, oval-face woman was seated behind an oak desk.

"Please be seated," she told him. "It's first come first served. Mother Hazel is with a client."

Rufus preferred not to sit between the two women seated on the brown couch. A big yellow tomcat occupied the only other available seat. Reluctantly, he sat down quietly between the two women.

Rufus suddenly became aware of the gray-haired woman in dark glasses, seated across the room. He felt his heart skip a beat. Her white woolly, unkempt hair and black skin bore such a striking resemblance to Olga! She could've easily been mistaken for her. He wondered if she, too, might've been one of Olga's so-called dead relatives that his Uncle failed to mention.

Suddenly, the woman lashed out at him in anger. She jerked the sunglasses off her face and rolled a pair of cloudy, angry eyes at him.

"You see somethin' you want, heffa? Why are you lookin' at me like you're crazy for!"

Rufus felt his body vibrate under the weight of her accusations. Feeling mortified, he quickly averted his eyes, willing himself not to look in her direction again.

"You better stop cock-watchin' me!" she accused, even though he was no longer looking at her. "You dog! I see you still looking at me under your lashes! You ain't fixin' this cock, if that's what you're here for. No way!" She locked her knees and pulled down the hem of her dress.

Rufus stirred in his seat. Hatred rose to its pinnacle inside him. He felt like mauling the woman with his hard fist.

He felt the eyes of the two women seated on either side of him resting on his pain-stricken face. His blood was boiling. He didn't know how much more of this woman's madness he would take.

"She's a lunatic," the woman on his right said in a low tone. "Don't let her get to you. Every time I come here, she's here, sitting in the same damn chair like it's hers. She thinks it's hers. She's crazy!"

Although Rufus tried to ignore the woman, her vulgarity continued to sting his wounded soul. He couldn't take much more of her, but he would not leave without a fortune reading.

Finally, he got up. He went and whispered in the ear of the oval-face woman.

She looked up at him. Her expression was concerned.

"My name is Rosalie," she whispered. "Make it ten dollars, but don't give it to me here," she whispered to him. She got to her feet. Pretending he was there on business, she looked up at him and said, "I'm sorry, Mr...."

"Poygoode." Rufus filled in.

"I'm sorry, Mr. Poygoode, for the mix-up. Mother Hazel didn't tell me she had somebody coming here on business. Otherwise, I would've taken you right in to her."

The crazy woman scrambled to her feet.

"Business my ass!" she shouted. "You all think y'all slick. He's here to cock-watch me. I read your lips. I know he offered you money."

Rosalie stared incredulously at the enraged woman. She had never known her to act like this before. Rosalie looked at Rufus, then at the angry woman, then at Rufus.

The woman continued. "But you go ahead," she told Rosalie. "Take the money! You need it for your hungry mouths at home. Well, go on. Take it, dammit! I know that's what you gon do, once you're out of here. Take it and get him out of here so he can stop watching my cock like a hungry ass dog. Shiittt! I didn't come here for this! You tell Mother Hazel what he was doing to me, you hear!"

Rosalie took a deep breath. Looking up nervously, she met Rufus' angry eyes.

"C'mon," she said, with urgency in her voice. "Let me take you to Mother Hazel."

She swung through the door, with Rufus right on her heels. When they got a measured distance down the hall, she turned around and faced him, and put out her hand.

Rufus gave her a fierce look and reached into his back pocket for his wallet. Ten dollars wasn't what he had in mind, more like a dollar. He handed her a ten-dollar bill and put the wallet back in his pocket.

Rosalie took the money; she turned her back and stuck the money inside her brassier, then she turned and faced him.

"Thank you," she said. "This money will go a long way...."

The conversation was abruptly interrupted by the loud screams of a female client. Rufus turned around just in time to see a short, rotund woman hurrying pass them with uplifted hands, shouting praises to God.

Puzzled, he looked at Rosalie. "What the hell...! What was that all about? Who was that?" he inquired.

"Sorry. I'm under oath," said Rosalie. "I'm not allowed to discuss the clients."

She started to giggle at Rufus' expression. She put a hand on his arm.

"Oh, don't you worry, none, Mr. Poygoode. Mother Hazel is hardly preaching the gospel. People act all kinds a way when they leave her. To tell you the truth, God ain't got nothing to do with what Mother Hazel's doing. Believe me, I know. I go to church. But, in any case, not everybody act that way...."

"That's good to hear," Rufus said. He was just about to say something when the door opened down the hall. His eyebrows shot up when Mother Hazel poked out her head. One look at the tall, handsome stranger set her passion afire. Her eyes lit up like a Christmas tree. She smiled, knowingly.

"Rosalie?" she called.

Rosalie turned and faced her.

"Send him in," she ordered mildly. "How many more customers do I have out there?" she asked.

Rufus studied Mother Hazel while she and Rosalie discussed her customers. From all appearances, she gave a good impression—like she knew her stuff. There was just something about her, something in her voice that gave him assurance. She sounded warm and personable.

"Three more," Rosalie replied. There was no need to speak about crazy Viola's behavior. She was one of Mother Hazel's best customers.

"Well, they have to wait," Mother Hazel remarked under her breath. "Thank you," she said loudly. Then her eyes slid back to Rufus, as he was walking toward her. "Lord, have mercy! Love from heaven!" she mumbled under her breath. "I sure wish I knew voodoo! Come on in here now, you handsome devil, and sit down," she said to herself. "I wish I knew hypnosis."

She held the door open for him.

Rufus stepped inside the room.

She closed the door and leaned against it. Then she motioned toward the chair at the round oak table. "Do sit down," she said.

Rufus sat down and crossed his knees; then uncrossed them.

Mother Hazel started a cheerful conversation. "It's not often men come here to see me, you know. You all are just too proud to seek help from a woman. And we're the ones who bring you all into this world. Yes Lord," she said, drooling over his fine good looks.

Don't tell me about women, Rufus thought. I just hope I'm not making a mistake by coming here to see you.

Mother Hazel went on. "Just give me a minute here. I have to light a few more candles. You've certainly come to the right place for advice. I'm the best in the business." Rufus didn't comment.

I hope so, he thought.

He looked around the orange room, trimmed with molding that had been painted brown. Orange curtains draped the tall windows. Incense sticks burned inside the brass tray. He stared at her outfit, wondering how many more she had like that, since it matched the room's decor.

She wore an orange blouse, a brown gathered buttoned-down skirt, and a brown turban around her head. He gazed at the tip of her thick fingers, and saw that her fingernails were painted orange. He wondered where this plain, fat woman, with silky smooth, black skin, and pleasant voice, got her powers.

...And you just had to be black, he thought. Good grief! He looked away. Then suddenly, Olga popped into his head, but he managed to push her out.

Mother Hazel blew out the match and dropped the stem into the incense tray. She sat down and faced Rufus.

"That will be ten dollars," she said.

He reached inside his shirt pocket and brought out a ten-dollar bill and a picture of Charlotte, and laid them on the table. Mother Hazel's body stiffened. Charlotte's picture resembled the woman who'd stolen her husband some twenty-odd years ago.

Rufus saw jealousy dancing in her dark eyes.

Mother Hazel grabbed the money and stuck it inside her skirt pocket.

"I gather she's your wife," she said. Her undertone was icy.

What, you're jealous of her? Rufus thought to himself. He now looked at Mother Hazel warily, wondering if she were capable of giving him an unbiased prediction.

"Yes. She's my wife."

"What's your wife's name?"

He stirred in his seat. "Her name is Charlotte." His voice was flat.

Mother Hazel picked up the picture and handed it back to him. "Put it away. I've seen enough."

Rufus took the picture and put it in his shirt pocket. He sat with the palms of his hands facing down on the table. There was silence. He stared at the table, wondering if he had made a mistake coming here.

Mother Hazel's attitude changed, as she smiled and took his hands, turning them palm up. She closed her eyes to the sensual feeling rippling through her body.

God! It's been a long time since I've gotten this close to a man, she thought. I'll be damned if I let some damn divination get in the way of my needs.

She squeezed the hungry muscles in her triangle, and relaxed them slowly. Her muscles throbbed with intense desire. He was the most handsomest thing she ever laid her eyes on: Hazel bedroom eyes and red, curly locks. She smiled to herself.

She began to conjure up a new way of divining in her head. If he wanted her prediction, he would have to accept her new way, even if it didn't make sense to him because it sure didn't make much sense to her either; but she would make it work.

"You'll have to close your eyes," she told him. "And you'll have to put your hand over my heart, so our souls can meet. When the spirit gets on me, I'll probably moan and jerk around a little bit, but don't be frightened. When this is all over with, I'll have some answers for you." She smiled.

Rufus had never been to a psychic before, so what did he know? Nevertheless, he felt a bit uncomfortable about touching her breasts.

"I want you to close your eyes now," she told him. "Slowly." "Relax." "Inhale." "Exhale." Relax."

At first, his eyelids fluttered. He had to force himself to relax.

Mother Hazel smiled. Flames of desire burned within her sixty-year old-body. She guided his hand to her breasts. When he touched them, Mother Hazel's hungry passion burst into flame.

Rufus was anxious to help her to get answers to his problems, so he asked her if it was okay to talk about them.

She sighed; her shoulders drooped.

"Go ahead. But be quick. The spirit is anxious."

I sure hope this doesn't take long, she thought to herself. I aim to get my own needs met here now.

Rufus was finally able to collect his thoughts.

"Well, he began, "I'm a big-time landowner. I'm concerned about not having enough children to help me work my land. You see, I would like to be able to keep most of my fortune in the family, and not have to pay for hired hands."

Mother Hazel looked at him. In her heart, she was wagging her head at him.

"There's this other woman in my life, too," he said. "Now, I can't say that I love her, because I don't. That kind of thing takes time. You know what I mean."

Mother Hazel rolled her eyes toward heaven.

Please get on with it, she thought.

"I can't get my wife to give me children, aside from the one we have. She gave me a daughter, then she quit on me."

Mother Hazel was suddenly listening intently. He had given her a basis on which to build her prediction.

Rufus went on. "This other woman is divorced with six kids. Unfortunately, she comes from a bad background. Her mother was a whore...."

Mother Hazel broke in irritably.

"And you want to know if she can be trusted?"

When Rufus didn't answer, she shifted impatiently in her seat. There followed a long interval of silence. She wanted him to finish babbling and let her get on with her business.

"The other woman has four young daughters and two teenage sons. And I need to know what I'm up against if I bring them all under my roof?"

Mother Hazel laughed to herself, watching him. You must think I was born yesterday, she thought to herself. What you really want to know is if you can get away with messing with those little girls. Who am I to judge? What you and that woman do are you all business. If it isn't you, it'll probably be someone else. That seems to be the way it is around here with stepfamilies.

"Well, let's see what the spirit reveals," she replied. "Just press your hand a little harder against my chest."

Her voluptuous, fleshy breasts left him feeling uncomfortable.

"Relax, son," she cooed. "There ain't nothing sexual going on here. I know that's what's bothering you. You're very tensed. I'm old enough to be your mother," she clucked.

Mother Hazel thought for a long moment about Charlotte, and what she was probably doing to keep herself from having children. She felt that Charlotte was douching—something she herself did when she was young. Now this other woman, she thought, is probably as poor as 'ol Job in the Bible once was after Satan destroyed his family and all his riches. She probably looks pretty much like me. Probably feels about herself, the same as I do. Reflecting on how she grew up, Mother Hazel would rather see the frog upstage the princess.

Memories of Mother Hazel's childhood flooded back to her. She was teased and ridiculed because of her dark, soft skin. It was unbearable. All that teasing made her feel insecure. She had a hard life, but she learned how to deal with it. She forced those memories to the back of her mind.

She wanted Rufus for herself.

Fat chance of that happening, she thought. I'm old and unattractive, but passion still burns within my old bones.

She sniffed. She had wasted enough time thinking.

"You must keep your eyes closed," she told Rufus. As soon as she said that, his eyelids started fluttering, again.

"Uh! Uh! Be careful. Try to keep 'em closed."

It was hard, but he willed himself to do as she said.

"I want to warn you again that when the spirit gets on me real hard, you're going to hear me making strange noises. I might even be moving around a little bit, depending on how hard it gets on me. But don't you concern yourself. You just keep your eyes closed, because after the spirit moves, I'll tell you what's going on with your wife and whether or not this other woman and her children will be good for you."

Hearing Mother Hazel's words, Rufus relaxed completely. The incense gave off a soothing aroma he never smelled before.

With great dexterity, Mother Hazel pushed the tiny brown buttons through the slits in her buttoned-down skirt. She spread her fat thighs apart and gently inserted a finger inside her throbbing womanhood. She began moaning in subtle ecstasy. She withdrew her finger and dried her hand on the hem of her skirt. Smiling like a satisfied thief, she looked at Rufus dreamily. She wished she could've had the real thing! If only she knew hypnosis! Finally, she said, "Open your eyes, now."

Rufus looked at Mother Hazel with great anticipation, but not knowing what had just transpired. She touched her tongue to her lip and smiled, and then proceeded to give him a spurious divination: "That pretty little thing that you're carrying around inside your pocket—well, she's been throwing your babies out with the bath water. I can almost guarantee that you'll find her douche bag hanging in back of her closet door." Mother Hazel felt happy to see Rufus clench, and then unclench his jaws. She hoped he would beat the daylight out of Charlotte, as he silently stared at the table.

She went on. "Marry that other woman! Encourage her daughters to marry early, so you can get the hands you need to help you work your land. The boys—well, you know male children. Expect a bit of trouble; but they'll probably leave home early."

She saw in his eyes the excruciating pain of betrayal. She hadn't meant to hurt him; she had only meant to hurt Charlotte because she couldn't stand her beauty. Pretty women irked her. "I'm sorry to be the one to tell you about your wife. But that's what you paid me for. Marry that other woman and get on with your life."

He lifted his cold steely eyes and glared at her. To hell with Maebelle for now, he thought. He could only think of Charlotte—goddamn her soul! He thought he had her under control. Women always betrayed him. He blamed Charlotte's deception on old Mrs. Daisy Carter, their next-door neighbor. He pushed the chair back, scraping the floor with the bottom of the chair, and stood. He was livid.

Mother Hazel got up too, and followed him to the door. "I hope I've been helpful to you." Rufus still said nothing. He opened the door and stormed out of the orange room.

"Please tell Rosalie to send in my next customer," she told him as she adjusted her turban on her head. He didn't answer, as she closed the door and leaned back against it. Boy! Do I feel like a spring chicken! If only I knew voodoo! she mused.

Rufus stormed pass Rosalie. Her farewell fell on deaf ears. Outside of her house, darkness had arrived; crickets and cicadas rasped like an off-key million-voice choir. All the windows were squares of yellow light. He was cussing and swearing as he swiftly crossed the street. Inside the pickup, he slammed the door hard. After he turned on the headlights, he raced toward the highway.

****

It took Rufus one day and half the night to get home, because his darn pickup broke down. He had to wait another day for the part to be shipped. At three o'clock, Wednesday morning, he sped into his yard and brought the pickup to a screeching stop. He felt tired, rubbing a hand over his face. He wanted Mother Hazel to be wrong about Charlotte, throwing away his babies.

"Does she really hate me that much?" he kept asking himself. "I always thought I had Charlotte under control." He opened the door and climbed out of the pickup, dragging his suitcase towards the house. Rover was wagging his tail as he greeted Rufus, and followed him to the door. He barely noticed his pet as they walked alongside each other. Storming up the porch steps, he unlocked the front door and entered the house. After a few seconds of fumbling in the dark, he turned on the light switch and set down his suitcase near the door. In a huff, he marched toward the bedroom. The door was ajar. He switched on the light and rushed toward the bed. He dug his fingers into her shoulders, jerking her out of her sleep.

"Wake up god-dammit!"

Charlotte bolted upright, wide-eyed and frightened out of her wits. At first, she thought it was an intruder. For a second, she lost her voice as she stared up at her towering husband. A surge of anger rippled through her, when she recognized him. "Rufus!" she snapped, "Why are you waking me out of my sleep like this? What's the matter with you?"

Rufus smacked her hard with the back of his hand. The blow took Charlotte by surprise. She fell back on her pillow, letting out a strangled cry. Sari, who was sleeping beside her, stirred in her sleep.

"Get your ass up!" Rufus ordered. "And bring your god-damn *doooche* bag with you. I'll be waiting in the kitchen." Rufus turned on his heels and stormed out of the room.

Shaking like a leaf on a tree, Charlotte lifted herself up on her elbows, wondering what in the world had happened to Rufus while he was away. She was panic-stricken and disgusted, as her low-down husband had violated her privacy. It was clear he didn't think she deserved any. Questions started racing in her mind as she remembered he just got back.

He just got back! she thought. "When did he find time to go through my things? My contraception!" She gasped. "Oh, God!"

Her heart slammed into her breast, as she threw back the covers and jumped out of bed, but tiptoed softly across the floor to her bureau. She heard Rufus pacing in the kitchen.

Charlotte pulled open the drawer and ran her hand under her clothes. The contraception was still there. She closed her eyes.

"Thank you, God," she whispered.

Charlotte pulled opened the bottom drawer and brought out the "damn" douche bag. "What should I tell him?" she muttered, clutching the douche bag to her breast. She didn't want to involve Mrs. Daisy. She had ordered the douche bag out of the old woman's catalog.

She moved awkwardly toward the door. Then she stopped, half turned, and looked back at her precious Sari. She stepped out of the room and closed the door behind her. Her fears suddenly dissipated, and were replaced by fury. She wasn't the traitor; he was.

She marched toward the kitchen with fire blazing in her eyes. It was sheer luck he hadn't found her contraception. She had wrapped them inconspicuously inside several pairs of panties, and stuffed them in the corner of her drawer. She wondered why it had taken him so long to bring up the fact that he had known about her douche bag. "Thank God he didn't find my contraception," she repeated.

One of Mrs. Daisy's sons, Aaron Carter, a young gynecologist with a practice in a small town in Wicker Valley, Alabama, had prescribed the pills to her. He had visited the summer she went into labor with Sari, and had helped deliver her healthy baby girl. That day Rufus was nowhere to be found. Charlotte had been shocked when Mrs. Daisy suggested that Dr. Aaron Carter prescribe something to prevent her from having more children.

"But only if you want him to." Mrs. Daisy said as an afterthought, considering Charlotte's own opinion. But Charlotte wanted him to prescribe contraceptives. Dr. Aaron Carter had been a "God-send," in her opinion. Each year, thereafter, when Dr. Aaron Carter visited his mother, he would examine Charlotte over at his mother's house.

Charlotte fought back the tears forming in her eyes. She would not appear weak in front of Rufus.

"I'm tired of your ass!" she muttered, flushed-faced. "Tired of you trampling over me. My mother is a strong woman; she didn't raise her daughters to be doormats. But I've let you be an ass of a husband. No more, Rufus! I've let you walk on me, just to keep a promise, I never should've made in the first place!"

As she made her way to the kitchen, she thought of her grandfather, and what he told her right before he died. 'I'm depending on you, Charlotte, to keep this land in the family. It's your great-great grandfather's legacy. Promise me you'll never let this land out of this family. I pray that God will let your first born be a son.'

"Well, God didn't answer your prayer!" she muttered. "And I've tried my best to live up to my promise. But at what cost! I could've been some place teaching school if I hadn't married this scoundrel! What about my dreams? I had only two years to go before I got my degree. But you—you had to go and get sick. And, of course, you expected your little girl to drop everything and come take care of you. I sacrificed my dreams—my life. But I'm tired now, Grandpapa. Tired of trying to keep your dream alive. Tired of low-down Rufus. This is the straw that broke the camel's back. I've had it!"

Charlotte summoned courage she never knew she had. She would give Rufus a tongue-lashing that he would never forget. It didn't matter if he beat her. But she swore this would be her last beating.

She stepped into the kitchen and stood with her shoulder against the door jam, hugging the douche bag against her chest, snorting fire.

You wanted to see it. Well, here it is, she thought. She didn't yet have enough courage to say the words out loud.

Rufus whirled around angrily, his eyes riveted on the douche bag in her arms. His gaze was drawn to the long syringe, then to the nozzle lying on the floor. He lifted his eyes and glared at her. She read in his eyes, the feeling of betrayal.

The sonofabitch, she thought to herself. What about how you've betrayed me—sleeping with every whore you can get your hands on.

Marching toward her, Charlotte swallowed. He looked at the darn thing like he would jerk it from her and cut it to shreds. It didn't matter because she had another one still wrapped in plastic.

"Go into the dinning room!" he ordered. "I want you to count the goddamn chairs! Then I want you to tell me how come we have more goddamn chairs than children!"

She looked him straight in the eye, as if he had lost his mind. Her piercing eyes struck him.

"Well, what the hell you staring at me for? Turn your ass around and go count the goddamn chairs! Then tell me where are the children to fill them up!" he demanded.

Charlotte stood as stubborn as a Mississippi mule. To hell with him! She wasn't counting shit—beating or no beating! Rufus could not believe that Charlotte dared to disobey him.

"You defying me, woman!"

She didn't answer.

You damn right, she thought. But she still didn't have enough courage to speak up to him, but she was working on it.

"Well, I'll tell you why we don't have enough children to sit in all them chairs since the cat's got your tongue. It's because of that—that damn snake-ass looking doooch bag you're hugging. You knew what I stood for when you married me! You and your smart-ass old man both knew. I'd have the children I needed if he hadn't dangled you in front of my face. He knew goddamn well what he did. He took my money then got his land right back because I married you! You were in on it. You think you're too damn cute to have my babies?" he asked with blazing eyes.

"Shut up!" Charlotte shouted. "You leave my grandfather out of this! You got Granddaddy's land for peanuts, you bastard! And you knew what I stood for, too!" She raised her chin slightly, having summoned the courage she needed.

"I wanted a real marriage; I wanted more than one child. Maybe not as many as you, but I wanted more than one child! But you—you started trampling all over me with your whores from day one! I was a virgin when you married me," she said through clenched teeth. "Next thing I knew, my vagina lost its identity! It smelled— smelled like every whore's rump you ever laid up with. I wasn't going to let you rot my insides! "So yes! I started douching. I started washing your stinking filth right out of me, along with your stinking, rotten seed! I guess you could say I've been throwing your goddamn babies out with the bath water."

Charlotte saw Rufus' eyes widen in a sort of horrified recognition. "Somebody's been talking to you about me, haven't they?" He didn't respond.

Mother Hazel's words beat inside his mind: *That pretty little wife of yours is throwing your babies out with the bath water.*

For a moment, Rufus felt he was sinking to the floor. His cold, steely eyes rested on Charlotte, as if she were a total stranger. Charlotte's face was taut and flushed. She wasn't afraid anymore.

Charlotte never cursed. She was a religious person, although he didn't allow her to attend church. But she was hot now; and she was sick of him. She laid down her religion. The venom started flying, striking at the core of his wounded soul. She called him everything, but a child of God.

Rufus felt electrified. He looked at her with fear and hostility, realizing for the first time that he didn't really know whom this quiet, beautiful monster was. He wondered what else she was capable of. Murder? For the first time, since he had known Charlotte, Rufus became fearful of her. Trying to conceal it, he glared at this stone, cold, enraged stranger, he called his wife.

Charlotte knew she took a grave risk, but she was determined to stand her ground. She folded her arms across her chest and moved toward the window, despite thoughts that he might strike at her. She couldn't stand looking at his miserable face any longer. She despised him, as she wiped tears from her face. Drawing the kitchen shade, she stared at the early gray dawn. Anger boiled inside her.

Minutes passed before he asked: "Just answer this one question for me, will you?" His voice was an eerie calm. It made her uncertain.

"What is it?" she said, refusing to look at him. Her voice was hard as stone.

"Where did you keep that—that douche bag?"

Charlotte's mouth fell open. Slowly, she turned and faced him. Their grievous eyes met.

"What!" she cried in disbelief. "Aren't you the one who told me I had it in the first place? Now you're going . . . Oh! I see. It was one of your bigmouth whores who planted the idea in your head, wasn't it? Well, why don't you ask her, or them where I was keeping it?"

Rufus' eyes were aflame. He said nothing.

Charlotte shuddered with anger, then turned her back to him and stared out the window.

"A low-down dog!" she muttered. She felt surprised she was starting to smell her own blood. It had never happened before.

Seconds later, she heard him leave the room. Then she heard the front door open and close. Before long, she heard him drive away.

Good, she thought. Go to your damn whores. Don't come back.

Charlotte moved toward the china cabin and pulled open the drawer and took out a pad and fountain pen and sat down at the table, and scripted her parents a brief letter.

Dear Mother and Papa,

How are you? I've been thinking. You and Papa haven't seen Sari since she was a tiny baby. She is growing like a ragweed. I want to bring her for a visit. Look for us next Saturday.

Love you,

Charlotte

She conveniently left out the fact that once she and her daughter arrived she planned on staying. She had just finished the letter, when Sari came running out of the bedroom, climbed onto her lap, and nestled her head in her shoulders. The child was shivering. Charlotte put down her pen and put her arms around her small frame and hugged her to her breasts.

"Everything is all right," she clucked softly.

She stared vacantly at the yellow prints in the wallpaper. She had to make a change; give Sari a chance to grow up in a peace.

****

On Saturday morning, Maebelle rose at the crack of dawn. She built a fire in the wood burning stove and made breakfast. She poured a cup of coffee, and sat outside. She sat on the kitchen step, sipping freshly perked coffee, listening to the cry of a lonesome dove somewhere deep in the woods. Her mind shifted back to Rufus. She was deeply troubled. "Where are you, Rufus? Why haven't you come by to see me? Why did you leave like that?"

A knock at the front door interrupted Maebelle. Thinking it was Mr. Klapper; she muttered to herself, "Mrs. Klapper can forget it. This is my day off; I'm not giving it up. I'm sick of looking in you all's faces."

Taking the cup of coffee with her, she went back inside the house to see who was at her door. She set down the saucer on the table, and tiptoed from the kitchen to the living room. She slightly drew back the curtain just enough to peek out. Her heart nearly leapt into her throat.

"Rufus!" she cried. Her voice was low, but full of excitement. Withdrawing her hand from the curtain, then eyeing herself in the nearly faded mirror on the wall near the door, she took some deep breaths, and moved toward the door.

"Who is it?" she asked, faking deliberate irritation in her voice.

"Rufus."

Maebelle opened the inner door and looked at him through the latched screen door. She adjusted her gaze upward to look into his handsome face. Her knees weakened, as she cautioned herself not to show how much she missed him.

Rufus smiled at her. Strangely, she didn't remind him of Olga any more. Olga was now old, frail, and crazy. But, he would always believe she was Olga's estranged daughter. Her dark skin required getting used to. All his life he swore he would not touch a dark-skinned woman. Not because they weren't attractive, but because they reminded him of his aunt Olga.

"What are you doing knocking on my door this early in the morning?" Maebelle scolded.

Rufus dropped his head.

"Oh, c'mon, baby. I'm too tired to fight." He looked haggard. He'd stayed at the juke house ever since Charlotte revealed herself. He pulled on the door handle.

"Maebelle, unhitch the door, and let me in, please!"

Feeling rather bold now that he arrived, she stood with her hands on her hips.

"Please what! You can't treat me just any old kind of way, Rufus, then pop up on my doorstep whenever you feel like it! I haven't seen you since last Sunday, when you drove off like some crazy person. Now here you are, knocking on my door early in the morning, thinking. . .."

"We need to talk," he said, cutting her off.

Maebelle kept staring at him before she finally unhitched the latch. She hoped her little charade had made a lasting impression. She didn't want him to leave, but she didn't want him to think he could treat her just any kind of way.

Rufus grabbed the handle, pulled open the door, and stepped inside the house.

Maebelle arms were folded tightly across her chest.

"May I sit down?" he asked.

She motioned with her hands, pretending to be aloof.

Rufus sat on the couch and reached for her arm.

"Don't touch me!" she yelled, swinging a hand at him. Her emotions were disturbing now, because she still actually felt rejected.

He grabbed her hand, anyway, and pulled her toward him.

"Listen to me, baby. Without getting into a long, drawn out explanation about last Sunday, I just want to say I'm sorry. I-I mean I had things on my mind; I couldn't wait around for you to finish carrying on with your tongue-wagging friend that day, before you decided to come back out. I knew if I told you, I didn't want to wait for you, you'd want to argue. I'm sorry, baby."

Why the sudden mood swing, she wanted to ask, but she was afraid he might leave if she started pressuring him for answers.

"Well, I don't care what your excuse was. I'm letting you know what you did to me was wrong. You embarrassed me in front of my friend."

"I said I was sorry, baby. What more can I say?"

Plenty, she thought, wriggling out of his grasp.

Rufus stared up at her, and then let his head loll back on the sofa. He closed his eyes.

"I'm a broken man, Maebelle. I need your loving. Charlotte has left me." He lied.

Maebelle's heart leaped for joy. Trying to control her happiness, she feigned a sympathetic expression.

"I've been out of town all week," he told her. "I just got in this morning. I still can't believe it. I got the shock of my life when I entered the house."

Maebelle straightened. She waited intently for him to share all that had happened.

Rufus opened his eyes and stared pitifully at her.

"She took my little girl, Maebelle. They're gone!"

The truth was, the scoundrel hadn't been home since his showdown with Charlotte, Wednesday morning.

Ever since Charlotte admitted to what the psychic had predicted, Rufus had a vendetta against her. He wanted her to leave and finally figured out a slick way to get her out of the house permanently.

Maebelle was the perfect bait. He knew Maebelle wanted his possessions. He'd give them to her because she had four beautiful daughters to reproduce for the sake of the land. He still wasn't sure about her sons, though. Getting her to give them up seemed reasonable. Yes, he would convince her the boys should be with their father.

"Come live with me," he said, surprising the heck out of her. "Live with me until I get my divorce. Then we can get married."

Maebelle felt her heart pounding to the rhythm of her joy. "You sure that's what you want? I mean, you don't think it's too soon for you to bring someone else into your home? Suppose your wife changes her mind?"

"She won't," he replied. "You know how you women are. Once you make up your mind, there's no changing it. But if you need time to think about it, I understand."

I don't need time to think about it, honey; I already have, she smiled to herself.

She had dreamed the impossible dream, according to Leslie. It was becoming her reality. The good life handed to her on a silver platter. She quickly sat in his lap, nestling her head in his hard shoulder. She felt like the luckiest woman in the world.

Leslie didn't think I could win you, she thought. Wait till I tell her the news.

Finally she said, "Give me a week to think about it. Okay?"

Rufus looked at her for a moment.

"Sure. Well, I have to get going. Make sure this is what you want, because once I get my hooks into you, there is no letting go. Charlotte slipped away, but I won't make the same mistake twice. Once you're mine, you're mine. So think real hard about it."

Maebelle smiled committed. "Don't let me go; I love you. When will I see you again?"

"What are you doing this afternoon?" he asked. "I'd like to come back and bring you to see the house, to help you make up your mind sooner."

He knew it would, for the house she was living in was small and run-down; the furniture was in poor condition. But, at least she was clean; he liked that about her. She kind of looked nice with her hair down around her shoulders, too, which was how Charlotte wore hers.

You have nice features, he thought. But your skin . . . He averted his eyes.

"I have no plans," she told him. "My 'ex' is picking up the children, so I'll be free!"

"Good. Then I'll see you—say 'round four o'clock."

"All right," she replied.

He stood, and gently planted her on the floor.

Maebelle walked with Rufus to the door. It was one of the happiest moments of her entire life. Unexpectedly, he pulled her towards him and planted a surprise kiss on her lips.

"See you later."

She opened her eyes and looked at him in a dreamy state.

"Later," she replied.

She stood on the top step, watching him head toward his pickup. Driving away, he waved good-bye from the window.

She lifted a hand with a jaunty wave.

"I love you," she called.

With the truck out of sight, Maebelle raised her hands in the air, swinging her hips sensually. She felt her life was finally coming full circle. She went inside.

A couple of hours had elapsed since Rufus' visit, but Maebelle was still too excited to keep her mind on her housework. She decided to pay Leslie a visit—surprise her with her good news. She moved toward the kitchen where the children were seated at the table eating breakfast.

"Lynn?" she called, before stepping inside the doorway.

Lynn, a lovely eight-year old, light complexioned, wavy-hair girl with pouty lips and big brown eyes, looked at her mother out the corner of her eye. She didn't say anything because her mouth was full.

"I'm talking to all of you, matter of fact," Maebelle said.

Lynn swallowed. "Yes, ma'am?"

"I said I'm not only just talking to Lynn; I said I'm talking to all of you!"

The other children turned around in their seats expectantly.

"That's better," Maebelle said. "Now Lynn, I want you and Jennifer to finish the wash I left in the tub. Jackie, I want you and Jinni to clean the kitchen; do a good job. I want this floor swept and scrubbed. Sam, I want you to clean the backyard. Jake Junior, you clean the front yard. Now, does everybody understand what's to be done? Or should I repeat myself?"

"We understand," they said in unison.

"Good! Then that means when I get back from Leslie's I'm going to find everything as I expect it to be."

"Why are you going to Leslie so early for?" Jennifer asked. "And why are you looking and sounding all happy all of a sudden. All week you've been acting so mad."

Maebelle smiled; she looked down leisurely at her left shoe.

"Yeah, Mama," Jake Junior interjected. "Why are you so happy all of a sudden?"

Maebelle laughed. "I was that bad, huh?" She propped a hand on her right hip. "Well, thank God I'm not feeling that way now. While you all were asleep, I had a visitor who gave me some really good news." She saw the children wide-eyed with excitement. She knew they were thinking it was their father she was talking about.

"You're talking about Daddy? Was he here?" Lynn asked. "Did he say us girls could come live with him, too? Cause it's not fair for him to only take Sam and Jake Junior just because they're boys. We're his children, too. We want to live with him, too. Please!"

"...And leave me without any of my children! I thought you all loved me." Maebelle said with mock hurt.

"We do," Jennifer said. "But we're tired of living in this old raggedly house. We want to go to Detroit with Daddy. So, was it Daddy? Did he say we could come live with him?"

Maebelle stared at the floor. Then she lifted her eyes and spoke in a low, even tone.

"Un unh. It wasn't your daddy; and no, you cannot live with him. That's all there is to it. It was Rufus; he wants to marry me. You girls are staying with me—I don't mean in this house, in his house. You all can live good, like your brothers. Rufus has plenty money. I'm going to go over there later this afternoon to look at his house. He wants me—us to move in with him whenever I'm ready."

Not only the girls, but the boys, too, stared long-faced at the floor—all except Jinni. The idea of Rufus having plenty of money sounded appealing. Now she could have all the things she'd always dreamed about. She would be the envy of the whole school.

"So what happened to his wife?" Jake Junior inquired emotionally. "I know he's got one because I've heard you and Leslie arguing about him. I can't believe you're taking that woman's husband!" he exclaimed. He looked her full in the face, not caring about the outcome.

"So you've been eavesdropping on grown-ups conversations, boy?"

Jake Junior didn't answer. He turned around in his chair, picked up his fork, and started eating.

Sighing heavily, Maebelle dropped her hands in exasperation.

"Ungrateful little wenches," she mumbled under her breath. "I'm doing this for all of us, not just for me."

"Mama, please don't move in with him," Jennifer said. "None of us like him. He can't even look me in the eyes when I look at him."

"We don't want no step-daddy," Lynn whined. "We like things just the way they are since Daddy won't come back. We even like this old broken-down house, right Jennifer?"

"I like him," Jinni interjected."

Seeing the shocked expression on the faces of Lynn, Jennifer, Jake Junior, and Sam, Jinni looked down at her plate. "I mean I like him a little—for you, Mama."

"That's because you think he looks like Philip Coon," Jennifer mocked. "And all because they got the same kind of eyes. But he's no Philip Coon, stupid!"

"Nobody said he was!" Jinni retorted. She poked out her tongue, stuck her thumbs in her ears, and wriggled her fingers.

Maebelle's back suddenly stiffened. She glared at Jinni. "Who's Philip Coon? I know y'all ain't messing around with no little boys—Jinni?"

Jinni didn't comment.

"He's just a boy at school," Jennifer replied. "And it ain't no y'all! And I didn't say she was messing with him. She just likes him. But you don't have to worry because he doesn't even know she exists. I guess she's too dark for him."

She gave Jinni a hard glance. The two girls were twins. But one would never tell by the way they sometimes treated each other, and the contrast of their skin. Jennifer had a light complexion like her father; Jinni, on the other hand, was dark-skinned, like Maebelle.

Rolling her eyes, Jinni mumbled under her breath, and stirred in her seat.

"When Rufus was here last Sunday he looked at Jennifer and Jinni kind of funny, and it wasn't because they were dressed up for church," Jake Junior blurted out, and then looked at Sam for confirmation. Sam didn't budge. "That's what you told me, didn't you?"

Sam shrugged his shoulders, and spoke under his breath. But he hadn't lied about what he had seen. (The night Rufus drove Maebelle home from his juke house she brought him in the house and introduced him to her children. Maebelle went to change out of her heels. Jake Junior went to bed. But Sam hung around keeping and eye on his two older sisters, until Maebelle returned.) Jake Junior looked at him annoyingly.

Jennifer sat opened-mouthed.

"But why—why me, I'm not the one who likes him! Jinni does." Jennifer looked around at Sam, and at Jake Junior, and then at Maebelle's taut face. She felt hurt and embarrassed. Now, she would always be conscious of Rufus' presence. She wished Maebelle wouldn't do this to them.

Maebelle swallowed hard. She felt her blood was starting to boil.

These little bastards trying to sabotage my life, she thought.

Her lips were a thin, taut line. "You know something, Sam, I'm glad you and Jake Junior are going to live with your father!" She glared at Jake Junior and said, "That wasn't a nice thing to say in front of your sisters." She snatched the head-rag off her head and stormed out of the kitchen, cussing under her breath. A few minutes later, they heard the front door slam.

"I sure hope Leslie can talk some sense into her," Jake Junior said. "And you'd think she would want to be here when Daddy picks us up. He told her he was coming early. I just hope to God Leslie talks sense into Mama's head. I know she's going over there to tell her, too. Like Leslie is going to offer her congratulations."

Jake Junior was sixteen, the oldest of her six children. Maebelle made him the man of the house when she and Jake split up.

"Well, she might as well turn around now, because Leslie is never going to side with her," Jennifer ad-libbed.

"Leslie won't be able to talk Mama out of nothing she doesn't want her to," Jackie remarked. "Mama is hardheaded. She done changed a lot since she met that 'ol thing. She used to listen to what we had to say, but no more—not since she met him." The conversation lapsed.

Troubled, Jennifer stared at the food on her plate. She was also thinking how much Maebelle had changed, how she used to be a nice mother. But now she was too infatuated with Rufus' good looks and money. She cared less about them. To think that Jake Junior was telling the truth about Rufus looking at her funny made her ill. I sure hope Mama knows what she's doing, she thought.

****

The dust bit at Maebelle's heels as she walked blithely down the dusty road. She dismissed the children's objectionable outbursts and accusations—what did they know. Children are children. She turned into Leslie's yard. She propped a foot on the bottom step and swiped the dust from around her ankle with a white handkerchief.

Leslie was looking at her through the screen, smiling. She was happy to see her, even though lately all they did was argue. She knew she'd be coming back once she got pleased. She moved toward the door. She hadn't wanted to leave for Harlem, New York City, without saying goodbye.

"Hi, girl.... Aren't we out bright and early."

Maebelle looked around in Leslie's direction. She giggled in startled surprised.

"Hi. How you doing?"

"Fine," Leslie replied, opening the screen door. "Come in. I'm really happy to see you."

Maebelle looked in agreement. "Oh, yeah?" She stuck a handkerchief inside her skirt pocket, walked up the porch steps and entered Leslie's house. Maebelle held her mouth open as she observed Leslie's living room. "Leslie, girl! What happened to your furniture?"

Leslie twirled around like a happy child. "Brandon took it over to Mama. Girl, I'm going to Harlem, New York City! Child, Aunt Thelma finally sent me that one-way ticket she always talked about." She started sipping the homemade plum wine her mother made. She was elated, as she wriggled her booty and snapped her fingers.

Maebelle's eyes opened wider. "Miss Holier-than-thou is wriggling her booty! And snapping her fingers," she said incredulously. "Why, I don't believe it. What happened to...?"

Leslie put a hand on Maebelle's shoulder and began pushing her toward the kitchen. "Oh! Come. Let's sit in the kitchen, girl. Now sit your behind down, and stop judging me." Her voice was mild.

Maebelle sat down at Leslie's makeshift twenty-five-gallon barrel, plywood table.

"Now, tell me what brings you out so early—and looking all happy, at that?" She didn't wait for an answer. "You know, I was going to get Brandon to drop me by your house before I left. Now I don't have to."

"When are you leaving?"

"Tomorrow. But today I'm going to Mama. I won't be back, of course, because I have no furniture.

"Hmm. So you finally made up your mind, huh?"

"Sure have. I'm looking forward to this change."

Leslie sat down, handing Maebelle a glass of wine.

"I never told you that I've been writing the songs my aunt sings in the nightclubs. She's been paying me, of course."

Maebelle looked at her over the rim of her glass. "Hmm, isn't it a sin for you to be writing them kind of songs?" she asked in a crass tone.

"No. As a matter of fact, they're clean songs, my aunt sings in those classy nightclubs." Avoiding an argument, Leslie abruptly changed the subject.

"So what has you all bubbly? I saw that twinkle in your eyes a while ago. Are you and Jake getting back together? The children would love nothing better...."

"Rufus' wife left him," Maebelle blurted out. "And he has asked me to move in with him until his divorce. He wants to marry me."

Leslie suddenly choked on the wine.

Enraged by Leslie's reaction to her news, Maebelle jumped up from the makeshift table and rushed toward the kitchen window. She could feel her tension burning, as she stared out into the yard, sipping on her wine.

"I should've known you'd act like this," she said. Neither woman spoke for a few minutes.

Leslie broke the silence. She felt it a necessity to rebuke Maebelle and her past improprieties.

"So once again you've taken someone else's man. There's no stopping you, is there? You took Jake from your sister Pauline. You let him knock you up, so he felt obliged to marry you. You caused your youngest sister Effie's marriage to break up. And now, though you've lived here a few weeks—maybe a month—you've wrecked Charlotte's marriage!" Leslie felt enraged. When would Maebelle change?

"Jake liked me better than he did Pauline!" Maebelle retorted. "Besides, I was twelve then; I was young. I didn't know what I was doing. And he wasn't married to her, for your information. He was engaged to her."

"I didn't say he was married to her. I said you took him away from her. You broke up her engagement! And don't give me that you were young bull. You weren't too young to get him in that barn and spread your legs. You were a fast-tail, selfish brat then, and you're still that way!"

Maebelle drained her glass.

"Here! Pour me another glass. Or should I get it myself!"

"Get it yourself, you heathen! You're not exactly a guest, you know!"

"Fine! I'll get it myself."

Maebelle moved toward the cooler, tilted it, and filled the glass to the rim.

"I can't help it if Jake liked me better than he did Pauline, now could I?"

Leslie swallowed the ill taste left in her mouth by that selfish remark. She glared at Maebelle, wondering where in the world Mr. and Mrs. Hawkins got her? She was nothing like her sisters, Pauline and Effie. She was a selfish, cruel, cunning person—stubborn as a mule.

Maebelle cut her eyes at Leslie. She thought of leaving after finishing her wine. I don't need this shit. First, it was my children. Now it's you! To hell with all of you, she told herself as she stood in front of the window gulping down the wine. There was a long, awkward moment of silence.

With Maebelle's back turned towards her, Leslie studied Maebelle's shapely backside. She wondered if Maebelle wore panties, because she never used to. She had heard it was her panty-less booty that had seduced Effie's husband, Scott Lloyd. She felt so annoyed with Maebelle, she could no longer restrain her hostility.

"You said you were young when you took Jake from Pauline, huh? Okay. So tell me, what were you when you went to Effie's house and sneaked out in the shed with Scott Lloyd?"

Maebelle swallowed hard, while nodding her head sideways, and looking at Leslie for a long moment. She turned to the window clearly recalling what happened on that awful day changed her life forever.

Maebelle felt she had done nothing wrong. It was all Scott's fault. She had convinced herself of that because of the outcome. He forced her to lie down. She had tried somewhat to fight him off, until he forced his tongue in her mouth. She still remembered his thrusts, and in retrospect she had sort of enjoyed Scott's rhythm, similar to that of a very good dancer. Still, she quietly cried afterward.

Maebelle pressed the half-empty glass against her cheek. She didn't care how good Scott made her feel; she knew she hadn't gone over there to be raped. And the dirty-dog had caused the breakup of her marriage—ruined her life.

Leslie broke into her thoughts.

"I just can't believe you've gone and broke up Charlotte's marriage. That man doesn't want you; he's looking at your girls, fool! Any fool would know that!"

Maebelle shuddered with anger. She turned and glared at Leslie.

"You know, Leslie, you really make me sick! I'm not breaking up that woman's marriage! How many times have I told you I didn't go to Effie's house to mess with Scott Lloyd! Every time you bring this shit up, I say the same damn thing over and over again! And I'm telling you the same damn thing again. I went there to borrow thread! Thread! You hear—thread!"

Leslie scrambled to her feet. She despised Maebelle's irresponsible attitude.

"You went there wearing no drawers, dammit!" Her eyes widened when she heard herself curse. She cupped her mouth and sat back down.

Maebelle glared at her, wondering how she knew she hadn't been wearing panties. I never told her that. Right now she hated Leslie so much she couldn't wait for her to leave town.

"I won't miss you after you're gone," she calmly told her.

"Don't try changing the subject," Leslie retorted.

The silence that followed included Maebelle looking out the window reflecting on her life and that fateful summer day she'd experienced with Scott. That reckless infidelity destroyed her marriage. If only Jake hadn't needed to borrow the lousy monkey wrench, she thought. If only it hadn't rained; if only the Devil's wind hadn't lifted her dress the moment Scott scooted out from beneath his car. Her throat ached. She had truly loved Jake, and had no intention to be unfaithful.

Jake had stopped by Scott Lloyd's, and finding his wife, he offered to take her home. As she and Jake climbed into the pickup and closed the doors, the sky suddenly opened up, resulting in heavy down pour. Jake rolled up the window on his side, and asked her why she sat there with hers opened. Knowing she looked stupid letting herself get drenched, she also knew if she rolled up that window, Jake would smell the aroma of sex.

Jake started the engine, drove a hundred yards or so, while looking at her like she was crazy. He quickly raised his chin and started sniffing like a dog. The sensual air permeated throughout the cab. Knowing she was in trouble, she thought about telling him right away what Scott did to her; but she didn't. Without warning, Jake reached across the seat and forced her thighs apart. His rough, stiff fingers dug inside her. She grabbed his arm, but it was too late. He brought out his wet fingers and looked at her thunder struck.

She reverted to the present, pushing those memories from her mind, but they lingered. Two weeks later, the tractor Scott Lloyd was driving turned over, crushing him to death. Days before his death, instead of clearing my name, he lied to keep his marriage, she thought.

Maebelle's mother had died of cancer a week after Scott's death. Effie and Pauline had chased her from the funeral home and burial site. Their father had passed away two years earlier. Now she had no one, except her children.

Maebelle raised the empty glass to her lips. She moved toward the makeshift table and set down the glass. She tilted her head down. "I was a fool to come over here," she lamented.

Leslie reached out and put a hand on her arm.

Maebelle drew back, as her eyes swelled with tears. "Don't touch me! If you were a real friend, you would not bring up my past. At least I'm not leaving my children behind, for somebody else to raise!"

"I'm coming back for my children as soon as I get settled," Leslie replied. "So come down off that kick, home-wrecker. I was only about to say God sent you over here. You were no fool to come here. And, I am your friend. You know that!"

"Bye, Leslie! You have a nice life and don't bother to write."

Maebelle staggered out the kitchen, holding her stomach, with one hand. Leslie started to chase after her, but changed her mind, as she heard the screen door open and slam hard.

"Go on, fool," she muttered. "When you get messed up, remember I tried to warn you, but it'll be too late. And don't worry about my writing you, either. That evil, funk man, Rufus, will never put his poison fingers on any of my letters."

CHAPTER 3

After making rounds on the farm, taking care of the livestock, but still not wanting to return home, instead Rufus went to the juke house.

All morning he had agonized over whom he could get to pick up Maebelle and drive her to his home. He was glad to see John's white, Chevy pickup parked out back of the juke house. However, he had a gut feeling that John might still be ticked off since he cut in on him and Maebelle on the dance floor. He hoped John was big enough to let bygones be bygones.

When Rufus entered the juke house, John was working quietly behind the bar re-stocking the shelves with clean glasses.

"Good morning, John," he said, heading toward him.

John turned and faced him.

"Morning, Rufus. I didn't hear you come in. I came in early to get this out of the way, so I could take my time when I come in this evening. So you're early, too, huh?"

"Well, yeah," Rufus said, scratching the back of his head. "Actually, I went by your house on the way here." He lied.

"Oh! What for?"

Still scratching his head, he moved closer to the bar.

"Well, I'm--I'm in need of a small favor. But you just said you came in early so you could have a little time for yourself. It is not right for me to impose on time you're planning for yourself."

John turned around and replaced a glass on the shelf.

"Yeah, I am looking forward to it. It depends on the favor, I still might be able to help you."

Rufus stared at the floor, crossing his fingers.

83

"So what is it?" John asked.

Rufus pulled his gaze from the wooden floor and fixed it on John's broad shoulders.

"You remember Maebelle, don't you?"

The moment he'd said that, John's back stiffened. Rufus could've kicked himself in the teeth for broaching the subject. Of course, John remembered her. He had danced with her, hadn't he and Rufus rudely cut in, right?

John's eyes were fiery as he faced Rufus.

"You cut in on us on the dance floor, didn't you? Now you're going to ask me if I remember her! Are you trying to start something, because I decided to let that go?"

Rufus stepped back. He put up an opened palm.

"Oh no, not at all. I was wrong. I apologize. It was just that when I saw her I thought she was someone I used to know. That's it." He still lied. "Anyway, she's related to Charlotte. At least, that's what she's claiming. Could've fooled me though. At any rate, she wants to pay Charlotte a visit." He lied, again. "Of course, I haven't mentioned any of this to Charlotte only because Maebelle asked me not to. She wants to surprise her. I think Charlotte will be happy to know she has at least one relative living close by.

"So I made plans to bring her over late this afternoon, but something's come up. I have a fellow coming here, from Ruby Creek—on business, of course. The problem is, he has to make a stop on his way, and he's not sure when he'll arrive. I can't afford to miss him."

John felt ticked off that Rufus had purposely gone looking for him.

"So why come to me? Why couldn't you ask Clarence?"

Rufus dropped his head. I need you—not Clarence, or anyone else to do this for me, he told himself.

A long tense moment of silence occurred between them. He knew he couldn't force John, but he sure hoped he could influence him to change his mind.

On second thought, John knew Clarence would not grant Rufus the favor—especially this one. He would have a hard time explaining to his wife, Claire, why he was driving another woman around on a Saturday afternoon at that! He supposed if Rufus could've asked someone else, he would.

On the other hand, he wouldn't mind seeing Maebelle again, but as for her and Charlotte being related—well, that didn't add up. But who was he to think otherwise.

"What time should I pick her up?"

Rufus breathed a quiet sigh of relief.

"How about four o'clock?"

"Four o'clock's good. And I accept the apology."

They shook hands.

"Thanks, John. I owe you one. You had me nervous there for a moment. I was afraid you'd turn me down. I'm glad I don't have to disappoint Maebelle again. You're a much better person than I. Don't ever change."

"Yeah, well, I don't plan to."

Rufus turned on his heels and moved swiftly toward the back to his small office.

"That apology meant shit!" he murmured. "That young buck got too much temper for his own good."

****

By the time Maebelle reached home, Jake had already picked up the children and gone.

"Shucks!" she muttered. "I forgot to tell them not to tell Jake my business. Shucks! Oh, well, I can't do anything about it now," she sighed, making her way toward the kitchen. The fresh scent of Lysol awakened her senses. She loved a clean house! She walked out onto the back porch and dragged an oval tin tub into the kitchen. Moving to the stove where a few coals still burned that kept the pot of water warm, she dipped her finger into the water. It was warm enough for a comfortable bath. She poured the water into the tub.

She found a bar of soap, a washcloth and towel on a chair. A smile traced her lips.

"Jennifer," she muttered fondly. "You're a thoughtful child in spite of your fresh mouth."

Maebelle kicked off her slippers, disrobed, stepped into the tub, sat down and extended her legs. Times like this without the children around was a rare treat, she told herself. She rubbed soap onto the washcloth and started bathing. Her mind drifted back to her argument with Leslie this morning. She and Leslie would never see eye-to-eye on anything.

After she stepped out of the tub, and reached for the towel, draping it around her body, she went to her bedroom, got dressed, and combed and styled her hair into a tight, sexy French roll.

When Maebelle noticed the time on the clock on her bureau, she was surprised how quickly the day had passed. She felt slightly tired. Knowing there was still time for a short nap, she went into the living room and reclined on the couch.

Later, Maebelle awoke from a strange dream that left her feeling anxious. She sat up, rubbing her eyes. In her dream, she gave birth to three sets of twins, all in the same year. In her last pregnancy, she gave birth to a girl and boy, but the boy died right after birth. Rufus went stark raving mad, accusing her of being careless with her pregnancy. He fired the midwife. He blamed her for the child's death as well. From then on, he eagerly ravished her at every opportunity, to replace their dead child.

"Oh, God, she said, rubbing her temple, it must be that plum wine I drank."

She heard the motor of a car. As she arose from the couch, she read the clock on the wall. It read three-thirty.

She heard the car door open, then close.

"He's early," she muttered. Her heart pounded with excitement.

She patted her French roll, smoothed down the wrinkles in her tight red dress, moved toward the window, and drew back the curtain. Her eyes widened in surprise.

"John!" she exclaimed. "What's he doing here?"

Maebelle opened the door and stepped out on the porch.

She gazed at John curiously, who was bowlegged, tall, dark and handsome. He looked exceptionally handsome in khaki pants and a long sleeve white shirt rolled above his elbows, sauntering across her yard. He was walking with his head down.

Maebelle yelled to him with a lithe of laughter in her voice.

"There is no use looking down! There are no apples on the ground!" She giggled.

John jerked his head up, and chuckled.

"Maebelle...hi! You know my mama used to say that to me a lot. It's a bad habit of mine. But, I only do it when I'm in deep thought.

Maebelle looked at him with curiosity.

"What are you doing here?" she inquired.

Without giving any sign he'd heard her, John complimented her dress.

"I remember that dress, you know. You wore it to the juke house, when I first met you. Red is becoming on you. It really looks good on you."

"Why, thank you," Maebelle said.

John climbed the porch steps. He reached for her hands and planted a wet kiss on her forehead. He noticed her confused look.

"I've been elected to be your chauffeur today, Madam Hawkins, in case you're wondering why I'm here." He bowed playfully. "You see I remembered not to call you Madam Blakestone." He laughed. "I remember how you'd nearly bit my head off before. Boy, that cat must've really hurt you! Anyway, I'm here at the request of Mr. Poygoode. He asked me to drive you to his house so you can see Charlotte. He said he had unexpected business to take care of, so I'm doing him a favor."

Maebelle was taken aback for a brief moment.

"Take me to see Charlotte? What the...." She blinked. She averted her eyes, hiding her shock, wondering what other lie Rufus had told John. She knew she had to play along. Yet, she felt embarrassed.

"So what are you to Charlotte, first or second cousin?"

The question startled her. She lowered her lashes, then looked up at him. "Must you be so nosy?"

Although her voice was mild, she saw John raise his brows. She felt like striking Rufus the next time she saw him.

"I take it Rufus wasn't suppose to tell me. I don't see what the big secret is, though."

"It's no big secret," she replied curtly. "At least not any more! Charlotte and I are third cousins, if you must know." She lied.

"Hmm!" Pinching his chin, John stared at her for a second. "Well, I guess we should get going."

He extended a hand to take her by the elbow, but she sidestepped him. She didn't feel friendly right now.

"Why don't you wait for me inside the pickup," she told him. "I have to go inside to get my purse and lock up. I'll only be a minute."

He looked at her half-smiling. Women, he thought to himself. They always got some last minute detail.

"Okay," he said. "But don't be long; I know how you women are. You'll say a minute, but you'll take fifteen or twenty, right?"

"I'll only be a minute. I promise."

She entered her house, cursing Rufus under her breath.

John momentarily watched her, and then returned to his pickup. He reached across the seat and opened the door, on the passenger side.

"What kind of mess is this?" Maebelle fussed. "Telling John me and Charlotte kin to one another! Huh! In her dreams!"

She grabbed her purse and keys off the couch and hurried out the door, locking it behind her. She felt John's gaze on her as she rushed down the steps, hurrying toward his white, Chevy pickup. She smiled at him as she climbed inside. She closed the door and purposely leaned against the passenger side.

For all she knew, Rufus could be testing her. After all, he had taken her away from John when they first danced, and upset John by his harsh remarks in front of everyone. Now, he was linking them together again. She wondered if John thought the same thing.

She gave him a sidelong glance and saw the humorous pleat at the corner of his mouth. She supposed he was laughing at her.

"You'd better close the door before you fall out of it, he teased."

Maebelle felt embarrassed. I closed it and locked it," she replied. He knew she tried to sit far from him, and that it was tightly closed. She unlocked the door, grabbed the handle, opened and slammed the door hard, and locked it. After rolling down the window, and sinking back in her seat, she fiddled nervously with her purse strap.

John gave her a serious sidelong glance, refusing to try to figure out her odd behavior. They weren't exactly strangers, but one might've thought so by the way she was acting.

John put the pickup in gear, and drove in the direction of Rufus' house. He waited for Maebelle to strike up a conversation. When she didn't, he rested his left elbow over the sill and started whistling.

Maebelle observed him from the corner of her left eye. His cologne and his mannerism reminded her of Jake: subtle and sweet smelling. However, she imagined John had a temper underneath his coolness, just like Jake.

Her eyes slid below his belt. She sniffed, turned her head, and stared out the window. She recalled how well endowed John was the first time that she saw him at the juke house. Boy! He made her rather hot when they were dancing, crotch-to-crotch, thigh-to-thigh. Her three-inch red pumps raised her to a perfect height—she'd felt his arousal. He was an extremely good dancer, and probably a very good lover.

Maebelle's body temperature was rising. It had been a long time since she had been with a man. She felt her body heat. She had to take her mind off him, and concentrate on the scenery outside: the weather worn fences; fat black spotted cattle; tall, fat red horses dipping their heads and pressing their noses into the lush, green, grassy meadow.

Finally, John interrupted her thoughts. He had waited long enough for her to get comfortable next to him. "I know Charlotte will be glad to see you."

"Unh-hun. I'm glad to be seeing her, too." She continued to stare out the window.

Damn you, Rufus! She thought to herself. Why are you playing games? Why couldn't you've just told John the truth about us! I wonder what you're hiding.

****

Rufus timed their arrival precisely. He drove the pickup into the woods behind the thick green foliage and cut the engine. He couldn't help chuckling. He anticipated a furious catfight between the two women.

"I put my money on Maebelle," he said aloud. "She smells money! And she'll fight Charlotte until neither one of them can see one another." He laughed.

He grabbed his binoculars and found a spot from where he could see them claw each other to pieces. He brought the binoculars to his eyes and saw Charlotte and Sari in the garden.

"Just as I thought," he muttered.

He moved to another spot; saw John's white Chevy traveling in the distance.

"Mmm-hmm! Yessireee boy! Hurry up and get here. C'mon! Let's get this show on the road!"

****

Maebelle didn't know the stately house she was admiring belonged to Rufus. Like an excited child, she leaned forward in her seat, marveling. John's chuckle made her turn to look at him.

"Don't be laughing at me," she scolded mildly. "That's a beautiful house! White folks sure have it good, don't they?"

"Mmm-hmm," John said smiling. "And some coloreds, too. That house happens to belong to Charlotte and Rufus."

John looked at Maebelle and laughed.

"Huh?" She looked stunned.

Damn, I'm lucky, she thought to herself.

Lilacs and trumpets, and rose bushes flanked each side of the house. A beautiful magnolia tree in full bloom kissed the front window. Maebelle smelled a waft of sweet fragrances from a distance. She was excited. She wished she could be honest with John, and tell him she and Rufus had formed a relationship, and that Rufus had asked her to marry him.

"He's got a rich man's taste," John remarked. "That gray-mist clapboard house to the left belongs to old, Mrs. Daisy Carter. She's like a mother to Charlotte. Nice old woman! Charlotte and Sari Rufus' little girl calls the old woman Nana Two." He laughed lightheartedly. "I'm sure Charlotte will introduce you to her."

Maebelle didn't comment. She wished he would stop talking about Charlotte as if she were still living in the house. He was making her nervous.

John went on and on as though he was a tourist guide. Maebelle gave him a look as though to say "shut up", but he didn't catch the hint.

"All this land," he said, "used to belong to Charlotte's Grandfather. Rufus worked for him, as a hired hand. Charlie Hanson liked Rufus for some reason. When his health failed him, he sold the land to Rufus for mere peanuts. Yep, Charlotte comes from a middle-class family—in case you didn't already know that."

"My parents used to say we had family who were well off. But I never really knew who they were talking about."

"Well, Rufus is one lucky sonofagun, I tell you. He was a poor boy who went from rags to riches. Talk about luck! But it's only because old Charlie Hanson would've done anything to keep the white man from getting his land. He referred to it as the family legacy."

John saw the question in Maebelle's eyes.

"That shouldn't be too hard to figure out," he said. "Isn't Rufus married to Charlotte?"

Maebelle felt foolish. She poked out her tongue good-naturedly.

John abruptly changed the subject.

"You know something, Maebelle? I've been sweet on you since the first time I laid eyes on you. Are you seeing anybody special?"

His question annoyed her.

"Forget it, John," she replied. She turned her head and looked away. "You're a twenty-one year old kid. There is nothing you can do for me." Her voice was dry.

He opened his mouth to say something but she cut him off.

"I'm twenty-eight. I don't date men less than two years younger than me."

John felt kind of insulted.

"Well, you could've fooled me the way you danced with me that night at the juke house. If Rufus hadn't cut in, I think I would've gotten a chance to park my shoes under your bed."

Maebelle kept her head turned. She chewed on the inside of her lip.

That might be so, she thought. But it's neither here nor there, now.

The conversation lapsed.

He observed Maebelle staring at Charlotte's house; saw the faraway look in her eyes, and said, "It used to be a lot smaller. Rufus added the top floor, built with his own hands. He did it thinking Charlotte would spit out a whole-bunch of crumb-snatchers for him."

Maebelle felt annoyed as she stared at him with her mouth agape. After all, she had six 'crumb snatchers,' if that was how he chose to describe people's children.

"What's the matter?" he inquired. "Why are you looking at me like that?"

"No reason," she replied, curtly. "You figure it out."

"Well, as I was saying, Rufus thought Charlotte was like women who spit out babies every year. He soon found out that is not what she was about. You could say they each had their own plans about what would happen in their marriage." John paused.

"One thing for sure, though, his plan failed. She knew his motive, and she didn't care for it. You see that Negro hates paying the cost of labor. And he thought Charlotte ought to, act the way farmers' wives act; you know what I mean.

"But, Rufus forgot she never worked the fields one day of her life. Her Daddy was a big-time principal at an all-Negro college in Tannimills, Kentucky. Her mother was a schoolteacher. Her family comes from money."

"Well, here we are," he said, turning onto a winding gravel path. He pulled up in front of the house and parked, leaving the engine running.

Maebelle's body trembled. Now that she was here, she didn't know how to act or what to say. She was in awe; her life was on the verge of coming full circle. The house was more beautiful than she had ever imagined.

Thank you Rufus for asking me to marry you. Oh, God, I'm lucky, she thought.

****

Where John parked the pickup, Rufus was unable to see them. Cursing loudly, he moved to another spot. He felt something strike at the heel of his boot. He whirled around and looked at a wide-mouthed snake in strike position.

"Aw shit!" he cried, almost stumbling. He searched frantically for a big stick. To his dismay, a second den of the deadly reptiles was a few feet in front of him. The poisonous creatures surrounded him, and some were ready to strike!

"What the hell...!" he cried. His heart slammed against his chest.

There were too many to shoot. Besides, he would only drawn attention to himself. His only chance of staying alive was to try and get out of there. He spotted a clear path; took it and bounded toward the pickup. Breathing heavily after he jumped inside the pickup, he sat until his nerves were calm. He had been scared as never before. Happy to be alive, he drove back to town. Watching Charlotte and Maebelle scratch out each other's eyes wasn't worth risking his life over, he confirmed.

"Damn snakes!" he scowled, hitting the steering wheel with the heel of his right hand.

****

After John parked, Maebelle reached for the door handle.

"Wait!" John said, reaching across the seat, then grabbing her wrist. She looked annoyed, so he released her.

"I'm sorry. I didn't mean to grab you like that, but I had decided to ask you this question the next time I saw you."

"What question?" Her voice was curt, as he was holding her up.

"That first night you were at the juke house—did you see how Rufus looked at you when you came strutting through the door?"

Maebelle grinned. But it was not a cheerful grin.

"No! But I sure heard all them whores who were sitting around the bar hissing at me like I'd come up in there to take their men!"

"You mean their man—like in Rufus," John remarked.

Maebelle's eyebrows shot up defensively.

"I'm talking the truth. But, why do you feel you need to defend his reputation? He's nothing to you, and he's been with all of them at one time or another. He's a lady's man. Doesn't respect them—but he sure loves what they're giving him! Any way, I found it strange how he stared at you, like he hated your guts. It was even stranger when he cut in on our dance!"

95

With her piercing eyes focused on John, Maebelle was speechless. She lifted her head sorrowfully.

John shrugged his shoulders with uncertainty.

"Sorry. I just thought it was weird. I had to mention it to you."

"Well, I didn't see him act weird. Maybe it was your imagination. Anyhow, thanks for driving me here."

Maebelle opened the door and climbed out of the pickup. She closed the door, and leaned through the window on the passenger side.

"Did he say where I could find the...?"

Before she could get the word out of her mouth, she saw John's expression change; she knew she had messed up. She knew John had known she was about to ask if Rufus had told him where she could find the key. All she could do now was to hope that her assumption was wrong.

"Why would you need the key?" he inquired.

Maebelle didn't answer. She kept her eyes lowered.

I've screwed up, she thought. Damn you, Rufus.

The muscles in John's jaws knotted.

"I've been had, haven't I? You and Rufus done used me!" he said through clenched teeth. "I knew you weren't any kin to Charlotte. I felt it the moment the words came out of Rufus' lying-mouth! The lying sucker! He's using me to help break up his marriage."

Upset that she had been caught in a lie, Maebelle became bitter toward John, instead of Rufus.

"Don't go talking about you been had! Ain't nobody had you but your mama!"

John's eyes were a ball of fire.

"Oh, yeah, smart-ass. To say I been had isn't good enough for you, huh? Well, then how about I've been used! How's that? How 'bout if I use the four-letter word? This ain't a damn lady I'm talking to. And you damn sure ain't no kin to Charlotte!"

"You don't know anything about me, John! So just shut up and leave! You've done what he asked you to do."

Despite John's ashen-face, he began pleading with her out of concern for Charlotte. He respected Charlotte. She was always pleasant to him.

"Don't do this, Maebelle. Don't use me to help you and Rufus break up his marriage. Charlotte's a good woman; she doesn't deserve this. I've known her for a long time."

Maebelle sighed angrily and threw up her hands.

"Look, John, I don't know why Rufus hid the truth about us. Maybe he thought it was too soon; I don't know. But Charlotte is gone. There is no marriage. Rufus told me she left him while he was away in Chancy, Louisiana. He shouldn't have lied. I just played along because I-I didn't know what else to do. And you're right I'm not kin to Charlotte. I'm sorry."

"But she's not gone, Maebelle! Listen to what I'm saying! I was here yesterday! I picked up whiskey from their house and brought it back to the juke house. She's home, I tell you! Don't let Rufus use you like this; he's lying to you. He means you no good." He paused, trying to avoid looking at her. Speechless, she shot him a baffled look.

"Look," he said. "This might hurt, but it's the truth. Rufus—well, the man doesn't like dark-skinned women, honey! I'm not just saying this to hurt your feelings." Maebelle swallowed hard. She was sick of people talking about the color of her skin.

John continued. "He's always saying you remind him of some old aunt he's hated all his life. Why? I don't know, but I think it's why he stared at you that night. He's asked questions about you ever since. He probably thinks you're related to her. At least, that's my impression, although I could be wrong. Then, again, I may be right."

His remarks brought troubled recognition to Maebelle. She wanted to ask him some questions, but changed her mind. She would let nothing get between her and the dream she was about to realize. She took a breath and tried to calm her nerves.

But John wasn't giving up—at least now.

"Think of your children. I swear to you, you don't want him around them. The man has no morals."

Now, that did it! She had heard enough from John. She stepped back and applauded. "Nice performance, John. I'll try to remember not to mention any of this to Rufus. Now go on about your business and stop butting into mine. You're saying all this because you're jealous."

"Suit yourself!" he replied. "Again, you'll be sorry."

John threw the pickup in gear and sped off.

"Sonofabitches used me! That's it! I'm quitting that damn bartender job. Let him look for somebody else to make a fool of."

****

Maebelle was left in agony. Her legs shook as she climbed the front porch steps. John was so adamant about Charlotte being home, that her confidence started depleting.

What if she had returned and Rufus didn't know? A silent debate began within her mind. No. She's not home. She's gone. John doesn't know what he's talking about.

She bent and retrieved the key from under the flowerpot. She straightened.

"John is just jealous," she muttered. "I'm not thinking about him now."

Still, her hand trembled as she fed the key into the lock. Opening the door slowly, stepping inside the spacious living room, left her breathless. "Oh, how beautiful," she whispered. She closed the door behind her. Absent-mindedly she opened her purse, dropped the key inside and snapped her purse shut.

"Oh God! Is this real, or am I dreaming?" she muttered, looking around nervously.

The calico kitten suddenly sprang down off the winged-back chair yowling loudly, and sprinted out of the room. Maebelle gasped, clutching her chest. "Oooh! Oooh!" She fell back against the door. "You nearly scared the piss out of me! You'll get used to me. You wait."

She moved toward the plush tapestry sofa, sitting down gingerly, as she looked around the room. The large Mahogany china cabinet, loaded with expensive china and stemware, awed her. She got up and studied the old portrait hanging above the mantel. An intelligent-looking, smiling old man with piercing dark eyes, and an old woman with hair down to her shoulder, stared back at her. She swallowed and looked away. A beautiful, old wing-backed chair caught her eye.

"I'm going to be living like rich people!" she exclaimed in a whisper, rubbing a flat hand over its rich fabric. "Lord, is this for real, or is this a dream?"

She returned to the sofa and sat down, lolling her head on the doily. Her eyes closed and she fantasized about the kind of life she would have from now on. Sinking deep into her thoughts, ordinary, every-day sounds escaped her senses, and she didn't hear Charlotte and Sari enter the house.

****

"Sari," Charlotte called. Her tone was soft. "Don't forget to wash your hands."

"I won't, Mommy. First, I want to say hello to Taffy."

Charlotte removed her gloves and straw hat and stored them inside the pantry shelf.

Sari kicked off her shoes and went running barefoot into the living room. She stopped short when she saw the strange woman sitting on the sofa asleep.

"Mommy!" Her voice was barely audible.

Maebelle woke up wide-eyed and startled. She scrambled to her feet.

"Shit! Y'all back!"

Poor Sari remained in a frozen state of panic. Her lips moved, but no words came out of her mouth.

"Sari!" Charlotte called. "Did you let anyone in the house?" Sari stood speechless; her legs trembled.

Charlotte stepped inside the living room just in time to see the angry woman reaching for her daughter.

"Sari!" she cried aghast, reaching out her arms. "Run to Mommy!"

Sari pried her feet from the floor. She wheeled and bounded toward Charlotte, and fell into her arms.

Charlotte pushed her round back of her.

"Please, Mommy!" Sari cried, huddling behind her. "Let's get out of here!"

"You better listen to her!" Maebelle cried. "You all aren't supposed to be here!"

While keeping an eye on the lunatic standing in the middle of her living room floor, Charlotte quickly glanced down at Sari. She had to get her out of harm's way. Instinctively, she knew by the crazy woman's stance, she had a hell of a fight on her hands, to recapture her home.

"Run to Nana-Two, baby! Go!"

Sari turned and bounded out of the living room. She pushed open the screen door so hard that it reeled against the wall. The calico kitten howled, as it darted from behind the stove, skittered across the kitchen floor, and dashed out the door before it had a chance to close. He overtook Sari as she raced toward the old woman's home.

Frightened out of her wits, Charlotte looked the crazy stranger straight in the eyes. She summoned courage unknown to her. She wasn't leaving her home without a fight.

"You should've left too!" Maebelle shrieked. "You aren't supposed to be here!"

"Who in the hell are you?" Charlotte cried. "You're the one who'd better leave this house now! You can't just go around breaking into people's houses and demand that they leave. Get your black ass out of here!"

Maebelle's eyes dripped with spite. Her lips formed a thin taut line. Propping her hands on her hips, an evil laugh erupted from her throat.

"Well, if you must know, my name is Maebelle Hawkins. And, yellow-shit, don't call me black any more! And I didn't break in; I let myself in!" She strutted over to the sofa and picked up her purse and opened it. Momentarily, she held up a key in front of Charlotte's face.

Charlotte felt horrified.

"You see," Maebelle gloated, "I didn't break in. As a matter of fact, John Puntier—you do know him, don't you? Well, he told me where to find the key."

"You're lying!" Charlotte retorted. "John did no such thing! Get out of my house!"

Maebelle shrugged. "You don't have to believe me. But, I'm not going any damn where! I'm Rufus' woman; I'm moving in. He invited me to see this house, to see if I liked it. I like it! I'm taking your place. I'll give him all the babies he wants. Can't wait until we make love."

She watched Charlotte's stunned, disappointed smirk.

"Does it surprise you that I haven't let him make love to me yet? Well, you see, I decided to make him wait because I want him to be real hungry for it. You get my drift, don't you?"

Charlotte stood dumbfounded, wondering if this was the sow that told Rufus about her douche bag. Not that she could've known for certain that she had one—but she had obviously made a lucky guess.

"I'll make it real good for him when I do give in. You know what they say—the blacker the berry, the sweeter the juice!" A sinister laugh erupted from her.

Charlotte glared incredulously. Not her Rufus, she thought. He would never touch a dark-skinned woman. He had told her as much.

Maebelle ranted off at the mouth.

"Rufus wanted me here so badly he had John to pick me up. He would've picked me up himself, but something important came up. He'll be here any minute now, so you really should leave."

Maebelle marched back toward the sofa, opened her purse, and dropped the key inside. She snapped the purse shut and strutted back to the center of the room. She stood in front of Charlotte, deriving satisfaction from her frantic expression.

Something told Charlotte this woman wasn't crazy, after all. This was a conniving plot that Rufus had arranged. He hadn't been home since she electrified his ass after the douche bag incident. She'd felt he would be up to no good—he had retreated too easily. Now this! ...And John? Where does he fit? No. The John she knew would never do such a thing! He would never knowingly be a party to such maneuvers. Without doubt, she knew Rufus had betrayed poor John like he had betrayed her, if the crazy woman was telling the truth.

As Maebelle strutted back and forth across her living room floor like some proud peacock, with her hands propped on her hips, Charlotte looked in disbelief.

Obviously, she won't leave, Charlotte thought. Neither am I! I won't give up my home without a fight!

Charlotte backed into the dining room and grabbed the bed slat she had left against the wall to be thrown out. This small action only caused Maebelle to wear a silly grin on her face.

"Now just who do you think you're going to hit with that bed-slat?"

"You!" Charlotte replied. "I'm going to bash your stinking skull in!"

Maebelle's face twisted in anger. No way in hell was she was going to give up this house; she wanted Charlotte out before Rufus returned. She had to admit that Charlotte was beautiful. She knew that if Rufus returned and found her there that he might have a change of heart. There was only one thing to do. She rushed at Charlotte like a raging bull. Charlotte brought the bed-slat down with all her might, only to have it miss its target. It crashed into the floor, sending bone-jarring pain through her hand and elbow. Maebelle grabbed the bed-slat; the two women tussled like bitter jungle foes.

****

Sari ran up the back porch steps and knocked frantically on the old woman's door. Startled out of her sleep, the old woman bolted upright in her bed. For a second, she thought it was just a bad dream. But Sari's cries set off her internal alarm. Intuitively, she knew it was her Sari, and knew the child was in deep trouble.

"Oh my Lord!" she cried in a panic. "That's Sari!"

She spilled out of bed and ran barefoot across the floor toward the kitchen. She jerked open the door and saw Sari's frightened face. Tears rolled down her cheeks.

"My Lord, child! What's the matter? Where's your mama?"

The old woman looked around for Charlotte. Sari was short of breath.

"A...a crazy woman . . .A crazy woman is in our house, Nana-Two! She'll hurt Mommy!"

"Good Lord!" the old woman cried. "Come inside, child."

She grasped Sari's right shoulder and pulled her inside and closed the door. "You--you wait here. I have to help your mother! Good Lord, Almighty!"

The old woman stuck her trembling feet inside a pair of run-down tennis shoes and grabbed her rifle from the corner of the kitchen. She hurried out the back door, sidling down the steps as quickly as she could.

Sari, not wanting to be alone, grabbed her kitten and ran after the old woman.

****

Maebelle lost her grip on the bed-slat and took a nasty spill onto the threshold. Charlotte fell backward onto the porch. Quickly, she scrambled to her feet. It was too late. Maebelle had already gotten up. She slammed the door and flicked the lock, and leaned breathlessly against the door.

"This is my house!" she mumbled.

Lolling her head against the door, she inched her back down the door, landing on the floor.

A sharp pain shot up Charlotte's ankle; she turned away in defeat. She started rubbing her ankle. She looked up, as the old woman and Sari rushed to her aide. Limping down the steps, she met them halfway across the yard.

"My God, who was that woman?" the old woman inquired. "I can't believe she closed the door in your face like that! What's going on? Who is she? And how did she get in the house?"

Charlotte lifted a hand and wiped a tear from the side of her nose.

"She said her name is Maebelle Hawkins," Charlotte replied, looking back in the direction of her home.

"Huh!" The old woman grunted.

Hawkins was her maiden name. She hoped this wasn't one of her detestable relatives.

"She kept telling me I was supposed to be gone."

"Suppose to be gone! Gone where? What is she talking about? That makes no sense."

Charlotte looked down at Sari, and then at Mrs. Daisy.

"Oh!" the old woman remarked, glancing down at Sari. "We'll talk later. Let's get you to my house."

Charlotte bent and kissed Sari's forehead.

"Honey, you go on ahead of us. We'll be right behind you."

Teary-eyed and frightened, Sari did as she was told.

Charlotte straightened and faced the old woman.

"I didn't want us to speak in front of her."

"I understand," said the old woman. "It's just that I'm so angry that I forgot the child was standing there. So what do you think? You think Rufus is behind this?"

"He's behind it, all right. She knows too much about us. And according to her, he got John to bring her over here. Would you believe that?" Charlotte's chin quivered.

"Got John to bring her over here? What kind of nasty stunt is Rufus trying to pull? John would never knowingly do anything thing like this."

The old woman looked over her shoulder at Charlotte's house. Nothing Charlotte said made any sense. She never imagined Rufus messing with anyone that dark-skinned, if for no other reason than his aunt was dark, and because of the things his aunt had done to him.

The old woman looked at Charlotte.

"Well, let's get you to my house. My son Harold will arrive tomorrow. I'm taking you and Sari back to Tennessee with me. Something isn't right about this. You could've been killed."

She took Charlotte by the arm, and they walked in silence. They walked up the porch steps and went inside the house. The old woman turned and locked the door.

"Try to make yourself comfortable," she said, pulling a chair away from the table, for Charlotte.

Charlotte sat down, crying quietly.

The old woman moved around in her kitchen, pouring warm water from the kettle into a washbasin and mixing Epson salt for a warm bath for Charlotte's sprained ankle. She took a towel from the closet and threw it across her shoulder. She set the washbasin on the floor in front of Charlotte, and handed her the towel. She examined Charlotte's injured ankle.

"I think you should let that ankle soak for a while. How's the water?"

Charlotte looked up at the old woman's kind face, then lifted her foot and placed it inside the basin of water. She sniffed.

"It's fine. Thank you."

The old woman stood back with her hands on her hips for a moment or two.

"Have you and Sari had your dinner?" she asked.

"Yes, ma'am."

The old woman looked before her. Her eyes were vacant as she stared out the window. She turned and looked at Charlotte, letting her hands drop to her side.

"Well, I'm going to go check on the little one. She's gotten mighty quiet back there. She didn't need to see any of this," the old woman muttered.

Charlotte didn't comment. The old woman went toward the spare bedroom. She found Sari fast asleep on the bed. The ball of calico fur lay near her head. The old woman's heart went out to the child. She undressed her with care, trying not to awaken her. Unfolding the sheet at the foot of the bed, she pulled it around Sari's shoulder, and then bent over brushing the red ringlets away from her face.

"You're the spitting image of your daddy," she whispered. "I just pray to God you don't take after him."

Suddenly an animal-like cry erupted from the kitchen.

"Good, Lord!" the old woman cried, and rushed out the room. She felt her heart pounding inside her chest. "What could be the matter now?"

Charlotte jerked her foot out of the washbasin, and hobbled across the room to grab the old woman's rifle.

"I'm going over there and blow that wench to kingdom come! That's my granddaddy's house. I'll kill her before she takes over! Who the hell does she think she is!" she exclaimed.

The old woman bolted through the doorway in the nick of time. She jumped between Charlotte and the loaded gun, and planted a firm, flat hand in Charlotte's chest.

"My God, child! What do you think you're doing?"

She saw pain and humiliation in Charlotte's eyes, but she couldn't allow her to ruin her life.

"You can't kill that woman," she told her. "You leave that heathen to God. Why do you think He says vengeance is mine? He didn't say that just to be saying it. You got to have faith! Now sit down and pull yourself together!"

Tears streamed down Charlotte's face. She glared at the old woman.

"I'm angry, Mrs. Daisy. Angry! That's my granddaddy's house! My house! I have every right to chase that whore out of it! Kill her if I have to!"

The old woman's face was solemn.

"Sit down, Charlotte," she said sternly. "You're not thinking straight."

Charlotte hobbled back toward the chair. She sobbed uncontrollably. The old woman's heart went out to her.

"I know how you're feeling, child. I feel like doing the same thing to her. You're like a daughter to me, and I can't let you do something you'll regret. Let's use good judgment. You got a child to rear. Put your mind where it counts, now. The Lord will take care of that 'ol whore and nobody will have to go to jail for it."

The old woman picked up the towel, and got down on her knees and dried Charlotte's foot.

"Didn't you write to your folks and tell them you were leaving him? I know you didn't exactly put it that way, but that was what you had in mind when you wrote them. What did you think was going to happen to that house once you left here?"

Charlotte stared blankly at the wall. She didn't reply. At the time she wrote the letter, she didn't care what happened to the house. But this was different.

"It's your pride that's hurt the most because you aren't leaving on your own terms. And besides, that isn't your granddaddy's house any more. Rufus paid Charlie for that house. I'm sure Charlie put most of that money aside for you. I know what you've been doing all these years. You've been holding on to Charlie's dream. But what he got you doing is wrong. You've made enough sacrifices for the dead. It's time you stop carrying out his wishes and start looking out for the living—yourself and that baby back there—and let that damn land go. And don't you worry, that woman will pay dearly for what she's doing. Just you mark my words!"

Getting to her feet, the old woman took the towel and threw it across her shoulder.

"Now hand me the washbasin," she ordered mildly.

Charlotte leaned forward picked up the washbasin and handed it to the old woman. Once again, Charlotte could not hold back her tears. She cried profusely.

"That's the way to do it," the old woman encouraged, looking back at her. "Flush out all that hurt and bitterness, so you can heal."

She set down the washbasin on the wooden table, and wadded the towel and dropped it on the floor in the closet. About ten minutes later, when Charlotte's crying nearly ended, she returned and put a hand on Charlotte's shoulder.

"I'm going to leave you alone for awhile," she said.

The old woman picked up the rifle and softly closed the door behind her. Once in her bedroom, she searched an old trunk for a few dresses for Sari—dresses that her granddaughters had left behind. She found a cute pink dress with a Peter Pan collar. She also found one of her own dresses from the time she was a young woman. It was flair-tailed, with large flowers and short bell sleeves. She would pass it on to Charlotte, now. And once they got to Tennessee, Charlotte could go shopping, and she would pick up the tab. She placed the dresses at the foot of the bed, and headed back toward the kitchen. She was surprised to find Charlotte sitting on the sofa in the living room, flipping through the pages of one of her old magazines. Charlotte's expression was sad, but at least she had stopped crying, and was trying to cope.

Charlotte looked up at her with sad red eyes, looking as though she would start crying any moment.

"Well, I found some things for you and Sari to wear tomorrow. I put them on the bed in the room where you and the little one will sleep. I've decided I want you to go shopping at my expense when we get to Tennessee."

Charlotte sniffed. "Thanks. But I was thinking that when Rufus comes home I could...."

"You were thinking what!"

Charlotte swallowed and looked away. Her eyes filled with tears again. She knew she shouldn't have said anything.

"Where are your senses, child? You must not believe that woman was telling you the truth. That's a hornet's nest over there. That man done told you plenty about how he feels about you just by the way he tricked John into bringing that woman over here."

Tears ebbed down Charlotte's face.

"But everything I own is in that house, Mrs. Daisy! I want mine and Sari's clothes."

Without saying a word, the old woman sat down on the sofa beside Charlotte and began to gently rub her back. Before she said anything, she got up and went toward the window.

Charlotte followed her with her eyes. The old woman's gait was most noticeable when she wasn't conscious that anybody was looking at her. Her shoulders stooped. Her soft, long, almost-completely, white hair graced her shoulders, making old age look graceful. She'd told Charlotte her stooped shoulders and swinging gait were legacies of toting water and bending over scrubbing white folks' floors, and everything else that went along with keeping their lazy-ass houses clean.

Her beautiful yellow skin had faded with the passing years. She had moles now—lots of them. Her laughter, though, was still youthful and chirpy. Hard work, she told Charlotte, was what kept her figure slim and fit. Her hands were thin and ropey.

She pulled on the tassel and lowered the shade. When she turned around, she saw Charlotte staring. She adjusted her posture as she crossed the room. Her gait was less visible now, as she was aware of Charlotte watching her. She sat down again on the sofa beside Charlotte, rested her head on back of the sofa, and closed her eyes, thinking about how to share what she knew about Rufus, without divulging her own family's notorious secrets.

It was on her mother's deathbed that the old woman had learned that Rufus and Olga were members of their family. She remembered her father had already passed, and her mother, realizing she was dying, confided in her. Of course, Rufus didn't know that they were related, and he never would, if she had to be the one to tell him.

She opened her eyes and stared at Charlotte for a long moment.

"I have something to tell you, and you must promise me you will never breathe a word of it to anybody."

"I promise," Charlotte replied. Her voice was low.

"Well, I once saw Rufus—when he was a boy, that is."

Charlotte looked at her, stunned beyond words.

"Close your mouth," the old woman told her. "Anyway, my Aunt Hattie Belle and my Uncle James Belle—both now deceased—used to live next door to both women who helped raised Rufus. Years later I found out that he and Olga, who is his aunt and surrogate mother, were members of my family."

Charlotte blinked.

"It's a long story, dear. Close your mouth."

Charlotte stirred. She closed her mouth in embarrassment.

"It's a long, ugly story, I tell you. So ugly, in fact, that Mother and Father kept it from me all their lives. Mother only told me when she was on her deathbed." She paused.

"My parents adopted my oldest sister Gina. Gina and Olga Berry were identical twins. Another family adopted Olga, Amber, and Lester—these were Gina's other two sisters and brother. Amber was Rufus' mother. The midwife killed Amber, delivering Rufus. Anyway, after Amber died, Olga took up with Jesse, who was Amber's husband. Can you believe that? That's how she ended up taking care of Rufus. But she did more than just take care of him. She used him to satisfy an ache between her legs—if you get my meaning. I guess the boy's father wasn't enough for her.

Charlotte swallowed the lump that had built up in her throat. Her heart went out to Rufus. Oh, God, she thought. Poor thing!

"One summer, a long time ago, I went down to Chancy, Louisiana, but I never got to see Olga while I was there," said the old woman. "She always stayed in the house. At that time, I didn't know about what I'm telling you. After Mother told me about her, I talked to my Aunt Hattie Belle, who told me more stuff about Olga. She told me that Jesse left Olga for another woman, and Olga and this other woman fought all the time. Can you believe that this other woman was also messing with

Rufus, at the same time she was carrying on with his father? Yep. This other woman followed in Olga's footsteps, doing the same thing to the boy!" The old woman paused.

"To make a long story short, the boy—well, he's no boy any more—he's ruined. Olga and that other woman ruined his boyhood; trained him to crave what's under women dresses."

The old woman put a hand on Charlotte's lap and said, "You once asked me what was wrong with him. I didn't tell you then because I didn't want you to ever know this. He'll never be capable of loving any woman. And as I said, that other woman followed right in Olga's footsteps and finished ruining him."

The old woman paused, frowning.

"I'm trying to think of her name." She snapped her fingers. "I got it!" She looked at Charlotte. "Her name was Dora—Dora something or other. I can't think of her last name. But she was the worst. She made that poor thing go down on her."

Charlotte groaned sorrowfully. There was a long moment of silence.

"His father?" she finally asked. "Did he know what those women were doing to Rufus?"

The old woman nodded. "Jesse Poygoode—he had to have known. He lived in the same house with them. But he only took a stand against Dora after she did that down-thing. Aunt Hattie Belle told me the story. Jesse was down in the cotton field when he heard what Dora did to the boy. Apparently, Rufus finally emptied his guts to somebody, and it quickly got back to Jessie. That must've really gotten to him. Aunt Hattie Belle told me Jesse tore out of that cotton field as if it were afire, and ran like a Jackrabbit toward the house.

"Dora was hanging out the wash when he got there. The boy had emptied out his guts on her nasty self. Jesse was a tall, raw-boned man, and Dora was heavy-set. Aunt Hattie Belle told me Jesse balled his bony-fists and hit Dora upside the head so hard that she hit the ground like a sack of potatoes. Dust flew in the air, and her paper curlers flew every which way." The old woman chuckled. "After that, Jesse took the boy and moved. By then he was already about eleven. My aunt and uncle never saw either one of them again." There was a long moment of silence.

"Why did his mother Amber and the others have to be adopted?" Charlotte inquired.

The old woman shook her head in a kind of sad way. She looked at Charlotte.

"Their mother," she sighed heavily. "Well, she used to cheat on her husband with different men. Somebody killed her. And their daddy drank himself to death that same year.

"I hope you don't mind my asking, but why did your parents adopt Gina?"

The question brought a look of stinging recognition to the old woman's eyes. She smiled sadly. "They wanted a child. I was told I was too long in coming."

She abruptly ended the conversation. She patted Charlotte's knee and got up.

"Well, my dear," she said, looking down in Charlotte's upturned face. "I must call it a night. It's been a rough day."

"I know. There's no reason for me to stay up, either," Charlotte replied, getting up.

"Well, you go on ahead. I'll cut out the light. I know my way around in the dark. I don't want you tripping over the furniture."

Charlotte stopped and looked back at the old woman.

"What is it, child? Why are you staring at me like that for?"

Then it dawned on her what Charlotte was thinking.

113

"You're wondering if I told Charlie about Rufus, aren't you? Yes, I most certainly did. I thought he would change his mind about offering your hand in marriage to Rufus; but he didn't. The trouble with Charlie was he didn't believe in what is known as generational sin."

Charlotte's eyes turned bitter.

"Don't make excuses for him. The truth is, he sacrificed my happiness and put his grandchildren in jeopardy, just to hold onto his precious land." Her voice was hard.

Charlotte stared at the old woman Sara called Nana Two.

"Now you want to get on me too, don't you? The question in back of your mind is why didn't I tell you? I think you know the answer to that. You were in love. You wouldn't have believed me. He was—and still is—a good-looking man. He's smart and talented—but he's also damaged goods. You wouldn't have believed me if I had tried to tell you back then! Now, go on to bed so I can cut off this light," she ordered in a mild voice.

Charlotte's eyes started to fill with tears. She turned and went toward the spare bedroom.

"Goodnight!" she called over her shoulder.

"Goodnight, child!"

Charlotte felt crushed.

"They both knew," she muttered. "How could they let me walk into a hornet's nest and not tell me, especially you, Grandfather? How could you've used such poor judgment? All you cared about was your damn family legacy. Well, it's gone now!"

Her throat ached. She felt almost as much anger toward the old woman. Nevertheless, she admired her for recommending her to get on birth control, and helping her rear her daughter. She finally understood.

Once inside the bedroom, Charlotte went straight to the window and stared out at her home. When she saw the light on in her bedroom, she felt upstaged, and gasped in horror watching her husband and the strange woman in the nude, standing up kissing. Her heart ached.

So that tramp wasn't lying about being his lover, she reminded herself.

She gaped with jealousy. Tears flowed like a swollen river down her cheeks.

"You could've cut out the lights!" she muttered. "You did this on purpose."

Glued to the window, Charlotte could not move. She staggered backward, watching Rufus grind. Rufus was a good lover, and he was giving himself to this woman standing up, with the shades up. Momentarily, something inside her died. She jerked the shade, lowering it, and left the window.

After removing her shoes, she climbed into bed fully clothed. With her arms wrapped around Sari, her sobbing resurfaced, as she reflected on the things Nana Two told her. A cold chill swept over her and she drew closer to Sari. Suddenly, what she had learned about Rufus tonight suggested she was lucky to be out of his life. Yet, it hurt.

Mrs. Daisy is right, she thought. My pride is hurt because I must leave him on his terms.

Again, the old woman's words were beating against her mind like bitter cold rain against a windowpane. *It's your pride that's hurt—you didn't get to leave on your own terms.*

"You're so right. No, I didn't get to leave on my own terms. It's painful."

Somewhere between the tears and a million other thoughts, she found respite in sleep.

****

Rufus rose before dawn. He took a suit of work clothes from the wardrobe and moved to the bathroom where he cleaned his teeth, shaved, and bathed. He stood before the mirror gazing at his clean-shaven face, and chuckling.

"She thinks I don't know what happened here yesterday," he muttered. "I wasn't here to see it, but I know a serious fight had to have taken place. Charlotte's no pushover!"

His thoughts shifted to John. He suspected John had discovered the truth about his little plot, which was why he hadn't returned to the juke house last evening.

"Well, that's all right," he muttered. "Wouldn't make a bit of difference to me if he never came back. Shit, I can always find somebody to take his place."

Rufus laughed. He felt happy that he had accomplished all that he had set out to do. "I knew I could count on the bee to drive the goat out of the house," he told himself.

He finished dressing, and left the house.

Maebelle had faked sleeping. When she heard the front door close, she quickly got out of bed and went and stood at the window, so she could watch Rufus drive away. She supposed he was going to the farm. She smiled, thinking of last night when he had asked her how she liked the house and found everything. She told him a little white lie. She told him everything had been fine; that she loved the house—which she truly did.

When the pickup was out of view, Maebelle dressed quickly and hurried onto the back porch, and brought in a cotton sack. Inside Charlotte's bedroom, she pulled opened the drawers in the bureau and removed Charlotte and Sari's clothes, placing them into the cotton sack. With the sack on her shoulder, she left the room. After she opened the front door and stepped out on the porch, carrying the cotton sack, she hurried over to the old woman's house.

After climbing the old woman's steps, she awkwardly placed the sack on her porch. She tiptoed down the steps, and rushed back toward the house. Closing the door behind her, she stood with her back leaning against the door, enchanted by the beautiful living room.

"This is my house! My house!" she exclaimed.

Hugging herself, she felt lucky. Now leaning back in the straight-backed chair, she crossed her knees, and gazed at the portrait of Charlotte's grandparents.

"You all are coming down from there," she muttered, pointing a stiff finger at the photograph. "You won't stare at me every time I come into this room."

When she uncrossed her knees and sat upright in the chair, she considered having Rufus take her home, to start packing.

"Finally, my life has come full circle," she heard herself say half aloud. "I'm so glad he didn't bring up Charlotte's name."

Instead, she and Rufus made passionate love late into the night. Afterward, he told her he hoped he had hit the bull's eye, and that she was already pregnant. He felt good when she told him, Jake, her divorced husband, would move to Detroit, Michigan, the middle of summer, and was taking their boys with him.

****

The morning sun shone through the window directly in Nana Two's face, wakening her. She thought about her guests and got out of bed. After she washed and dressed, she went to the kitchen to make breakfast.

She waited for the biscuits to brown. She went to the living room, raised the shades, and looked out the window. Surprisingly, she saw a stuffed cotton sack lying on her porch. Something told her Charlotte and Sari's clothes were inside the sack. A surge of anger struck her—one of those devils had put that sack on her porch. She opened the door and cautiously looked around. Her heart sank when she looked inside the sack. "Lord, have mercy! You all are some cruel bastards," she muttered. "May you both rot in hell!"

She seized the sack by the strap, and dragged it into her house. She didn't want poor Charlotte to wake up and find her clothes stuffed inside a cotton sack, left on the porch.

Moving quickly, she sat down on the sofa and sorted the clothes into neat piles. Then, she went to her bedroom, took an old suitcase from her closet, and returned with it to the living room. As she picked up one of Charlotte's skirts to put into the suitcase, a small, neatly folded, somewhat thick, brown, paper bag fell on the floor. She gazed at it suspiciously before picking it up and opening it. She felt elated when she saw the wad of money inside. She took the money from the bag and counted it to see how much was there. It was money Charlotte's grandfather had given her for a rainy day.

"Whoo!" she cried. "You were smart to do this, Charlotte. I know it was you, God, who didn't let them heathens see this money!"

The old woman put the money back inside the paper bag, and put the paper bag back inside Charlotte's skirt pocket. She finished packing and closed the suitcase. As a surprise, she left Charlotte and Sari an outfit each on the sofa.

Returning to the kitchen to check on breakfast, the old woman removed the biscuits from the oven and buttered them. She turned off the flame from under the pot of rice on the stove, and took the sausages from the frying pan and put them in a covered bowl.

With Charlotte's welfare at heart, she returned to the living room to destroy the cotton sack. She picked up the cotton sack, and went out the back door now angrier than a rattlesnake. She marched across the yard to Rufus' house.

"Bastards!" she muttered, tossing the sack, as hard as she could, on his back porch. Mission accomplished, she turned on her heels and headed back toward her house, mumbling under her breath.

Maebelle heard the thump on the back porch. She opened the door cautiously. She saw the cotton sack on the floor and looked up in time to see the old woman making her way across the yard. Grinning sheepishly, Maebelle called after her.

"Ah, excuse me!"

The old woman stopped abruptly; she whirled around. She was taken aback when she saw Maebelle for the first time. She looked in disbelief at the young dark-skinned woman standing on Charlotte's porch. It was as though she was looking into the face of her deceased adopted sister, Gina Hawkins. Her mouth fell open in amazement. When the old woman swallowed, she heard the noise her throat made. She couldn't believe her eyes.

"Oh, God!" she exclaimed. "Could it be possible that this girl is Gina's granddaughter?"

The old woman recalled Gina's wild, risky ways. She broke up many marriages in her day. She gazed sternly at Maebelle, as she descended the steps, to her astonishment. Maebelle boldly started a conversation as if they would be neighbors.

"Good morning! I'm Maebelle. I take it you're Mrs. Daisy Carter. John told me a lot of nice things about you." The old woman didn't answer. She was too stunned. The nerve, she thought to herself.

"I see you brought back the sack. You could've kept it, you know. We have lots of them. Tell Charlotte I was the one who packed her things and brought them over. I didn't tell Rufus she had tried to come back."

Nana Two shook with anger. Not only did Maebelle look like Gina, she was also feisty. "If I were a younger woman, she retorted, through clenched teeth, "I'd beat the shit outta you! You got some damn nerve talking to me like you know me! Where you from, anyhow?"

"My name is Maebelle. I'm from Beulah Creek, Mississippi."

The old woman choked. Beulah Creek was the town where Gina had gone and given away her illegitimate son, James Hawkins, to a total stranger.

"Whose girl are you? What's your daddy's name?" the old woman inquired.

"I'm Lula Mae Hawkins' girl. My father was James Hawkins—they're both dead now."

The old woman suddenly felt faint. She tried to regain her composure.

"And what was James Hawkins' mama's name?" she inquired further.

"You mean my grandmother? Her name was Gina Hawkins. (The old woman's parents gave Gina their family name.) She wasn't married when she had Daddy. Do you know me?"

"Hell, no!"

That wasn't exactly a lie. She didn't know her; but she had known her grandmother, Gina.

"Now keep your ass off my property because if I ever catch you on it, I'm liable to shoot you."

Maebelle swallowed.

"And start lowering the shades," the old woman told her. "Nobody's interested in seeing human beings act like dogs in heat. I saw you on your knees last night. He rode you like a---"

Maebelle chuckled, making the old woman more furious.

"You're standing there grinning now," she told her. "But some day you'll be crying and *slinging* snot like a damn fool. And are you sure he isn't your kinfolk?"

The grin slid off Maebelle's face; her antennas went up. She wondered what the old woman meant by that remark. First, it was Rufus, then John, now this old woman, suggesting some kind of relations existed between her and Rufus. Maybe she did have folks she didn't know. But who didn't? But one thing she was sure of, she wasn't related to Rufus, she thought. The two women stood glaring at each other.

"You're just like your grand-mammy used to be," said the old woman. "She never did stop to think about what it was she was doing, or who she was hurting."

She saw the bewildered look in Maebelle's eyes.

"You're confused, huh? Well, that isn't all you're going to be. Just you wait!"

Maebelle swallowed her anger. She started walking toward the angry, old woman, who seemed to know more about her folks than she did.

"Do you know me?" Her voice was concerned.

The old woman put up a refraining hand.

"Don't come any closer. And hell, no! I already told you I didn't know you. But I do know this one thing. Rufus isn't in love with the likes of you. And I'll tell you another thing: if you got any girls you're going to end up having to pull him off 'em. That's the only reason he would be interested in the likes of you."

Hearing the old woman's prediction of doom and gloom, Maebelle felt shocked and deceived. Shivering, she stared at the old woman, nearly afraid.

"Why are you putting a bad mouth on me?" she asked. "You're just doing this because of Charlotte, aren't you?"

The old woman saw fear in Maebelle's eyes. Now it was her turn to laugh. It felt good that she had put the fear of God into this heathen. Feeling satisfied, she turned on her heels and headed back toward her house.

"You were cursed the day you were born. You don't need me to curse you!"

Maebelle felt shaky. She had no one to corroborate the old woman's accusations. "You're a liar," she muttered. "You just want Charlotte and Rufus back together, but it'll never happen."

Maebelle went back in the house.

****

Nana Two glanced up at her house. The curtain moved at the window. She knew Charlotte must've been watching, but she wouldn't tell Charlotte the woman inside her house was her great niece. She went up the porch steps and entered the house. Charlotte and Sari were seated at the table eating breakfast.

"Good morning," she said.

"Good morning," Charlotte and Sari chorused together.

"I see you found the clothes I put out for you." Charlotte didn't answer, although she was curious about who'd brought them. She was afraid of what the answer might be. She would rather Rufus had brought them over.

Charlotte followed Nana Two with her eyes, as she moved about.

The old woman moved toward the stove, and poured a cup of coffee.

Sari jumped up from the table and started chasing her calico kitten.

"Who brought them over—the clothes?" Charlotte finally inquired.

The old woman gazed inside her cup at the black coffee; then looked at Charlotte. "I don't know who brought them over. I found them on my front porch when I got up this morning."

She didn't feel badly about telling a lie. Charlotte didn't need to know that that heathen had put her poison fingers on her and Sari's clothes.

"I saw the two of you out the window. What were you all talking about?"

The old woman raised the teacup to her lips. She saw Charlotte looking directly at her.

"Well, I found out she's got girls. I figured that would be the case. You remember what I told you about Rufus last night? Well, I as much as told her he's going to plunder them girls of hers right in her presence. It's not her he's after, I tell you. You can mark my words. There's more to this situation than meets the eye!"

She replaced the cup in the saucer with a click.

Charlotte nodded down at the table, thoughtfully. A knock at the front door broke into her thoughts, making her jump.

The old woman walked over and patted her on the shoulder.

"Don't you fret none; I'll get it. I've already told her she better not set a foot on my property. It's probably my boy Harold. He said he might be getting here early."

Charlotte heard the door open and close, and the old woman clucking like a mother hen.

"Hi, my schoolteacher son!" she exclaimed. "Thank God, you decided to come now!"

Charlotte's thoughts drifted. Absentmindedly, she got to her feet and started washing the dishes. Then it hit her like a ton of bricks—she was single again! A free woman! One with no plans, no skills! Well, she was almost free. There would be a divorce. She felt funny going home to live with parents, she hadn't seen in over four years, whom she had never confided to about her sad marriage. Her mind traveled backward.

She thought about how long it had taken her to get pregnant with Sari. Two whole years had seemed like a long time to her. Now, she was not only a mother, but also a single mother. She wondered if it was too late to return to college. She'd had only two years to graduate. At twenty-five, she wondered if she was a little old to return to college. She would do what was necessary. She thought about the people she knew during her college years, wondering if they were still around, and what they were doing with their lives. Were they still married, or about to get divorced like her? She still wanted to become a schoolteacher, so she had to go back and finish those last two years of college.

Lost in her thoughts, Charlotte didn't hear Harold walk into the kitchen.

"Hi, Charlotte," he said, snapping her back to the present.

She grasped her chest. She looked up at Harold and forced a smile. She had forgotten how deep and husky his voice was. Harold was tall and good-looking, with salt and pepper hair.

"Hi, Harold! I-I was in deep thought. How are you?" They shook hands. "How's Sherry?"

"She's fine," he replied, taking a good look at her.

Charlotte withdrew her hand and stepped backward.

"So I hear you and Sari are going to see your folks."

She looked beyond him at Nana Two, then at him.

"Ah, yes. I-I hope you don't mind if we ride along with you—as far as Tennessee, of course."

"Of course not! Don't be silly. You and Sari are family."

"That's right!" Nana Two, ad-libbed. She asked Harold if he wanted breakfast.

"No thanks. I had a continental breakfast at the hotel."

She had figured as much. Her son looked neither hungry nor tired. "Well, let's get going, then.

Charlotte watched Nana Two go inside the pantry and come out with the hammer and pail of nails.

"Here, son, I kept these close by" she said. "The boards are on the back porch. Nail them over the windows for me. Nail them tight."

Harold raised a curious brow.

"But why? Won't Rufus be around?"

The old woman placed a hand on her hip.

"Yes, he is. But, I've decided I want to be near my grandchildren. After Sherry has the baby, I want you to

124

find me a little place of my own. It doesn't make sense your driving all this way to see me all the time. I'm getting much older; starting to think about my health. I should be living closer to my grandchildren while I can still be of some use to them."

What about the land—are you going to sell it to Rufus?"

"Hell, no!" she exclaimed. "He's already too big for his breeches. I'll give it away before I sell it to him. He already owns half of Derriene Crossing. Maybe after a year or so I'll go ahead and sell it to the Reid's."

Charlotte couldn't bear to hear Rufus' name called. She left the kitchen.

"Excuse me. I'm going to go make sure Sari won't leave anything behind."

Harold gave Charlotte a peculiar look, as he took the hammer and nails from his mother.

"Make sure you put the boards on good, now!" his mother instructed, before she followed Charlotte.

Harold looked at his mother's retreating back, studying her. Then he went outside, got the boards from the porch and began boarding up the windows. In the meantime, Charlotte and Nana Two put their belongings in the car. Sari carried the kitten in her arms.

****

After Harold finished boarding up the windows, he re-entered the house and locked the back door. He returned the hammer and nails to the cupboard, and moved toward the living room, where his mother had left her trunk in the middle of the room for him to take out to the station wagon. He hoisted the trunk on his shoulder and stepped onto the porch. Slowly, he lowered the trunk to the floor and locked the front door, thinking that he would have to come back later in the season to retrieve the rest of his mother's things. He loaded the trunk onto the station wagon.

"We're all set," he said getting into the driver's seat. He started the engine.

Without anyone noticing her, Maebelle came around to the side of the old woman's house. Sari looked up wide-eyed and frightened at the black face peeking at them. Her scream made everyone turn and look in the direction that she was pointing.

"Who the hell is that? She's peeking at us!" Harold said, with concern.

Charlotte grabbed the door handle to get out of the car and confront Maebelle. Her blazing eyes met the old woman's warning eyes. The old woman shook her head, quietly warning Charlotte to stay inside the car.

"Oh, she's just some lunatic stranger wandering around. She's the reason I told you to board over the windows," his mother told him.

"You sure you don't want me to speak to her?" Harold asked.

"No! She's a bit crazy. Let's just go."

"Well, all right," he replied looking at his mother, and then at Charlotte.

He put the station wagon in gear and drove away slowly. Charlotte put her arms around her daughter.

"It's okay, baby," she told her. "You can stop crying now."

When the station wagon was out of view, Maebelle came and sat down on the old woman's steps. But not before she noticed the license plates.

"Hmm, I wonder how he got down here so fast," she muttered. "I guess the two of you must be gone for good, seeing how the house is all boarded up. You put a curse on me, and then you leave. I know you only did it because of Charlotte. Well, I hope both of you will keep your behinds away. I'm starting my new life, and I don't want either one of you around trying to mess things up. Good riddance."

Chapter 4

At the end of June, Jake Blakestone and his sons, Sam and Jake Junior, moved to Detroit, Michigan. Jinni, Jennifer, Lynn and Jackie started a whole new way of life on Rufus' farm.

Those first few weeks Rufus behaved like a "normal" stepfather, except he insisted on them calling him daddy, which they all hated. No one could ever take the place of the girls' natural father. And no matter how nice he pretended to be, Jennifer felt leery of him. He still couldn't look her level in the eyes. She tried to catch him looking at her and Jinni, the way Jake Junior had said, but was never able to. Still, she always made sure she kept her distance.

At first, it had seemed like a dream. Life was so wonderful. The house was roomy and more beautiful than they ever imagined. At their old house, the four girls had shared the same bedroom. Now, they slept two to a room and they each had their own bed. There was plenty of food to eat. But there was also lots of hard work. They didn't mind, for they were the richest Negro family around, and Rufus' farm seemed to stretch forever.

They were assigned chores: The responsibility for cleaning up the old barn was Jennifer and Jinni's. But working in the barn was a pleasure since it provided a nest for their dreams. They would lie for hours dreaming about the future. In the barn Jinni wrote love letters to Phillip Coon, although he never responded. The barn provided solitude for Jennifer for reading and writing poetry. Lynn and Jackie were too young to do work in the barn. Their chores mainly consisted of helping around the house.

On a bright, sunny day, in October, both Jinni and Jennifer discovered that the old barn was no longer safe. The twin sisters realized that to be found there alone would make them prey for the hunter—Rufus—their stepfather. That day Jennifer, followed by Jinni, each lost their virginity. Afraid and ashamed, they kept their frightening secret from each other; and, of course, from their mother.

In the months that followed, the girls lost their tempers easily. And both of them were surprised that their breasts began swelling, and their bellies grew rounder. They both dropped out of school. They both dreaded it, especially Jennifer. Her dreams of becoming a schoolteacher had ended.

* * *

Maebelle was fit to be tied that Jinni and Jennifer were pregnant. She often sat alone at the kitchen table mumbling to herself, with her brows tightly knitted in skeptical despair. She considered her twin daughters trifling traitors. Her fantasy world crashed. She refused to believe that Rufus had raped her girls, daring not to confront him with their confession. She pitied herself. Out of frustration, she frequently pounded a hard fist into her thigh, although she felt sore afterward and regretted her actions. "You're both trying to destroy my marriage. I wish to God that I'd let you all go and live with Jake. But, when I'm through with you, you all will change your story!" she began telling herself.

One morning Maebelle jumped up from her chair. She rushed out the house and retrieved the hatchet from the back porch. She waddled down the steps to the nearby underbrush. Swearing, she tromped around cutting small bunches of saplings to bring back to the house. "You all will tell me the truth!" she fussed.

After gathering enough saplings, she trudged back to the house and up the porch steps. She put away the hatchet and sat down on the top step and began stripping away the leaves from the saplings, transforming them into twigs. She carried her twigs through the kitchen and stacked them in a corner where the girls would see them. Her mission accomplished, she went to her bedroom.

* * *

At dinner, there was ominous silence, except for forks scraping against the plates. Dinner was like that since the girls' bellies began swelling. Jinni and Jennifer ate dinner as quickly as possible, to get out of Maebelle's presence. They would return as soon as Maebelle left, to wash dishes and clean the kitchen. Today, Maebelle lingered long after she ate dinner. She sat at the table, staring vacantly, eyeing the papered wall.

Rufus would come home soon, expecting his kitchen to be cleaned. For some strange reason, on Friday evenings, he preferred eating dinner alone in an immaculate kitchen.

Jinni and Jennifer were reluctant to return to the kitchen with Maebelle there. She hadn't looked right to them. The twigs she had stacked in the corner puzzled them, since no one had done anything to merit a beating.

They had no choice but to return to the kitchen, as quietly as two thieves. They looked at their mother chewing a chicken bone. Her face was stern, as she continued staring at the wall. The twin sisters exchanged wary glances. "She's been chewing on that same chicken bone since we left!" Jinni whispered.

Jennifer placed her right index finger on her lip. "Shhhh!"

They both moved softly toward the sink. Jinni swallowed the nervous feeling in her stomach. She turned on the faucet to a gentle stream of water. "You think she's waiting to finally confront Daddy?" Jennifer whispered.

Jinni looked over her shoulder at Maebelle, then at Jennifer. "Uhn-uhn. And I don't think she knows how late it is, either. She knows she better not be in here when he gets home on Friday. Let's stop whispering before she catches us."

The dishes rattling in the sink disrupted Maebelle's thoughts. She snapped her head around, gazing angrily at the two girls. In silent rage, she sprang to her feet; crossed the floor, and grabbed a twig out of the corner. She started harshly lashing her daughters across their backs repeatedly, one after the other.

With their hands flailing in the air, they screamed in agony.

"I want the truth from y'all!" she cried.

"We've told you the truth!" Jennifer screamed, trying to block those stinging blows. "Please, Mama. Stop beating us! We didn't do anything wrong!"

Jinni saw an opportunity and bolted out of the kitchen to her bedroom. She grabbed her lightweight sweater and fled. She didn't stop running until she reached the stream. Later, the evening, autumn air started to feel chilly. She braved the cold, trembling, while rubbing her wounds and sobbing uncontrollably, as any place felt better than home.

* * *

Rufus arrived home to the sound of Jennifer's helpless screams as they echoed throughout the house. He rushed through the living room, through the dinning room, and entered the kitchen. He stopped short when he saw Maebelle's angry, twisted face. "What the hell . . .!" He rushed upon her. He grabbed her arm, and wrung the twig out of her hand. "What the hell do you think you're doing?"

Maebelle stepped backward stunned at Rufus' words. Her chest rose and fell rapidly. She didn't answer him, though she gave him a menacing glare.

Jennifer rose from the floor, badly bruised and hurting. She felt the baby turning inside her womb.

Rufus caught sight of the twigs stacked in the corner, and confronted Maebelle. "Have you lost your mind, woman? Get this shit out of here! Don't nobody beat ass around here but me, you hear?"

Jennifer was taken aback by Rufus' expression of anger. Up to now, he'd never hit them, but she could hardly appreciate his pathetic, kind gesture. You're the cause of this, she thought to herself. Why don't you just tell her the truth, you dirty dog.

"They done brought shame to this household!" Maebelle cried.

"Girls make mistakes," Rufus told her, glancing back at Jennifer. Facing Maebelle, he said, "Nothing has happened here that's bad enough for you to go crazy over! Now you leave her alone!"

Jennifer swallowed hard. The gall! She couldn't believe his hypocrisy.

"And where's Jinni?" He inquired. "I suppose you've beat her, too."

Maebelle folded her arms across her chest. She felt too angry and distraught to fight with him. She went and stood in front of the window thinking. This is supposed to be a happy time in our life. "I'm the only one who should be having babies in this house," she snapped.

"Yet, you stand there saying what they've done isn't anything to be going crazy over? Well, I didn't raise them to be lying up with some little 'ol boys! I know it's that Logan boy, they've been with. He's the only boy who has been around here! Besides, people look up to you. What will they think about this family?"

Rufus looked at Jennifer. She immediately gave him her back. "I hate you! I hate you!" she cried in her heart.

Rufus joined Maebelle at the window.

She kept her eyes lowered.

"Woman, you listen to me. It's nobody's business what goes on in my home. I'm the head here. I'll determine what's shame. You think I care about what those poor Negroes think about me? I keep most of them alive—half of them work for me." He paused. "Besides, I need the extra hands in the field. Nobody will starve on account of a few more mouths being added. If they get knocked up again, it's nobody's business! Now you leave them alone! Don't let me catch you hittin' them again. It's not healthy...."

Jennifer felt her heart sank deep into her stomach. Oh, God! We're in trouble, she thought to herself. Please Mama! Wake up! Look what he's doing to all of us. Just ask him if he raped me and Jinni. Please! She shivered, as though a North Pole wind had blown into the room.

Then, as if it were an omen, the numbers and days suddenly disappeared from the calendar hanging on the wall in front of her. All that was left was an ominous black page—no writing—no nothing. She could see it as clear as day. Her legs felt wobbly. This is my future, she thought. Oh, God!

Jennifer thought about her father, Jake. If only she could find the piece of paper she had written his address on. She knew she had put it inside her pocket book, as did Jinni. But neither of them could find their paper with their father's address. They believed Rufus had gone into their pocket books and taken them. Still shivering, she ran out the kitchen, leaving Rufus and Maebelle to argue. She had expected to see Jinni when she entered their bedroom. But, Jinni wasn't there. She also noticed that Jinni's sweater was missing, and knew she had gone down by the stream. She would join her, and tell her what Rufus had said, but darkness was setting in. She would wait for Jinni.

* * *

Rufus gathered up the twigs and stored them in his pickup. He would dispose of them later. Headed back to the house, he stood on the porch steps for a while, looking out absently at the darken horizon.

Meanwhile, Maebelle pulled a chair from the table and sat down exhausted. She felt her baby move inside her. In spite of everything, she felt relieved she was released from the vow, she now realized she couldn't keep. She had vowed to beat the two girls until they confessed the babies inside their wombs belonged to the Logan boy. She felt her life had turned into a nightmare. In despair, she carried on a silent conversation in her mind. They've never wanted me with Rufus. That's why they've done this. He's a good man, taking up for them like that, though she didn't agree with him. She couldn't imagine his reaction if he knew that they'd accused him of ... She couldn't bring herself to say the word. "You're a good man, Rufus. However, why did you encourage Jennifer that they could keep having babies?" They're my girls, she thought.

She got up slowly and finished washing the dishes and cleaned the kitchen. When she was finished, she heard the front door open and close. Rufus entered the house. His footsteps led to their bedroom. She knew he was giving her time to clean the kitchen and put his dinner on the table. She did so and left the kitchen.

Later, Jinni retuned home and found Jennifer asleep—the only means of escape from their troubles. Jinni quietly slipped into her nightgown and crawled into bed.

* * *

In the wee hours of the morning in late July, both girls went into labor only hours apart.

At 6:00 a.m., Rufus went to get the midwife, Hailey Richard, just as she was leaving her house. She was en-route to go see one of her patients. She was a rather plain, tall, stout-built woman, with a noticeably wide nose. Upon seeing Rufus, her large, brown eyes opened in surprise. "Rufus!" She switched the medical bag to her other hand. "I-I was just on my way out. Are you here to see Daniel?"

Rufus stood midway down the steps. "Good morning, Hailey. Ah, no. I'm here to see you. Mae--Maebelle--my--my wife sent me here to ask for your service," he stuttered. "She's in the family way."

Hailey studied him for a long moment. She felt nothing but contempt for him. Wife my foot, she thought to herself. You can barely say her name. She was, however, curious to see what the woman looked like. Her nephew, John, had told her how Rufus had tricked him into driving Maebelle to his house in an attempt to break up his marriage. "Well, I guess my other patient can wait," she said. "When I'm done at your house, I'll drive out to see her later."

Rufus sighed with relief. He was glad Hailey had agreed to come. "I appreciate it. Thank you." He knew she could have turned him down because the girls were not her patients.

"You're welcome," Hailey said, grudgingly.

He turned on his heels; he went down the steps ahead of her, got into his pickup and sped away.

Hailey took just enough time to lock up the house before rushing off with her medical bag in hand. "He sure didn't waste any time fattin' her belly," she murmured. "Talking about 'my wife.' Wife my foot! Who does he think he's fooling? Everybody knows they're not married." She opened the door and climbed quickly into her green Dodge. She drove in the direction of Rufus' place.

Half an hour later, she parked in front of Rufus' house, got out of her car, closed the door, and dragged her medical bag with her. Quickly climbing the porch steps, she knocked on the door, then stood back admiring the blue shutters and the white lace country curtains draped over the windows.

A harried-looking Maebelle appeared in the open doorway. "Hailey Richard?" she asked, reaching out her hand.

"Yes. I'm Hailey," she said, as they shook hands. Hailey's eyes were drawn to Maebelle's smooth dark face and then to her enormous belly. She wondered why Rufus hadn't allowed her to become her patient, considering how he could easily afford her services. "And you must be Maebelle." Of course, she knew who she was. John had described her to a T.

"Ah, yes ma'am. I'm Maebelle."

"Your husband said you requested my service."

"Ah, yes, ma'am. Please come in."

Hailey stepped inside the spacious living room. Just as she was about to sneak an appraisal, two distinct agonizing screams echoed from one of the bedrooms. "Whose screams are those?" she inquired.

Maebelle rubbed a flat palm over her swollen stomach. "Ah, my daughters...they're in labor. You're here for them." She saw Hailey's stunned expression and knew that as soon as Hailey left the house the family secret would be out.

"Well, you lead the way. Have they been seen by any other midwife?"

"I'm afraid not," Maebelle replied. She led Hailey through the arched doorway, to the large bedroom on their left. She opened the door and Hailey stepped inside the room. Hailey was astonished to see that the girls were nearly babies themselves, and twins. She turned towards Maebelle. "As young as these girls are, you mean to tell me you've never allowed them to be seen by a midwife!" Maebelle swallowed. She didn't answer. She turned around and closed the door.

"Lie down, children!" Hailey cried, rushing to the nearest bed, which was Jinni's. She set down her medical bag on the polished Mahogany night table and brought out her stethoscope. "Lie down, honey!" she said to the hysterical girl. "You'll break the baby's neck bending forward like that!" She looked over her shoulder at Maebelle. "Well, don't just stand there!" she barked. "Take care of that other girl! I only got one pair of hands! How long have they been in labor?" she inquired. Her voice was concerned.

"Since last night."

Hailey rolled her eyes heavenward. "That isn't' telling me anything! At what time 'last night'?" Maebelle didn't answer, not because she was trying to avoid Hailey's question, but because Jennifer had violently objected to her even putting a hand on her and cursed at her.

"Well, there might be complications seeing how young they are, and given the fact they've never been examined. What kind of mother are you?" she accused. Maebelle glanced down at her own stomach. She was far along herself and she, too, had not seen a midwife. She'd been too distraught to take care of herself. She guessed she should let Hailey examine her before she left.

"I'm going to need your help," Hailey told her once more. "So be prepared. It's never been required of me to attend dual births before. I'm already nervous." She took a deep breath; shook her fingers. "How'd you let this happen to both of your girls?" she emphasized. "Don't you watch them? And what I can't understand is why you didn't let them see a midwife. It can't be because you don't have the money."

* * *

Maebelle reached out a hand to Jennifer. "Let me help," she said.

"I said, don't touch me!" Jennifer cried in anguish. "I don't want you touching me!"

Hailey straightened. "Now honey," she called across the room. "You're going to have to let your mother help you. I've only got one pair of hands."

A knock at the door brought both women's heads around. Rufus pushed the door open and entered the room.

Hailey's eyes widened. "You aren't allowed in here!" she shrieked.

"But I heard you say you needed somebody to help you."

Hailey glared at Maebelle, then at Rufus. "Are your crazy! You know full well I don't mean you. You can't be in here!" She glared hard at Maebelle. "Well, why are you just standing there? He's your husband! You should be the one chasing him out of here. These are your girls, for heaven sake!" Hailey cried incredulous!

Maebelle, frozen in her spot, lowered her head. She had seen Rufus' stubbornness before, and it was useless of her to try persuading him to leave the room. She wanted to escape the shame and humiliation he was causing her. Finally, she found her tongue.

"I'll go get the water," she announced. Then turned on her heels to leave.

"What's this over here in these pots!" Hailey called, watching Maebelle walking away.

Maebelle stopped short in disgust, and then she turned around. Uncertain of what to do, she stayed near the door.

The girl's anguished screams drew Hailey's attention away from Rufus. She didn't know which girl to attend to first. Since Jinni seemed closer to delivering, Hailey went to her. Jinni's screams hit high heavens when she felt the hot tearing pain. Warm fluid gushed out between her legs, then numbness. Jinni refused to look when Hailey held up the small, pink, mottled, bundle of pain. "It's a girl," Hailey flatly remarked.

There was nothing joyous about this birth. She cut the cord and tied it with twine. Then she looked around and saw Maebelle still standing near the door with her lashes lowered and her hands clasped in front of her. "Well, don't just stand there like a fool," Hailey scold. "Come over here and get this baby!" she ordered. "You should be trying to help that other child! Don't you see Rufus, over there, messing with her!"

Maebelle unclasped her hands, and languishingly moved towards Hailey.

"Here! Take this baby, so I can go help your other daughter before that fool ends up killing her and the baby!"

Peering down at the child, Maebelle's eyes opened wide. She was stunned after Hailey placed the baby girl in her arms. Her heart stumbled, as her knees were knocking together uncontrollably. The Logan boy was dark-skinned—a far contrast from this pink bundle with reddish hair. Now she knew Rufus had fathered this child. She immediately remembered the old woman's prophecy. *"You're laughing now, but some day you'll be slinging snot and wrangling your hands. He'll rape your girls in your presence."* Suddenly, she saw Jinni glaring at her. Maebelle knew, Jinni knew, the moment of truth was upon her.

Before Hailey could get to Jennifer, she had to turn right around, because Jinni was pushing her second child into the world. "Jesus!" Hailey cried, her hands flailing in exasperation.

While Hailey was in a quandary, Rufus was busy humiliating Jennifer—dangerously helping her with her delivery. He put his flat hand on her stomach and pressed down with the weight of his shoulders. Poor Jennifer let out a horrific howl. "You're killing me! Somebody get him off me!" She felt herself lose control of her bowel. Simultaneously, she felt a hot searing tear and a gush of warm fluid between her thighs.

Before Hailey could reach Jennifer's bed, Rufus had delivered her baby. "It's a girl!" he announced. "There's nothing to it," he said. "I figured I could do this!" he exclaimed and half turned and looked at Hailey. For a moment or two, Hailey stood immobilized and astonished. She watched in horror as Rufus lifted the child from between Jennifer's feet. She glared at Rufus with deepest indignation. This was a nightmare. This man doesn't respect women, she told herself. What kind of human being is he! Does he really think child birthing is a plaything? She saw Jennifer's agitated expression. Slightly regaining her composure, Hailey quickly clipped the umbilical cord and tied it with twine. Out the side of her eye, she saw Rufus watching her every move. She suspected his interest went beyond giving her a helping hand, all of which she found criminal.

With Rufus pressing down on her stomach a second time, Jennifer's sudden howl brought Hailey rushing back to her. "Lord, have mercy! What are you doing man? Good Lord. How many children are being born here today!" Hailey yelled for Maebelle. "Come get this baby! Why are you standing around like somebody crazy! You should've been the one helping that girl! What kind of mess is this!" she exclaimed. Her forehead was beaded with sweat.

Maebelle moved quickly toward Hailey. Hailey practically threw the baby into Maebelle's arms. Maebelle took the baby girl from Hailey's arms. To her consternation, the baby had the same striking feature as her twin sister. Maebelle felt her heart shift to her stomach. This was her worst nightmare.

Hailey moved apprehensively to Jennifer's side, fearing that Rufus would not allow her to intercept. Surprisingly, he moved out of her way. A moment later a little red-haired, mottled boy arrived into the world. Rufus watched intently as Hailey cut the cord and tied it off. For sure this low-down scoundrel is trying to learn child-birthing techniques, she told herself. She noticed how badly her hands were shaking.

"Come get this child!" she ordered Maebelle. "You been fiddling with them others long enough to know who their daddy is!" Hailey glared at Rufus when she said that.

He averted his eyes.

Too distraught for words, Maebelle came and stood beside Hailey with her eyes cast toward the floor.

Hailey handed her the squalling baby. "Take him and clean him up!" she demanded. "So this is what you fought Charlotte for, huh?" You got some mess on your hands!" she told her. "You fought and won you know not what." Hailey wasn't a woman who minced words. Maebelle didn't answer. She took the baby grudgingly. Glaring quickly at Jennifer, she avoided her eyes.

Jennifer glared back. What you got to say now? she thought. You beat us for nothing, and let him rob your daughters' dignity. She turned over on her side. You ain't no kinda mother, she thought, sobbing. I wish I never knew your name.

Lost in her misery, Jennifer had forgotten Hailey was standing nearby. When she felt a gentle hand on her shoulder, she jerked her head around.

"I need to finish attending to you," Hailey said softly. "Then you can rest."

Jennifer looked up at Hailey's kind face. Her expression was concerned. Jennifer sniffed. She saw Rufus across the room, standing in the middle of the floor, looking from her, to Jinni. She wished he would go now. There was nothing else for him to see. She wanted to die. Why me? Its Jinni who thinks she's in love with you. She closed her eyes. "I'm in pain," she said, looking into Hailey's troubled eyes.

"I figured you'd be," said Hailey. Her voice was soothing. "I already told Maebelle what to give you."

* * *

Maebelle suddenly quaked. The babies were turning inside her. She could actually see ripples of movement as she glanced down at her stomach. She suddenly felt thunder-struck. It dawned on her that all three of them were carrying twins. She remembered the dream she had right after Rufus had asked her to marry him. She held on to the crib and let out a low, strangled moan.

* * *

Hailey finished attending the two girls. Jinni was sleeping now. Hailey lifted a tired hand and brushed away a few unruly gray strands out of her face. Her brain felt numbed. As she picked up her medical bag, she glanced at Jennifer. The poor thing was weeping. Hailey's heart went out to her. She felt ashamed for her own womanhood. She understood Jennifer's torment.

"I'm out of here," she told Rufus. "Where is my money?"

"Here," he said, touching her arm with the envelope. She drew up short.

"I wouldn't think of not paying you. What kind of man do you think I am?"

"A dog!" Hailey barked, with a penetrating stare. "I won't be a bit surprised if some day, I hear, you've done the same things to your own!" She snatched the envelope out of his hand and stormed off.

Rufus studied her from behind. I'd like to smash your wide nose, flatter than flat, he thought. "You should know a man has a right to rule his house the way he sees fit," he shouted. "This will teach them to keep their legs closed."

Jennifer, still awake, overhead Rufus' comments. Her eyes were riveted on him. She felt used since he was blaming them that he raped them.

"You see I know how to put a stop to things." He half turned and glared at Maebelle. She shivered, not knowing who he was anymore. She imagined what Hailey must think about her.

"It's better than the whipping Maebelle been putting on them!" he exclaimed.

Hailey didn't answer. She kept walking. When she reached the door, she turned around and stared the Devil in the eyes, gauging the depth of his madness.

"I put enough money in that envelope for you to keep your mouth shut," he added.

Hailey's eyes were blazing. She squeezed her hand tight around the envelope, feeling its thickness for the first time. "I can't be bought, you bastard!" she retorted. In all of her thirty years of midwifery, she had never witnessed such mess. She couldn't wait to get out of his house. She left the room, walked through the living room, and stepped out on the porch. Rushing down the steps, she hurried to her car. Inside the car, she opened her medical bag and put the envelope inside. Her hand shook as she turned the key in the ignition. She started the engine and drove off, telling herself she was too exhausted and disturbed to drop in on Lottie Mae.

* * *

Three months later, Hailey parked her car in her yard. She was returning from delivering Lottie Mae and Ernest Albert's baby boy. Yawning, she rubbed a tired hand over her face. Moisture filled her eyes. Thank God the baby came into the world healthy, she told herself. She had seen the relief on Ernest's face when she'd told him he had a healthy baby boy. They're good people, she thought. She shivered. It was a chilly November mornings. Reaching for her medical bag, after she had half opened the door, suddenly Rufus, pulled up behind her. She swore. After slamming the car door, she hurried toward the house. She wanted nothing to do with him.

Rufus pulled up along side her and rolled down the window.

Hailey stopped short, glared at him, and then started walking again. She knew why he was there. But she had vowed never to set foot in his house again.

"Good morning, Hailey. I'm glad I caught up with you. Maebelle is in a bad way; she needs your help."

"Get somebody else!" she barked. Her voice was tremulous from the chill in the air. She pulled her jacket collar up around her neck and kept on walking.

"There's nobody else," he said, rolling along side her. "Not within twenty miles."

"Oh, yes there is! What about yourself? Now get out of my yard, you heathen!"

Rufus swerved the pickup in front of Hailey, cutting off her path.

She stopped abruptly in astonishment. Her eyes were blazing. "I'm not playing games with you, Rufus! I said get out of my yard! I'm not Maebelle!"

He jutted his elbow out on the sill. "Please, Hailey. I'm not playing games. Maebelle really needs you. She slipped and fell this morning." He lied. "She's in a bad way." That much was true—and he had been responsible. It all started when he lured poor, ten-year-old Jackie in his bedroom, after she complained to him the light bulb in the bathroom had blown. Taking Jackie as his prey, he inflicted unbearable pain on Jackie. Her petrified, anguished, screams pierced the darkness, waking the household. Maebelle tried to peel him off Jackie's small frame, but he was like an animal in heat. He got off Jackie, fought with Maebelle, crushing her stomach. Maebelle passed out. Meanwhile, three pairs of frightened, terrified eyes watched in horror as he climbed back on top of Jackie.

"Please, Hailey," he begged.

Hailey closed her eyes and gritted her teeth. Damn you! She thought to herself. Why did his timing have to be so perfect? Why couldn't he have come while I was still at Lottie Mae's house! She sighed, looking up at the sky. The rosy sun had crept upon the horizon. She was looking forward to making breakfast for her husband, Daniel. Now she wouldn't have time, especially if Maebelle was in as much trouble as he claimed. Thank God the stroke hadn't totally incapacitated Daniel. He would have to fix himself a hot bologna sandwich, which was nothing new. She was often called upon at odd hours, and he would have to fend for himself. She took a deep breath. Boy! I dread going back to that house. "Never say never!" she muttered. She stopped; turned and stared at Rufus, for a long moment. He avoided looking her in the eyes. "Tell me something," she said. You aren't planning on being there, are you? Because if you are, I'm not going!"

He sniffed, and looked before him, so as not to meet her eyes. "I got to go feed the livestock. The key is under the white flower pot on the front porch."

"That's what you said before!" she said. Rufus didn't comment. "Arrogant bastard!" she mumbled under her breath. "I guess you won't be there! She's your wife!" He still didn't answer.

Reluctantly, she went back to her car. A minute later she drove down the road headed to Rufus' house.

As Rufus passed her car in his pickup, she told herself, I'm glad you won't be there. She made up her mind to talk to those girls. Jinni and Jennifer had been on her mind too long, and she had promised herself if she ever saw them again she would do her best to persuade them to run away from home.

* * *

Later, she parked her car in the winding driveway. "Oh, what a beautiful home," she muttered. "Looking at it from the outside, no one would believe the misery behind these walls." She exited the car, carrying her medical bag that she thought was unusually heavy. Then she recalled taking Daniel's gun, because she had left the house in the wee hours of the morning to deliver Lottie Mae's baby. The key to the front door was underneath the white flowerpot just like Rufus said. She unlocked the door and entered the house. It was so quiet, except for the ticking clock. She guessed everybody was asleep, except Maebelle, of course, poor soul. It suddenly dawned on her that she had forgotten to examine Maebelle, when she was there last time. She guessed Maebelle had also forgotten. Things had been so crazy that day, delivering so many babies. She couldn't wait to get out of there!

She saw the dining room door slowly opening. A frail girl poked her head inside. "Hi. I remember you," she said. "I'm Lynn. I'm the only one up. I'll show you to Mama's room."

Hailey looked at her in surprise. She was a friendly girl. "Good morning, Lynn. I'm Mrs. Hailey Richard. I don't recall seeing you when I was here before."

"I know. Mama made us stay in our rooms." She led Hailey down the short hallway to the room on the left. "It's this one," she whispered, pointing a long, thin finger. Lynn was a cute, lanky girl, with dimpled cheeks, with two thick braids, reaching her shoulders. "This used to be Jennifer and Jinni's room," she confided. "They're upstairs with us now."

Hailey raised a brow in suspicion. How many girls does your mother have? She wondered.

Lynn spoke freely without any prodding from Hailey. "Mama told them not to sleep on the same floor with her and Daddy anymore." She looked up in Hailey's kind face. "Well, I have to go now." Hailey had found the young girl's brief conversation interesting.

"Well, thank you, Lynn, for taking me to your Mama's room."

Lynn didn't answer, as she grabbed the stair rail, running softly up the stairs.

Hailey knocked on the door.

"Come in."

Hailey opened the door and entered the immaculate bedroom. Lovely lace curtains hung at the window.

Maebelle moved her head on the pillow, looking at Hailey, who noticed the worry-lines etched in Maebelle's forehead. "Good morning," Maebelle remarked weakly. "I'm so glad you could come. I'm in so much pain."

"Good morning," Hailey said softly. She placed her medical bag on the seat of the rocker and moved toward the bed. "Your husband told me you slipped and fell. Is there any bleeding?"

Another sharp pain shot through Maebelle's stomach. She jerked upright; stifled a scream. When the pain subsided she lay back down.

"That's not how you work with the pain, honey. You know you can't jerk up like that. You'll break the baby's neck that way, Hailey told her."

146

"I'm having twins. I don't want to lose them," she confided.

Hailey looked stunned. "Damn! Three sets of twins all in the same year! *What's he got inside that thang of his?" she mumbled.*

"Did your water break?" she asked. She then saw blood on the bed.

Maebelle mumbled incoherently. She felt intense anguish as the throbbing pain rippled through her stomach. She hated Rufus for putting her and the babies' lives in danger. He had become so dangerous. It was as though someone had put a curse on him, causing him to do horrible things to her and her daughters. She blamed the old woman for their troubles.

"Well, I have to examine you." Hearing only one heartbeat, Hailey frowned. Time passed, and Maebelle endured excruciating pain, her water still unbroken.

Fretful, Hailey rose from the rocker. "Well, I'm going to go out for a breath of air, and say a prayer for you."

Maebelle miserly nodded on the pillow and looked at her. She said nothing.

Hailey left the room, entered the kitchen, and pulled a chair away from the table and sat down listlessly. Worry-lines etched deeply into her forehead, feeling that one of the babies had definitely expired.

She stood and went over in front of the window, whispering a prayer for Maebelle. She looked out at the nimbus clouds drifting in the early morning sky, while sighing heavily. She brushed the unruly gray strands of hair away from her face, hoping the rain would hold off. Her arthritis started flaring up. After she got done here—providing she had energy left—she would drag herself over to Stella Moore's house, and explain to her what was going on here. Until now, she hadn't told anyone, not even her husband Daniel, but she couldn't keep this to herself any longer.

She felt a tug on her elbow and whirled around. She stared down at Lynn's upturned face. "Why, you're like a cat!" she kindly stated. "Do you always get around so quietly?" Lynn didn't answer.

She crooked her finger and beckoned for Hailey's ear. "I wanna whisper something in your ear."

Hailey was anxious to hear what Lynn had to say, as she bent down at once.

Lynn brushed back Hailey's tousled gray hair, and cupped her hands over her ear. "Daddy did that to Mama. He's the reason she's sick." Lynn's hands dropped to her sides. Hailey straightened. Lynn looked at Hailey, detecting her confusion.

"I don't understand!" Hailey replied in a low voice. "What did he do to her?" She bent her waist again.

Lynn cupped her hands over her ear, as she whispered. "He threw Mama against the wall last night when she tried to pull him off Jackie. Then he did something else to her this morning."

Hailey stood erect. She swallowed hard. A cold, frightening chill spiraled down her spine. "Who's Jackie?" she asked in distressed.

"My sister."

"Shhh," Hailey said. "Whisper. You don't want anybody to hear you telling me this. How old is Jackie?"

"She's ten and a half. And I'm nine," Lynn confided. Then she crooked her finger and beckoned for Hailey's ear.

Hailey bent down again.

Lynn pushed back Hailey's gray hair, whispering in her ear. "He made Jackie take off all her clothes! He was on top of her. *We saw his thing.* Jackie woke up the whole house screaming. Then Daddy and Mama started fighting!"

Maebelle's screams reverberated through the walls and ended their conversation. Hailey's heart jumped. She shoved Lynn out of her way. "Excuse me, child! I have to go see about your mama!"

"Don't tell anybody I told you!" Lynn called.

Hailey half turned and looked at her. "I won't," she said, dashing from the kitchen. She opened Maebelle's bedroom door and stepped inside the room. She was shocked. "Rufus! Why are you here!" she exclaimed. "You said you had to feed the livestock." Turning his head, he peered at her, with a smirk, without answering. He began wiping Maebelle's forehead with a washcloth.

Hailey shuddered with anger, because she didn't hear him enter the house. Again, he had lied to her; reminding her of a preying animal, sneaking up like a slithering snake. "I guess the animals weren't hungry after all," she remarked, and then moved toward the bed. "This will be a very difficult birth! Please don't assist me, in any way!" Her feelings surpassed anger.

"Nah. I'm helping!" he decreed, to her dismay. "And don't tell me she's not my wife, either. I told you before that a man has a right to set rules in his own house. I will deliver this one myself. I just needed you here, to make sure everything goes right."

Hailey stood enraged. Everything started seeming like a nightmare, surreal, just like before. Her blood froze. She remained speechless, knowing the dirty dog was up to something. She didn't trust him. She wanted to grab her medical bag and flee. But, then, felt responsible for Maebelle, who was already in danger, possibly with one dead fetus inside her.

Helplessly, Hailey placed her fist to her mouth, watching Rufus in horror, place his flat palms on Maebelle's stomach, pushing down with the weight of his shoulders. Maebelle howled loudly. After a long horrifying moment she felt numbness.

A look of terror masked Hailey's face.

Rufus looked at her with a silly grin. Later, he announced: "It's a girl! Bless her soul! Well, c'mon. Let's see you cut the cord.

Hailey's feet were anchored to the floor. "The nerve—I mean the nerve of you—"she stammered. "Who the hell you think you are, using me this way?" For the child and Maebelle's sake, Hailey cut the umbilical cord and tied it with twine. Then she grabbed the infant and bathed her. "I hope you know she's having twins!" she cried, as she nervously bathed the baby, then dressed her in a tiny, white undershirt, cloth diaper, and wrapped her in a receiving blanket.

Maebelle began screaming at the top of her lungs.

Hailey felt drained by tension. She could do so little because Rufus was Maebelle's so-called husband.

Maebelle pushed as hard as she could, until the stillborn fetus spilled out on the bed. She fell back on the pillow, in unceasing pain. For the first time in hours, she finally closed her eyes, as she felt an eerie silence.

Not hearing her second baby cry, Maebelle opened her eyes. Rufus looked dumbfounded as he held the dead child. She sat up on her elbows. Rufus' jaws became taut. "Oh, God! My baby is dead," she wailed, blaming Rufus for its death. His shoulders were slumped, and then he laid the dead baby on the mattress, at her feet. His face looked weird, as he glared at the child's grotesque lip. He flew into a wild rage and started mauling Maebelle with his hard, bloody fist. "You've been whoring around with Thomas Wright! These ain't my damn babies!"

Maebelle let out a strangled cry, hiding her face inside the pillow. "I don't know a Thomas Wright!" Her voice was muffled. "They're your babies! Please! You're killing me. I just gave birth!"

"Je-sus!" Hailey cried, pivoting on her heels. She moved quickly across the floor. "What are you doing, man? She just gave birth!" Hailey became more alarmed when she saw the dead infant was still attached to the umbilical cord. Maebelle, in trying to escape Rufus' brutal fist, had a foot hanging precariously off the mattress, while the other rested on the dead baby's neck.

"My Lord," Hailey cried. Desperate to rescue Maebelle, she quickly scrambled onto the bed and leapt on Rufus' back. Catching him around his neck, she wrapped her thick legs around his thighs, and brought him to his knees.

He gagged a few strangled words: "Turnnnn-me loose, black monkey! You chokin' me! "

Hailey withdrew her arms and legs. In two, long strides she was near her medical bag, with her hand on her husband's revolver. One false move and she would blow his brains out. "Get out of here! You crazy *sonofabitch!*"

Holding his throat, Rufus slowly got on his feet. He eyed Hailey out the corner of his eyes. He shook his shoulders and stuck out his neck. She glared back at him, breathing heavy, with her finger on the trigger.

He faced Maebelle. "You give that damn baby girl to Jennifer. You will not hold another man's baby in your arms. Not in my house. Don't feed her; don't wipe the shit off her ass! You hear me!"

Hailey saw Maebelle's eyes filled with distress and fear. She sat up on her elbows, pleading. "Rufus, please! Please don't do this. This is our first child!"

"First child, hell! Do what I damn well tell you! Or I'll give it to a total stranger."

Maebelle nodded, then sank back on her pillow. He stood, irately, waiting for her reply. Her voice cracked. "I'll give the baby to Jennifer."

He turned and faced Hailey. "Your damn money is on the dresser! And don't you ever try that again! You finish in here, and then get the hell out of my house! I don't want to see your monkey-looking ass back in here after today!"

Hailey didn't reply; and she didn't move, except to thump her right index finger on the revolver. She would have loved to put him six feet under.

Rufus turned and stormed out of the room.

Hailey cut the umbilical cord and then attended to Maebelle. She bathed and dressed the dead infant and wrapped him in a receiving blanket. Then she pulled the drawer out of the bureau, emptied the contents, and put the dead child inside the drawer. She expected Rufus to at least give it a proper burial upon returning, but that wouldn't happen. The farmland, down by the stream was the burial site for Jennifer's baby boy, who'd later died. This child would also be buried there. There would be no death records for these children. Rufus saw to that.

After Hailey put the dead child in the drawer, she stood dazing with her hands on her hips. Not in her thirty years of midwifery had she ever seen a situation like this. "Where are you God?" she asked. She looked at Maebelle. Then she went over and perched on the edge of the mattress. "What are you going to do, child? You can't continue staying here with this mad man and let him treat you this way, and running through your girls. Things won't get any better, you know."

"I'm trapped, Mrs. Hailey. And I'm scared to death of him. You see how he is. Besides, I have nowhere to go. My parents are dead. And my sisters—well, they want nothing to do with me. I don't know where they are, anyway." She wiped tears from her eyes. "I think he's doing this to us because he thinks I'm related to a woman who mistreated him when he was a child, and he's taking out revenge on me and my children!" She wailed.

Hailey sniffed. "Hmm. That's too bad," she remarked. "I guess you wished you'd listened to John, now. She saw Maebelle's astonishment. "Oh, yeah. I know all about you. This is a small town. John's my nephew. He told the family how you and Rufus set him up to help you and Rufus break up his marriage to Charlotte. He figured Rufus would do something like this. He said he pleaded with you, but you wouldn't listen. You thought you were getting yourself somebody special, huh?" Maebelle didn't answer. "Well, a hard head sure makes a hard bed. Look at you now. You're trapped by insane fear." There was momentary silence. Hailey sat back on the mattress. "Well, this is only the beginning. But you keep staying with him because you're "scared!"

Maebelle turned away from Hailey. Her heart was torn, her arms felt empty, and her fantasy world had ended. She really didn't want to think about what she had done—wrong or right. But yes—a thousand times yes, she wished she had listened to John, to Leslie, to Sam, and Jake Jr. and, yes, even that old woman. Nevertheless, she blamed the old woman for her troubles, wondering how she had predicted the outcome of her future so precisely. She probably went some place and worked voodoo on me; made this happen, she thought to herself. That's probably the reason she upped and moved so quickly. She thought about her boys, Sam and Jake Junior; and wondered why they hadn't written to her, or their sisters, with their new address. Unknown to Maebelle, the boys had written, and so had her friend Leslie, but Rufus had intercepted every single letter mailed to the house. Finally, he started writing on the envelopes: return to sender; address unknown. They stopped writing her and the girls, believing that they had abandoned them for their new life.

Getting to her feet, Hailey yawned and rubbed a tired hand over her face. "Are you going to name these children, or not?" she asked.

Maebelle shook her head. "No."

"Hmm. Well, I better take this baby in to Jennifer so I can get going. I put your son inside the drawer. I hope when your husband comes back he'll give the child a proper burial." She took her pay envelope, placing it inside her medical bag. Then she took the baby out of the crib, picked up her medical bag and headed out the door.

"Thanks for pulling him off me," Maebelle called.

Hailey stopped and turned toward Maebelle. "And who'll pull him off you next time?" She didn't wait for an answer, knowing she was disgusted with Maebelle. She went upstairs to find Jennifer, who was waiting at the top of the stairs. Hailey followed her to her room.

"This little bundle is for you," Hailey told her. "You look like you were expecting us," she said placing the child in Jennifer's arms.

"I heard everything," Jennifer remarked.

"Well, she hasn't been named. I guess you know that, too! She noticed the painful look in Jennifer's eyes. "I'm just tired, child. Pay me no mind. I don't mean to be rough with you."

Jennifer swallowed. She peeled back the blanket and stared into the face of the sleeping child. The baby batted her eyes rapidly. She smiled, never completely opening her eyes. "She looks like my Nora," Jennifer remarked. "They could pass for twins." There was a tinge of sadness in her voice, as she wagged her head.

Hailey moved toward the crib, looking at Nora. She's right, she thought; they do look alike. She looked around the room. A crib was missing. And so was Nora's twin brother. Hailey swallowed. Her mind was still fuzzy concerning the birth of Jennifer's babies. This house is full of shame, she thought. She couldn't recall if she'd made sure the baby was breathing before she passed him on to Maebelle. She bore a startling expression, considering that it was odd, almost an omen, that both male children had died, if in fact Jennifer's child was dead. On the other hand, she felt she might be jumping to conclusions. But the crib was obviously missing. She walked back over to Jennifer. "So what will you name her?"

"Tara," Jennifer replied. "I'm naming her Tara, after the girl in my essay," she said, looking up at Hailey. "Tara lived in England. Her father rejected her, too, because she was a girl. He had wanted only boys. But, Tara grew up strong and twice as wise as her six brothers." She paused, and looked away abstractly. Finally, she said, "When their father fell desperately ill, and the family farm was in trouble, it was Tara who kept the farm from going under. Yet, her father still favored her brothers." She shrugged her shoulders carelessly and said, "Some day this little 'ol baby girl will grow up and pay Daddy back for all the ugly, mean things he's done to us. I'm the smartest in this house, and I'm the strongest. I'll raise her to be just like me." She paused, fighting back tears. "I can't fight Daddy by myself . . .." Her voice trailed off.

"Well, you'll have an awfully long wait for this little one to grow up and help you, don't you think? Seems to me there's enough of you all to over-power that man."

"Oh, I want to!" Jennifer remarked. "Its Mama standing in our way. As scared as she is, I believe she would give us up if she found out we were trying to defend ourselves. I wouldn't dare ask her for help." She blinked back tears, and changed the subject.

155

"You know, Mrs. Hailey, Mama changed, like she's under a spell."

Poking her head inside, Lynn interjected. "Especially after last night and this morning." They jerked their heads around, looking at her with their mouths open.

"Can we come in?" Lynn asked.

"Yeah! And next time knock!" Jennifer snapped. "Don't be sneaking up on people, like you're a damn cat! You're always sneaking around like a cat!"

"Shut up!" Lynn retorted. Jackie and Jinni followed her in the room, crowding around the newborn, and taking turns peeking at her.

"She looks just like Nora!" Jinni remarked, flatly.

"I bet Daddy is to blame for our baby brother dying," Lynn remarked.

Hailey's brow shot up in a curious arch.

"He did something bad to Mama this morning," Lynn blurted out. "And she was screaming! I saw 'em." Everybody's eyes were riveted on Lynn.

"What did he do?" Hailey asked. The lying dog, she thought. She figured there was more to his story. She didn't trust him any further than she could throw him.

Jennifer elbowed Lynn. "Shut up!" she told her. "Daddy was right about you! You do have a big mouth! You're the reason why you and Jackie can't go to school! You big mouth!"

"I don't have a big mouth! And I'm not the cause of Jackie and me not going to school! Daddy is!"

"Now don't you all be arguing," Hailey ordered mildly. "Lynn is right, Jennifer. Your stepfather is to blame for all you all's troubles."

"I know," Jennifer conceded. "I know."

"Go on, Lynn, and tell us what happened this morning," Hailey urged.

"I saw Daddy put his gun up Mama's nose. He was fussing about last night. He made her get on her knees and he pulled up her dress and got behind her." She flicked a glance at Jennifer. "I know you all *musta* heard Mama screaming. Daddy was calling her Olga Berry, the Second. Then I heard him tell her there was plenty enough of him to go around." Lynn froze, as she saw everybody looking at her in shock. She shrugged. "I wasn't spying. The reason I saw him is because I woke up scared; and I was going to Mama's room so I could get in her bed.

"Anyhow, he told Mama she was lying about not being kin to somebody name Olga Berry. He said she knew she was kin to Olga Berry. Then he said weren't nothin' wrong with what he did to you, Jackie." She looked at Jackie.

Jackie started to shake. She lowered her eyes and stared at the floor.

Hailey staggered backward. But Lynn went on without distraction.

"I turned around and ran back to my room before he had a chance to see me!" They were speechless for a few minutes.

"Well, Hailey, said, "Let me go before he gets back."

"I'll walk you to the door," Jinni told her. "Can I talk to you, Mrs. Hailey?"

Hailey turned her head, looking at Jinni. She didn't answer, as Jinni followed behind her. When they got down the steps, Hailey half turned and faced her. "Well, make it quick. I don't want him to come back and find me here." Jinni still did not answer, so Hailey kept walking to her car with Jinni trailing behind. Hailey squeezed the handle and opened the car door. "Stand back, out of the way. I don't want to hit you with the door," she told her.

Jinni stepped back.

Hailey slid the medical bag on to the seat and climbed inside the car, closing the door behind her. She started the engine, while looking at Jinni impatiently. "Well, what is it child! Spit it out so I can go!"

With her eyes glued to Hailey's face, Jinni began fidgeting with the end of her long braid. "When Daddy is on me, I pretend he's this boy I like at school," she blurted out.

"Whoa!" Hailey blinked.

Jinni jumped.

"Child! Child! I know what you think you're doing! But you—you can't make-believe with stuff like that! You got to stop that! And why are you telling me this stuff? My heart is already burdened! Good-Lord!"

Jinni shrugged. "I don't know. I guess because you're the only person I can talk to. Jennifer hates him, so I can't talk to her, and she wouldn't understand. I keep telling myself he isn't kin to none of us. He's not married to Mama." She gazed at the ground. "It's just that I have these feelings."

Hailey put up a refraining hand. "Look! I have to be going! You—you think about what I just told you! Now stand back out of the way." She put the car in gear. "Oh, and another thing before I go. I want you to help Jennifer with Tara. It's going to be hard for her to take care of three babies." She said that purposely, to find out if Jennifer's other child was still alive.

"Jennifer's baby boy didn't make it. She didn't tell you?"

Just what I figured, Hailey thought. "Ah no. She didn't tell me. Well, you go on back in the house. Help her, anyway. I'm sorry to hear that her baby boy died. I have to be going now."

"Bye, Mrs. Hailey."

"Bye, child."

* * *

Hailey drove straight to Stella Moore's house. As she pulled into the yard, Stella came around the corner of the house carrying an empty laundry basket. Hailey parked and got out of the car.

"Hailey! I thought I heard a car motor. I just thought about you while I was hanging out my wash. It's been so long since I seen you." She stopped and stared at Hailey's expression. "What's the matter, Hailey? You don't look so good. Is it Daniel?"

"Nah! My husband is fine, all things considered. It's that damn Rufus!"

"Rufus!" Stella frowned.

"Yes! Rufus! Can we go sit on your porch? I'm about dead tired on my feet."

"Certainly." Stella said. "C'mon. Let's sit on the swing."

They climbed her porch steps, and sat down on the swing. Stella held the laundry basket on her lap. "What is it, Hailey? You look like you're about ready to explode."

"Hailey sighed deeply, as she sat sideways on the swing. "You remember about a year ago, when everybody was talking about Rufus got some woman to chase his wife out of the house?"

"Yeah. I remember. I thought that was real low-down of him—and of the woman that did that!"

"Well, I've met her."

Stella's eyes widen. "You've met her! When? What does she look like! Is she really as black as they say she is?"

"Uh, huh." Hailey nodded. "Yeah. She's as black as midnight, all right, but cute. Anyway, I delivered a set of twins from both of her twin daughters' three months ago. I think it was three months ago. Time goes so fast. Those girls can't be more than thirteen or fourteen years old." She put a hand on Stella's arm. "Girl! I have never seen anything like it before. That fool man is molesting them girls right in her presence!"

Stella's mouth hung open in dismay.

"Stella, Girl! You haven't heard anything yet! I'm telling you, the man thinks he's a midwife! He insisted on helping me with the birth of one of them girl's babies! And with Maebelle, his so-called wife!" Stella's mouth fell open. "I just left there. I found out that one of the babies died—the one he delivered. I went over there to deliver a set of twins from Maebelle. Well, girl, he delivered the last baby himself. 'Ol dog tricked me into coming over there just in case he ran into some trouble."

"What! " Stella cried. "Hailey, you're lying!"

"And he jumped on her, too—started to beat her senseless as soon as she gave birth to her last baby—all because the baby has a hair lip! He accused her of sleeping with Thomas Wright."

Stella swallowed.

"You know old Thomas Wright."

"Of course, I know Thomas Wright! He does have a hair lip. But boy! That man is so old he can hardly put one foot before the other." Stella wagged her head. "And he looks like he's such a nice man—Rufus I mean!"

"Looks can be deceiving," Hailey replied. "There is nothing nice about him."

"Well you know, Hailey, it will be un-Christian of us if we don't try to do something to help those girls. That woman is probably getting what she deserves. But those innocent girls—we must help them. How many girls are there?"

"Four."

"Umph! Plus the ones being born," Stella remarked. "In the years ahead, he's gon have himself a bigger feast. He won't stop with just his stepdaughters, you know. I done seen that kind of stuff. It's sickening. Yes! We have to stop him. Let's go talk to Reverend."

"I was hoping you would say that! I was thinking the same thing, but I didn't want to go to his house by myself."

"Have you told Daniel?"

160

Hailey shook her head. "No. If my husband knew what was taking place there, he wouldn't let me go back. Besides, I'm too ashamed. Ashamed for my own womanhood."

"Well, let me put my laundry basket in the house and lock up."

Hailey got up. "I'll wait in the car for you."

"Okay," said Stella. "I'll only be a minute." She put the laundry basket in the kitchen and went to the bedroom to change shoes, and to get her pocketbook and house keys. "Stinking dog!" she muttered on her way out the door. "Somebody has got to put a stop to him." She locked the door and rushed down the steps. She went to the passenger side and climbed inside.

"I was just looking at your hair," Hailey remarked. "You dyed it jet black, but it looks good against your brown skin. I have been thinking about putting dye in mine."

Stella patted down her tight bun. "Thank you. I look ten years younger, don't I? And you will too."

Hailey smiled as she backed the car out onto the road. "Yeah. You look younger than your forty-seven years, all right. I'm sure its due in part to the fact you haven't put on any weight like most of us have."

"Well, I'm always watching my figure," Stella replied. "I never could stand the old-age spread, you know."

Hailey smiled, as she straightened the wheels. She gave Stella a sidelong glance. She remembered how Stella had panicked when she had her first experience with the change of life. Stella described the fire in her bosom as streaks of lighting, and she thought she had become ill. When Hailey explained the change of life to her, Stella was both surprised and disappointed that her youth was leaving her. 'That's for old people,' she told Hailey. Stella was forty-four at the time. Since then, she denied ever having any more hot flashes. Hailey smiled to herself.

The two women clucked like two mother hens all the way to Reverend's house.

He was sitting in the yard under the oak tree when they drove up.

"Umph!" Hailey said, "He's out enjoying this unusual warm weather. Like me, I guess he's glad it didn't rain. Looks like he'd doing some Bible study."

"Look like he's sleeping to me," Stella remarked.

"You may be right," Hailey said. "I hope he's feeling well." She pulled into the yard and cut the engine. The two women exchanged glances, then opened the door and climbed out of the car. Stella purposely slammed her door hard.

"I told you he was sleeping," she said. "He didn't even hear me slam the door." She waited for Hailey to come around to her side, and then they walked over to Reverend. "Boy! He looks so old," Stella whispered.

"He is old!" Hailey replied.

"I'm nervous," Stella admitted.

Reverend Kincaid suddenly awoke. Hailey heard Stella's soft, nervous intake of air. "Relax Stella! Put your hand over your mouth and breathe deeply, like you're yawning."

Stella covered her mouth, inhaling and exhaling. "I think it worked!" she said.

"Now move your hand from over your mouth," Hailey told her.

Reverend leaned forward. He studied the two women from behind his wire-rimmed spectacles. He put a marker at the page he was reading and closed his Bible. "Afternoon, Hailey, Stella," said Reverend Kincaid, as he stood, and momentarily sat back down.

"Afternoon Reverend," the two women chorused.

"To what do I owe this visit? Or did you all come here to see Maelie? She's in the house gettin' us some tea. God done seen fit to make a change in the weather for us. Have a seat, ladies."

The two women exchanged glances. They sat in the chairs opposite the old preacher.

"We came to see you," Hailey told him.

He looked surprised. "Oh! What about?"

"About Rufus Poygoode."

Reverend sat quietly. He glared suspiciously at Hailey. "I'm listening. Go on."

Hailey leaned forward. "Reverend, I'm going to be blunt with you."

Reverend Kincaid chuckled. "Hailey, Hailey. Don't go changing on me now. You were never one to mince words. I don't know how poor Daniel put up with you all these years."

Hailey raised her chin a fraction. And I don't know how Maelie puts up with your old ass, she felt like saying. "Rufus is siring children with his stepdaughters, Reverend. I delivered two sets of twins from his two oldest stepdaughters about three months ago." I think it was three months ago, she thought to herself. She had trouble keeping track of the weeks, since Rufus' mess. "The girls can't be more than thirteen or fourteen years old. It's a disgrace what he's doing over there. I think the community should do something about this—the church, I mean."

Reverend's expression suddenly changed. His jowls quivered.

The two women exchanged knowing glances.

"Well, Reverend?" Stella said.

"Well, what, Stella!" He glared at Stella for a long moment. He said nothing.

Hailey felt anger rising inside her. Why is this old fool looking at Stella, she thought, when I'm the one who's talking? She didn't like Reverend's attitude. And no force on earth was going to keep her from giving him a piece of her mind, if he didn't start acting like he had some sense.

Reverend sniffed; turned his eyes upon Hailey. "Ah, listen ladies, especially you Hailey," he said, pointing a thick, stubby, shaky finger. "I don't know if what you all is sayin' is true, or not. There are two sides to every story. If you haven't got the other side, you ought not to be going around spreading them kind of nasty rumors. Rufus is a well-liked man. He has a lot of power in this town. It could make him mighty mad if this ever got back to him." His eyes shifted to Stella. "And Stella! I'm surprised at you!"

Stella swallowed. She lowered her lashes.

Maelie returned with the tea. She brought along extra cups. "Hi . . . ladies.

The two women's greetings were barely audible. "What's going on?" Maelie asked puzzled. "Reverend, I could hear you shouting at these ladies way back at the house. Why are you screaming at Stella and Hailey?"

"Because!"

"Because what?"

"Because they come over here with a bunch of lies. Talking 'bout Ru--Rufus." He stammered. "Talking about Rufus is siring his stepdaughters. If it's true, it's because they're putting their little fast selves on him. Everybody knows Rufus is a fine and outstanding man in this community. Just because a man doesn't go to church that ain't no reason to crucify him!" He glared at Hailey. Her eyes were steadily upon him. White spittle showed at the corners of Reverend's mouth.

Hold my tongue, Jesus! Hailey said to herself, because I'm about ready to fire your anointed one ass up!

Maelie set down the tray on the wrought iron table, and placed an arm about her husband's shoulders. "First of all, you need to calm down, Kincaid! Here. Have some tea. You can't even talk straight." He pushed her hand away.

"Stella and Hailey aren't like that," she told him. "I'm certain they wouldn't have come way over here if they thought anything less than the truth about this whole thing."

Absently, Maelie tried to hand him the cup of tea again.

He lifted his hand and shoved the cup away. "I don't want any tea!" he shouted looking up at her. "What's the matter with your hearing!" He pressed a hand down hard on his unruly thigh, to keep his foot from patting the ground.

Maelie tried to pass the cup around. "Would you all like some tea? Hailey?"

"No thank you."

"How about you, Stella?"

"No thanks," she said with her eyes still on Reverend.

Maelie shrugged and set down the cup on the tray. She sat down beside Reverend. "Quite frankly," she said, "whenever I hear stuff like that, I believe it. It's only the men who don't believe. A man isn't going go against another man that easily."

"This is ridiculous!" Hailey blurted out. "You'd think we committed a sin by telling Reverend what that dog is doing to those girls!"

Maelie reached over and put a hand on Hailey's knee. "Un-uhn. You haven't committed any sins. It's just that Rufus helped us out awhile back and, well, how can Reverend go to him with what you all done told him."

Reverend Kincaid glared up at Maelie. "Quiet, Maelie! You don't need to be telling the family business!" His jowls quivered. His steely eyes swiveled to Stella.

"Does Roy know you're here, Stella?"

Stella lifted a hand and patted her bun, while looking at Reverend, before she looked away. "No. I don't need his permission to come see the good Reverend, now do I?" She glared at him levelly.

"Well, you should have talked to him before you come driving over here. He still owes Rufus money, doesn't he? For fertilizer he bought two years back!"

Stella flinched at him, and then she turned her head. She wondered what Roy would have to say once he heard she had been over here with Hailey and was talking about Rufus behind his back.

"And your Daniel, Hailey? He's a sick man. You never know if he'll need to borrow- - -"

"He won't!" Hailey snapped, cutting him off in mid-sentence. "He's been a smart business man all his adult life. We'll do just fine!" She got to her feet.

"C'mon, Stella. Let's go. You can see why I don't waste my time in the church, especially Reverend's church. Hypocrite! They're all probably in Rufus' pocket!"

Maelie stood. "I'll walk you all to the car." She put a hand on her husband's shoulder.

He looked up at her, and put his hand on top of hers.

"I'll be right back," she told him. "You should have had some of that tea. You don't look well. Look at you. You look like you're about to have a heart attack."

Hailey and Stella exchanged glances. "Old fool hypocrite is going to have a heart attack he's so mad," Hailey remarked to Stella in a low, angry voice

Maelie looked back over her shoulder at him, as she walked with Stella and Hailey to the car. "This must be hard on you, Hailey," she remarked. "You don't have to keep going back there, you know." She followed Hailey around to the driver's side.

Hailey opened her car door and climbed inside the car. She slammed the door hard.

"Good-bye, Maelie!" Hailey said tersely. "You better go back and check the pillar of the community. Seems to me he was foaming around the mouth pretty badly."

Maelie raised a limp hand. "Oh! Don't be cruel, Hailey. I think if he were a younger man, he'd try to do something. He's too old."

Stella grunted. She opened the passenger door and got inside the car. She closed the door.

"Good-bye, Stella, Hailey," Maelie continued.

"I've already said my good-bye!" Hailey snapped.

"You better go take care of your husband," Stella remarked.

After starting the engine, Hailey put the car in gear and backed onto the road. Shifting gears, she headed for Stella's house.

"I don't see how Maelie can stand to look at him," Stella remarked. "She's so young compared to him."

"Maybe it's the church members' money keeping them together," Hailey suggested before she changed the subject.

"Well, Stella, so much for Reverend, the community. It seems that you and I are the community. And we don't have a prayer. According to Reverend, Rufus has everybody in his pocket. And I'm not saying that to slight you. You know that, don't you?"

"I know," Stella said. "Old fool! He needs to come down out of that pulpit! I'm finding me another church!" Hailey looked at her out the corner of her right eye. She didn't respond to that. She knew Stella wasn't going any place else.

Hailey drove one-handed, with her left elbow jutted out on the sill. "I'm so tired," she said. The two women talked off and on, although they rode in silence for most of the ride to Stella's house.

Later, they were back at Stella's house. "Since you're tired," Stella said, "you don't have to drive into the yard. You can pull over and drop me off here."

Hailey pulled over to the shoulder of the road. She turned and faced Stella. "Thanks for coming with me."

"You're welcome." Stella opened the door and got out. She closed the door. Holding on to the door window, she asked Hailey what she would do about working for Rufus?"

Hailey looked at her for a long moment. "There is nothing I can do. He already told me not to come back. But if he changes his mind...Well, I'm a midwife, Stella. What can I tell you? If the heathen sends for me, I'm sure I'll go. Besides, I'm the only contact those girls have with the outside world. I would still like to help them, if I can."

"Well, just stay off Rufus' back." Stella teased. She laughed.

"Oh, that!" Hailey said. She waved a hand. "Well, I better get on home. I'll see you soon."

"Bye. And be careful," Stella called.

* * *

Hailey reached her house some twenty-five minutes later. She dragged herself along with her medical bag, into her house. It felt good to be home. She tossed the key on the couch, and set down her medical bag on the floor. "I'm home, Daniel!" she called.

"I'm in the bedroom," he replied.

She moved toward their bedroom, and perched on the edge of the mattress. Daniel was grinning. "It's sure good to see you, honey. I worry about you when you're out all day."

Hailey kicked off her nursing shoes and drew her feet up in the bed. "It's been a long day, Daniel. I want to lie here for a little while, then I'll get up and make dinner." As much as she wanted to, she restrained from talking to her husband about Rufus. Maelie's words echoed in her mind. *Men don't go against another man that easily..."*

Chapter 5

The spring and summer of 1950 were fleeting. And autumn soon turned into winter. The autumn leaves faded, withered and fell to the ground. By early November, the earth was hard—nearly frozen over—ready for a deep sleep. The winter months were the worst.

The girls yearned to be in school—where they felt they belonged. Jennifer's vision of becoming a schoolteacher had died. As for Jinni, well, all she could think about was Philip Coon—a boy who didn't even know she existed. And Jackie and Lynn—well, they just wanted to be with their school friends.

On days in which it was absolutely too cold to work outside, they spent their time sitting around the gas heaters, longing for the impossible. Given the improbability of ever going back to school—and trying hard to adjust to their fate—Jennifer was rather glad she had Tara and Nora to care for. She knew she could never forget that Tara really wasn't her child. Nevertheless, she treated Tara like she was Tara's natural mother. The two children helped to fill up her time.

Not trusting that Rufus would allow these children to attend school either, Jennifer tried planning her babies' future. Before they learned to walk, she drew alphabets and numbers, and cut pictures out of catalogs and magazines for Nora and Tara to learn by. As soon as they learned to talk, she began educating them.

* * *

Jennifer had begun to feel frightened for Jinni, for it was hard nowadays to tell if Jinni was losing her mind, or if she was using this Philip Coon thing to shield her pain. She had gone beyond the theory that Rufus and Philip looked alike—which was insane to begin with—to actually calling him Philip, and he let her.

Jennifer carried so many heavy burdens. She lived daily with the pain and jealousy reflected in Maebelle's eyes. She felt that one day her mother would despise her for acting like she was Tara's mother. She had no choice. This was what Rufus demanded of her. And, in taking care of Tara, she had grown to love her like she loved Nora.

* * *

One morning Jennifer went downstairs to the kitchen to prepare the children's milk. She boiled the sweet cow milk, added a pinch of sugar, stirring it frequently to keep it from scorching. When the formula cooled, she filled the baby bottles and set them inside the refrigerator, except two, which she would take upstairs. She moved to the window and drew back the curtain. She saw Rufus coming toward the back door. Her heart slammed into her breasts. She ran out the kitchen and up the stairs. She flung the door open and stumbled into the room. "Mama! He's coming in through the back door. You better go!" Maebelle's eyes widened with fear.

Jennifer sat down the bottles on the bureau and reached out her arms to take Tara. "Give her to me! You got to hurry, Mama." Jennifer's heart was pounding inside her breast.

Maebelle quickly planted a kiss on beautiful Tara's forehead, then handed her over to Jennifer and ran out the room. She nearly stumbled on the stairs. She opened the door and entered her bedroom, and closed the door behind her. She felt her heart beating wildly. If she was ever caught near Tara, she knew she'd be in trouble. Rufus, she thought, would even give Tara away to a stranger. The thought of losing her precious child forever was unbearable.

She went and stood in front of her bedroom window, pressing her head against the cold windowpane. Her heart ached. She watched the brown leaves blow across the yard. She imagined having wings like a dove, and grabbing Tara, and flying away to a better place. "Why can't you see that she's your daughter? Why?" Her eyes filled with tears. She looked down at her full stomach. What if this baby meets with the same fate? Suppose she has a hair lip, too? The thought of losing another child to one of her children hurt. She lay down on her bed, waiting to be called when breakfast was ready. Staring up at the ceiling, thinking about the mess she had made of her life, deep down inside, she knew that her daughters weren't to blame for Rufus' molestation. She still believed that the old woman and her curse caused all their problems.

A soft knock on her bedroom door brought her back to the present. She rose upon her bed. "Come in," she said, keeping her eyes glued on the door.

Jennifer opened it and poked her head inside. Maebelle saw her troubled expression.

"I got bad news, Mama." She entered the room and closed the door behind her.

Maebelle bolted upright, wide-eyed and scared. "Is it Tara?" She studiously watched Jennifer as she approached and sat perched on the edge of the mattress.

"No, Mama. Tara is fine. It's Jackie. Mama, I didn't want to say anything until I was sure. She's been throwing up a lot recently. I thought Daddy had stopped messing with her until now, Mama!"

Closing her eyes, Maebelle fell back on her pillow. She didn't comment. Staring at the foot of the bed, Maebelle was also so sick of her daughters bringing her bad news about what Rufus did to them. Didn't they know by now that she couldn't help? Why don't you all just disappear, she thought?

Jennifer shifted on the mattress and said vehemently, "Mama, stop letting Daddy do this to us! You must do something!" Crying, she swiped her tears from her cheeks, with both hands.

Maebelle turned onto her side. "When will breakfast be ready?" she asked.

171

Jennifer's throat throbbed. She wanted to tell her that she and Jinni were expecting, again, and that she had wasted her time putting them in the bedrooms upstairs. But she knew that wouldn't change things, as she kept glaring at her mother, in disgust.

"You'll have to ask Jinni about breakfast. It's her turn to cook," Jennifer told her, as she left the room in a cloud of despair and anger.

* * *

At breakfast, Rufus chided Jackie for not wearing a sweater. He frowned. "I told you to start wearing your sweater, didn't I? You look like a sick frog. Now I won't tell you again, hear?"

Jackie lowered her lashes. "Yes, sir. But I'm not sick. My stomach is just upset all the time. I keep throwing up every time I eat."

He looked at her without a clue.

Jennifer stirred anxiously in her seat.

Silence returned—except for the hurried forks scraping against the plates.

Then Lynn opened her mouth and said the damnedest thing.

"Daddy?"

He grunted. His mouth was full of food.

"Jackie doesn't have a cold, Daddy. She's just sick because she throws up so much, like she said. I think she got a baby growing inside her stomach, just like Mama. Mama used to throw up a lot, too, and . . ." Then she stopped.

Everyone stopped chewing; their forks suspended in the air.

Rufus eyes arrested on Lynn. One never knew what was going to come out of Lynn's mouth. She always talked too much.

Lynn grinned nervously, as she began picking hair out of her grits, not noticing Rufus glaring at her, and everyone else's startled eyes that landed on her. "I been thinking, Daddy," she said, pulling a long strands of hair out from her food. She frowned. "I don't want to be the only one around this house with no baby. Could you do me? I think Mama won't mind so much like she did before, when she pulled you off Jackie because she doesn't pull you off her any more." Lynn turned her head and looked at Maebelle for approval. "Right Mama?" she said.

Rufus choked.

Maebelle looked down, sliding way down in her chair. She felt something die inside her. She no longer loved her daughters. How can they try to put themselves on my husband right in front of my face, she thought?

Rufus looked from Lynn, to Jackie, then back at Lynn. But Lynn still didn't detect his angry stare. She had just found a sliver of hair in her eggs. She pulled it out; dropped it on the floor; and flicked a disgusted glance at Jinni. "You need to start covering your head!" she chided.

Poor Jackie shivered, afraid she was in trouble, but she hadn't told Lynn anything. She kept their little dirty secret, the way he made her promise she would. Lynn was like a cat. She always snuck around. No one could keep anything from Lynn.

Jennifer stuck out her foot and kicked Lynn in the ankle.

"Ouch!" Lynn cried. "Who kicked me?" She looked at Jinni, then at Jennifer.

Shut up, stupid, Jennifer's eyes told her.

Though Lynn was going on ten, she often exhibited the mentality of a seven-year old. And then again, there were times when she seemed quite older than normal for a child her age.

Rufus put down his fork sharply. His face was flushed with rage and embarrassment.

Jennifer and Jinni exchanged sad glances, and poor Jackie sat with her hands in her lap, staring at the table.

Rufus pushed himself away from the table, scraping the floor with the bottom of the chair. Upon leaving the dinning room, he grabbed his coat and hat off the coat rack. He wanted to wring Lynn's scrawny, little neck. How dare she invite herself on him like that! How many times had he told her, she talked too damn much? He couldn't stand her little emaciated ass.

When the front door opened and closed, everybody breathed with relief, except Lynn. She still didn't realize she had said something wrong. She couldn't quite figure out why everybody was so upset. But she knew to shut up, watching Maebelle's stern face.

Jennifer quickly jumped up from the table. Boiling words spewed off her tongue. "This is just too much! Mama!" she screamed. "How could you sit here and hear Lynn ask Daddy to do her—and say nothing? Lynn's stupid! You know she doesn't know what she's saying. And as a mother, you sit there saying nothing?" Silence ensued, as if Jennifer had been talking to the wall. Finally, Jennifer was reduced to tears.

Suddenly, Jinni couldn't take it any more. She jumped up from the table. "Them just wasted tears!" she told Jennifer. "I stopped crying a long time ago. She didn't speak up because she's a coward! She has no damn courage—except for when it comes to us. She beat the shit out of us—remember? She ain't no kind of damn mother. As far as I'm concerned, none of us are her damn daughters. We all are Daddy's damn women! From the youngest to the oldest." She glared at Maebelle and said; "Now maybe you all can understand why I call Daddy, Philip. It make it easier to burn the mid-night oil with him." She crooked her thumb and pointed toward her crouch. "Stop it! Just stop it!" Jackie cried, tearfully. "Mama can't help us. She tried to help me, remember?"

"But not no more," Lynn interjected. Her voice was low this time.

"She can't help us!" Jennifer cried frantically, waving her arms. "Why not? She's the one who caused this mess. She wouldn't listen to Sam and Jake Junior, when they tried to tell her about Daddy. Even Miss Leslie told her Daddy was no good. But no! She didn't listen, because she wanted his money, and she didn't care if he had a wife, and we're all suffering now. It's not right!"

Maebelle, no longer tolerating the degrading words from her daughters, exploded. She harshly pushed back the chair from the table. "Dammit! What do you all want me to do?"

"Kill him!" Jennifer cried. "Before he ends up killing us. He could have killed me when he called himself helping me deliver my babies. And you stood back and let him!"

"That's right!" Jinni remarked. "He could have killed Jennifer. I say kill the sonofabitch. I'm about tired of him riding me. I want my own damned man. I wanna go back to school, so I can be with Philip. Be with a boy my own age."

Maebelle's face became a mass of twisted anger and fear. "You all must think I'm crazy! Y'all trying to get me killed!"

For a long moment, they all became silent. Four pairs of startled eyes studied Maebelle.

"Well! Well!" Jennifer remarked. "I guess we all heard that! I don't know about anybody else, but from now on, no one will ever hear me call you Mama again! From now on, I'll call you by your first name," she said, frowning at Maebelle. "Because, just like Jinni said, you're no kind of mother." One by one, the girls left the dinning room. Jinni was the last to leave.

Maebelle reached out and grabbed her wrist.

Jinni stopped short, wrestling her wrist from Maebelle's hand. "Let go of me!"

"Just you wait a damn minute!" Maebelle barked, grabbing Jinni's wrist again. "You never fooled me with your Philip Coon mess, pretending you're half crazy. You know damn well what you're doing. You're in love with my husband! This isn't a just-now thing. You've had your eyes on my husband from day one!"

Jinni peeled Maebelle's hand her off her wrist. She had long since disrespected her. She gazed down in her upturned, twisted face. "He isn't your husband, heffa! Seems to me—he's all our husbands because he does nasty to all of us. And for your information, I don't love that dog. I'm just making the best of this damn life that I have no say over." She started mimicking Rufus: 'I want you to act like you glad to see me. Don't I make it feel good to you?' She paused because she was bursting with anger, and her eyes blazed with anguish. "And guess what?" she announced to Maebelle, looking her straight in the eyes, "I say, yessir, to every damn thing Rufus says to me. I learned the hard way." Jinni stormed out of the dinning room.

Maebelle folded her arm; rocked to and fro with her eyes closed, tears gushing down her face. Her recollection of the old woman's curse returned. She felt helpless.

* * *

Several bleak and tragic years passed since that last heated argument occurred between Maebelle and her daughters. In fact, the girls all lost hope of Hailey ever returning. Word got back to Rufus that she had gone to the Reverend on him. After that, he permanently barred her from his house. In his madness he forced Maebelle to help him in their unfamiliar role of midwifery. All four of her daughters became mothers of his children. They each lived in their own houses that Rufus built, except for Lynn, who was slated to get Mrs. Daisy's house. After the old woman passed away, her son sold the property to Rufus. Of course, Rufus would eventually add more rooms to that small house.

* * *

When Lynn reached adulthood, she still remembered what she asked for on that fateful morning long ago. She wished she could turn back the clock. As the youngest sister, she felt foolish. Rufus kept her stomach pumped up, like she was being punished for asking him to do her. But Jennifer knew differently about Rufus.

Jennifer lay on her bed reflecting on the fate she and her sisters were still enduring. Fate once led her, so long ago, down to the house where old Mrs. Daisy once lived. She had seen the old woman's son, Harold, removing boards from the windows. She thought they were getting neighbors. She didn't know Harold. But she took for granted that this new neighbor of theirs might have some daughters; and if he did, she was anxious to meet them. She made sure Rufus' pickup was nowhere in sight, when she snuck down toward the house. Without saying hello; nor introducing herself, nor asking him his name, she asked him if he were moving in, and if he had any daughters.

She felt crushed when he told her his daughters lived in Tennessee, and that he wasn't moving in. He told her why he was removing the boards off the windows. Their conversation lapsed. But Jennifer couldn't quickly leave. He was like a breath of fresh air to her.

Then to her surprise, not knowing who she was, he unlocked the secrets to Rufus and Maebelle's dark past. Jennifer let him believe she was one of Rufus' disgruntled tenants. It blew her away when she learned how her family moved in with Rufus: Maebelle went to Rufus' home, and picked a fight with his wife, Charlotte, driving her from her home; then she moved herself and the kids in with him. Her mother, Maebelle, didn't know that her grandmother Gina was Rufus' mother's sister. Or that his aunt Olga Berry also his mother's sister, had reared and sexually abused Rufus. And that Rufus' mother Amber had died after giving birth to him. She turned her head to keep Harold from seeing her horrified facial reaction.

Then Harold put down his hammer and told her, "Wait here. I have something for you." She watched him climb the porch steps and enter his mother's house. Her heart raced, and she willed herself to relax a bit before he returned. Momentarily, he returned with a box filled with old textbooks, coloring books, crayons, pencils, and lined paper. "This is for you. Its better you have them than they go to rot."

He placed the box in her arms. "I'm a retired school teacher," he told her. "When my children were small, they spent their summers with Mama. Mama made sure they kept up with their reading. You can do the same with your children."

Jennifer looked at him strangely, with mixed emotions. She felt happy and afraid at the same time, wondering if the books were an omen. She had often feared that when the children reached school age, Rufus wouldn't let them go to school.

The box became heavy in her arms; but she had lifted things much heavier, so she willed strength from within, since she still wasn't ready to leave. It never occurred to her to set the box on the ground. The contents were too precious.

She looked up in Harold's solemn face and took in every bit of him. She had never been this close to any man, except the one she hated. He caught her eyes for a split second. Then he looked away. He had gentle eyes, she recalled. His brows had specks of gray. His side burns were salt and pepper. She had a feeling about him, which she couldn't describe. It felt like she had known him all her life, like an old friend.

She decided to leave the man so he could do his work. She felt her body shiver as she walked quickly back towards her house, trying to avoid being seen by Maebelle, who would cause trouble.

Harold's stories about Rufus and Maebelle unraveled the mysteries surrounding Jennifer and her sisters. He answered a particular question that had haunted her for years: Why did Rufus taunt Maebelle, calling her Olga Berry?

Jennifer never told Lynn or anybody about her encounter with Harold. Although Lynn was no longer that giddy little string bean, getting around on her feet like a cat, she still suffered from loose-lip syndrome. And poor Jinni, well, she was just lost, altogether. And Jackie, well, she had her own troubles. She passed out a lot whenever she became too afraid. So Jennifer had to live alone with her secret.

In late autumn, Lynn moved into the old woman's house.

* * *

The disparaging years came and went, and Rufus held on to his decree that the children would never set foot inside the schoolhouse door. Jennifer continued to pray, and continued teaching the children in secret. All her teaching materials were used over and over again, as there were no other resources available. When she reached her limitation of her own creative imagination, a miracle happened. Her mind shifted back to the present.

She crawled out of bed, and went to the kitchen to wash the breakfast dishes. Time seemed to pass fast now that the children were in school. Her mind continued to drift. She stood over a sink full of dirty dishes, remembering the miracle that was responsible for the children being in school.

It was in the spring of 1962. She remembered it just like it was yesterday. The clouds were drifting lazily in the sky, as she stood over a sink full of dishes just as she was presently doing. Rufus was out of town on business.

Momentarily, she glanced out her kitchen window and saw the dizzy-looking blond woman from the Census Bureau park her green and white Buick in her yard. Her name was Cathy Winterhope. She knocked on the door, carrying a large, brown envelope in her hand. A pocket

179

book hung on her left shoulder. Jennifer quickly opened her door, unaware that the woman had already visited the houses of Maebelle, Lynn, Jackie, and Jinni.

Cathy was appalled by what she had seen and heard from Jinni, Lynn, and Jackie. And she thought that Maebelle lied about all the children being too sick to go to school. Cathy announced who she was, raised the identification tag that hung around her neck. Jennifer felt a mixture of excitement and fear, as she invited Cathy inside.

Cathy asked non-census related questions—all of which Jennifer was glad to answer, hoping that emptying her guts, might result in deliverance. She believed Cathy had been jealous of their riches, and if for no other reason, she would surely report what she saw and heard, which was fine by Jennifer.

In Jennifer's mind's eye she could still see Cathy Winterhope, with her stringy blond hair, standing in the drizzling rain between the house and the worn-out Buick, staring at the ground. She suddenly wagged her head and threw up one hand. She looked back at Jennifer's house for a long moment then rushed toward her car. She got in her car and slammed the door. Jennifer saw her through the windshield shaking her head before she started the engine and drove away.

Later on, Lynn stopped by the house filled with excitement. She told Jennifer she had told the Census woman everything. This was one time Jennifer could say she appreciated Lynn's loose lips.

By September, the first generations of Poygoode children were all in school.

Rufus exploded. For the life of him, he couldn't figure out how his dirty secret got out. Nobody was talking, including Maebelle, for she had grown to despise him. He was a mean husband. He was so bitter that he started cracking a mean wicked whip. He made all their lives bitter, and Sunday was no longer a day of rest.

Every able-bodied person, no matter how small, how old, worked in his fields from dawn to dusk.

After school, the children had to work in the field until it was too dark to see. He rigged light poles outside the house and down by the barn, so they could see how to get the other chores done—after they stopped working in the field. They ate dinner late; did their homework late into the night. Nevertheless, he demanded good grades from them, but only as an excuse to severely punish them if they didn't do well.

In spite of their routine agony, the children got excellent grades because school—and a chance to learn—had become their lifeline.

Maebelle's two oldest boys Zeke and Elliott stopped fighting so much. In fact, they discovered they really did like each other. Of course, there were still occasions when they put their mean, hard, tight fists to each other's body. Jennifer felt Zeke was destined to become a murderer. She believed his angry, dancing eyes suggested more than a fistfight. The lashes he received from Rufus left him scarred and bitter.

Jennifer finally finished stacking the dishes into the safe, and closed the door. She began humming, as she folded her arms across her chest and leaned her back against the safe and letting her mind drift again.

She recalled a lot of things, like it was yesterday. On the children's first day at school, she and Rufus arrived at school with a pickup full of Poygoode children. Under normal circumstances, she would've felt embarrassed, but these weren't normal circumstances. She saw so many benefits of the children getting an education. Nothing else mattered. With the younger children being exposed to outside influences, she believed that some day, they would rise up and break the yoke Rufus had placed on their family.

The principal, Mr. Dale Davis, watched them come up the walkway. There were twenty-one children following Jennifer. Mr. Davis opened the door before they reached him. He was tall and dark and as thin as a reed, but he looked handsome to her. His hair was neatly cropped. He had salt and pepper sideburns. He was recently widowed.

"Good morning, I'm Mr. Dale Davis, the school principal," he said, with a deep voice.

"Good morning," the children chorused

"Good morning," Jennifer replied. "I'm Jennifer Poygoode."

Mr. Davis extended his hand to her, but withdrew it when he realized she wasn't going to take it. Instead, she nodded her head, and hoped he understood. Then he looked beyond her and the children, at Rufus sitting inside the pickup, watching her closely. Mr. Davis held the door open, as Jennifer and the children filed inside. "Follow me to the cafeteria," he told them.

Inside the cafeteria, right away, Jennifer recognized her former sixth grade teacher, Mrs. Ora Blunker. Jennifer drew up shyly; seeing that Mrs. Blunker looked quite the same, except her short black hair was now, pretty much gray, and she had put on weight.

"This is Ms. Jennifer Poygoode," Mr. Davis said to Mrs. Blunker and the other young teacher, Ms. Kizzie Flowers. "Ms. Jennifer is here to enroll the children in school."

Mrs. Blunker spoke without a hint of recognition. "Hi. We've been expecting you all."

Ms. Flowers was smiling. She looked so young.

"I want all the older children to be tested," Mr. Davis told them. "Hopefully, they'll do well enough that we can put them in the classroom with children their own age. And if they don't—well, we'll put them in with them, anyway. We'll all just have to work twice as hard." He then looked at Jennifer, now smiling.

They'll do well, she thought to herself.

Ms. Flowers and Mrs. Blunker marveled over how pretty the girls looked and how handsome the boys looked in their white shirts and blue slacks. They were especially taken by Nora and Tara's gray-green eyes, reddish hair and sun-baked golden skin. The two girls could easily have passed for twins.

"I've never known black people to have red hair and green eyes," blurted Ms. Flowers. Mrs. Blunker jabbed her gently with her elbow.

"Are you all twins," Ms. Flower asked Tara.

Jennifer held her breath.

"No," Tara and Nora chorused. They looked at each other and smiled, and turned toward Jennifer.

Jennifer smiled nervously. Tara and Nora were the same height and weight, born three months apart. But Jennifer told them they were born exactly a year apart, which she thought was best. It was forbidden that Tara should ever know who her real mother was.

"You all may be seated," Mrs. Blunker told the children.

Jennifer stood back clutching her purse and staring at Ms. Flowers. She guessed that Ms. Flowers was her own age. It hurt her that she had been denied her dream of becoming a schoolteacher. Ever since she could remember she'd wanted to teach, as she looked around the cafeteria. In a sense, she reckoned she was a teacher, since she had taught the children all that they knew. She knew Mr. Davis would be surprised to find out just how smart they all were.

Mrs. Blunker began asking Nora for her full name, address, her date of birth, and mother's name. Jennifer stayed long enough to hear Nora say, "My mother..." Then Jennifer turned to Mr. Davis and requested to use the bathroom.

"I'll walk with you," he said, surprising her. "If you would like to leave afterwards, I'm certain the older children can give us the information we need to get everyone enrolled."

Jennifer felt relieved. Unable to speak, she simply nodded, holding her purse strings with both hands. They walked out into the hallway. She suddenly felt she no longer had to pee.

"The bathroom is to your left," he said, pointing a long, slender finger.

"Thank you." She felt like telling him she had once attended the school in the old building next door, but then decided not to. It used to be a combination of elementary school and high school. The new building was now the junior high, and high school.

Mr. Davis stopped and slightly turned. She stopped too. "My office is back that way," he told her. "If you need to speak to me before you leave, that's where I'll be. And Ms. Jennifer, we'll do all we can to help the children compete with our other students. Do any of them know how to read?"

"Yes sir!" she replied excitedly.

He gazed at her. "Well, that's a start. As I said, we're going to help them as much as we can. I'm new in town; I can see there hasn't been a sense of community here. I'm hoping to bring about change. It has begun already—with your bringing the children and getting them enrolled in school." He paused. "I'm going to say good-day to you, now."

She stared up in his thin face. "Good day, Mr. Davis."

He pivoted on his heels and left.

Jennifer stood for a second watching him stride down the hall. Still hopeful, she continued down the hall toward the bathroom. When she entered the small, immaculate bathroom, she looked at herself in the mirror above the sink. She no longer had to pee. She knew it was just nerves, and stayed in the bathroom long enough not to draw attention to her. She left and walked briskly down the hall toward the front door, hoping to get out of the building before Mrs. Blunker or Ms. Flowers came looking for her. She passed Mr. Davis' office, whose back was toward the door, sitting behind a desk talking on the phone.

Jennifer felt emotional. Blinking back tears, she pushed open the door and stepped out into autumn's early morning air. She saw Rufus watching her through the windshield. She pretended to look straight ahead, although she did as much looking around as she could out the corner of her eyes; at the houses; the parked cars; and the yellow school buses parked on the curb. The world felt new and strange, thinking about the life she could have had.

With dread, she opened the door and climbed in Rufus' pickup. She avoided his eyes, though she felt him looking at her. He cleared his throat, and she knew what that meant. She hated the power he held over their lives. She kept her lashes lowered. "They didn't really need me. The principal said the older children could answer questions for the little ones." Rufus said nothing. Out the corner of her eyes she saw the hard look on his face.

He turned the key in the ignition and started the engine.

She began staring out the window. No words were spoken between them, but she felt pleased that someone had finally forced his hand. She wondered if Mr. Davis had anything to do with it.

* * *

That afternoon, Jennifer waited anxiously on her front porch for the school bus to show. When the bus arrived and the driver opened the door, nervously, Jennifer counted each child as they descended the bus. They were all there—all twenty-one of them—all stair-steps. They all came to her house. They had big grins on their faces, as they came up her porch steps.

"Whoa!" she said, happily. "Where do all you think you're going? You all better get on home." Her voice was happy.

"We just wanted to say thank you," they all chorused. "It's because you taught us that we were all put in class rooms with children our own ages."

"We all passed the tests they gave us," Nora remarked.

Jennifer cupped her hand over her mouth excitedly. Tears filled her eyes. "Thank you God!" she exclaimed, stretching her arms towards the heavens.

Tara handed her a letter from the principal. Jennifer hands trembled as she ripped open the blessed envelope. She bent her head; read the letter narrowly. Then she hollered and grabbed Tara and Nora embracing them tightly. "The rest of you all—go on home. I'm happy for all of you. My prayers have been answered."

"Thanks again," they chorused. Then they all left.

Jennifer read the letter again and again. Tears slid, sometimes streamed down her cheeks. It didn't matter that she'd been addressed as Mrs. Poygoode. All that mattered was that her prayers had been answered.

* * *

Dear Mrs. Poygoode:

The children have all been carefully tested, and were found to be extremely bright. Tara and Nora have brought fame to Derriene Crossing High School. They are the first geniuses to ever attend our school, since its establishment in 1910. They both have been placed in ninth grade, strictly on their intellectual abilities. You are welcomed to visit any time you wish.

Sincerely,

Mr. Dale Davis, Principal

* * *

"Well, what does it say?" Tara and Nora inquired.

Jennifer looked at them. She lifted her free hand and wiped tears from her eyes. "I think you already know," she said. It says you all have been placed in ninth grade. And that you all are geniuses."

A click at the front door intruded upon Jennifer's thought. She heard the door open and close, followed by familiar footsteps. "Daddy!" she muttered. A knot formed in the pit of her stomach. It was hard pretending she was happy to see him; but that was what he demanded—and that's what she did.

When she entered the living room, he was standing in the middle of the room staring blankly out the window. The fragrances of lilacs, honey suckles, and roses had attached themselves to him. All of their houses were flanked with lilac, honeysuckle, and climbing roses. Nora once jokingly said the roots must have been airborne, since nobody took credit for planting them. But it was Rufus who'd planted them. He just never told them.

Years ago, when he was in Chancy, Louisiana, he fell in love with the landscapes, and the idea entered his head to bring some of these landscape ideas home, thinking that when people saw his beautiful, manicured lawn they would never think unhappiness existed there.

Something seemed to be weighing heavily on his mind. Jennifer stood quietly, staring at his broad back. Finally, she said, "Hi, Daddy." The knot inside her stomach grew tighter.

He turned around facing her. She felt surprised to see him with a cigar in his mouth, but it wasn't lit. As long as she'd known him, he had never smoked or drank, except on holidays he'd have an alcoholic drink. He took the cigar out of his mouth; held it between his index and middle fingers. He sat down in the winged-back chair and crossed his knees. "Sit down," he ordered.

She sat down on the sofa watching him. It was a long moment before he said anything. She felt more nervous with each passing moment. She wished he would cut the suspense and just say what was on his dirty mind.

"I been thinking," he said. "I want Tara up at the Big House."

187

Jennifer's eyes went round. She felt her heart stumble. "But why, Daddy?"

He put the cigar in his mouth, then took it out, and held it between his index and middle fingers. "Because the farm has gotten too big for me to run by myself. And I want to get rid of my foreman in the not-so-distant future. That's one salary less I'll have to pay. I want Tara to help me manage my property. I've seen that she's a born-leader. After I'm gone"—he looked at Jennifer—"not that I'm planning on dying any time soon, but after I'm gone, I want to make certain the farm stays in the family. I don't want the white man getting his hands on my land."

Jennifer averted her eyes to hide what she was thinking right then. I wish you'd drop dead right now, she thought.

He continued. "I want her up at the Big House, so I can teach her about the business of farming, and how I keep my books." He paused. "I'm buying a new cotton picker and a new combine; and one of them brand new John Deere tractors. I'm going to teach her how to operate 'em, and then I want her to teach what she knows to the others. You got any objections?" His voice was terse.

"No sir. You know what's best for them." She kept her lashes lowered. I don't believe this, she thought to herself. This sick lunatic is going to try to keep Tara and the other children on the farm!

She got up and went and stood in front of the window. She folded her arms across her chest. She kept her back turned to him and forced herself to speak calmly.

"You know, Daddy, Tara and Nora have their hearts set on going to college next fall. Tara wants to be a lawyer. And Nora wants to study medicine—I think she wants to be a children's doctor." She felt so nervous that she couldn't think of the proper term at the moment.

Rufus sniffed. "Mmm hmm. Well, I'm the one who's making plans for everybody living on my land. They're going be what I tell them they can be. But, if it'll make everybody feel better, I'll be putting them all on payroll after they finish with their schooling."

And where will they go to spend the money she felt like asking him.

"But don't you say a word. Let them keep on dreaming, you hear?"

Jennifer closed her eyes. "I hear." Her voice was barely above a whisper. He's trying to destroy my last dream; my last hope, she thought. We'll never get away from him if Tara and Nora let him do this. I hope to God they'll run away, even if it means leaving me behind.

Rufus stood, and headed for the door.

"Can Tara at least stay with me until school is out? It's only a few more weeks."

Rufus stopped and looked at her. "I can wait," is all he said, then he opened the door and left.

Jennifer shivered. She didn't like the sound of his "I can wait." She felt afraid for Tara. How could she keep this from Tara and Nora? They needed to know, so they could start making plans other than for college. She felt helpless.

* * *

Tara arrived at the cafeteria late. Nora, Rhoda, and Trudi had been unable to save her a seat because the cafeteria was nearly packed when they reached it. Tara stood in the middle of the room holding her tray. There was only one seat left, and it was at the rear of the room, next to the boy she had often seen eyeing her in the hallway. "Oh, God!" she said to herself.

He looked up and saw her gazing at the empty chair beside him. Their eyes met and held. Then he pointed to the empty chair. Tara's stomach caught butterflies.

She took a deep breath, then exhaled and restored her sense of balance. She walked over and put down her tray on the table beside his. "Thanks," she said.

He pulled the chair out from the table for her.

Tara sat down. "Thanks," she said coyly. "I was beginning to think I would have to eat standing up."

He looked at her and smiled. "Now that wouldn't have been any fun." His voice was deep and crisp. She couldn't help but notice his accent. "I'm Dion St. James," he said. "I see you in the hall a lot—when we're changing classes. I didn't think we'd ever get this close."

Tara looked at him coyly. "Me too. I mean I see you in the hall a lot, too. I'm Tara Poygoode. But I suppose you already know my name."

Dion smiled broadly. Tara noticed his pretty white teeth. His skin was a dark, rich texture. " Of course, I know your name," he said. "But, only because you're famous because you're so smart."

Tara smiled proudly. "You're very kind," she told him. She took a bite out of her bologna sandwich. Tara didn't know she was talking to an altruistic person; or that he would eventually play an important role in her and her family's destiny.

Fate had brought Dion to Derriene Crossing. When his uncle fell off the tractor and broke three ribs, Dion volunteered to change schools at the end of his junior year, so he could be with his uncle, and help out on the farm until he was well.

Dion loved Tara from the moment he first laid eyes on her. Loved her even more when he heard the ugly rumors floating around the school about her father. If she let him, he intended to do something about her situation. Though he didn't know what just yet.

He peered at the novel lying on her tray. Tara had just checked it out of the library. She had gotten permission from Ms. Sandra Macklin, the librarian, who gave her permission to sign out as many books as she liked, to read over the summer. *"Where My Heart Is, Now,"* he remarked.

"Huh?" She looked at him quizzically.

"I was reading the cover of your novel."

"Oh!" Tara replied. "I was wondering what you were talking about." There was a lilt of happiness in her laughter.

"You started reading it yet?"

"No, not yet. I just checked it out of the library a few minutes ago. That's the reason I'm late for lunch. I told my friend, Trudi, to save me a seat, but I guess she couldn't. She's sitting over there with my sister Nora, and her friend Rhoda."

She changed the subject.

"I see the margins in your Science book are pretty marked up. There's no room for anyone else to write. That's for sure. Still studying for final, huh?"

"Sort of," he said, then he closed the textbook and put it inside his book satchel.

"Don't do that!" she cried. After noticing his startled expression, she was surprised by how authoritative she sounded. "I'm sorry. I didn't mean to yell at you. What I meant was don't let me keep you from studying. Maybe I'll find another seat." She started getting up.

He put a hand on her arm. "No. Sit down—please. You aren't keeping me from studying. I'm just filling up my time. I'm one of those persons who always have to have his head in a book. My father is a college professor. He teaches agriculture at Joshwald College. He taught us kids the importance of reading."

For a moment, Tara looked at him without speaking. Her mind was traveling. "Where's Joshwald College?" she asked eagerly.

"Oh, it's nowhere around here."

She waited patiently for him to tell her where, but he never did. She finished eating the sandwich, and watched Dion write something. He ripped the page out of his loose-leaf binder and folded it, and handed it to her.

"Here," he said. "It's my address—where I'll be living after I leave here."

Tara felt disappointment. She started wondering where he was moving. She read the paper. "Lagoona, Indiana. Is that where Joshwald College is?" she asked.

"Yep. It's also my home town."

"Where were you born, Dion? Your accent . . ."

He smiled coyly. "I was born in Haiti, but I've lived in this country since I was three. My father was the Chief of Agriculture back in Haiti. He was forced to leave because of his radical views. Plus, marrying my mother didn't help. She was too dark for his high-class colleagues. He and my grandparents had to leave the country—they all had radical views. My grandparents settled in Tennessee. Anyway, I thought I'd lost my accent."

"But why would you want to lose it? It's different. I think it's cute."

He looked at her for a long moment. "You really think so?"

"I wouldn't have said it if I didn't. I'm looking forward to going to college, too. But I don't know of any colleges that aren't around here."

"Oh, there are lots of colleges all across the United States," Dion told her. "I'm only going back home after graduation because that's where I want to be. I only came here to help my aunt and uncle. He got into a bad accident last year. But he's better now, so I can go back home."

"Oh," was all she could say right then. She knew it was silly of her, but she felt he was letting her down. Here they were just meeting, and already she'd begun to look forward to a long friendship. Well, for what it was worth, she at least had his address, which she would have to hide, and which she, of course, could never use. She stuck it between the pages of her novel. The conversation lapsed.

Dion reached inside his book satchel and pulled out his Science textbook, and started reading again. But he really wasn't concentrating. He was more focused on Tara, thinking about the rumors floating around the school about her father, and the bad things he does to his family. He stole a sidelong glance. In spite of what he'd heard about her, she looked so pretty. How could any father hurt such a tender, beautiful flower, he thought? Finally, he closed the textbook and broke down the friendly wall of silence between them.

"You mind if I ask how old you are?"

Tara smiled. Slowly, she lifted her head and flashed those gray-green eyes that made him shiver with desire. "I'm fourteen."

Dion blinked. "And you're in eleventh grade!" he exclaimed.

"Um-hm." Tara smiled proudly. Thanks to Mama, she thought.

"So it's true that you're a genius?"

"Um hm."

"Wow! Well, I'm--I'm eighteen. Does that matter?" Then he wondered why he'd said that, for fear Tara might think he was too old for her. He loved everything about her. But he knew he would only be around till graduation. Then he would be gone. But if she would let him, he would at least try to lay the groundwork for her to escape from her mad-dog father. It would be then that he would ask her to let him take care of her for the rest of his life.

It took awhile for Tara to find her tongue. That was a loaded question. Did he mean what she thought he meant? She felt her heart pounding inside her chest.

Having finally found her tongue again, she said, "Not really." Then she reversed the question.

"Does it matter that I'm thirteen and a half?" She looked at him with those flashy gray-green eyes. He found her irresistible.

He sort of chuckled. He shook his head. "No. Not at all." He looked up at the front of the room, and then looked at her. "We still have time to go for a walk, if you like."

Tara looked at him in surprise. She felt her heart doing the jumping jacks. "I don't mind," she told him. "It is kind of stuffy in here."

They stood at the same time. Tara took her novel off the tray.

Dion hung his book satchel on his shoulder.

Tara stared at the two trays, debating whether or not they should leave them there.

Dion reached across in front of her; took her tray and placed it on top of his, and left them sitting on the table. He caught her right elbow and ushered her out of the cafeteria. They passed the table where Rhoda, Trudi, and Nora were seated.

At first, the three girls stared at Tara opened-mouthed. Then Trudi put up her right thumb. "He's cute!" she mouthed. Tara heard Trudi say to Rhoda and Nora: "He's the best looking boy in Derriene Crossing High!"

Tara flicked her a quick glance and smiled. Dion acted like he didn't hear them admiring him.

He opened the school door, and they stepped outside into the warm spring weather. The sky was tranquil blue. Tara lifted her hand and shielded her eyes from the bright sunshine.

Dion stepped in front of her; he reached inside his back pocket, and took out his wallet. He opened the wallet and pulled out his senior picture and gave it to her. "I want you to have it. Hide it so your father will never find it."

If there had been any doubt before, Tara knew now that he'd heard the disgusting rumors about her father. The moment her fingers touched his picture, her heart skipped a beat, and butterflies fluttered in her stomach. No boy had ever come this close to her. Oh, she had caught them staring at her lots of times, but none of them ever had the courage to approach her. She stuck his picture inside the novel on the same page she'd put his address.

"Come," he said. "Let's sit under the tree out of the sunshine."

They sat down under a tall oak tree. The air smelled of freshly cut grass. Dion reached inside his book satchel; he brought out a sketching pad and pencil. For the next fifteen minutes, no conversation was exchanged. He felt excited. Once in a while he would lay the pencil and sketching pad aside, cup Tara's face between his hands, turning her face this way, then that way. Then he'd pick up the pad and pencil and continue sketching her. She burned from the touch of his hot fingers. No boy had ever touched her before. Her heart kept pounding. "Is this how love feels," she asked herself.

When Dion finished, he handed her the sketch.

She took it.

"I'm keeping it for myself, if you don't mind," he told her, staring down in her upturned face. "I'm just sorry I couldn't capture the color of your eyes, your hair, and pretty skin."

Tara forgot how hard she was staring at the girl in the sketch. Am I really that beautiful, she said to herself? Dion captured a hint of sadness in her eyes. Tara realized she was as beautiful as she had often heard people say. She smiled and looked up at him, and returned the pad back to him.

She watched him close the pad slowly, as he gazed admiringly at his work. He bent, picked up his book satchel, and put the pad and pencil inside, and hung the book satchel on his shoulder.

"I didn't know you could draw," she remarked.

He chuckled. "Of course, you didn't. How could you? We've just met, remember?"

He stood, extended his hand, and helped her get up from off the ground. "We probably should head back," he said. "Which class are you going to now?"

"English," she replied, with a ripple of sadness. She wished they could've had more time to be together.

"Me, too," he said.

They walked back toward the school, not saying much of anything. She thought they were wishing the same thing: That they had more time to spend together. Dion opened the school door and then made a wide sweep with his free hand. "Madam Tara Poygoode," he said.

Tara looked up at him and smiled.

As soon as they entered the building, the bell rang.

"Well," Dion said, studying her beauty. "We've got to get to class. See you on Monday." The undertone of his statement had sounded more like a question. She enjoyed being with him. Of course, she wanted to see him again.

She nodded. "See you on Monday."

Her classroom was a short distance from where they stood. She leaned a shoulder against the wall and watched him move in and out of the crowd. He was sort of bowlegged. He had strong, broad shoulders, standing tall above most of the other boys. Tara suddenly felt a hand on her left shoulder. She turned around slowly, hating to take her eyes off Dion.

"Hi," Nora said. "Sorry, kiddo, but you have to stop looking at him for now. Let's get to class."

Tara smiled at Nora and turned back and watched Dion, until he disappeared around the corner. "I know," she remarked. "I know."

"Well, tell me all about him when we get home. Right now we gotta get to class," Nora said. Nora was cheerful. She felt happy that Tara was doing something that their father couldn't do anything about.

* * *

One day when things were quiet at home, Tara and Nora went off together to their room. They perched beside each other on the edge of the mattress; and sat with their heads together, looking at Dion's picture, and discussing and planning their future. A knock at the door caught the two girls off guard.

Slowly, the door opened. Jennifer poked her head inside.

Tara jerked Dion's picture out of Nora's hand and hid it behind her back.

"Didn't you all hear me calling! It's dinnertime. And what's that you hiding behind your back, Tara?"

"Nothing," she replied.

Jennifer entered the room. "C'mon, now. I saw you snatch something out of Nora's hand. You two look like the fox that got caught stealing the chickens. You all got something. I know it. Now let me see it. I promise I won't get mad."

The two girls exchanged unhappy glances.

"It's okay. Let her see it," Nora told Tara.

"Well, all right," Tara said reluctantly. Bringing her hand from behind her back slowly, she handed the picture to Jennifer, and held her breath, awaiting Jennifer's response.

Jennifer took the picture; brought it close up to her face. Her brows shot up curiously. "Hmm! He's cute. To which of you does he belong?" she asked, unable to pull her eyes away from the picture.

Like an unsure child, Tara slowly raised her hand.

Jennifer gazed at her. "He's cute. What's his name? How old is he?"

"God!" Nora exclaimed. "Why so many questions, Mama?" She and Tara exchanged agitated glances.

"His name is Dion St. James. And he's eighteen," Tara said, then held her breath. The two girls saw Jennifer's expression change, but neither of them could decipher what was going on inside her head.

Jennifer looked at Tara curiously. "Don't you think he's a little too old for you?"

Tara responded by jerking the picture out of her hand.

Nora flew off the handle. "What difference does it make how old he is? It's just a school thing! It's not like he's taking her out; or he'll see her after school is out. He's going back to Lagoona, Indiana." There was silence, as they began hoping Jennifer would leave.

Jennifer thoughtfully stared at Nora, whose temperament was really starting to worry her. "You know, Nora, you're so full of anger that it scares me sometimes."

"And you're not!" Nora snapped.

Jennifer looked away vacantly cupping her elbows in either hand and stared at the wall in back of the bed. She didn't approve of the girls' sassiness, but she would never think of hitting them.

"Now, can we have our room back?" Tara barked.

Jennifer sniffed, also disturbed by Tara's angry expression. "I'm sorry," she said. "Nora is right. What difference does it make?" Knowing Rufus's plans for the two girls, she added as an afterthought: "Grab all the happiness you possibly can. And find a safe place to keep that picture." After standing around for another minute or so, she left, closing the door behind her.

* * *

Dinner was long over by the time Tara and Nora reached the kitchen. They were deliberately late. Jennifer heard them coming. She grabbed the hem of her skirt and dried her eyes, after just finishing crying for the lost years of her youth. She was now twenty-eight years old, with a few unruly gray strands in her temple area, and she had never experienced her first love.

Tara and Nora stopped short when they saw that she was still seated at the table. They exchanged disappointing glances. "Sorry we're late," Nora announced.

"Huh? Sorry my foot!" Jennifer remarked. She forced her voice to sound cheerful.

The two girls took a plate out of the safe and moved toward the stove. Nora lifted the lid off the black cast iron pot and let out a loud, desperate holler. "Mama! They ate up all the pinto beans!" Jennifer didn't reply. Nora slammed the lid down on the pot with a loud bang. Her face flushed with anger.

Tara reached across her and lifted the top off the pot of rice, and slammed it right back down. She half turned and looked at Nora. "Do you believe this? Mama sat here and let them greedy hound dogs eat up all the food!"

Nora stomped the floor with her barefoot. "I'm going to kill Millie and Tony! They knew we hadn't eaten! I bet it was them two greedy pigs that ate up all the food from us." Tara checked the last two scraped pots. Tears nearly filled her eyes, but she fought them back.

The two girls walked over to the table and put down their plates sharply. They dragged the chairs from the table, and sat down hard. Propping their elbows on the table, they cupped their chin in their hands, while watching their tearful mother with dismay.

Suddenly, Jennifer burst out laughing. "Your food's in the oven fools! I figured I'd fix your wagons. Teach you to come to dinner on time, next time."

The two girls jumped up and raced toward the stove. Tara pulled opened the oven door. She touched the plates with her fingers. "We don't need the pot holders," she told Nora. She gave Nora a plate and took the other one for herself. She closed the oven door with her free hand.

They sat down at the table with great big grins on their faces.

"You all are something else," Jennifer remarked. "You should've seen your faces!"

Tara and Nora looked at each other and started laughing. They chattered non-stop about the kids at school, about homework, and about their desire to go away to college.

Jennifer wanted so much to tell the girls that they might not get the opportunity to go away to college. She also wanted to tell Tara that she was going to have to go up to the Big House to live once school was out, but she couldn't bring herself to spoil their happiness.

* * *

On Sunday, when the sun had cast a long, slender shadow and the sun had sunk low behind the trees, Jennifer went to see Jackie. She walked up the porch steps and looked into the house through the screen. The living room was dark. She opened the screen door and entered the house, closing the door behind her. The light was on in the kitchen. "It's me, Jackie," she called. "You'd better get on these kids about leaving this door open when it gets this late. Anybody could walk in here on you all."

"I done told them kids at least a hundred times about leaving that damn door open! "

Jennifer moved toward the kitchen. She framed the doorway, and folded her arms and stood with her shoulder leaning against the door jam.

Jackie looked up from her cup of tea. "Hi. Come sit down. I'm on my second cup. Fix your self a cup," she told her, then changed the subject.

"Did Lynn tell you she had to pull Rudi out of Carol? He thinks that just because Carol isn't his whole sister it's okay for him to put his penis in her. Lord, I tell you, that boy is going to be just like his damn daddy. He ain't looking like him for nothin', I tell you. No female is safe around this place!"

Jennifer felt her heart slam into to her chest. Too shocked for words, she wanted to fold up and die. Finally her speech returned, as she calmed herself. There was no use getting her pressure up over stupid Rudi.

"This is the first I heard of it. I--I don't know what to say." Jennifer felt deeply troubled. Every time she turned around there was a crisis of some sort.

200

"There is nothing you can say about a cesspool," Jackie remarked emphatically. "Lynn threatened to tell Daddy, though. But, then she changed her mind. She knew Daddy would've killed Rudi. She did tell Rudi to stay his fat behind up at the Big House from now on. One thing for sure, he isn't allowed at my house, any more. Come sit down and have a cup of tea with me."

"I don't want any," Jennifer replied. She sighed heavily, as her arms fell loosely. "When school is out, I have to send Tara up to the Big House to live. She has to live there from now on."

A grotesque look covered Jackie's face. She looked intently at Jennifer for a long moment. "Don't tell me," she said, her thin finger pointed upward. "Daddy's behind it, isn't he?"

"Who else? It sure isn't Maebelle."

Jackie stared at the floor for a long moment. "Jennifer, are you ever going to start calling her Mama again?"

"Hell no!" Jennifer barked. "She ain't no damn mother. Shit nah! All she ever done for any of us is ruin our lives. She acts like she doesn't have an ounce of good sense left!"

"I know," Jackie concurred. "I know. It just doesn't seem right for you to be calling her by her name all these years. But calm down and let's talk about Daddy. Do you think he still believes Tara isn't his?"

Jennifer pulled a chair from the table and sat down wearily. She took Jackie's cup and sipped some of the tea. Then she replaced the cup in the saucer shakily.

"Hell, no!" she exclaimed. "That bastard would have to be blind in one eye and cock-eyed in the other, to still claim that child isn't his. Her hair is just as red as the rest of them."

"Did he say why he wanted her up there? I mean after all these years...!"

"He claims he wants her to take over the farm after he dies, the bastard! I wish he'd drop dead, like yesterday," she declared. "He claims he wants to teach her how to keep the books and do some other things."

Jennifer saw Jackie quaking. "Why are you shaking like that?"

Stirring on her seat, Jackie snapped her head up and looked at Jennifer groaning. "I don't know. It's just that I have bad feelings about Tara going up to that house. I'm shaking because I'm thinking about the first time that Daddy did it to me. I was a lot younger than Tara, remember?"

Jennifer swallowed, glancing away to avoid the pain in Jackie's eyes, and vice versa. How could she forget, she thought? Jackie had awakened the whole house that night, screaming. Neither of them had never spoken about their ordeals to each other.

Jackie went on. "I remember his penis looked so ugly. It was all swollen. Yuk! I still can't stand when he touches me." She shivered, watching Jennifer, who couldn't face her.

"He had no mercy on me," Jackie said, now standing, as she picked up the cup out of the saucer, and moved toward the stove. She lifted the kettle and filled the cup with hot water and put in a fresh tea bag and a slice of lemon, adding two tablespoons of sugar.

Jennifer sat quietly reflecting. That first time Rufus attacked her he'd cornered her inside the old barn. Later that evening, she saw Jinni running home from the barn crying. Rufus walked out behind her.

Jackie broke into her thoughts. "So how does Tara feel about all this?"

"I haven't told her. He told me not to, but to wait until the last day of school to tell her."

"That's this coming Wednesday, you know?"

Jennifer frowned. "Yeah. I know."

The two sisters talked late into the evening. When Jennifer left the house, the silvery moon had risen in the expansive black sky.

Chapter 6

In her junior year, as the school year drew to a close, Tara began to grieve deeply, for she had found a very special kind of love with Dion; and now she was about to lose him forever. He was so warm and caring, causing happy butterflies to grow inside her stomach whenever she saw him. Those past few weeks were the happiest times of her life. She brought sandwiches to school, so they could spend more time together outside on the grounds. Their days together were warm and happy days.

* * *

A day before school was to close Jennifer pleaded with Rufus to let Tara stay with her until the beginning of the next week. She felt surprised when he obliged. Still, she wasn't allowed to tell Tara about her impending transition, until the very last minute.

* * *

On the last day of school, behind a huge oak tree, Dion surprised Tara with a long, steamy kiss. She felt her womanhood awaken. He was her Prince.

Dion promised her he would help her escape her life at home once she graduated, if that was what she wanted. She wanted it. He promised to keep in touch. He promised to send letters to her via her friend Trudi's address. Trudi agreed to receive Dion's letters for Tara.

* * *

On Sunday, Tara went reluctantly to the Big House. Jennifer told her it was a temporary arrangement that would last until Rufus taught her how to run the family business. Then she could come back home. Oh, how Jennifer wished that was true.

Tara hated living at the Big House. It was cold and uninviting. And she missed Nora so much, and she hated sharing a room with Adie, Maebelle and Rufus' fifth child.

Besides being too young to engage in teenage chatter, Adie's frequent nightmares kept Tara up at night. They got worst on Friday nights. All night long, Adie woke up with her fists clenched tight, fighting demons from a very recent past.

Late one Friday night, Tara woke to Adie's desperate screams. "No! No!" Adie cried. " I don't like it. Mama!"

Tara bolted upright from sleeping. She swung her legs over the mattress and rushed to Adie's side. She climbed upon the bed; straddled Adie; clutched her small wrists, and forced her back down on the mattress.

"No!" Cried Adie. "Don't take off my panties!" Adie twisted her body vehemently.

"Adie! Adie!" Tara exclaimed in a frantic whisper. "Wake up before you wake up the whole house!" When Adie wouldn't stop, Tara slapped her hard across her face.

Adie woke up frightened. She finally realized that she'd been dreaming and that it was Tara who was straddling her. Still, she was angry because Tara had struck her hard. "You didn't have to hit me in my face like that!" she snapped. "Get off me!"

"I'm sorry," Tara remarked. "But I had to keep you from waking up the whole house. You know how Daddy can be. And who did you think I was, anyway? You've been having bad dreams ever since I arrived here." Tara released Adie's hands, and sat back on her haunches.

"It's not just a bad dream," Adie told her. "It's real!" she said, and pushed Tara in her chest. "Get away from me!"

The smoky light from the silver moon illuminated their room. Adie saw Tara hang her head. After a moment or two, Adie leaned forward and put her thin arms around Tara's shoulders. "I'm sorry I pushed you; I'm sorry for yelling at you. You care about me, don't you? I wish you were my mama. She wouldn't stop Daddy from taking me to town so his friends could do things to me."

Tara's mouth fell open, as her heart stumble. The things Adie said were incomprehensible. She wondered if Adie was fully awake and knew what she said. She peeled Adie's arms off her and held her at arm's length.

"How long has Daddy been taking you to town?" she demanded. Adie hesitated. Tara crawled off to the side of the bed, and sat on the edge of the mattress and waited for Adie's response. She sat sideways on the mattress looking at her. "Talk to me, Adie!"

Adie looked at her. "He doesn't take me any more. But he used to. The men got scared somebody might tell the sheriff what they were doing to me."

"What men? Where did Daddy take you? I mean where did the men do those things to you?"

"In the back room, at Daddy's juke house," said Adie, rubbing her eyes with the heel of her hand. They made me touch their you-know-what, and they peed white stuff in my hands." She looked up at Tara's bent silhouette, as Tara held her forehead, while her other hand was over her heart. Adie knew Tara cared.

Tara swallowed hard, trembling. Tears slid down her cheeks. She felt so sorry for Adie. She knew Adie must have been confused about the men's pee being white, though. That can't be, she thought, even though she knew very little about male organs, and thought it had to be something other than pee that came out of their *thing.* "You sure you're not making this up, Adie? " It sounded so awful.

Adie pursed her lips, and folded her arms across her chest. She felt deeply hurt that Tara didn't believe her. "You wouldn't make a good mama," she told her. "Get off my bed. Go on, get away from me!" There was a silence, but Tara wanted to believe her.

She reached out and touched Adie's knee. "I'm sorry. I believe you're telling me the truth. "You said you told Big Mama. What did she say?" Adie didn't answer right away.

Finally, Adie said, "When I told her, she acted scared. She said she couldn't stop Daddy from doing nothing he wanted to. She told me the men would soon get tired of me. But they didn't. They only got scared because they might go to jail. I saw them giving Daddy money, too."

Tara's body rocked. She felt rage toward Maebelle. That's typical of grandma, she thought. She recalled once over-hearing a conversation between Jennifer and Lynn. They were mimicking Maebelle. They'd said the same thing Adie said.

Tara got to her feet. She looked down in Adie's upturned face. Adie looked so much like Maebelle. She wandered if Rufus had done those things to her, because she looked so much like her. Adie's skin was very dark, with Maebelle's puppy dog eyes. Tara had a feeling he really hated Maebelle, and he'd do anything to torment her. She sighed deeply.

"My heart can't take this," Tara murmured, and went back to her bed. "I never thought he would do this to his own children." She stood near her bed, not knowing what to do, as she hugged her elbows and observed the room glowing from the moon. She started wondering about the real reason Rufus wanted her at the Big House. Maybe to take Adie's place. I'll kill him first, she decided. I swear to God! She looked back at Adie, and her heart went out to her. "If you want to, you can sleep with me from now on. Maybe it'll help.... " She was too distraught to finish her sentence, and got in bed.

Adie had always wanted to sleep with Tara, but she was too afraid to ask. Quickly, she threw back the white sheet; climbed out of bed, and climbed in on the left side of the bed. She pulled the sheet up, around her small shoulders.

"Please don't tell Mama I told you. She'll get mad at both of us."

"I won't," Tara replied.

Adie turned on her right side and faced Tara's back. "She doesn't like you, you know. I see the way she looks at you when you're not paying attention."

"You didn't need to tell me that. I already know she doesn't like me." Adie got quiet. Tara felt glad Adie wasn't able to see her face in the dark. She would've seen her terrified expression, with tears rolling down her face. Since a child, she felt that Maebelle didn't like her, because she never had more than two words to say to her. But she was always clucking to Nora and the other children. Tara felt she resented her for coming to the Big House, since she barely said two words to her since she arrived. She laid awake for most of the night thinking about Adie, and hearing her snore.

* * *

Tara rose before dawn. She got up this way every morning since coming here. She didn't want to see any of them, especially Maebelle and Rufus, and even more so now. After she bathed, she put on a long sleeve cotton checkered shirt, old faded jeans and timberland boots. She thought this little education about the family business would only last through the summer, and then she could go home. She hated not seeing Nora, now working in the field, with the rest of the family, far from the house.

Maebelle's four boys, Adam and Rudi, and the twins, Elliott and Zeke, had to dig up stumps from the lower east end of the pasture, and prepare it for farmland. Tara's job was to oversee the work the boys did in the pasture, and to lend them a hand, if needed. Before she could start helping with the removal of the stumps, she had to clean out the barn and get it ready for fresh bales of hay soon to be harvested. Later on, Rufus promised to train her on the combine and cotton picker.

She would in turn train Elliott, Zeke, and Rudi. Adam was too young. Adie had to help Maebelle baby-sit all the children who were too young to work in the field.

Routinely, Tara went downstairs to the kitchen, kneaded dough, and made two large biscuit sandwiches with sausage patties and scrambled eggs. One sandwich was for breakfast and the other one was for lunch. She filled a quart size jar with buttermilk from the fridge. She screwed on the lid and set the jar on the table. Then she proceeded to clean the kitchen.

Afterward, she ran softly up the stairs to her bedroom to bring down her book satchel. She opened the door softly and stepped inside her room. It felt good to see poor Adie sleeping peacefully. She grabbed her book satchel and ran softly back down the stairs, toward the kitchen. She took the sandwiches and the jar of buttermilk and put them inside her book satchel. With the book satchel hung over her right shoulder, she opened the kitchen door and stepped out into the gray dawn. The birds chirping in the tree branches and the doves singing plaintively inside the woods brought the morning air to life.

Tara took long strides down the smooth path to the barn, thinking about Adie and the weeks ahead. She could hardly wait for summer to end, so she could return home. She wondered how Dion was spending his summer. She thought about Trudi, wondering if Trudi had received any letters from Dion, and was holding them for her; or if he'd changed his mind and decided to wait until school started to write her. The latter had made more sense, since he knew that she and Trudi wouldn't be seeing each other until school started.

She reached the old barn. The door creaked loudly as she opened it. She stared at the hinges and made a mental note to oil them later. She went inside, closing the door behind her.

Soon the sun peaked on the horizon. Slivers of light filtered in through the cracks. She sat down on a pile of straw; removed her book satchel off her shoulder, and took out the biscuit sandwich. She drew her knees, leaning back against the wall. It felt peaceful inside the old barn. It was in excellent condition with all the work Rufus had done on it. He gave it a fresh coat of red paint last summer. Tara downed the sandwich and finished drinking the buttermilk. Then she got up and began the daunting task of moving old bales of hay toward the front of the barn. She worked steadily. All the time her mind was inundated with the curse she felt her family lived under.

Before she knew it, it was lunchtime. The Uncle Ben clock inside her book satchel whined loudly. She threw down the hayfork, and retrieved her book satchel, and shut off the alarm. The book satchel hung on her right shoulder, as she pushed open the door, and stepped out into the fresh air and sunshine. She lifted her hand, shielding her eyes from the bright sunshine. Tara preferred being by herself, since she couldn't be with Nora. "I think I'll take a walk down by the stream," she muttered.

On the way down to the stream, she met up with Zeke, Elliott, Adam, and Rudi, on their way to the house. Tara saw Rudi looking at her with a strange expression on his fat, round face. He cut across in front of her. She stopped short and stared him straight in the eyes. She knew he was trying to start something, and she was ready.

Zeke, Elliott, and Adam stopped to watch.

"The house is *thataaway*," Rudi told her, pointing. Then he got right up in front of her face. "What, you think you too good to eat with the family? Everybody knows you been getting up before daybreak and making your breakfast. I guess you made lunch again, too, huh?"

Tara's blood started boiling, as she put her hands on her hips. Her lips were tightly pursed. "That's right!" she snapped. "You got a problem with it!" She felt like slapping Rudi's pudgy jaws. His stupid dominating ways reminded her a lot of Rufus, with his controlling ways.

Rudi turned sideways and made light of her. "Y'all hear that? She wants to know if I got a problem with her cooking her own breakfast and lunch," he said, facing her.

"Leave her alone," said Elliott. "She's not bothering anybody."

"Yeah, leave her alone, boy," said Zeke. "She's not used to being around Mama. That's all that is."

Tara glanced at Zeke.

"That's bull," Rudi said. He held his menacing eyes in hers. "She thinks she's better than anybody else. Just because she and Nora are graduating next year."

Tara smelled his hot breath, and tightened her fists. She had enough pent-up anger inside her to unleash a tornado on his fat, round rump.

"Back off, fat fart! You're just like your damn daddy. You can't control me. Now get the hell out of my way!" When Rudi didn't move, Tara dropped her book satchel on the ground and balled her fists into tight hard knots. But Rudi just laughed in her face.

He stood on his tiptoes and got even closer. His lips were taut, and his eyes challenging. "He's your daddy, too, remember?" He laughed. "Daddy got five women!" After he said that, he stepped backward and gyrated in front of her.

A look of horror crossed Tara's face. She looked out the corner of her eyes, at Zeke, Elliott, and Adam. They didn't seem shocked, except Adam was staring at Rudi's round gyrating butt.

"Some day I'm going to be just like Daddy," Rudi remarked, proudly. "Girls ain't good for nothin' but humpin.' But, you needn't worry," he said looking up in Tara's angry face. "You're too ugly for this." He grasped his crotch.

Tara felt a lump catch in her throat. She forced back rushing tears, daring him to ever lay a hand on her. He'd be deader than dead, she told herself.

"Quit it, boy!" Elliott said. "Tara's our sister!"

Rudi turned around looking at Elliott. He turned back towards Tara. "She's not our whole sister. We didn't come out of the same belly. But I don't want her anyhow. Like I said. She's too ugly for my *thang*. I got my eyes on Adie. She's gon be my woman."

Tara was stunned speechless, swallowing hard. If he touched Adie, she, alone, would kill him.

"You and Adie are whole sister and brother, stupid!" Zeke remarked. "Boy, you're crazy."

Rudi shrugged. "*It don't matter.*"

"Adie don't even like you," Adam commented.

Rudi looked back at Adam. "Shut up, you little runt. *It don't matter*, and girls don't matter, I'm telling y'all. I heard Lynn and Jackie them talking about Daddy's their stepfather, and that he shouldn't be doing nasty to them. But Daddy makes them do him. So you see Adam, it don't matter what girls think. Ain't nothin' wrong 'bout humpin' no girls. That's what they are made for."

Tara felt mortified. She hated Rudi.

"You better not let Daddy hear you say that," Zeke told him. "You aren't grown. Besides, Tara would tear you apart if you ever tried that on her. And I'm not helping you."

Zeke turned and faced Elliott. "C'mon. I heard enough. Let's go. I'm hungry."

"Me, too," said Adam. "Enough is enough".

When Rudi saw they'd left him at Tara's mercy, he suddenly backed away. He was jealous of Tara because Rufus always bragged about how smart she was. It was for that reason he wanted to make her miserable. He ran off to catch up to Zeke, Elliott and Adam.

"Hey! Wait up!" he called. He overtook them, and looked back at Tara, grasping his crotch.

"You don't have nothing down there but a nipple!" she called. Sweat rippled down the side of her temple.

She swore and picked up her book satchel, and she continued toward the stream.

Rudi called her. She ignored him, until he said, "Daddy won't let you and Nora leave the farm. Ha! Ha! I heard him say it with my own ears. Ask Mama if you don't believe me."

Tara pretended she didn't hear him. Her anger now combined of fear and dread. She felt a chill snake up her spine. She believed him. There was no reason not to. She would tell Nora what Rudi said about Rufus not letting them leave the farm, and what Rudi had done to her.

As she neared the stream, she felt trapped in a sea of madness. Rudi was already posing a threat to her, but mostly to Adie. She knew he wouldn't always be a little roly-poly, eleven-year old. Some day he would grow up to be tall and strong. She swallowed hard, pushing the sick thought out of her mind. "I got to get away from here," she muttered. "That's all there is to it. And I'll take Adie and Nora with me." She pulled herself together. Once in a while she looked over her shoulder.

* * *

Tara strolled along side the quiet stream, eating the sausage biscuit and doing a lot of thinking. She felt thirsty, but the buttermilk was gone. By now it would have been spoiled anyway, she thought. She would wait until Elliott returned with the water bucket, for a drink.

The summer heat was unbearable. Tara sat under the sweeping branches of a weeping willow tree, on a patch of soft green grass. Resting against the trunk of the tree, she slipped the book satchel off her shoulder, and reached inside and brought out Dion's picture. She lingerly stared longingly at him, remembering his kisses––the way he'd touched her. He has gentle hands, she thought, yearning to see him again. She brushed away the tear falling down her face. She sniffed, putting his picture back inside her book satchel, to avoid ruining it with her tears.

The leaves rustling in the soft, cool breeze made her sleepy. Just in case she fell asleep, she set the alarm on her Uncle Ben clock. Then she lay down on the soft green grass. She felt a mound pressing against her back. She sat up and looked behind her. Surprisingly, there appeared to be three tiny graves that she was lying on. Carpeted with tiny wild flowers, they were barely visible. Tara was puzzled, but naturally assumed these were human graves, while wondering whose babies were buried in them. Whoever these children were, she thought, they seemed peacefully rested beneath the earth, protected by long sweeping willow branches. Tara wished she had died before she'd gotten to know herself. Instinctively, she knew she wasn't supposed to be here on these gravesites. It was as though a still, small, voice had told her that.

Suddenly, there was rustling in the tall grass. "Rudi!" she cried. It sounded as though he was running straight toward her. Quickly scrambling to her feet, she grabbed her book satchel and ran out from under the branches, crouching down motionless, behind a thick oak. When she thought it was safe, she peeked out from behind the tree. She let out a sigh of relief when she saw that it was two Jackrabbits rumpling around in the grass. "Thank God!" she muttered. Straightening up, she reminded herself to go back and look at the small graves. Suddenly, fear gripped her. What if someone really was out there? What if the Jackrabbits happened to be there at the same time? She looked around cautiously, as she slowly walked from behind the oak tree, heading back toward the stream, to the barn.

On the other side of the stream, far out in the distance, she could hear a church choir singing *"Savior don't pass me by!"* Reminding her that today was Sunday. She stopped to listen, looking up at the crystal blue sky. How she wished the Savior would come and carry her

213

home. She had always wanted to go to church, but Rufus didn't allow religion. To her disappointment, the choir stopped singing. A moment later, she heard the preacher. His voice rose and fell, so she only caught bits and pieces of his sermon. *"If you take one step, aha! God will take two. Aha!"* She wondered what the preacher meant by 'Aha!' The rest she understood. His voice rose again. *"Fear God! You got no business fearing man. Aha!"*

The alarm on her Uncle Ben clock whined loudly. She reached her hand inside her book satchel and shut it off. She wished she could've stayed and listened to the preacher longer, but she had to return to the barn. In any case, he gave her food for thought, as she made her way back to the barn.

* * *

What Rudi had told her about Rufus was true. She worked and stayed at the Big House that summer. As the weeks of summer wore on, Rufus drove Tara harder and harder. Learning to balance the books and writing checks were the easiest parts of her tasks. She only wished her name were on the bankbooks. She had difficulty learning to drive the great big cotton picker and the great big combine. Initially, she feared the monstrous machines. They were nothing like the tractors she had driven since she was eleven. She told Rufus she was afraid. However, he ignored her excuses, so she learned to master her fears. Later, she taught Zeke, Elliott, and Rudi to drive those monstrosities. Missing Nora so much, she tried persuading Rufus to let her teach Nora, too. First, he said yes. The next day he said no. She was disappointed as that was the only way she could see Nora that summer.

Tara grew to hate Rudi more than she thought possible. She desperately wanted to tell Nora about him. Sometimes she felt like beating the living daylights out of him. But she managed otherwise.

* * *

It was an early afternoon, when Tara finished her outdoor chores, deciding to go home to balance the books. She went into Rufus' bedroom and sat down at his desk. She pulled opened the drawer, and brought out the ledger. "Damn!" she muttered, when she accidentally knocked over the caddy of pencils. They spilled on to the floor, rolling in every direction. Tara dove after them, narrowly missing two that had rolled under his bed.

She got down flat on her belly and crawled under the bed. A cotton rug, conspicuous because of where it was, caught her attention. She forgot about the pencils and focused on the rug spread over a small area. She lifted a corner and saw the loose floorboard. She rolled back the rug carefully lifting the board, put it aside, and looked inside the hole. "A churn!" she muttered. Although her heart was pounding, she proceeded to look inside. She removed the cover. Her eyes swelled, as she saw lots of money. She instinctively knew that she couldn't be found here, and especially by Rufus.

Quickly, she placed the cover on the churn and replaced the floorboard. She rolled the rug back exactly as she'd found it. Grabbing the stray pencils, she crawled from beneath the bed, and picked up the rest of the pencils, and arranged them neatly in the caddy. She grabbed the ledger and a pencil and rushed out the room.

When Tara went into the dinning room, she decided she would work there from now on. "All that money," she muttered. "Why is he hiding it? We're so rich!" She knew now that the books he had her keep didn't reflect their true worth. She started thinking of ways to grab the money and run. But she couldn't just think of herself, she would take everyone with her— except Rudi. She would do it after graduation, and her family could buy a small farm somewhere far away. She and Nora could attend college without worrying about how they would pay their tuition.

A strong hand suddenly touched her shoulder. She felt her heart jump inside her breast. She jerked her head around and looked up in Rufus' face. She swallowed hard.

"Kind of jumpy, aren't you?" he remarked.

"Ah, no sir. You just startled me; that's all. I was kind of in deep thought. I was thinking how I used to be scared to climb upon the combine and the cotton picker." She thought she sounded convincing. Rufus didn't comment, as he looked at the ledger. He handed her the thin paper bag he held in his hand.

"What's in it?" she asked politely.

"Just your heart medicine."

She took the bag and laid it on the table. She was sick and tired of Rufus trying to play doctor. She had long ago stopped taking her so-called heart medicine. She felt just fine. Anyway, the pills always made her dizzy, and Trudi had said people shouldn't take anything stronger than an aspirin unless they'd seen a doctor, and he'd prescribed it. Tara had never seen a doctor.

"You're still taking them I hope," he said.

Tara flinched. "Yes, sir." She picked up the pencil and thumped it on the ledger.

He flashed a quick glance at her. She hoped he believed her.

"Well, I dropped some new tools off at the barn. Be careful when you put them away. Don't mix them with the old ones. There is a place in the back of the barn where I keep the new tools. Put them there."

"Do I have to put them away now?" she asked. "'I'm balancing the books, now."

"I think its best. You might forget it later. It might rain." When he saw her hesitating he demanded: "Do it now! You spend much to much time on the books!"

"Yes sir," she replied softly, as she put down the pencil. "Why didn't you put them away yourself," she muttered under her breath—after he walked away, of course.

Tara returned the ledger to Rufus' bedroom and went upstairs to get her book satchel. As she walked through the living room on her way out, she saw Maebelle dusting, with her back turned toward her. Tara stopped short and gazed at her. She's at it again, she told herself. Maebelle had become a nervous wreck, always flittering about the house dusting things that didn't need dusting and sweeping the floors that didn't need sweeping. Tara tried to tiptoe across the floor, but the boards creaked, drawing Maebelle's attention. She quickly turned around.

"Tara?" she called, authoritatively.

Tara took a deep breath, as she dropped her head and gazed at the floor.

"Look at me when I talk to you, gal."

Tara sucked her teeth. What do you want? she thought to herself, as she studied her grandmother.

"Why is it that every time I see you, you got that-- that book satchel with you? What's inside it that you got to be carrying it with you everywhere? Look at it, it's filthy!"

Tara held her eyes in Maebelle's, challenging her. A nosy wench, she told herself. It's none of your business what I have in my book satchel. She started leaving without responding.

"Don't you walk away from me, gal! You answer me when I speak to you. I'm yo,yo..."

Tara became enraged. "You're my what! Look at you. You can't even get the words out of your mouth! You haven't said two words to me since I been here. You're not my grandmother! Why don't you go pick on Daddy? And why didn't you stop him from selling Adie's body?" Oops! It was too late. She had betrayed poor Adie's confidence. She didn't mean to.

Maebelle's eyes were riveted on her in shock. Her face turned a shade darker, as she rubbed a flat palm down the side of her skirt. She turned fiercely, as if she were looking for a hiding place. Nevertheless, Tara hadn't won the battle, although she thought she had.

Tara started walking away, but Maebelle wasn't finished. She had a lot of pent-up rage inside her, resenting Tara's affection for Jennifer. She no longer wanted her grandmother! And she bet Tara hid love letters from some little 'ol boy inside her book satchel.

"Wait a minute!" She demanded in a shrill tone.

Tara stopped short, skinning her lips, and trying desperately to control her temper, but Maebelle was making it hard. She glared back equally hard.

"Don't stand there like you're crazy. I asked you what's in that nasty ass book satchel!"

Tara's muscles flinched. She wondered if Maebelle had lost her senses, thinking she would allow her to control her, when the whole family knew she was a pussycat with Rufus—no matter what he did to them! She didn't have time for this. "It's books! Books!" she screamed. "You satisfied!" Leaving the Big House in a huff, Tara lifted her right foot and kicked the screen door open, bounding down the steps, and cussing all the way to the barn. She saw the new tools lying on the ground near the barn. She cursed profusely. "What the hell we need with another chain saw. The one we have is in perfect condition?" she complained. "And what the hell we need with more hoes and rakes?" She kicked them with her booted foot. "You could've put these things away your own damn self!"

She opened the barn door and picked up as many tools as she could carry and brought them inside the barn. After she finished storing them away, she lay on the floor, on her back, using her book satchel as a pillow. She drew up her knees and folded her arms across her chest. Before long, she dozed off.

* * *

After inspecting the job that Zeke, Elliott, Adam, and Rudi were doing with the stumps, Rufus stopped by the barn to see how Tara had stored the tools. He felt upset that she left the barn door open. He would scold her. He went inside, and to his surprise, he found Tara asleep, snoring on the floor behind the tall bales of hay. He stood over her admiring her firm, round breasts. He cupped his chin, and looked around. He went back and locked the barn door, before he came back and knelt down beside Tara and lightly unbuttoned her shirt. As he unsnapped her jeans, Tara awoke frightened. Rufus' eyes danced with lust. She bolted upright. "Daddy! What are you doing!" she cried, grabbing his hand. "Daddy, no!" She bent her head and bit his arm as hard as she could.

He began squeezing Tara's neck.

Tara saw the lights go out, slowly. When she came to, she realized she was raped, as she lay naked. A shrill cry from the deepest part of her soul filled the old barn. No one heard her. "You're my father!" she cried, searching for her clothes. "How could you do this to me?" Hot tears streamed down her cheeks, before she spotted her clothes lying in a heap nearby.

She dressed quickly. "I have to leave here," she muttered. She grabbed her book satchel, and ran toward the front of the barn. She flung the barn door open wide, and ran out the barn.

She spotted a fallen tree when she reached the stream. It stretched to the other side of the stream. Despite her inability to swim, she precariously walked carefully on the fallen tree, to the other side of the stream. She saw gray smoke floating above the trees, and ran in that direction. A small house, the color of gray, mist stood secluded behind the trees. After running up the steps of the house, she banged frantically on the door. "Somebody please help me! Help me!" she cried. No one answered, and she fell to her knees in deep despair. Suddenly, the door lock clicked. As she stood on her knees, the door opened, and Hailey Richard poked out her head.

"My, Lord!" she cried, and reached down and hoisted Tara off the floor and helped her inside the house.

She closed the door and locked it. "Who's after you, child?"

"He--He raaaped me!" Tara cried.

"Who? Who raped you?" Hailey's voice was deeply concerned.

"My daddy!" Small ropes stood out on the sides of Tara's neck.

Hailey became horrified, and cupped her mouth. Peering at the redheaded young girl, she believed she knew who she was. She drew her hands away from her mouth and gestured to the ladder-back chair. "Sit down, child. I'm Mrs. Hailey Richards. Lord, have mercy!"

Tara sat down, holding her book satchel on her lap. Her knees kept knocking together, and her feet kept patting the floor.

Hailey sat down regretfully studying her. "I think I know who you are, child. You're one of the Poygoode girls, aren't you? Is your mother named Jennifer?" she inquired.

Tara nodded to both questions because she couldn't get her mouth to work.

Hailey grunted. She threw up her hands. "I knew it! Just as sure as my name is Hailey Richards. I knew this would happen! Stella predicted it."

Tara stared at Hailey in surprise.

Hailey reached inside the pocket of her black, gathered skirt and brought out a white handkerchief. She blotted Tara's face. "Umph! Umph! Such a pretty child as your-self shouldn't be going through stuff like this. It's a damn shame that the community has sat back all these years and let that skunk get away with this kind of mess!"

Hailey calmed down. "Might your name be Tara, or Nora?" she asked.

"I'm Tara." She wondered how this woman knew so much about them.

"Oh, my God!" Hailey cried. The sound of her cry woke Daniel.

"Hailey!" His voice resounded from their bedroom.

Tara jerked like lighting had struck.

Hailey put a comforting hand on Tara's trembling shoulder.

"What's all that racket? Who you done let in this house?"

"It's one of the Poygoode children, Daniel. She's been hurt. You go back to sleep. I'm taking care of her," said Hailey gazing at Tara's troubled face. "Daniel is my husband. He's had two strokes."

"Get her out of here!" he called. "Don't you go gettin' mixed up in them folks mess!" he ordered.

Tara was shocked to learn that both Hailey and her husband were aware of their peril and hadn't lifted a finger to help them, not even now. She looked at Hailey pleadingly.

Hailey touched her on her knee, while yelling at her husband. "Oh, hush, Daniel! You're scaring this child, almost to death." She dismissed him with the wave of her hand. For a moment, Daniel was quiet. But then he started up again.

"You heard me, Hailey! I mean it! You get her out of here!"

Hailey couldn't hear herself think. Daniel was getting on her nerve, as a surge of anger arose inside her. "Shut up you old fool!" she shouted. "This is women's business, stay out of it!" She got to her feet and moved swiftly toward their bedroom. The door was half ajar. With bristled shoulders, she stepped inside the room. "I'm sick of your mouth!" Tara heard her shout. "Where's your heart, old man? I said she's been hurt!" She grasped the doorknob.

Daniel lifted his head off the pillow. "Whatta you doing? Leave that door opened! Don't you dare close that door, Hailey!"

She slammed the door hard and came back into the living room. She sat down and faced Tara, as Daniel carried on, until his voice faded.

"Look at you," Hailey said. "Sweat is pouring off you. Would you like a glass of water?"

"Yes, ma'am."

Hailey got up and went into the kitchen. She took a glass out of the cabinet, opened the icebox and filled the glass with ice water.

Tara opened her book satchel to see if Rufus had gone through her things. She stuck her hand inside the thin paper bag and brought out the pastel compact. With shaky hands, she removed the seal and some of the pills spilled onto the floor. She was down on her knees picking them up when Hailey returned with the glass of water. She saw Tara close her hand quickly.

"Why do you need to take so many?" she inquired. "Get up off your knees, and give me all of those pills," she ordered. "You won't kill yourself in my house. I know that's what you're planning on doing."

Slowly, Tara got to her feet. Her face was drenched with tears. Like a flash of lighting, she brought her hand to her mouth.

Hailey moved swiftly and slapped Tara's hand. The pills flew every which way.

"No!" Tara screamed, shaking frantically. "I don't want to live any more." She started to bend down to retrieve the pills, but Hailey grasped her arm.

"Hailey?" Daniel called. "You still got that girl here?" Hailey ignored her foolish husband.

She set down the glass on the coffee table, and reached out cupping Tara's face between her hands. She intensely focused on Tara. "Yes! Yes, you do want to live! You must live! God has an assignment for you. At least your mother Jennifer thinks so. And she thinks she knows what it is—God knows I hope she's right. Don't let her down." She paused thoughtfully. "You're not thinking straight right now." Hailey reached for the glass and gave it to Tara. "Here. Drink some water; cool yourself off. Don't give that 'ol Devil any more power over you. Don't let him make you take your life, child."

Tara looked pitifully at Hailey. She took the glass. Hailey placed her hand around Tara's to help steady the glass. Tara gulped down the cold refreshing water, as she looked over the rim of the glass, at Hailey. Hailey let her hold the glass on her own. Hailey knelt down, picking up the rest of the pills. She stared quizzically at the pills, until she realized what they were. She looked at Tara in suspense by the time she stood up.

"How long have you been taking birth control pills?"

Tara set down the empty glass on the oak coffee table. "They're heart pills," she replied.

"Listen, child, I'm looking dead at them. I know birth control pills when I see them. I get them for my patients. I'm a midwife. I helped bring you into this . . . Well, I would've, had it not been for that low-down dirty dog taking over my job."

Tara looked startled.

"That's right," Hailey said, slipping the pills inside her skirt pocket. She walked over to Tara and began picking pieces of broken straw out of her soft, long, red braids. "I guess he took my place because he hasn't sent for me in over thirteen years," Hailey said, without further explanation. She sat down, folding her hands on her lap. "Sit down, child," she told Tara.

Tara sat down slowly, not taking her eyes off Hailey's face.

"That low-down dirty dog," Hailey remarked. "Got you thinking you got heart trouble. Did he take you to see a doctor before he started giving you these so-called heart pills?"

"No, ma'am. He started off giving them to Mama, to give to me. He told her you said I should take them when I turned eleven because I was born with a heart condition. But I didn't know you were the midwife that he and Mama were talking about."

Hailey's mouth fell open, and she wiggled her head. She glared at Tara. "Well, he's a liar! I told him no such lie! I never saw you since the day I helped deliver you. Midwives don't practice medicine." She jumped to her feet, resting her hands on her hips.

Tara looked up at her and asked, "What's birth control pills, Mrs. Hailey?

Hailey jerked around. She glared down at Tara.

"What? You mean to tell me... Lord!" Hailey flustered. "They're something to keep women from having babies, honey! I guess he's got a different plan for you, than he had for your aunts. Now I hope you've been taking these things daily." Tara swallowed hard, panicking. No. She hadn't taken them daily, or otherwise.

"No ma'am. I haven't been taking them. They made me feel ill."

Hailey's eyes widen in hysteria. "You haven't!"

"No ma'am."

Hailey sighed deeply. "Oh, what a tangled web that 'ol fool has woven for himself. Well, this one might very well back fire on you, you 'ol Devil." She looked at Tara, hoping wholeheartedly that Tara hadn't conceived. She wondered why he made Tara take the pills. Outwardly, there was rock silence. But inwardly, both of them were in turmoil.

"Well, I don't know if this is good advice I'm fixing to give to you, seeing he done already put his seed in you. But I have a good mind to tell you to start back to taking those pills. And take them religiously. She reached inside her pocket. "Here. Let me give these back to you. But, of course, if you're already pregnant, you'll harm the baby, you may even lose it, taking those pills," she warned. Inwardly, she hoped Tara would loose the baby. "Only you can decide what's best for you."

"I don't need them. I have a fresh pack he gave me today," she told Hailey.

Hailey groaned. She looked beyond Tara, staring vacantly.

Tara felt trapped. She wanted to lose the baby. She would take the pills religiously. And she wouldn't blame Hailey if anything went wrong.

She didn't want to go back home, though.

"Can I ask something of you, Mrs. Hailey?"

Hailey focused on her intently. "What is it, child?"

"May I please stay with you and Mr. Richards? I won't be any trouble. I promise."

Hailey felt like crying. Her heart went out to Tara, but she knew Daniel would never agree to let her stay. "I'm so sorry, baby. You heard my husband. He doesn't want any trouble. We're two old people living our days. I told you my husband done had two strokes.

"Besides, we're no match for your daddy. He's got too much money and too many Negroes in his pocket. Even got that old stupid fool, one-foot-in the grave-one foot out-of the grave, preacher in his pocket. That's Reverend Kincaid I'm talking about. Of course, you probably never heard of him, so I don't know why I bothered to mention him to you." He must be close to ninety, she thought. "He'll split hell wide open, when he hits inside it." She questioned Tara.

"Let me ask you something, child. Did he ever let you children go to school? I know Jennifer wanted that more than anything. She put her whole future in your hands, from the moment I handed you over to her. She said, with such conviction, that some day you would set them all free. I thought she was making believe, when she said it, but I guess her faith has kept her going."

Tara appeared puzzled. "You know a lot about us, don't you?"

Hailey nodded. "More than I care to. And you've come over here to show me more, without planning to." Her voice sounded troubled. "But I didn't know if he'd let you all go to school, or not. You see I'm retired from my profession. I don't get to hear the latest news since my best girl friend, Stella, passed away. She used to bring me all the news."

"You asked me if Daddy let us go to school. The answer is yes."

Hailey clasped her hands in front of her. "Thank God! I guess Jennifer must have been sending up a whole lot of prayers. What grade are you in?"

"Twelfth," Tara replied. She saw Hailey's brows raised in sheer joy. "The teachers tested me at school. They told me I'm a genius. So is my sister Nora. We were skipped a lot of grades." There was silence. Hailey was thinking.

"Well, seems to me two geniuses ought to be able to figure out a way to get themselves out of that 'ol Devil's grasp. You don't have to go back there, you know. Seems to me you already have enough education to get along out there in the world. Steal some of your Daddy's money. He's got plenty of it. Steal it child, and leave from round here! Take Nora with you. God will forgive for stealing because it's for a good cause." Tara stared steadily at the floor. "What's the matter?" Hailey asked.

Tara lifted her head, and turned towards Hailey. "You don't understand. We can't leave the rest of the family behind. They're all Nora and I have," she cried, wiping her tears off her cheek with her shirt.

"Besides," she said, " We wouldn't know where to go, or how to get there. We've never even been to town, except to pass through on the school bus." She paused. "I do plan to leave, but not before I get my driver's license and my high school diploma. They're teaching drivers education at school this fall. Nora and I are getting our drivers' license. My girlfriend promised to sign Mommy's name on the consent slips for us. We all know it's not right, but we have no choice."

Hailey looked happy. "Don't worry about the rights and wrongs of it. It's necessary; thank God you have such a friend. You young people just keep putting your heads together. Things will work out." Still, Hailey sighed heavily like someone carrying a heavy load. She stood, watching Tara, dreading the decision she was forced to make. "Well, let me get you home before he finds out you're gone."

Tara swallowed hard. Her insides shivered. She couldn't believe Hailey would return her back into the arms of her tormentor. "But I can't go back there!" she cried, with her tears flowing again.

Hailey put a hand on Tara's shoulder. "Oh, baby. I know you don't want to go back, honey. I don't want to take you back, but I can't keep you here. Besides, he'll only find you. Then we'll all be in trouble. I must take you back. Now c'mon." She grabbed her keys off the coffee table. "Get your book satchel and lets' get you back home."

* * *

Hailey opened the door. Tara walked out ahead of her. They descended the steps together, and walked along side each other toward the car. "Where do you think he is now?" Hailey asked. Tara could tell by the sound of Hailey's voice that she was taking a grave risk having her in the car with her.

Tara looked up at the sunset. Then she looked at her shadow. "He's probably picking up everybody from the field and bringing them home."

Tara rounded the hood of the car to the passenger side. She felt afraid. If only she knew someplace else to go. Hailey and Daniel had let her down.

Hailey squeezed the handle, opened the door, and got into her car. She closed the door.

Tara opened the door, then stood there panic stricken. Having no place to go, or hide, feelings of betrayal crept over her. Wagging her head, reluctantly, she got into the car.

With tears in her own eyes, Hailey told her, "Well, let's pray I get you there before he brings the others home from the field." She started the engine and drove in the direction where Tara lived.

A dangerous melee in the field prevented Rufus from getting home at his usual time. Jinni, Yvette, and Yvonne argued heatedly ever since they returned from lunch. Jennifer had done her best to separate the girls from their mother, but Jinni wouldn't allow it. Yvette and Yvonne were Jinni's twin daughters, whose swollen bellies had begun to show. Jinni, in a warped frame of mind, had accused them of seducing Rufus, whom she continued to refer to as Philip Coon.

Five minutes before quitting time, the sudden violent clashing of hard metal drew Jennifer's attention. She turned around. "Oh, my God!" She called her daughters Nora and Mattie. "Come and help me! They're going to kill each other." The girls reacted spontaneously, dropping their hoes, as they ran along side Jennifer. They saw Yvonne and Yvette fiercely fighting. Jinni was crazy, with the strength of an elephant.

"Help us!" Yvonne cried out. Jinni, Yevette, and Yvonne were all recklessly waving their hoes in a tangled mass. The silver, sharp blades glistened in the evening sunlight. Jinni's eyes blazed. "I'll kill both of y'all. Philip is mine! Y'all got no business opening your legs to him."

Nora squinted upward and studied the tangled mass of sharp metal. Her heart beat rapidly, as she tackled Jinni from behind, toppling her to the ground. Jinni flew forward, losing her grip on her hoe, as it landed nearby with the blade pointed up. Jennifer picked up the hoe before Jinni regained her balance. Yvonne and Yvette lowered their hoes to the ground, and stood back trembling, glad to be alive.

* * *

Amidst the chaos, Nora heard a loud motor roaring toward them. She looked back and saw the pickup heading towards them. "It's Daddy!" she cried. "Oh my God!" She couldn't imagine what he would do to them, seeing they had stopped working and gathered into a crowd. He would think that they were conspiring against him, she thought.

Rufus reached them. Slamming on the brakes, he brought the truck to a screeching stop. He threw the gear in park and left the motor idle. He opened the door and jumped out. "What the hell...!" He pushed through the crowd, stunned when he saw Jennifer and Mattie sitting on top of Jinni, trying to hold her down. But when Jinni saw Rufus, her strength increased. She managed to free herself. She grabbed her hoe and rushed forward with it, swinging it wildly at Rufus.

He staggered backward; quite aware she had narrowly missed his flat stomach. He swore.

"What!" Jinni cried. "My stuff isn't good enough any more! Huh?"

He held up his opened palms and started pleading. "Now listen to me, Jinni. Please. Put down that hoe. This--this is your daddy talking to you. Nobody will hurt you."

Nora rolled her eyes toward the sky. Dirty dog! Suddenly you're her daddy, she thought.

Rufus turned slightly, looking at Jennifer. He gestured to her to come to him. "Talk to her. Tell her it's her daddy talking to her. Well, go ahead! Don't just stand there looking at me like a damn fool," he demanded, breathing harshly.

Jennifer looked at him, as she swallowed. Not trying to disrespect him, she, however, could not utter a word.

"Go on, girl, and tell her what I just told you! Don't just stand there like a damn fool!" he shouted vehemently.

Why is he trying to get Mama to save his stinking hide, Nora thought, detecting Jennifer's fear? Every angle of Jinni's stance implied death. Determined to stop her mother from sacrificing herself, Nora pushed her aside. "Why don't you shoot her, Daddy?" Nora suggested, unaware of what she just said.

Jennifer fastened her eyes on Nora. What is wrong with you? she thought

"You got the gun, don't you?" Nora said, challenging her father. "You can always say she was crazy, and you were only trying to defend yourself."

Jennifer's blood dropped to zero.

Everybody became startled and terrified.

Looking at Nora, he chuckled. He sounded nervous. "You--you don't know what--what you're saying, Nora. You--you get back now before she cut you with that hoe."

"I'd rather be dead than end up like Yvonne and Yvette!" Nora cried. "I know I'll probably be next. So she can kill me now if she wants to because sooner or later she'll have to kill every girl in this field and back at the house, too. All because of you, Daddy! You know what you do to us is wrong!" Poor Nora had momentarily lost her senses, as she folded her arms across her chest and stood there. Rufus said nothing, as he stood ashen-faced.

Nora continued. "But I tell you one thing, I'm already as good as dead—because if you rape me, so help me God, I'll kill you, Daddy! I mean it!" She broke down crying.

Rufus swallowed hard. What he'd done to Tara flashed through his mind. He looked at Nora and staggered backward, flashing a quick, nervous glance around him. Every one's eyes fell upon him. He suddenly felt enraged. Nobody had ever challenged him and got away with it. He'd get Nora, in time.

Poor Jinni felt insanely confused, as she clawed Nora out of her way with her free hand. "Move! I'm gon kill you, Philip!" She swung her hoe wildly.

He barely jumped out of her way.

"Oh, God!" Jennifer cried, biting her nails. She felt sure someone would die today, and it wouldn't be Rufus. His face was taut and fierce, as death wishes beamed in his eyes.

Quickly, she crooked her finger and beckoned to Jinni's sons, Troy and Roger. They rushed over to her. She whispered in their ears. The boys nodded, then forced themselves from the group. Returning, they came up behind Jinni. Roger bear-hugged her, as Troy wrestled the hoe from her.

Jinni slumped in Roger's arms, and let out a wild, strangled cry.

Just when they thought the crisis was over, Rufus whipped out his gun. Vulgarity spilled off his fiery tongue. His eyes were filled with red, live coals of fire. "If any of you all think you'll walk away from here with any bright ideas, drop them now, dammit!" He fired the gun into the ground.

Everybody screamed, except Nora infused with a death wish. Like the rock of Gibraltar, she stared outrageously at Rufus. He knew she wanted a challenge. She didn't mind if he killed her, because if she ended up like Yvonne and Yvette, she'd rather be dead. She was tired of being afraid; and tired of being driven like a slave. She felt ready to die.

Rufus held his eyes in hers. She didn't blink. Having felt a sudden premonition, he averted his eyes. He knew Nora and he shared the same mean blood. He could see that now. He realized he had two dangerous crises: Jinni and Nora. Nora had a death wish, or wished him dead. And Jinni was crazy. He had to leave Jinni alone. He had a gut feeling Jinni might kill Yvonne and Yvette, if he didn't remove them from her house.

He looked for Jennifer in the crowd.

"Jennifer?"

"Yes, sir?"

"Come over here."

Jennifer swallowed hard. What now? she thought. With her knees knocking together, she approached him.

"From now on, Yvonne and Yvette will live with you. If you don't have enough room, let Mattie and Hattie stay with Jinni. I don't think she'll hurt them."

Jennifer was aghast, as she opened her mouth to speak, until Rufus put up a refraining hand. "I'm not done. Yvonne and Yvette should not be near their momma. When you all are in the field, I want at least fifteen rows between them and their momma. You understand me?"

Jennifer swallowed hard. "Yes, sir."

She turned and saw her daughters Hattie and Mattie looking with disgust. Why are you continuing to break up my family, Jennifer thought. First, it was Tara——now, its Hattie and Mattie. She hated him with all her soul.

Rufus turned to Troy and Roger and told them to put Jinni on the truck and to keep an eye on her.

"The rest of y'all go get on the truck," he ordered. "And whoever can't fit, walk. I'll come back for you later."

* * *

An eerie feeling came over Hailey, as she drove fast to get Tara home before Rufus arrived. It was like she just heard Rufus say he had to get home. She started to wish she hadn't taken the long way around, but she was avoiding being seen by as many people as possible. Glancing down at Tara sitting on the floor, she drove faster.

Tara looked up at her.

"Child, I wish with all my heart I could do more for you," Hailey told her. "But it takes more than just myself to get you out of this mess. If I tried to do this alone, I'd start a bigger mess."

"I'm so scared, Mrs. Hailey."

"I know, child. But I can't keep you. I have to give you credit, though. You're the first one of them to ever run away. The others just stayed and took whatever he did to 'em."

Tara looked down. Hailey's remarks didn't make her feel any better. Yes, she ran away, but what good had it done? She couldn't believe Hailey was returning her to the arms of her vile father. She felt betrayed. Wishing to God she knew where Trudi lived. I know Trudi would help me, she thought. But wishing was getting her nowhere. Her luck now lay in getting back home without her father's knowledge. There was stony silence. She wished she were dead, and that she had taken the pills before Hailey had had a chance to see her.

Just then she remembered the tiny graves under a willow tree. She wondered if Hailey knew about them since she knew so much about her family. She willed the courage to ask.

"Mrs. Hailey?"

Hailey glanced down at her. "What is it, child?"

"I came across three tiny graves under a willow tree, down by the stream, on our farm."

Hailey flinched. She didn't take her eyes off the road. A long moment occurred before she responded. She had a feeling about those graves, at least two of them. She believed both Maebelle and Jennifer's sons were in those graves. But she had no clue about the third one. She glanced down out the corner of her eyes at Tara, then looking at her. "Are you asking me or telling me?" she said. "Because if you're asking me, I can't answer you. All I do is deliver babies. I don't bury 'em." Tara didn't comment. She felt the car slow down. "We're almost there. And guess what? I don't see your father's truck anywhere," Hailey said, trying to comfort her.

Panic welled up inside Tara's head. She felt hopeless. "Mrs. Hailey, I thank you for keeping it a secret that I ran away. But I have to say what's in my heart. I know what you've told me about not being able to keep me. But I can't believe you're returning me to Daddy. You know what he's done to me; and in my heart, I feel you haven't really tried to help me."

Hailey touched her forehead. She felt bad about taking Tara back there. What else could she do? It never occurred to her to go to the town's police department.

"Tara, honey. I'm an old woman. My husband is old, and bed-ridden. You have to understand!" Suddenly, she saw Maebelle sweeping the front porch. Damned fool, she thought to herself.

She changed the subject.

"I'll drop you off in back of the house, if that's all right with you? Your grandma is sweeping the porch. I don't think you want her to see you, do you?"

Tara looked up wide-eyed and scared. "No, ma'am!" she replied. She started shaking. That was all she needed—to be seen by Maebelle. My nightmare will get worst, she mused.

"I didn't think so," said Hailey. "We'll get pass the house, and I'll pull over on the shoulder of the road. Be prepared to get out. Hide inside the bushes once you get out. I'll make my U-turn and drive back by the house. If she has left off the porch, I'll toot my horn, meaning it's safe for you to come out of the bushes. Just be careful, though, because she could be out back. Okay?"

Tara clutched the book satchel to her chest. "Yes, ma'am," she replied, with her voice trembling. She couldn't stop crying.

Hailey pulled over to the shoulder. "Get ready to open the door. And remember what I told you about getting yourself out of this mess."

Tara nodded. "Thank you, Mrs. Hailey, for driving me.... I probably would've drowned if I had had to cross the stream again. I'm afraid of water; I can't swim."

Too many things were evolving in Hailey's head to reply. She rolled the car close to the edge of the road at a very slow speed.

Tara got off her knees and sat on the seat. She opened the door, positioning to leave the car.

Hailey stopped the car and flashed a quick glanced in the rear view mirror. She looked at Tara misty-eyed. "Make haste, child," she said nervously.

Tara got out of the car and disappeared into the bushes.

Hailey reached across the seat and closed the door, all the while watching Tara crouched low inside the bushes, waiting for her to give the signal. Tara heard the gravel crunching under the wheels. She could tell by the sound of the gravel that Hailey had completed her U-turn, but Hailey didn't toot the horn. Maebelle had sat down on the porch swing.

Tara anxiously waited inside the bushes, waiting for the sound of the horn. Not hearing it, she assumed Maebelle was still on the front porch. Remembering that Hailey had warned her to be careful, she emerged from the bushes with great care, and crossed to the other side of the road. She ran half bent alongside the cotton field. When she considered it safe, she straightened, looking for Maebelle. She didn't see her, and quickly dashed up the back steps and entered the house. She tiptoed fast, through the kitchen, into the dinning-room, and finally upstairs to her bedroom, closing the door behind her.

She felt sore and dirty between her legs. She went to the wardrobe; took her robe and went back downstairs to the bathroom. She locked the bathroom door. She turned on the spigots, and combed out her two long braids. She took the soap and tossed it into the tub. She took a towel and washcloth off the brown wicker table and threw it into the tub. She dropped the towel on the floor nearby. She disrobed.

Tara's soul ached at the sight of blood in her panties. Tears flowed, knowing her wicked father had invaded her. She stepped inside the tub, bathed and washed her hair.

Picking up the towels, she dried her hair; then dried her body. After she dressed and collected her belongings, she sneaked upstairs to her bedroom. In bed crying profusely, she began to sober, thinking about what to do, which was nothing, for now. She vowed that after her high school graduation, she would win. She didn't know exactly how, but she had plenty of time to plan. She imagined shielding her soul, knowing this was only the beginning of her ordeal. For now, he held the power, but in the end she would pay him back for what he'd done to her.

Chapter 7

When the long, hot, tragic summer of 1965 began to fad into autumn, Lord knows the Poygoode children couldn't have been happier. School would commence shortly, and God knows the twenty-three, Poygoode clan looked forward to an easing of those around-the-clock, daunting tasks, that made their lives bitter. With each passing school year, their desires grew stronger for a better life. They all hoped their education would finally free them from the jaws of Rufus Poygoode, their ruthless, monstrous father.

On the other hand, Rufus felt resentful. On Sunday, one day before school started, Rufus stood at the top of the front porch steps, with his hands in his pockets, staring at the abundant, fluffy white cotton spilling out of their red crowns. The gilded sun hung low on the Western horizon. "Damn that Board of Ed. Damn 'em for interfering in my life! Again I to have pay good money to get this shit harvested. He drew his hands from his pockets. He sat down on a chair, tilting the back against the wall, and began reminiscing about wild things that had happened this summer.

His thin lips curled into a crooked, sadistic smile. He had slaughtered Nora's white rabbits: Tibby, Libby, and Bibby, to teach her a lesson after the stunt she pulled in the field the day Jinni lost her senses, threatening to kill him. Because of his indiscretions, Nora claimed she wanted to die. He decided to show Nora that day the ugly reality of death, as he watched her at a measured distance, minutes later, sitting on her haunches weeping frantically because her rabbits' throats were slashed.

He grinned briefly. Unfortunately, killing Nora's rabbits failed to tame Nora's ill temper. He still considered her meaner than a bulldog. He wanted her, but knew if he took advantage of her it wouldn't be without consequences. He got up from the porch chair, stretched his arms above his head. His eyes moistened. He left the porch and climbed inside his pickup, and drove off to make his final round of the farm for that evening. Tara and Nora weighed on his mind. They were like two peas in a pod. But he didn't think Tara told Nora what he kept doing to her.

It was past mid-night when Tara returned from Rufus' bedroom. She thanked God that Adie was always asleep when she left the bed they shared, and when she returned. Although she'd tried building armor around her little heart, her soul wept whenever he touched her. "Why, God, is he doing this to me?" She'd asked God that question a thousand times, since Rufus started raping her. There was never an answer. She turned on the lamp and quietly plumped up her pillows. She took her pen and notebook off the bedside table, and climbed upon the bed quietly. She rested the notebook against her bent knees; and with the stroke of the pen, poured out her heart to God in a long, poignant poem. Tears blurred the blue lines and smeared the ink, but she kept on writing.

I vow that I shall never see another summer liken to thee.

Oh hellish summer...
O lonely summer...
Oh, God. Why me!

It started a long time ago, God.
My daddy raped Big Momma of her children.
Wouldn't let her be a mother.
He raped Jackie right in her presence!

In Her Presence: A Husband's Dirty Secret

*Then, started hiding in the shadows, preying on the
others.*

This summer . . ..
Oh, God, he started raping me!
My soul tries to flee his stinking touch!
My heart hurts so much.

I vow that I shall never see another summer liken to thee.
O hellish summer...
O lonely summer...
Oh, God, why me!

He takes the babies from between our feet.
He cares not that we lie there and weep.

I vow that I shall never see another summer liken to thee.
O hellish summer...
O lonely summer...
Oh, God, why me!

I thought I'd die when I saw him in the barn
Towering awkwardly behind my brother.
I suspect he's doing the same to the others.
He made him bend over a bale of hay.
Made him say things he didn't want to say.

I vow that I shall never see another summer liken to thee.
O hellish summer...
O lonely summer...
Oh, God, why me!

What I'm thinking causes me dread.
I'm telling you the truth, Lord.
With all my heart, I want him dead!

*I vow that I shall never see another hellish summer liken
to thee.*

239

O hellish summer...
O lonely summer...
Oh, God, why me!

Tara stared at what she'd written, and wiped tears from her eyes with the heel of her hand. She gazed down at Adie, wagging her head in sorrow. At least, for now, he'd left poor Adie alone. Imagining what Adie had endured from the men who had violated her was too shameful. Pushing those images out of her mind, Tara noticed the clock on the bedside table indicated that she had a few hours to sleep. Placing the pen inside the notebook, she closed it, and placed it on the bedside table. She shut off the light. Rearranging her pillows, she slid down between the sheets and cried herself to sleep.

* * *

In the morning, the sun streaming through the window woke Tara. She rolled over, pushed in the alarm button, and spilled out of bed. She looked back at Adie, sleeping peacefully. That made her happy for Adie. Inside the bathroom, she got excited about the first day of school that always felt like a long awaited gift. For the first time in months, she was thrilled. School was her life, just as Dion had been. Oh, how she missed him. She looked forward to the letters he'd promised to write her. She could hardly wait to see Trudi, to pickup Dion's letters. After Tara washed, dressed, and combed her hair, she walked over to Adie's side of the bed. "Adie, wake up. It's time to get up," she said, shaking Adie's right shoulder.

Adie awakened wide-eyed. "Oh, my God! I'm late for school," Adie declared.

"You're not late, silly," said Tara. "I just got up early that's all. Tara stood back and spread her arms. "So how do I look?" she asked.

"Good," Adie replied, without as much as a glance. She threw back the covers and got out of bed. She jerked the stocking cap off her head and threw it on the foot of the bed. It left a ring around her forehead that made her look funny.

Tara looked at her and smiled. She knew Adie was too excited about going back to school to pay her any mind. She had grown to like Adie. When she first came to the Big House, she felt angry because she and Adie had to share the same bedroom. Of course, it was Adie's room, and she had the right to be there. But still, she had felt angry just the same. But now Adie was like a little sister who needed a big sister to keep her secrets. Tara felt glad Maebelle didn't scold Adie for having told her that Rufus had sold her small body like a piece of meat. The aroma from the coffee pot perking on the stove made its way up the stairs.

"Hmm! That coffee sure smells good," Tara remarked. Her voice sounded happy.

"And you can't have none 'cause you ain't grown," Adie told her.

"Shut up peep squeak. Nobody asked your opinion. I'm going downstairs for breakfast."

"Me, too," said Adie, forcing the last button through the buttonhole on her white blouse.

"But you're not washed."

"So? I'm clean. I bathed last night, and I brushed my teeth too. So there!" She stuck out her tongue.

"You better keep that tongue in your mouth before you lose it." Tara smiled when she said that; she then wagged her head good-naturedly.

* * *

Maebelle was at the window, holding a cup of coffee in her hands. She set down the cup in the saucer and turned sideways looking at the two girls. Tara felt surprised when Maebelle commented on how nice she looked. That was the kindest thing Maebelle had said to her during her entire lifetime. Tara spent the whole summer avoiding her, especially after their big showdown over her book satchel, which she still carried despite Maebelle's stern objections. Tara still didn't like her, and that comment meant nothing to her. Nevertheless, she managed to drag out a dry, "Thank you."

"Good morning, Adie," said Maebelle. "You look nice, too."

Adie glanced at her out the corner of her eyes. "Morning. Thanks." Adie had decided that she no longer liked Maebelle, because she knew Maebelle didn't like Tara. Adie admired Tara, and also loved her for her kindness, and because she could confide in her.

Maebelle glared at the sand in Adie's eyes, and said nothing. "I didn't set the table," she told them. "Besides, you all have to fix your own plates," she said, as she resumed staring out the window.

After they fixed their plates, they moved quickly inside the dining room, to escape Maebelle, even though she'd been too busy staring out the window, until she turned around and dragged a chair away from the table, over to the window. She sat down and began gazing at Lynn's house. Her heart ached for her boys. She wished she hadn't given away her boys to Jake, her former husband, because she knew Jake Junior would have protected his sisters.

In her anguish, she visualized Lynn and Rufus in bed together. She groaned loudly, and slapped her thigh with a hard flat opened palm. Her tears swelled because she wanted her husband, but for the past two years he ignored her in bed, forcing himself on her daughters.

She recalled how things used to be when she and
Rufus were first together. He used to bring her to insane
ecstasies. "Now, he never touches me," she sighed, with
rage for her daughters. "They've taken over my husband,"
she complained half aloud. "I'm not that old; I'm only
forty-two. Next thing you know Lynn'll be knocked up
again, and I'll have to help him deliver her baby. She
examined her fingernails, thinking how often they were
stained with the blood of her children, giving birth to....
"Why did this happen to me, Lord? What did I ever do to
deserve this?"

She suddenly recalled her dream from way back,
when she and Rufus were dating, right after he'd asked
her to move in with him. (She was still waiting for him to
legalize their marriage.) The dream had been surreal.
She had had three sets of twins in the same year. A silent
argument began in her mind. I don't care what has
happened. I won't believe some silly old dream. It's just a
coincidence we've all had twins. It's that old woman! I
know she did this to me! Maybe she and Charlotte did
this to me! Charlotte must've gotten a hold of my hair
while we were fighting, and gave it to the old woman. She
was willing to bet her life that was what happened,
because that was the only way the old woman could have
cursed her!

Tara and Adie hurriedly devoured their hot grits,
bacon, and eggs, and minutes later placed their dishes in
the sink.

"I'm leaving," Tara shouted from the dinning
room.

Maebelle snapped back into the present. Tara saw
her, out the corner of her eyes, peering at the clock on the
wall, and look at her. Before she opened her mouth to
speak, Tara cut her off.

"I know! The bus won't come for another half-hour.
I don't care; I'm not hanging around in this awful house!"
She saw Maebelle's angry gaze shift from her, onto Adie,
and back to her.

Tara left the kitchen in a huff, with Adie following on her heels. "You make me sick!" Tara mumbled under her breath. "You're always trying to take a stern hand with us, when you won't un-part your cotton-picking lips to Daddy about what he's doing. You're nobody to me."

Maebelle shuddered with anger. "And you're another one," Maebelle muttered. "I watch you sneaking into Rufus's room. You're not fooling anybody." She blamed Jennifer for Tara's sassiness.

Unlike her aunts, Tara never confided in Maebelle, or in Jennifer. Even the boys never told what Rufus did to them. They all figured it didn't matter to Maebelle.

Tara went down the front steps, staring down at the shiny pennies in the slit of her brown leather loafers. The sunshine and the birds' chirping brought life to the early morning. She strode toward the bus stop, and unfortunately as she glanced over her shoulder, she saw Rufus' pickup parked in Lynn's back yard. Anger overcame her, as she turned her head quickly and ran as fast as she could. When she slowed down to walk, she thought about Maebelle standing in front of the window. "I figured that was the reason you kept staring out that damn window," she muttered. "All you do is sit back and spy, but don't do shit!" She walked with her head down.

Tara wondered if Maebelle ever saw her leave and enter Rufus' room, late at night. She always tried to be careful. She felt ill just thinking about the way her daddy put his penis inside all of them. She felt so helpless--so angry with Maebelle. "How can you sit idly by knowing he's humping us, and later help him deliver the babies!" She could barely breathe. She decided to push Rufus and Maebelle from her mind before she lost her sanity. "Oh God," she muttered, looking up at the sky. She forced back her tears. "I'm so lucky to be on the pills. I know why he put me on them—thank God."

A familiar voice snapped her to the present. "Wait up!" Nora called. "Wait for us!"

Tara turned around and looked. To her horror, she saw Yvonne and Yvette waddling along beside Nora, like two over-stuffed ducks. "Ah! Come on now! Just where do they think they're going! They can't be letting people see them!"

The three girls caught up to Tara.

"Oh, straighten your face!" Nora snapped. "Ain't nothing wrong with them walking with us to the bus stop. I already told them they have to leave the minute we see the school bus coming. And they've agreed." Tara peered at Nora.

"You don't mind, do you?" Yvonne asked, ignoring Tara's expression, and how Nora had rebuked her.

Tara peered at Yvonne, for a long moment. Her answer was restrained in spite of Nora's scolding. Nora looked at her in a certain way. Tara knew what that look had meant. But, for the grace of God there go I, she thought. Only she and Nora knew about her miscarriage. It was all Nora knew. She never told her she had run away and had been returned to the arms of her tormentor by a woman who knew all about them, and had delivered her and Nora. She withheld from Nora that she learned the so-called heart medicine was really birth control pills; and she takes them daily to avoid pregnancy. And Nora never learned about the money she'd found under Rufus' bed; or her plans to run away. She had reasons for keeping all these things a secret....

It was Rudi who had caused Tara to miscarry. He'd aggravated her ever since she arrived at the Big House. It was inevitable they'd fight. One hot day, toward the end of summer, they finally tore into each other like two mad dogs, outside the house. He'd caught her off guard when he slammed a hard, tight, angry fist into the pit of her stomach. She folded like an accordion, hurting like hell.

Seconds later, she had felt hot blood running down her pants legs. Although it had hurt like hell, she was glad she'd lost the baby; but she dreaded she gave that rotund, fat fart the impression he could beat her, though she still felt he couldn't, and that he'd caught her off guard. It pleased her that Nora had jumped in and picked up where she was forced to stop. Rudi had limped away looking like he'd been in a series of catfights, and the cat had won every round. After that, he left her alone.

Nora was losing her patience, while Tara stood reminiscing. "Tara!" she snapped.

Tara blinked. She looked at Nora, then at Yvonne. "I don't mind," she said. "But for the grace of God, I guess I could be walking in you all's shoes."

Nora nodded, approvingly. Then the four girls entwined their arms and walked on toward the bus stop.

Suddenly, the screen door flew back on its hinges so hard it brought the girls' heads around. Their arms dropped loosely beside them.

"Wait for me!" Adie yelled."

Tara laughed. "Boy! Look at Adie running," she said. "The girl is running like a caged animal set free."

"No. It's more like she's running for her life," Nora remarked.

"She is, in a way!" said Yvette. "School is our life outside of here. It's the only time we get to meet and talk to other people. But Daddy took that away from me and Yvonne." Her voice cracked, as she became misty-eyed, gazing at the ground, wondering why Rufus chose her and Yvonne over Nora and Tara. She thought that maybe he felt Tara was too pretty, and Nora too mean, and he feared her. She willed herself not to cry.

When Adie caught up with them, she wrapped her thin arms around Tara's small waist, and stared up in her face laughing. "Thanks y'all for waiting for me."

"You're welcome, but don't knock me over," Tara said pleasantly.

"I wasn't trying to knock you over," Adie replied.

The five girls walked the rest of the way in silence, seemingly listening to the gravel crunch beneath the sole of their shoes.

Pretty soon the whole troop of eager-faced, school-aged Poygoode children were anxiously waiting for the bus to show up that arrived shortly.

Tara and Nora hugged Yvonne and Yvette and said good-bye. "Some day—hopefully," Tara whispered to them, "you all will get back into school, if y'all want to. Mark my words!"

Yvonne and Yvette exchanged skeptical glances, before looking at Tara. Although they nodded their heads, they wondered how she would make that happen. Would she kill Rufus, since he'd told them they weren't ever going back to school? Yvonne and Yvette said good-bye, as they glanced over their shoulders, and waddled back home.

* * *

Forty minutes later, the bus arrived at the school. The driver pulled into the parking zone, and stopped the bus. He opened the door. Tara and Nora were the first two to step off the bus. Trudi waited anxiously on the curb when the door opened.

They ran to Trudi.

"Trudi!" they chorused. "Hi, girl! It's so good to see you!" Tara said.

"It's good to see you all, too!" The three girls embraced.

"Oooh, Trudi!" Tara marveled. "I can't get over how pretty you look in red. That's a pretty dress! Right Nora?"

"Yes, it is," Nora, agreed.

"And I see you all finally decided to dress like twins, huh?" said Trudi.

Tara and Nora both wore a short sleeve hunter, green blouse and a black pleated flannel skirt.

"Well, not really," Nora replied, winking at Tara. "We weren't together when we made our orders. It's a long story," she said, waving a hand. "Anyway, when we found out we had ordered the same outfits, we looked at each other—shrugged our shoulders and said, "why not?"

Nora changed the subject.

"Have you seen Rhoda?" She stood on her tiptoe, looking around. "You'd think she'd be waiting for me the way you are for Tara. Some friend she is!"

"Well, yeah. I saw her," Trudi replied. "She was with the town-girls." Trudi slightly bent her index and middle fingers on either hand. "They were bragging about how much fun they had in Chicaaago! You'd think there were no other cities in the whole United States for these Mississippi Negroes to visit. And, of course, this little country bunny went with her Mama and Daddy to Boston." She wrinkled her nose distastefully. "Well, it wasn't a real vacation. Daddy had to attend the Baptist convention."

* * *

Tarrence Dowel walked up behind them, holding a white envelope. "Hi," he said, coyly. "Which one of y'all is Tara?"

The three girls turned around, facing him suspiciously.

"Dion described one of y'all," he said. "But I still can't tell who is who because y'all both look alike to me. I just want to make sure I give his letter to the right person. Oh, and by the way, I'm Tarrence Dowel, Dion's cousin."

Tara's eyes lit up. She felt her heart fluttering like an excited bird just learning to fly.

"She's Tara," Nora said, pointing. "And I'm Nora."

Tarrence turned in Tara's direction. He looked at her with delightful admiration. "Hi, Tara."

"Hi." All the while she kept her eyes on the envelope.

"Dion told me to give this to you." He handed her the envelope.

She took it and clutched it to her breast. "Thank you. Thank you so very much."

"You're welcome," he replied, smiling. Then he backed away. "Well, I have to find my friends now. I'm a freshman. We'll probably run into one another sometimes. Bye."

"Bye. And thanks!" Tara called, beaming with joy. "Oh, God. I'm so happy!" she exclaimed to Nora and Trudi. But I wonder why he didn't send it to your address, like we agreed?"

"Maybe he lost it," Trudi told her. "Who knows? The important thing is he wrote like he said he would. Girl, you got yourself a cute boyfriend."

Tara swallowed the happiness rising inside her. "You're right," she said. "He wrote me. That's what's important. You all don't know how much his letter means to me!"

Trudi put a hand on Tara's arm. "We think we know. Right Nora?"

"Yeah. I think I do, even though I've never been in love—don't think I'll ever be."

"Neither have I," Trudi admitted. "But I still think it feels good to be in love." Trudi was eighteen, and she wasn't allowed to date until she turned twenty-one. She didn't seem to mind, though. A long moment of silence occurred.

Dion was on Tara's mind all summer long. Oh, God! Thank you. Thank you, God! she praised silently.

"Aren't you going to read it?" Trudi asked.

"Not until I get home," Tara replied.

"Well," said Nora. "I'm off to find my friend Rhoda. I'll catch you all later. Bye."

"Bye," Trudi and Tara chorused.

Tara put the letter inside her new book satchel, and glanced at her watch. "We better go," she said. "The school bell will ring soon."

As soon as they stepped inside the school building, the bell rang. Trudi reminded Tara to pick up a consent form for the driver's education class. "Remember, I'll do what I promised, kiddo."

"Oh, I need you to do that," Tara replied.

Trudi curtsied. "Okay, Madame Tara Poygoode! Catch you at lunch. And get one for Nora, too, just in case she forgets. Bye." She turned on her heels and left.

"Bye."

* * *

Those beautiful, warm days of autumn soon evolved into winter. On Sunday, November 28th, the first gentle snowflakes of the season fell. It caught Tara by surprise, as she focused on the stream, covered over in a thin sheet of ice. She hadn't walked this far down the stream, since running away last summer. A tear slid down her cheek, taking with it the snowflake that landed under her right eye. She gazed at the fallen tree, wondering how she once made it to the other side without falling and possibly drowning. She looked at the sky and noticed smoke billowing over the trees from Hailey's chimney. She wondered if Hailey ever thought of her, because she thought of Hailey a great deal.

Tara drew a mental picture of Hailey sitting by the fire, darning a pair of her husband's old socks. She still had mixed emotions about Hailey's indifference toward her plight. She would never forget that Hailey had returned her to Rufus, her tormentor, fully aware of her circumstances. Running away was another misery she had endured. "When you're in trouble, you stand alone," she mumbled to herself.

As the light snow fell, it became windy. Tara pushed up her coat collar, and headed back toward the house. She had taken the liberty to grab a little solitude while Rufus was gone, after announcing he had to go out of town—to most of the family's relief. She moved on. The brittle foliage and dry twigs crunched under her booted feet. A lone squirrel skittered across her path, climbed upon an acorn tree, and disappeared into the leafless tree branches.

The snow stopped, not amounting to much. Tara made a detour, and sat on a pile of dry foliage, under a willow tree. It was not the one where she had discovered the three small graves last summer.

She stuck her gloved hand inside her book satchel and brought out Dion's letter. It was the sixth letter. They were now sent to Trudi's house; and Trudi had been right, Dion had misplaced her address. Eventually, he found it tucked between the pages of a suspense novel he'd been reading. Tara unfolded this letter and read it for the fifteenth time.

My gray-green-eyed girl,

I'm glad you and Nora are doing well with the driving lessons, and that Mr. Davis is still pretending not to know you all are underage drivers. (Smile.) In any case, it gives me a great deal of satisfaction knowing you're at least doing something your father doesn't know anything about and, therefore, can't stop.

I have what might be promising news. Grandfather and Grandmother, in Tildarose, Tennessee, are thinking about selling their one hundred and sixty-acre farm come this spring. [Not a lot, of course, by your daddy's standards. But it's enough to make a good living on]. Question: Do you think your mother would be interested in buying the farm? I know you can get the money, considering you've found the old devil's treasure. Let me know what I should tell Grandfather. Don't forget to burn this letter, too. Don't want to put Trudi in jeopardy.

All my love,
Dion.

Tara held the letter close to her heart. Then she took a match to it the way Dion had told her to do. She took the blue ballpoint pen and spiral notebook from her book satchel and answered him right back.

My Guardian Angel,

You'd never believe where I am right now. I'm down by the stream, hiding out under a willow tree. It was snowing a minute ago, but it has since lifted. I read your letter for the fifteenth time. I've just burned it, which is always so hard to do. I love you.

Tell your grandparents we'd love to buy the farm. I have to be honest with you, though. I didn't talk to Mama about it. I can't. So, I'm making the decision for her. The reason I can't tell her is because Daddy has a way of blistering the truth out of us.

I'm sorry I can't send you a Christmas card. You know I'm not allowed in town. I didn't feel right asking Trudi to pick one up for me. So please consider this letter as my Christmas greeting to you. Merry Christmas and a Happy New Year!

All my love,
Tara

She folded the letter and put it inside the envelope. She addressed and sealed the envelope. She licked a stamp and glued it onto the envelope. She stuck the envelope inside the notebook and put the notebook and pen back inside her book satchel.

She stood. She brushed the foliage off her coat. After kicking dirt and dry foliage over the charred paper, she headed back toward the house, as the frigid wind pushed her along.

She was about to dash up the back porch steps when she heard two loud motors at the front of the house. She ran to the corner of the house and peeped. As she stared at two large, flatbed trucks, carrying tons of lumber, her first thought was Rufus was preparing to build houses for her and Nora. But then a bell suddenly went off inside her head. "No!" she muttered with great relief. "He's getting ready to build houses for Yvonne and Yvette. "Oh, God!" she lamented. She couldn't believe he'd been serious about never allowing Yvonne and Yvette to go back to school! Her entire body shook with fear.

The cold wind made Tara run toward the back of the house. She ran up the steps, entered the house, and closed the door behind her. "I can't wait to graduate, so I can get out of here!" she exclaimed to herself. She anticipated that one day Rufus would stop giving her the pills, telling her that her heart had gotten better. She ran upstairs to her bedroom.

* * *

On Christmas Day, everybody came to the Big House. The most unusual thing happened at the dinner table: Rufus was happy. He even held up the wishbone and asked Maebelle to come make a wish. They all were stunned. The frown lines suddenly eased on Maebelle's forehead, and her troubled face lit up like a Christmas tree, as a rare smile creased her lips.

She sat at the opposite end of the table. Pushing her chair from the table, she moved toward him. She reached for her side of the wishbone, but he jerked it away. She placed her right hand across her heart with embarrassment.

"Go sit your drawed-up ass down. What you got to wish for?" Rufus said sternly, frowning at Maebelle.

Maebelle groaned like a wounded animal. Her dark face mirrored her pain and humiliation.

Everyone's disturbed eyes focused on Maebelle. They sat dumbfounded. Maebelle appeared confused, turning this way, then that way, before retreating to her seat. Finally, she sat down quietly at the end of the table and held her head down.

Now that Rufus made it apparent, Maebelle looked *drawed up*, as he had coldly put it. The contours of her hips were lost in her waistline; permanent worry-lines creased her forehead, and her hair seemed too gray for a woman of forty-three.

Nora looked under her lashes at Rufus. You're one cruel *sonofabitch*, she thought to herself. The woman that birthed you surely must've been cursed.

Rufus placed the wishbone on the side of his plate, and leaned back in his chair. He sucked the roast turkey out of his teeth. Everybody could tell he would say something that nobody wanted to hear.

"We had a good crop this year," he announced. "Made six hundred thousand dollars."

So where is our portion? Jennifer thought to herself. I guess you're saving it up to bribe Tara and Nora.

"You can't make that kind of money working anywhere else," he said. His hazel eyes turned in the direction of Tara and Nora. The girls averted their eyes.

Nora kicked Tara's foot gently. The two girls exchanged glances.

Try to make it sound good all you want, Tara thought. Just as soon as I graduate I'm out of here. You low-down bastard!

Nora stirred restlessly in her seat, glancing at Maebelle. She could tell by her expression that he'd probably ran a similar line on her, and she had bit into it hook, line and sinker. Everybody remained quiet, and Rufus ordered Maebelle to serve desert.

* * *

The winter months were cold, long, and lonely, but after a while Old Man Winter began giving up his reign. Each passing day grew a minute longer—the sun lingered a little longer on the western horizon as well. Before long a new, sweet spring, strolled into this little old delta town with exquisite pomp, spraying the fields and meadows with new grasses and an abundance of wildflowers.

The chattering voices of elementary schoolchildren, playing on the monkey bars on the grounds of the red brick annex was heard through the open windows of the high school next door.

In town the sheriff was busy cleaning out the jail cells in anticipation of arresting many drunken Negroes to be locked up for talking "out of character" to the lawman.

The juke houses were bustling again, and liquor flowed.

The school year would soon end.

* * *

Mrs. Elaine Shackleman, a tall, slim-built, good-looking, middle-aged woman, with short-cropped, dyed, black hair, pushed her chair out from her desk. Momentarily, she stood in front of her desk, wearing a tight navy blue skirt; a red short sleeves blouse and tall red pumps. She perched on the edge of her desk, and crossed her ankles. "Class, may I have your attention, please," she asked softly. "We all know that in a few weeks school will be out for the summer, and we'll all go our respective ways."

She looked down while brushing the chalk dust off her skirt with her right palm.

Trudi was elated because she had been accepted into St. Stillman College, although she only shared her good news with Nora and Tara. She purposely left Rhoda out of the loop, with good reasons. She reached across the aisle and held Tara's hand. Rhoda and Nora saw them, and they held hands, too.

Mrs. Shackleman lifted her eyes. A smile creased her lips, as she looked at the four girls. "I wonder how you girls will live without each other after graduation. You remind me of four peas in a pod.

"Now that you already have my attention, I'll start with you Trudi. Tell us what your plans are after graduation?"

"I would like to- - -"

Mrs. Shackleman didn't wait for Trudi's answer.

"You're a very creative writer, Trudi. You should think about studying journalism."

Trudi closed her mouth and looked at Mrs. Shackleman strangely. Mrs. Shackleman paused. Having decided which career Trudi should pursue, she then directed her attention to Tara.

"And you, Tara? What are your plans after graduation?"

Tara stirred on her seat, flashing a glance at Trudi, and fixed her eyes on Mrs. Shackleman. Aside from running away from home and taking Aide and Nora with her, Tara's dream was to become a criminal lawyer. "Well, actually, I'll study criminal law if ever I get to go to college."

Mrs. Shackleman marveled at such high aspirations. "You're looking to become a pioneer, huh? That's a good field to study! The world needs some smart, Black women lawyers—judges, too. There is so much injustice in the world—right here in our community."

Tell me about it, Tara agreed to herself. Although she smiled because Mrs. Shackleman approved of her choice, nevertheless, she judged Mrs. Shackleman for not lifting a finger to help relieve them of their situation.

"And you, Rhoda? What are your plans after graduation?"

Rhoda raised her chin a fraction. "I've been accepted into Dahlia College. I want to teach."

Nora, Trudi, and Tara exchanged glances, all thinking that Rhoda thought she was the only one of them accepted into college. Trudi hadn't told Rhoda that she had been accepted into St. Stillman College, because she knew Rhoda would've tried to make Nora and Tara feel bad.

Mrs. Shackleman nodded. "Teaching is a noble profession, if I must say so myself."

"And what about you, Nora? What are your plans after graduation?"

As always, Rhoda answered for Nora, or at least attempted to. "She wants to- - -" Mrs. Shackleman put up a refraining hand. "Please, let Nora speak for herself, Rhoda." Her voice was terse. "When are you going to learn that people prefer not to have someone else speaking for them?"

Trudi squeezed Tara's hand, and the two girls looked at each other knowingly. But you just did the same thing to me, Trudi thought to herself.

Rhoda lowered her lashes.

"Now go ahead, Nora," Mrs. Shackleman said.

A faint smile creased Nora's lips. She felt sort of glad Rhoda had gotten a good scolding, even though they were supposed to be friends. But recently Nora wasn't so sure about their friendship. She had heard about the nasty rumors Rhoda was spreading about her and Tara. Nora looked at Mrs. Shackleman. "I would like to become a pediatrician—but I don't know. My Daddy wants to keep us on the farm." She looked at Tara. Tara nodded.

Nora went on. "He wants to teach us to become good farmers, and take over the farm when he dies." Immediately, she wished he were already dead, while watching Mrs. Shackleman's composure change.

Mrs. Shackleman uncrossed her ankles, got on her feet, and placed a hand on her hip. She was a woman ahead of her time, regarding liberal views and a woman's right to make her own choices. As a matter of fact, Mr. Davis admired her for her views and wished he had more faculty members like Mrs. Shackleman. She never minced words. She once threatened to visit Rufus when she heard the rumor floating around the school that he was having sex with his daughters, but her husband forbade her interfering. She also had many arguments with some other faculty members over the same issue. Mr. Davis would support her, provided the full faculty unanimously agreed. Not all faculty members were in agreement, so neither Mr. Davis nor Mrs. Shackleman proceeded. When he told Mrs. Shackleman that, she answered, "bullshit!"

She continued. "I have no doubts about your father's love of farming! But God has given you girls a very special gift! Don't waste your God-given gift turning over dirt for your father! You've done enough of that already!"

Tara and Nora were surprised when the class applauded. Before Mrs. Shackleman could finish what she was saying, the bell rang. "I'll see everyone on Monday!" she said. Her face remained taut, as they left her classroom.

* * *

The last few weeks of school went by swiftly. On Wednesday, the last day of school, at two-fifteen p.m., Mr. Davis' voice came over the PA system. "To all seniors," he said. "To those of you who've decided not to attend your graduation ceremony, since this will be your last day at Derriene Crossing High School, I want to say congratulations for a job well done." He paused. "May you leave here today with high hopes. Pursue your dreams with great tenacity, whether they are to enter college or to get a job." He paused again. "School will dismiss thirty minutes early for all graduating seniors. However, you must—and I repeat, you must remain on the school ground. Have a pleasant summer. God bless you all." The PA system clicked off.

* * *

On the school ground, Trudi had gotten lost from Tara. She looked for her among the crowd. Suddenly, she felt a hand on her shoulder. Whirling around, she came face to face with Vanessa Creamerspoon. "Vanessa! Hi. Have you seen Tara and them?"

"Hi, Trudi. Nah. I haven't seen 'em." Vanessa was a petite, dark-skinned girl, with black, curly hair. Trudi was so taken by Vanessa's looks, that she couldn't help staring at her. She admired her creamy, luscious, dark skin. She had great features. Tara blinked. "Ah. Have you seen Tara? Or Nora and Rhoda, for that matter?"

Vanessa peered at her strangely.

"I just told you. No. I'm looking for Tara myself."

"Oh!" What for?"

Vanessa tried to hand Trudi a letter. "For this. Can you give it to her? It's a letter from me to Mr. Poygoode. Tell her not to open it."

Trudi looked stunned. She staggered backward.

"Oh! Don't act so surprised!" Vanessa said tersely. "None of us in this school are hardly virgins. A lot of girls mess with him." She grinned like a slick fox. "We all heard he had a big you-know-what!" She giggled. "And we want to try him out. I don't know about anybody else, but he pays me every time I go out with him. Now I have enough money to go to Chicago. I'm leaving tomorrow morning. That's what this letter is about. I don't want him wasting time looking for me in town tomorrow night."

"And you-you want me to give that letter to Tara! How dare you! And don't give it to her, either!" she demanded. "You-you ought to be ashamed of yourself! Get out of my way!" Trudi stepped around Vanessa, and ran off to find Tara. "How dare she tell me to give her letter to Tara! Slut!"

Later, Trudi ran into Vanessa's brother Frank. She couldn't stand Frank.

He was slouching toward her grinning like a jolly hyena. Tara rolled her eyes heavenward. *"Jesus!"* She complained. "What is this? Fools' Day!"

Frank got right up in her face. She had to stop short to keep their noses from touching. She narrowed her eyes, then frowned at his thin, black face.

"How come you're not with your girlfriend?" he asked. "Unless, of course, you were waiting for me." He grinned.

Trudi sighed hard. She tried to sidestep him, but he blocked her. She looked up at him and barked really loudly. "Get out of my way, Frank! You Creamerspoons are sick people."

Frank laughed. "Un-huh," he concurred. "I know."

Trudi glared up at him. "Well," she said. "Since you got your 'ol crazy self all up in my face, I might as well ask you. Have you seen Tara? Well, have you?"

"Yeah. Yeah. I saw them." He half-turned and pointed toward a group of students about thirty yards away. "They're over—over there," he said.

Trudi strained. "Where? I don't see them."

Frank turned and looked at her and decided to change the subject.

"Now how 'bout you giving me a little good-bye-kiss on the last day of school? He bent his head, closed his eyes, and pursed his lips.

Trudi backed away, glaring at him. He was making her mad. She happened to look over his shoulder. "I see them!" she exclaimed. "Now get your crazy self out of my way!"

Frank straightened his posture.

Tara planted a hand on his chest, and pushed him hard, causing him to stagger.

"Do that again!" he teased. "I love when you touch me like that." When he noticed Trudi's furious expression, he stepped out of her way.

Trudi ran toward Tara. Frank stood there, lusting after her firm, round hips.

Running his tongue across his teeth, Frank tilted his head and gazed hard at her butt. "Hey, Trudi!" he yelled.

Trudi stopped, glancing back until her eyes rested on his tall, lean frame. His hand was rubbing his crotch. "Nasty fool!" she shouted. She pivoted on her heels and ran, though he began laughing loudly. "Sick fool!" she muttered. "I wonder if he knows Vanessa is messing with Tara's father. Probably does," she said to herself. "Vanessa probably gives him some of the money she gets from Mr. Poygoode."

Tara was crying, and Nora was trying to comfort her, when Trudi found them. Rhoda stood by calmly with her arms folded across her chest, staring indifferently.

"What's the matter?" Trudi inquired. Her voice was concern.

"Ask Rhoda!" Nora retorted.

Trudi placed a hand on Rhoda's arm. "What happened, Rhoda?"

Rhoda shrugged her shoulders. "Well, I guess I said something I shouldn't have. It just slipped out."

Trudi's brows crinkled quizzically. "What did you say that 'slipped out,' Rhoda? "

Rhoda couldn't face Trudi, until Trudi pawed her on the shoulder. "I asked you what happened," she snapped, with anger.

Rhoda answered, with her eyes fixed elsewhere. "I just asked if she's daydreaming about her daddy when she sits in class, since she's always staring out the window, while the teacher is teaching."

Trudi became tense. Tara and Nora looked at each other, as feelings of betrayal crept over them.

Trudi frowned, placing her hands on her hips. "You asked her what? I don't believe what you just said! What's wrong with you, Rhoda? Why would she daydream about her father?"

Rhoda turned her eyes toward Trudi. "You know, girl! You like playing dumb! He's probably paying 'em. You see how much better they dress than all of us. Everybody around here knows he's messing with 'em. You do too! You just don't want to admit it."

Tara once told Trudi that Rufus was messing with her older half sisters, but he'd never touched his biological children. Although Trudi believed Tara, she still didn't like what he was doing to her aunts.

Nora felt so angry she grabbed Tara's trembling hands and held them tight. Doing so, kept Nora from physically pouncing on Rhoda, like she felt like doing.

Rhoda and Trudi's eyes met for a slight moments. Fire ignited inside Trudi. "I don't like being falsely accused of anything, Rhoda! You don't know what you're talking about. Stop listening to gossip!" she fumed.

"You're just in denial!" Rhoda barked.

Trudi felt a rush of righteous indignation, causing her to throw down her book satchel, and kick Rhoda hard in her butt. Rhoda tumbled down on the ground, remaining there—afraid to get up.

Trudi picked up her book satchel. "Let's go!" she said, "before I stomp her behind in the ground!"

The three girls looked down at Rhoda tearfully sitting on her haunches, staring up at them, until Trudi, Tara and Nora proceeded to leave. "I can't stand y'all, anyway," she muttered.

* * *

"You shouldn't fight over us," Tara said.

"What fight!" Trudi replied. "Who was fighting?" she asked, facing Nora. The three girls laughed. But Tara and Nora really felt hurt.

"I could've beaten Rhoda down to the ground if I had wanted to," Nora remarked. "But I didn't because I know I could easily kill somebody if I'm not careful. I know it!"

Trudi arched her brows, glaring at Nora. Nora watched Trudi slightly glance at her. This wasn't the first time Trudi heard Nora say she could kill. She was starting to believe her, but hoped she never would hear that Nora was in prison for killing someone.

"Well, here's Dion's map and instructions," Trudi said, handing Tara the envelope.

Tara took the envelope and put it inside her book satchel. It contained the highway map and instructions on how to get to his grandfather's house in Tildarose, Tennessee. She had asked Trudi to keep them until school was out.

"I put my address to St. Stillman College in there, too. Remember, I'm staying on campus."

"I remember," Tara said. Thank you."

Nora was quiet, as she stared at the ground thoughtfully.

"Well, we better go catch our buses," Trudi said. "But wait! First, let's say a little prayer." They all bowed their heads. Trudi prayed: "Lord, may you watch over us always. And thank you, God, for bringing Dion and me into Tara and Nora's life. Give them wisdom, Lord, to do what they must to do. Amen." They opened their eyes. Tara's eyes were moist; Nora's eyes were hard. Trudi pretended not to detect what was in Nora's eyes, but she worried about Nora, because she didn't believe in God. "No loving God would sit idly by and let Daddy do these things to us," she often told Jennifer, whenever Jennifer would tell her to keep praying.

"Well, I guess this is it," Tara said, as she had already begun missing Truidi. "I'm going to miss you, Trudi. You're such a good friend, and thanks for making it possible for Nora and me to get our drivers licenses. We owe you so much."

Nora's demeanor had softened. "It's true," she said. "If it wasn't for you, we wouldn't have them. You've been such a good friend, too." Nora thought about Rhoda and wagged her head. "Too bad Rhoda turned out not to be." Moments of silence filled the air.

"Look, y'all. I'm trying really hard not to cry here, but you all aren't making it easy for me," said Trudi, with misty-eyes.

"Well, I can't help it," said Tara, wiping her tears with the heel of her right hand.

"Now make sure you all write me, and tell me the good news about your family's escape. I gotta catch my bus. Good-bye, and don't forget me."

Nora and Tara waved good-bye enthusiastically in spite of their broken hearts.

* * *

That night, Tara tossed and turned all night long. Two people who really cared about her were now out of her life. Their addresses were useless since she couldn't write to them, or they to her. She wouldn't spend another day on the farm if possible. Her urge to escape remained constant, knowing it would be tough escaping. It would take a miracle to take all thirty-one of her family members with her. She knew she had to at least try; otherwise, how could she live with herself?

She flopped over on her belly. "Lord, help me! Please!" she muttered into the darkness. Restless lying there imagining, suddenly an idea popped into her head. "The cattle truck!" she blurted out. "Oh, God! Thank you." Everybody can fit into it, she thought! "We can even take a little furniture!" She was wide-awake now. Her thoughts shifted on finding a way to incapacitate Rufus. As her mind raced in turmoil most of the night, somehow she fell asleep.

* * *

Tara rose at the break of dawn the next morning. After washing and dressing, she tiptoed down the stairs to the kitchen. She opened the refrigerator door and took out a pack of ground pork sausages. She closed the refrigerator door and stuck the frozen pack under her shirt. She tiptoed back up the stairs to her bedroom.

Tara quickly entered her bedroom and closed the door behind her. Adie stirred without waking up. Tara moved to her side of the bed, got down on her hands and knees, and pulled the shoebox from beneath the bed. She lifted off the top and put the meat inside. She closed the shoebox and pushed it far back under the bed. "I'm fixing your wagon," she muttered. "Botulism, salmonella— whichever it decides to grow is fine by me." She stood, looking around the room. Well, she mused, if this works, I won't see you too much longer."

She left her bedroom and rushed, tiptoeing back downstairs to the kitchen. She took a small bottle of Clorox, a three-gallon pail, and the straw broom and went out the back door, heading nervously down the path to the barn.

Tara half-filled the pail with water from the well and poured half the contents of the Clorox bottle into the water. She carried the pail, along with the broom, and placed them in the back of the truck. She climbed upon the truck and proceeded to sweep off the cow manure. She scrubbed down the truck until it smelled clean and fresh.

* * *

It was late afternoon, when Nora came up to the Big House with the highway map and instructions Dion had sent. Tara saw her from the kitchen window. She ran out of the house to meet her. "Hi, Nora! Where's the map and instructions? Tara asked, as they walked toward the barn."

"I have them folded inside my brassiere," she said, pointing to her chest. Daddy took so long leaving!" she exclaimed.

Tara didn't know how much money was inside the churn, but she believed it was enough to buy Dion's grandparents' farm twenty times over.

Nora suggested they might have to shoot Rufus.

"What! Who's going to do the shooting?" Tara asked frightened.

"I will!" Nora said, without a hint of remorse or fear.

"But suppose the gun misfires. Suppose you miss him, then what?"

"Then you come up with a better plan!" Nora snapped.

"I will! Just give me time," Tara replied. She wasn't about to tell Nora that she had made plans for Rufus to get sick by ingesting sausages tainted with salmonella or botulism. In case he died, no one else would be implicated. She learned about salmonella and botulism in Home Economics. She wished Rufus would die from the poison meat; nevertheless, part of her wanted him to live, so he could know she had out-slicked his ass. Rufus always boasted that nobody had ever out-slicked him and lived. She thought he'd only said that to scare them. He didn't look like a killer to her. On the other hand, she considered burning down his whole farm, turning everything into ashes, except the livestock, because she didn't want to hurt them.

"Why are you so quiet?" Nora inquired.

Tara shrugged. "Just thinking."

"Well? Did you come up with something?"

"Not yet. But I will." She proceeded to open the barn door. They sat down on the barn floor and studied the map. They agreed to make the trip. Nora folded the map and instructions and returned them inside her brassiere. They got up to leave.

Tara pushed open the door and the two girls got the shock of their lives. Tara staggered back onto Nora's foot. "Daddy!" she gasped. "You-you scared me!" She looked back at Nora, then at him.

Nora's expression was a culmination of fear and anger.

"So I scared you, huh? I wonder why!" he said, glaring at Nora. "So! I got two *dykes* on my hands, huh?"

The two girls exchanged shocked glances. They barely spoke, as Rufus detected their confused reactions.

"Cat got your tongues, huh? Well, don't confess to anything yet. But you will. Get on up to the house and stay there! I'm going to look around. Maybe I'm wrong," he said, gazing at Nora. "Maybe some little 'ol boys are hiding out in here," their father said suspiciously, while nodding his head and entering the barn.

Nancy Weaver

The girls walked fearfully toward the house. Nora looked disturbed at Tara. "I hate 'im, Tara! How could he say that about us? He doesn't want us together! All last summer he kept us apart. And I snuck up to the house like I wasn't a part of the family. You still carrying Dion's picture inside your book satchel?" Nora asked.

Tara nearly stumbled, as she clutched her book satchel. "Yeah," she said, with a sigh.

"Well, after today, take it out and hide it, because he's on the hunt for dick. He just might tell you to let him look inside it, since you're always carrying it with you."

Tara's heart stumbled. She knew Rufus could've demanded to look inside her book satchel, had he thought of it. After today, we'll be gone, she thought to herself.

"He's getting worse," Tara remarked.

"Tell me?" Rufus shouted. "Who cleaned the cattle truck? I'm mainly talking to you, Tara?"

The two girls turned around and looked at him.

"Oh, God!" Tara moaned. "What should I say?" She shook with fear.

"Tell him you cleaned it! Somebody had to clean it sooner or later. You just volunteered. That's all."

Tara swallowed hard.

"I did!" she shouted. Rufus didn't comment, as he turned around and re-entered the barn.

"I told you he just wanted to know," said Nora.

"Yeah. You were right. Damn! He's a nosy dog!"

"I'm going home!" Nora remarked.

"You can't!" Tara said, grabbing her arm. "He told us to go to the house, remember? If you're not in the house when he gets there, you'll be in a whole lot of trouble, and he'll really think we're guilty."

Nora looked at Tara for a long moment then said, "All right!"

They went up the steps and inside the house, and looked out the kitchen window. "Oh, God. He's coming," they chorused.

Rufus walked toward the house in long deliberate strides.

"Let's go in the living room and cut on the TV," said Tara.

"Okay," Nora agreed.

The two girls went into the living room. Tara turned on the TV and sat on the couch beside Nora. Nora felt her chest, making sure the map and instructions weren't conspicuous. She stood and started pacing.

"Sit down!" Tara ordered.

Nora looked at her, and sat down on the couch beside Tara. They heard the door open and close. Right away Rufus started screaming for Maebelle to come into the kitchen. She rushed out of her bedroom and entered the kitchen.

"What's the matter?" They heard her ask, frightfully. Then they heard Rufus say, 'I think I got two dykes on my hands—Tara and Nora. I caught 'em coming out of the barn together. I want you to feel inside their panties and tell me if they're wet or not."

Maebelle's eyes crisscrossed, looking at Rufus in utter disbelief.

The girls' eyes stretched wide open, as if they were being threatened by a tornado.

"Well, don't stand there looking at me like a damn fool, Maebelle! Go find them and do what I told you!"

"Oh, no!" Nora muttered and jumped off the couch. She headed for the front door. But before she could get the stupid door opened, Maebelle had already entered the room.

"They're in here!" she called.

Nora wrestled with the door but for some reason she couldn't get it open.

Rufus rushed inside the living room. "Nora!" he shouted. "Sit your ass down! Prove to me that you weren't puttin' your tongues on one another. Check 'em, Maebelle!" he demanded.

Maebelle looked at Nora, then at Tara. She didn't want to do this to them, but what choice did she have? She moved toward Tara.

"Don't do it, Big Momma!" Tara cried. "Don't let Daddy make you do this!" Maebelle ignored her. With Rufus standing guard, she would do what she had been told.

Nora stood, as she tried sneaking toward the door, until Rufus saw her.

"I told you to sit your ass down!" His eyes were aflame. Nora felt like a trapped animal. She wanted to run, but she wasn't sure if she would be able to open the door in time, so she came back and sat down on the couch next to Tara. She watched as Maebelle kept trying to ram her arm between Tara's thighs.

When Maebelle's knuckles touched Tara's crouch, Tara screamed loudly.

Maebelle brought out her hand from under Tara's skirt and rubbed the tip of her fingers together. Then held them up for inspection. "She's not wet," she told Rufus.

Glaring at her fingers, his brows raised. He gestured at her to check Nora.

Nora raised her hands in self-defense when Maebelle started toward her. "Don't you touch me!" she cried, digging her nails into Maebelle's fleshly arms. "You ain't no kinda grandmother! Get off me!"

Maebelle let out a howl.

"Sit your ass still!" Rufus ordered. "And open your damn legs, before I open them for you!" His threat fell on deaf ears. Nora kept struggling with Maebelle.

"Get off me! Mama was right. You ain't no damn kinda mother. I hate you!" she cried. Maebelle had unbelievable strength. Suddenly, Nora felt Maebelle's hard fingers raking across her private part. Her eyes widened in horror. Her voice left her and she couldn't utter even a sound. She swallowed the sick feelings over and over, as they came over her. She felt too stunned to scream. She watched teary-eyed as Maebelle rubbed the tip of her fingers together.

"Unh-unh," she said, shaking her head. "She ain't wet, either."

The two girls saw Rufus's brows shoot up in surprise.

But surprised or not, Nora vowed in her heart to kill him, if this was the last thing that she ever did. She sprang to her feet. "May I go home now?" she asked again wiping her teardrops.

Rufus nodded, speaking in a low, stern tone. "Go on. Get out of here."

Nora wrenched open the front door, kicking the screen door open with her booted foot, sending it reeling hard on its hinges, slapping the wall like a bolt of lighting. She ran down the steps cussing and threatening to kill both of them. She dried her eyes on her shirtsleeve. She decided not to tell Jennifer about their encounter with their father. What good would it do?

Tara ran upstairs to her room. "I hope to God you die from that meat tomorrow morning!" she mumbled. "I hate the both of you!"

Adie was standing in the doorway when Tara reached the top of the stairs. She opened the door and stood back, looking up at Tara.

Tara stormed into the room without a hint that she saw Adie. She fell upon the bed and cried uncontrollably. Poor Adie avoided consoling her. For Tara's eyes had told her she couldn't be comforted. Adie closed the door, and perched at the foot of the bed. She felt Tara's anguish and she cried in silence for her.

* * *

It was 2:00 a.m. and Tara still hadn't slept a wink. She arose from her bed and slipped into her robe. The full moon illuminated the room with a smoky light. She got down on her hands and knees and pulled the shoebox from beneath her bed. She removed the soggy pack of meat and returned the shoebox under the bed, reeking of rotten meat. She would throw it away, later. She got to her feet, moving softly across the floor. She opened the door and tiptoed down the stairs to the kitchen, praying that Maebelle had taken out ground sausages for Rufus' breakfast; otherwise, she would have to repeat today's ritual tomorrow. If she couldn't carry out her plan, she wouldn't try to stop Nora from shooting Rufus down like the dog he was, if that was what Nora chose to do.

She cut on the light. She stared excitedly at the pack of ground pork on the butcher block. "Good!" she muttered. She moved to the butcher block and pressed the tip of her index finger into the pack of meat. It was soft. "Good." Her heart began racing, as she proceeded to do something that could go either way. Rufus could get very sick and live, or he could get very sick and die. She no longer cared if he died. She had to hurry. She tilted her head and listened carefully for any kind of movement that indicated someone was coming. Quickly, she removed the wrapping from the rotten meat, pinched off a generous portion, and mixed it with the fresh ground pork. She sniffed it. It smelled tainted. "Oh, God," she groaned. She added a generous portion of chopped onions, and sniffed it again. This time, it mainly smelled of onion. Good, she thought. Rufus was the only person she knew who liked onions mixed with his sausages. She spat in it, too, before re-wrapping it.

Tara opened the back door and tossed out the rest of the meat to the dogs, and stood in the doorway and watched them gobble it down. She closed the door quietly. After placing the soiled wrapping at the bottom of the garbage pail, Tara moved to the sink and washed her hands. She wiped down the doorknob until it was nice and shiny. Finally shutting off the lights, she tiptoed back up the stairs.

* * *

In the morning Tara awakened frightened and anxious. She quickly washed and dressed, and later went and stood in front of the window, with her arms folded across her chest, waiting for Maebelle to rise and fix breakfast.

Fifteen minutes later, below her, she heard cabinet doors opening and closing, and pots and pans rattling. After a long while, the stench of rancid meat and onions floated up the stairs. Panic overcame her. She was at a crossroad. There could be no turning back, no mess up. "Please, God," she muttered. "Please don't let them pay attention to the smell. Please God." She paced to and fro, praying and hoping. She heard the muffled voice of Rufus talking to Maebelle, and stood real still. She listened intently, but she couldn't make out what he said to her. She wished she knew what he was saying, but she felt too afraid to go downstairs. She wondered if he was complaining about the rancid smell.

Adie awoke and saw Tara standing at the window and bolted upright. "Oh, my God!" she cried. "I'm gon be late for school! Why didn't you wake me, Tara?"

Tara jumped like a frightened rabbit. She turned around and glared at Adie.

"Girl! Why are you screaming like a damn fool, scaring me like that? You know dog-gone well school is out!"

Adie fell back on her pillow. She stared at Tara's back for a long moment. She recalled yesterday evening, when she had thought Tara was angry enough to kill somebody, because of what Maebelle and Rufus had done to her and Nora. She didn't want Tara to be angry with her too, so she apologized. "I'm sorry. I didn't mean to scare you. I thought today was a school day."

Tara didn't comment. She had no time for Adie. There was a long silence.

"I bet I know what you're thinking," Adie said, further agitating Tara. "You're thinking about what Daddy made Momma do to you and Nora. Momma should be ashamed of herself. You and Nora ain't no dykes." She paused. "Whatever a dyke is." She shrugged her shoulders, hoping Tara would define it for her.

Instead, Tara gritted her teeth. She wished Stupid would keep quiet. She was trying to listen to what was going on below in the kitchen.

Suddenly, Tara heard Maebelle let out a loud scream. Then it sounded like a chair had fallen to the floor, followed by a muffled thump. Rufus had tried to stand, but excruciating pain gnawed at his guts and he fell back down again. His eyes rolled back in his head. Tara swallowed hard. Her heart was beating faster. Her knees felt wobbly. "Oh, God! He ate it!" she mouthed. Tara closed her eyes. Oh, God! Oh, God, she thought to herself. I did it!

Tara whirled around, looking startled at Adie. Adie had timidly sat straight up in bed; her eyes blinked.

"Well, don't just sit there looking stupid!" Tara snapped. "Go see what happened!" Tara's body was shaking almost out of control.

"But I'm not dressed - - -"

Tara grabbed Adie's robe off the chair and threw it at her. It landed on top of Adie's head. "There!" she said. "Put it on, and go see what happened! And come back and let me know!" I sure hope that *sonofabitch* dies, she thought to herself.

Adie slid out of bed and slipped into her robe. She jerked the stocking cap off her head and threw it on the bed. Tara was already holding the door open for her. "Hurry!" she said.

Adie glanced at Tara and ran out the door. She descended the stairs, and moved toward the kitchen.

Someone was at the front door knocking frantically. Tara swore. She rushed down the stairs to get the door. "Who in the hell is knocking at this hour!" she grumbled. She didn't want anybody there who could rescue Rufus. She drew the door wide and looked down into the upturned, weatherworn face of a short, stocky white man. She was furious at herself for opening the door. She damned sure wouldn't have opened it had she known it was he. "What the hell do you want!" she snapped, surprising her own self.

The man briefly looked at Tara, and stood on his tiptoes, peeping over her shoulder into the house. "W-What's all that commotion in there?" he asked, fidgeting with his Stetson nervously.

Tara raised her shoulder a fraction of an inch. "Can I help you!" she snapped.

The man looked up at her. He stepped back. "Ah, yes. My name is Mr. Travis McGee. First, you should show some respect, young lady. I'm a white man you're talkin' to!"

"I don't give a shit who you are!" Tara barked. "You're on my Daddy's property! Now what do you want?"

Travis McGee's face turned red. He looked up at Tara. "I'm--I'm here to buy some cattle from your daddy. Is everything all right in there?"

Maebelle kept screaming Tara's name.

"I have to go," Tara said.

"Did I hear right? Did that person say something happened to - - -?"

Travis McGee's words got lost as the door slammed in his face. When Tara stepped inside the kitchen and saw Rufus lying helpless on the floor, on his belly, a strange feeling overcame her. She felt a mixture of power and fear. I did it, she concluded, glaring down at his long torso. I've conquered your ass. We should've done this a long time ago, she thought, realizing only now how easy it had been to render him into the helpless animal that he was. There he was—his forehead beaded with sweat—his eyes half closed, stretched out on the floor like a helpless dog. Die! You *sonofabitch!* she thought to herself.

Then her eyes met Maebelle's.

Maebelle's eyes were full of fear and anguish. She moved toward Tara and lashed out at her. "Gal, didn't you hear me calling you! What took you so long! We got to get your daddy to the doctor. You're smart. You could drive that pickup into town. I know you could."

Tara felt livid. Her face was full of hatred. She glared at Maebelle with enough fire in her eyes to cause a volcano. Have you forgotten what you two did to Nora and me yesterday, she thought to herself, or does it matter? She glared down in Maebelle's dark, ashen face. She felt incensed that Maebelle didn't have enough sense to at least take advantage of this opportunity and leave this devil. Instead, Maebelle was worrying about helping him. She hated Maebelle for being weak and stupid.

She turned, glaring at Rufus. Then she turned and looked at Maebelle, staring at her for a long moment, and told her, "You're right. I am smart. I'm smart enough not to help that dog!"

Maebelle bristled. As she lifted a hand to strike Tara, the fire in Tara's eyes caused her to withdraw her hand.

"If you want him to see a doctor, you find a way to get him there!" Tara told her. "Because I'm gettin' the hell away from here while he can't do shit to me! And don't try to stop me!"

Maebelle swallowed hard. She felt helpless, as she glanced around at Adie, Adam, and Rudi, now down on their knees staring at Rufus. Rudi tried shaking Rufus, hoping he would awaken.

Tara glared at Rudi. He's dumb, she told herself. She courageously announced: "I'm leaving here. Anybody wanting to join get up and stand beside me now!"

Adie and Adam straightened and rushed to her side.

Maebelle's eyes darted from Adam to Adie. Swallowing, she stared fixedly at Adie and Adam. And they steadily stared back at her.

"Anybody who wants to stay here with Daddy got to be crazy!" Adie remarked.

"I know," said Tara, while placing her arms around Adie and Adam's shoulders, and bent down whispering in their ear. "Both of you go and pack some clothes in a cotton sack. I don't know if Elliott and Zeke are in the house." She paused. "Before you all do anything, find them first. Tell them Daddy done fell out and it's time for us to leave here while we can. Tell them to knock on everybody's door, and let them know that I said I'm leaving here, and that they're welcome to come with me. Tell Elliott we're taking the truck that we used to haul the cattle to the market. Tell Elliott to fill up the gas tank. Hurry up! Tell him to make sure they knock on Mama's door first!"

* * *

The kitchen door slowly opened. Travis McGee peeped, then stepped inside. Adie and Adam glanced up at Travis McGee absent-mindedly and ran pass him. Shocked to see Rufus lying on the floor, Travis McGee backed up into the doorway. All he could think of was he'd come sixty miles for nothing. He looked into Maebelle's frightened faced. "W-W-What's going on?" he asked.

When Tara heard Travis McGee's voice, she whirled around speechless. Then she remembered she hadn't locked the door.

Maebelle had a hard time finding her tongue.

Travis McGee walked over to Rufus. He knelt down and checked Rufus' pulse. He looked strangely at Maebelle. "His pulse is faint," he announced. "You can see, his color isn't right and he's sweating a hellva lot. I'd say your husband been poisoned, ma'am."

Maebelle drew up short, in confusion. "I didn't poison nobody!" she exclaimed.

"I'm not the one you should be trying to convince, ma'am. I just want my cattle. I come sixty miles. I-I don't wanna leave here without my cattle."

Travis McGee reached inside his back pocket and pulled out a brown leather wallet. He turned, facing Tara. "Here's the money right here, you see. Give me my cattle, and I'll pay you and be on my way." Tara gazed at him. Sounds good to me, she thought to herself. McGee pointed to Rudi. "G-Get that young man to take me down to the pasture. He can help me."

Tara and Rudi's eyes met. Rudi stood slowly, as he tried stopping his tears from flowing. "You want me to get the cattle for you? Then first take my daddy to the hospital. When we come back, I'll help you get your cattle."

"Yeah! Yeah!" Maebelle remarked. "Take my husband to the hospital. Then come back and we'll see to you getting your cattle."

Travis McGee staggered; he put up his free hand, and said, "Now don't y'all go making me responsible for him. Y'all do what you'd do if I weren't here. I'm here for business. All I want is my cattle. Here's the money." He opened his wallet and took out the money and held it in front of Tara's face. But she didn't see it, since she was busy looking back at Rufus, thinking how she didn't want his filthy blood on her hands. She knew if he died, Maebelle would probably be blamed. The white man had already as much as said that without having the facts. She despised Maebelle, but not enough to see her go to penitentiary for something she didn't do. She didn't want anyone to have to suffer on a kind of Rufus. He had caused them enough suffering to last a lifetime. All she really wanted to do was to escape with her family—get them far away from him.

Tara moved toward Travis McGee. "Listen, Sir," she said anxiously. "In absence of my father, I'm second in charge of his business."

Travis McGee's face lit up.

"I'll handle the sale. Plus, I'll throw in a bonus of three more cattle if you get him to the hospital." She lied on both counts. Oh, she didn't care if he took every single cow for nothing. But more importantly she intended to be long gone by the time Travis McGee got back.

Travis McGee showed his full set of tobacco stained teeth. "Now that sounds like a bargain, I can't pass up! Here," he said happily, "hold my Stetson."

Tara took his hat.

He ordered Maebelle to stand back. Then he got down on one knee and hoisted Rufus upon his broad shoulder. He stood and reached for his hat with his free hand. Tara gave it to him. He placed the Stetson on his head at an odd angle.

Tara put her mouth to Rufus' ear and whispered words she hoped he'd never forget. She knew he'd heard her because she saw his eyelids flutter like wings on a frightened bird. "You don't make mistakes, huh? Well, you made one when you brought me into this house."

Rudi ran ahead of Travis McGee, opening and holding doors, as he came through the house with Rufus. Maebelle followed close behind, crying and carrying on.

Tara dashed inside the pantry; she grabbed the largest brown paper bag on the shelf, and dashed out of the kitchen heading for Rufus' room. Entering the room, she carefully closed the door behind her.

She threw the bag on the floor near the bed. Then lifted up the footboard and swung it to her left. She dropped to her knees, rolled back the rug, and removed the loose floorboard. Her heart pounded, as she moved quickly, lifting the lid off the churn; and set it on the floor. Grabbing the paper bag, she reached inside the churn and took out the money and threw it inside the bag. She felt her heart racing, as she expected that after Travis McGee left Maebelle would look for her to try to stop her from leaving. But no force on earth would keep her from gaining freedom.

Travis McGee slowly sidled down the steps toward the truck.

Maebelle stood irritably on the porch. If Rufus survives, she thought, he'll blame me. And if he dies, the law will blame me. She knew she wasn't the one who'd poisoned him, but she had a good idea who had. Ain't nobody did this but Tara, she told herself.

Rudi opened the door on the passenger side. Travis McGee maneuvered Rufus' limp body onto the seat. "Step back, sonny," he said, then closed the door and rounded the back of truck to the driver's side. Rudi opened the door on the passenger side and climbed in beside Rufus.

Travis McGee leaned forward and glared at Rudi. "Whoa! Wait just a minute. You ain't ridin' with me, boy! You just go make sure them five cattle the little Missy promised me is put with the rest of them cattle."

"She told you three!" Rudi snarled, pursing his lips.

"Well, whatever. You just make sure they're ready, because I'll be back. Now get down out of my truck. You're wasting precious time, boy!"

"But why can't I go with you and Daddy? How 'bout if Momma go with you, then?"

Travis McGee sank back against the seat. His face grew taut. He glared out the windshield at Maebelle, then leaned forward and glared at Rudi's fat, round face. "Look, boy! Don't make me lose my sensitivity. Now get out of my truck and close the goddamn door!"

Reluctantly, Rudi climbed down out of the truck, and slammed the door hard. All he wanted was to be in the hospital room when Rufus woke up, so he could win his love. Show him that he'd stood by him.

* * *

Tara worked feverishly. The last thing she brought out of the churn was a small stack of unopened letters. She scanned them hurriedly. "Whose Jake Blakestone, Jr.?" she mumbled. She looked at the forwarding address. "Mama!" she muttered surprised. She felt stupid because she never knew Jennifer's real surname was Blakestone. Jake must be her brother, she thought. "Oh, God! Wait until Mama sees this." There was one other letter addressed to Maebelle Hawkins, from Leslie Wills. "Oh, my God," Tara muttered. It suddenly dawned on her how little she knew about her family. She never knew Maebelle's other last name, either. Must be her maiden name, she thought to herself. She glanced at the postmarks. "Oh, my God!" she exclaimed. "These letters were written before I was born!" Her hands were shaking.

She heard the loud motor, and the truck drove away. Her insides shivered. She knew Maebelle would look for her now. She threw the letters into the bag, put the lid on the churn, put back the floorboard, and covered it with the rug. She pushed the bag aside. Then she stood; she grabbed the footboard, and swung the bed back perfectly into position.

With bag in hand, Tara slipped out of the room, running up the stairs toward her bedroom. She opened the door and stepped inside the room. She felt annoyed and surprised that Adie was nowhere to be seen. Nor had she packed. "Lord!" Tara muttered. Then she saw the two empty cotton sacks lying at the foot of her bed. She set down the bag of money and hurriedly packed the basics for herself and Adie. Lastly, she threw in her precious diary full of painful, ugly secrets, her book satchel, and Adie's book satchel. Then she tied the mouth of the sack.

Tara grabbed the bag of money with her left hand and the sack with her right hand and dragged it toward the door. She propped open the door with a shoe and dragged the sack through the door, down the short hallway, down the stairs, and through the living room. She kicked open the screen door with her booted foot. When the door swung back, she jerked the sack out on the porch, coming face to face with Maebelle. Tara felt enraged, seeing Maebelle sitting on the swing, gazing into space, like a crazy person, when there was so much to do in such little time. It helped, though, to see that Maebelle had at least packed her own things. The tightly, stuffed, five-foot cotton sack lay at her feet. She didn't acknowledge Tara's presence. It made Tara too angry for words, since it was obvious Maebelle was only thinking of herself.

Tara felt equally disgusted with Rudi, acting as selfish and stupid as Maebelle. He was packed all right, and she knew he had only thought of himself. Sitting on the steps hunched over, with his elbows on his knees and his chin in his hands, he frowned intently.

"God, help me," Tara muttered. "I wonder if I've done the right thing trying to get everybody away." She couldn't believe Rudi, especially after Rufus started poking him in the butt. "Since they're not here, has anybody packed Adam, Zeke, and Elliott's things?" Tara inquired. Her voice was harsh.

Maebelle sat stone-faced. She didn't even look in Tara's direction. And Rudi only looked back at her nonchalantly, and shrugged his shoulders carelessly, and then turned his head.

Tara swore out loud. "To hell with their stupid ass."

She let go of the sack's strap, turned and opened the screen door with her free hand and ran back into the house. She ran up the stairs and opened the door to the boys' room. None of the boys had time to bring in a cotton sack. She remembered that Adie had brought in two sacks, but she had only used one for both of their things. "Well, all the boys' things are going to all go into the same sack," she determined. She wheeled around and ran out of the room to her bedroom, grabbed the cotton sack off the bed and ran back to the boys' room. She put the bag of money on the bed and went to each boy's dresser, packing only the basics. She stuffed the sack right up to the mouth. "They'll have to tie it up themselves," she muttered.

She opened the door and propped a pillow against it. Then she grabbed the bag of money and the sack and dragged it out to the porch. She kicked the screen door with all her might and sent it reeling like a rocket headed for outer space. She jerked the sack through the door. The screen door slapped back like a hard bolt of lighting. In spite of her tirade, Maebelle and Rudi still didn't acknowledge her. Tara couldn't believe the way they were acting, especially Maebelle. Wasn't she happy to be leaving here? If Tara had not wanted to fix Rufus' wagon, she would've made them stay, even if they changed their minds. She despised them.

She had to hurry. By her calculation, they had exactly fifteen minutes to get on the road or risk running into Travis McGee on his way back to the house.

She dashed inside the house one last time for medical supplies. She entered the kitchen and stopped abruptly. Her heart flipped when she saw the rifle lying on the table. "Rudi!" she muttered and glanced over her shoulder. "What does he need with a gun?"

* * *

Elliott was riding the horn like crazy. That was his cue signaling that it was time to get on the road. Tara's heart leapt for joy. She couldn't wait to see Nora and Jennifer. She forgot about the gun. She ran to the window and drew back the curtain and looked out. Elliott was driving like a maniac across the vegetable patch. Heads bobbed up and down in back of the truck. Tara felt happy and nervous, simultaneously. The fact that they all stood with her brought tears to her eyes. "I have to hurry!" she muttered frantically, then made a mad dash for the pantry. Her body kept shaking. She set down the bag of money, and grabbed a large bag off the shelf and threw in medical supplies. To her surprise, the first thing she saw was Maebelle's high blood pressure medicine. "How could she forget her blood pressure medicine?" she grumbled, as she threw it in the bag. She packed a box of St. Joseph Aspirin, the Keopectate, three boxes of saltine crackers, two jars of peanut butter and two jars of blackberry jam.

* * *

Elliott rode the horn feverishly, as he sped into the yard and braked hard. "I'm coming! Tara exclaimed. Her whole body was shaking.

Elliott opened the door and jumped out of the truck. He left the motor idle.

Zeke opened the door on the passenger side and got out quickly. He went with Elliott to the house. They moved swiftly.

Rudi was sitting on the steps still hunched over, with his elbows propped upon his knees and his chin in his hands. "Where 's Tara?" Elliott asked. "Why you ain't helping her?" He gave Maebelle an edgy glance, expecting one of them to say something. His animosity flared when neither of them answered. "Where's our stuff!" He snapped. "You didn't pack for us, boy!" Rudi still didn't answer. Elliott's fist curled into a hard knot.

Zeke looked up and saw Elliott's flannel shirt sticking out of the mouth of the cotton sack. "I think that's your stuff, bro," he told Elliott. "I see your shirt sticking out." Zeke climbed the steps and rushed toward the cotton sack. He bent over, inspecting the contents. "It's all three of our clothes in here, Zeke told Elliott, with relief. "Tara probably packed them. That's why that sorry punk, Rudi couldn't answer you." Zeke straightened his posture, directing his words to Adam. "All our stuff is in the same sack, Adam."

"Well, we gotta get going, now" said Elliott. He turned to tell Maebelle something, but she had gone inside the house. He guessed Maebelle went to get Tara.

Rudi squinted at Elliott. "I'm feeling all kinds a thangs, bro. Did anybody tell you I was crying like a baby?"

Elliott glared down in his upturned face. "So that's why you weren't talkin'!"

"I feel shame. I was the only one crying." Rudi took his hands away from his face. "I know Tara and Nora ain't gon ever let me live this down. I--I thought that if I helped Daddy, maybe he would . . . Aw, forget it, bro! I don't wanna talk any more about it."

Elliott rubbed his neck, while peering down at the top of Rudi's head. He knew what Rudi was hinting at. But still he'd felt surprised that Rufus was doing Rudi, too. He'd thought he was the only one Rufus was trying to turn into a gal boy. He hadn't meant any of the things Rufus made him say. He liked girls. And once they got away he was going to find him one, and he was going to hump her brains out. He wasn't going to be nobody's gal-boy!

Zeke was standing within earshot listening to Rudi. He sniffed. He shot a quick glance at Elliott, and then looked out at the horizon. It didn't make him feel no better learning he wasn't the only one Rufus was humping. He'd always thought he was the only one Rufus was doing like that. He hoped Rufus would die.

* * *

Tara spent the next few seconds going over her mental list. And just when she'd gotten the things she needed and thought it was safe for them to leave, she found herself faced with an unimaginable angry and frightened foe: Maebelle! Maebelle planned to hold Tara hostage until Rufus returned. She pressed the cold, gray metal gun against the back of Tara's neck. Tara nearly peed on herself, thinking it was Rudi. Her knees knocked uncontrollable. She was speechless, although she pleaded in her heart for Rudi not to shoot her. She wondered why he wasn't saying anything. She imagined he wanted to scare her. Still, she wasn't certain if she should turn around. She wished Nora would hurry up, and come see what was taking her so long.

* * *

Nora and Jennifer jumped down off the back of the truck and ran toward the house. They hurried up the porch steps. "Where are Tara and Big Momma?" Nora asked. "And why aren't you in the house helping them?" she asked Rudi.

"Mama! Tara! Let's go!" Elliott cried.

Maebelle jumped and crisscrossed Tara's neck with the gun.

"Rudi!" Nora barked. "Boy! Don't you hear me talking to you? Why aren't you in there helping them?"

Rudi looked up at her. "They didn't ask me!" he barked. "Now stop bothering me!"

Nora glared down at him, and kicked him with her right knee. "Boy! You make me sick with your fat butt! I heard you were crying like a baby. Maybe we'll leave your butt here with Daddy, since you're so in love with him."

Rudi chewed on the inside of his jaw, thinking he would be glad when he grew up. He would beat up Nora. He pinched his itchy nose, and thought of his siblings teasing him.

"Come on, Nora," Jennifer said. "Let's go in and see what's keeping them. We gotta leave here before that white man gets back here. You never can tell. He might bring the sheriff back with him. Remember, Adie said he thought Daddy was poisoned."

Jennifer turned sideways and looked at Elliott and Zeke. "You all get that stuff on the truck. We'll go inside and see what's holding up Maebelle and Tara." She and Nora went up the porch steps and entered the house.

"C'mon, boy!" Elliott said to Zeke. "Get these sacks on the truck."

* * *

An eerie silence filled the house. "Wonder which room they're in?" Jennifer said.

"I don't know," Nora replied. "They're probably searching the house for Daddy's money. But we have to go now. Money won't do us any good if we get caught."

"You'll right about that," Jennifer agreed. "But I sure hope they find it because I only got a little bit of money." She put a hand on Nora's arm. "Well, I'm thirsty. I'm going to get a quick drink, then we'll leave."

"I'm thirsty, too," said Nora. "I'm coming with you."

When they stepped inside the kitchen, they halted in shock. Jennifer staggered back on Nora's foot, watching Maebelle pointing the gun at the back of Tara's neck, shuffling in a way that indicated she wasn't sure what she'd do with the gun. "Grace of God!" Jennifer shouted. "What are you doing? For *Chrissake*! Maebelle!" Will you kill your own daughter for that bastard! Don't you realize Tara is helping us?"

When Tara heard it was Maebelle pointing the gun at her, she felt the bottom drop out of her heart, realizing that all of them were in grave danger. At least Rudi would only want to scare her. But Maebelle would keep them here against their will. Her body shivered like a frigid wind was piercing through her small bones.

Nora jerked her head, and stared open-mouthed at Jennifer and then at Tara. 'Kill your own daughter!' It hit her like a ton of bricks. "You mean Tara and I are not sisters!" she could barely mutter. She flashed a deadly glare at Maebelle.

"Yes. I'll kill her!" Maebelle declared. "She--she's gon get me killed!"

Resistance shot through Nora so fiercely, she suddenly blurted out, "You heffa," clearly remembering what Maebelle had done to her and Tara last evening. Since then, Maebelle had become enemy Number Two. The thought of Maebelle touching her and Tara's private parts, made Nora bitterer.

Maebelle was rambling incoherently and shifting her feet. The gun barrel shot pass Tara's ear and pointed toward the wall. "If--if Rufus comes back and we're gone, he'll hunt me down and kill me, thinking I tried to poison him. But it wasn't me! It was Tara! And we--we gon stay right here—and tell him the truth. I'm not dying for something I didn't do!"

Tara's life flashed before her.

Any minute, she thought the gun would go off.

* * *

Nora saw that the gun barely missed Tara's ear. She knew this might be the only chance she could save Tara's life, and possibly her own, knowing that Rufus would link them together in this. If he returned home and caught them there, he'd kill them both.

She'd had enough of Maebelle and Rufus.

Her eyes searched the kitchen for a weapon. The butcher block was too far away. But the stove was close enough. A cast iron skillet sat on the cold burner. Although to her, it wouldn't matter if it had sat on flame. She'd grab it—with her bare hands. She tiptoed across the floor, grabbed the skillet, turned around, and moved up behind Maebelle.

Jennifer saw murder mirrored in Nora's eyes. She knew Nora was about to kill Maebelle, but she didn't want Maebelle's blood to be on Nora's hands. She commended Tara and Nora for their courage. They were doing what she should've done a long time ago. Jennifer eased toward Nora; put a hand on Nora's arm. "Give me the skillet," she mouthed. Nora shook her head. Jennifer pleaded with her eyes.

Reluctantly, Nora handed over the skillet. Jennifer jerked it out of her hand and tipped up behind Maebelle. She lifted the skillet in the air and brought it down on Maebelle's head. Bam! "I'll knock you out! You crazy wench!" Maebelle slumped to the floor. The gun hit the floor with a loud thud, but it didn't fire. Jennifer thought Maebelle had cocked it, but it wasn't cocked. Maebelle was an amateur with guns. "You scared butt, mother. I always knew you'd try to stop us if we tried running away." Jennifer lifted the skillet to strike her again, but halted, as she stood screaming with anger.

Tara closed her eyes and sank to the floor, weeping bitterly.

Jennifer tried lifting Tara off the floor; but Tara drew back. Her eyes immersed with dread. "I'm so sorry," Jennifer nearly whispered. "I'm so sorry, y'all," she said, looking back at Nora.

Nora's demeanor really hardens as she watched the small pool of blood forming near the back of Maebelle's head. She felt no sympathy for her, and she called for Zeke and Elliott.

"Zeke! Elliott! Come in here!" The urgency in her voice brought the two boys racing up the porch steps and in the house. When they got to the kitchen and saw Maebelle on the floor and the gun lying beside her, they froze wide-eyed and terrified.

"Oh, my God!" they chorused. "Who did Momma try to kill? Tara?" Elliott asked, with passion.

"Yes! Look at her!" Nora snapped, and pointed at Maebelle. "That scary heffa! "Now get her up and put her crazy self on the truck! Tie up her hands. I don't trust her! She never did nothing for us, and when we try helping ourselves she is gon try to kill Tara!" Nora's face was drenched with tears.

"Damn!" Zeke shouted. "That's messed up! Shit! Let's leave her here. She might try it again! Right? We want peace once we get away. We don't need that woman!" He cried.

Elliott put a hand on Tara's shoulder. He, too, was misty-eyed. Tara looked up at him in awe. "This is hard for me to say," he said, "because nobody has ever told me they loved me. "But I love you, sis. Thanks for not leaving us behind. C'mon. Okay? Calm down and lets get out of here." He reached, and caught her arm and helped her off the floor. "We can leave her. Just say the word."

Tara sniffed.

She stood slowly, and glared down at Maebelle in despair. She cast a pitiful glance at Jennifer, then at Nora. When she finally faced Elliott, though feeling emotionally torn, she refused to be deterred from her mission. She would keep her vow to strip her father of everything he had. Her deepest regret was she was unable to sell his land from under him. Nevertheless, she was determined to change her destiny—escape from her hellhole, and try not to leave a soul behind for him to batter, including Maebelle, as much as she hated her for being weak. "Don't think it hasn't crossed my mind to leave her crazy self behind," she said. "I've thought about it many, many times, especially since yesterday evening." She would never forgive Maebelle for touching her private part. "I hate her!" she declared. Her chin quivered. "But we're taking her, anyway. Only because I won't leave a single, living, breathing, soul back here for Daddy to destroy! It'll hurt that low-down dog more if he comes back here, finding only the dogs and chickens."

As Tara stared down at Maebelle again, Tara heard a small, still voice speaking to her that Rufus is alive, and that he would surely return home.

She was startled as she looked at Elliott with an amazingly, shocking revelation. "Hurry up! Put her on the truck! We got to get out now! Something just told me Daddy is coming back! I don't know when, but let's go!" She bent down and picked up both paper bags. She handed the bag with supplies to Jennifer. She looked down at the gun for a second before stepping over it. "Come on everybody!" she cried.

Zeke grabbed Maebelle by her arms, and Elliott grabbed her feet. They rushed out the house and put her on the truck, explaining rapidly to the others what had happened and why her hands had to be bound.

Elliott told Adie to find something to tie Maebelle's hands with. Then they climbed upon the truck. Adie handed Elliott her jump rope.

* * *

Tara opened the door and climbed behind the steering wheel. She set the bag of money on her lap, and closed the door.

Nora and Jennifer hurried around to the passenger side. Jennifer opened the door. "You get in the middle," she told Nora. At first, Nora glared in protest. But then she realized this was not the time to argue over a window seat, and protested no further. Jennifer climbed in after her and closed the door. They all began breathing deeply.

Tara willed her hands to stop shaking. She wasn't quite sure about driving on the highway, nor was Nora. But she had to drive if they wanted to escape. Aside from their Drivers Ed class, early on the girls had acquired their driving skills, driving around on the farm and dirt roads. Both of them wished they had more highway-driving experience.

Tara was pleased that the gas gage read full. She took another deep breath, before putting the truck in gear and pressing down on the accelerator. She sped down the back road, over to the highway, in case Travis McGee was heading back to the Big House. Hailey had driven on this road when she returned Tara home after Tara ran away last summer. Everybody was real scared, and no one said a word, either in the cab or in the back of the truck for a very long while.

* * *

Some forty-five minutes later, a bell went off in Jennifer's head. She scooted to the edge of her seat and looked across Nora at Tara wide-eyed and scared. "Tara!" she cried.

Tara felt her heart slam into her chest. Her eyes riveted to the rear view mirror, then the side mirrors. Her first thought was Travis had caught up to them and was trailing her.

Nora snapped her head around and glared out the back window. "What? What's the matter! I don't see anybody."

"Tara doesn't have a driver's license, girl! Oh, my God! What if the sheriff pulls us over? O, God! O, God!" She cupped her shaky hands over her mouth.

"Aw shucks, Mama!" Nora said. "You're going to make Tara have a wreck! And for what! You're not supposed to scream like that when people drive! We have our drivers' license! We got them in school. Jesus Christ, Mama! You think we would get on the highway without a license?"

Tara managed to control her temper. When she spoke, she forced herself to talk calmly. "Nora's right. Don't scream. You can make me turn this truck over and kill everybody. I'm already nervous."

Jennifer sank back in her seat. "I'm sorry, y'all. But if y'all had told me, I wouldn't have gotten so scared." She felt so strange and remained quiet for a long moment, until the next time she spoke. "... And where are we going to live; how are we going to live? I only have a little bit of money," Jennifer calmly explained.

Tara flicked a quick glance at Nora.

"I didn't tell her," Nora said, looking at Tara, "because you told me not to."

Jennifer scooted to the edge of her seat. "Oh no, she told you what?" she asked. "Well--can you all at least tell me now?"

Tara wet her lips. "Well, if we get away from here alive, we're going to be going to Tildarose, Tennessee, where Dion's grandparents live. We'll live and work on their one hundred and sixty acre farm." As Tara spoke, she looked in the rear mirror, keeping a look out for Travis McGee's truck. She'd already determined she would out drive him, if he tried to over take them.

Jennifer sat stunned. "You all—you all mean to tell me that little 'ol boy is behind all this!"

Nora and Tara exchanged glances.

"Yes ma'am," Tara replied. "And my friend Trudi, and Mr. Davis. He knew we were too young to take the drivers' education course, but he let us. I think he knew we were planning on running away."

"And Trudi forged your name," Nora said. "Not that anybody ever knew what your handwriting looks like, anyway. Still, she forged it."

Jennifer fell back against the seat. "Why bless her little heart—and Mr. Davis' too. I thought he seemed like a nice man." The conversation lapsed.

None of this seemed real to Jennifer—she hoped she wasn't dreaming. All their years of suffering had just suddenly ended. She didn't care if Tara had poisoned Rufus; it didn't matter. If Tara did it, Jennifer mused, at least she had the nerve to do what no one ever dared to do. She promised not to question Tara or Nora about it, but she knew one of them poisoned Rufus.

"We'll be sharecroppers," Nora said. "That's how we'll pay for the farm." Tara hadn't told Nora about the money. She planned to pay cash for the farm, and would save her surprise for when they arrived in Tennessee. Tara felt so good that she was going to be able to give her family something to finally rejoice about.

* * *

Upon approaching the highway, Tara took a deep breath, as she slowed down, and came to full a stop. She checked for traffic in both directions before she accelerated onto the highway. She gazed at the speedometer to make sure she was maintaining the legal driving speed. That had been a big accomplishment. Now she could relax a little. She felt glad they were all silent. It helped her to concentrate on her driving, until she got the full feel of the road. Jennifer and Nora looked out the window marveling at the open plains.

* * *

Two hours later, Tara crossed the county line, carrying her precious human cargo. They all started to feel at ease, and Nora started a conversation.

"Mama?"

"Hmm."

"Do you think Big Momma would've really killed Tara?"

Jennifer looked out the corner of her eyes at Nora. She wished Nora hadn't asked that question, at least not in front of Tara. "Child, I don't know. I really don't know," she said. Silence prevailed.

Tara cleared her throat. Her emotions ran deep, and she wished Nora hadn't asked that question in front of her. Yes! She would've killed me, she thought to herself, hoping not to become an emotional wreck.

"Mama," Tara said after a long moment. "I have an honest question for you."

Jennifer glanced at Nora. "I've always been honest with you girls. I didn't tell you I wasn't your real mother because I was instructed not to. Daddy would've killed me. But I've loved you like you were my own. I named you. And I ---"

"Mama! That's not what I'm talking about! As far as I'm concerned that thing in the back of this truck will never be my mother! Please don't ever mention her like that to me again!" She wagged her head.

"What I want to know," she said, "is who's buried in the three small graves under the willow tree, down by the stream, at the east end of the pasture?"

"Huh?" Nora shoved to the edge of her seat, fastening her eyes on Tara, and then on Jennifer. Tara stared straight ahead at the road. Yes. She had kept that from Nora, too. She hoped that keeping secrets from Nora wouldn't change their relationship. She had done what she thought was best, given their circumstances.

Jennifer nearly murmured, as she glanced out the corner of her eyes at Nora. She couldn't see Tara; because of the way Nora sat on the seat, blocking her view of Tara's face. Jennifer felt glad she couldn't see Tara. Jennifer stared out the window for quite sometime before she answered Tara. Tara was opening wounds that hadn't and possibly would never heal; and Jennifer began recalling those painful memories associated with those children in those graves. One of the children was hers from her first pregnancy that Rufus delivered over midwife Hailey's protest. In doing so, he robbed her of all her dignity. "Look, y'all," she said, "a lot of bad things have happened in our family. There are lots of secrets." She paused.

I can identify with that, Tara agreed silently, knowing she held secrets too. Still, she wanted to know more.

"But to answer your question," said Jennifer. "Tara, one of those graves has your twin brother in it." Tara gripped the steering wheel so hard her knuckles began hurting.

"Nora, one of those graves has your twin brother in it." Jennifer's eyes met Nora's long enough to see her digest the hard facts, as her head wagged. "The other child belongs to Lynn; and they were all boys," she whispered. She couldn't bear answering anymore of their questions. Chills now made her body shiver. "Look!" she said, rubbing her temple. "I'm getting a headache. Don't ask me any more questions; at least not now. Let me sit here and look out this window, and suck up this feeling of freedom," she said, not believing this experience was real. She turned her head and began smiling at the rolling-meadows, the fat brown horses, and the fat white spotted cattle grazing on lush green grass.

Tara and Nora looked regretfully at each other, without a word between them.

Nora had her hands folded on her lap, observing how the big roaring truck swallowed up the long, gray ribbon asphalt. We're moving on to a different kind of life, she reflected. She couldn't wait to see the world, promising she would work hard, so they could buy the farm. Then she would go away to college and become a pediatrician. And Tara can study criminal law, she thought.

* * *

At five o'clock that afternoon, Rufus signed himself out of the hospital against Dr. Joseph Kramer's orders. Dr. Kramer warned him to stay one more day for further observation. He was diagnosed with a severe case of botulism. Rufus sat in the waiting room hoping someone he knew would come by the hospital, so he could catch a ride with them. A half-hour later, the door swung open and John Puntier stepped inside. Rufus looked up. His eyes were sunken in his head. Their eyes met.

"John! Is that really you?" Rufus' voice was weak.

"In the flesh," said John. They shook hands. "I heard about you in town. I came by to see how you were getting along. Who's coming to pick you up?"

"I guess you!"

John chuckled. "Well, I'll be happy to drive you home, if that's what you want."

Rufus stood slowly. "I'd like that."

"Well, okay," John said, and then opened the door. He motioned for Rufus to go ahead. Rufus stepped out of the hospital into the late afternoon sunshine. John walked out behind him.

"The car is parked over there," John told him, pointing toward his vehicle. "So what happened to you, man? You look like death. You sure you ought to go home?" Rufus didn't answer, because he was not in the mood for conversation. He thought he'd feel better once he was off his feet.

"You know that white guy who brought you to the hospital, cussed you out like a dog. I was at the gas pump, when the tow truck pulled up with his cattle truck hooked up behind it. Seems he broke an axle trying to get back out there to your place. You really trust that white man to take only what he was paying you for?"

Rufus grunted. Hell no. He didn't trust Travis McGee! Travis McGee hadn't even paid him. But he trusted Tara would've taken care of business properly.

John walked with him around to the passenger side. He opened the door. Rufus got in the car. John closed the door, and rounded the hood to the driver's side. He pulled out of the parking lot and drove in the direction of Rufus' house.

"Sorry about your mother," Rufus said. "She was eighty-nine, wasn't she?"

"Thanks. Yeah. She had a full life." The conversation lapsed.

"I'm surprised you would come by to see me after what I did to you," Rufus announced.

John looked at him slightly grinning. "Well, Rufus, I'm a forgiving man. I later understood that what you did worked for Charlotte's benefit, as well as mine's. I have no regrets. I'm just sorry for Maebelle. But I tried to warn her about you. I heard Charlotte is happily married to a professor." Ha! Ha! Ha! "She has a few more kids, too!" He gave Rufus a sidelong glance, noticing that Rufus' jaws were rigid.

Rufus changed the subject.

"Nice car. I've been thinking about buying a Buick. And I see you got a little gray in your hair, too. You look good, though. The North suits you. How's Clarence and Claire, by the way?"

John glanced at Rufus. "They're fine. Clarence and I own a liquor store together. Yes, we're doing fine for ourselves."

Rufus didn't see a ring on John's finger. "Still not married, huh?"

John chuckled. "Still haven't found the right woman."

He changed the subject.

"I hear you and Maebelle got a real plantation now. By the way, how's she?" John was prying. He knew very well how Maebelle was faring. Hailey had told him everything. He glanced at Rufus, waiting for a response, but Rufus kept his head turned. He knew Hailey had talked about him like a dog to John. He didn't answer.

John continued. "The word in town is you're aping the slave masters. I heard you got five or six houses filled with your own litter." Rufus felt agitated and kept on looking out the window. If he knew John would start giving him the low down, he would've waited around for someone else to drive him home.

A *sonofabitch!* John thought to himself. You can't even look at me when I'm talking to you. The things Hailey told him at the funeral about Rufus had sounded incredulous, but now he knew she hadn't been exaggerating. He guessed Maebelle would be shocked to see him. He also bet she wished a thousand times she had listened to him. The conversation remained one-sided, so John quit talking.

* * *

An hour later, John pulled into the yard. Rufus' strange gaze caught his eye. He saw Rufus gaping at the house, so he followed his line of vision. Two gleaming black dogs stood in the doorway. John chuckled. They looked funny to him, standing in the doorway, especially in the rural countryside.

"So you've become such a big-shot you're lettin' the dogs have full reign of the house like the city folks, huh?"

Rufus snapped his head, glaring at John with penetrating eyes. John's laugh quickly faded.

"Big-shot my ass!" Rufus growled. He opened the door and climbed out of the car, and shut the door with an ineffectual click.

John went over to the passenger side of his car. Rufus looked at him with aggravation. "I'm only gone— not even a full day and the damn house goes to the dogs! What the hell is wrong with Maebelle?" John said nothing. But he sensed the house was deserted. The dogs looked too comfortable.

"C'mon man," Rufus said. "Help me get up these steps."

John lifted his right arm, and Rufus slipped his hand inside.

The dogs came down the steps as quickly as they made their way up the steps. Rufus glared angrily at the animals. Ordinarily, he would've given them a strong, swift kick in the rump, but he was too weak. His face was enshrouded in grief.

They entered the house. "Maebelle!" he called. He stopped abruptly and stared curiously at a pair of unrecognizable men's boxers lying on the floor. He kicked them to the side and turned slightly and looked at John. "What the hell is going on!" he snarled.

"I don't think anybody is home, man." John said. His voice was concerned.

Rufus became irritated. "What kind of nonsense is that!" he retorted, as he held on to John's arm, walking through the living room, through the dining room, and into the kitchen. They stopped abruptly. Rufus staggered, and gaped at John, then at the rifle lying on the floor.

The dogs had raided the pantry. Flour, sugar, and breadcrumbs littered the floor.

John refrained from commenting, until he saw more. He stooped and picked up the rifle, sniffed the barrel, and sighed at Rufus with relief. "It hasn't been fired," he said, placing the rifle on the table. So far, there was no sign of a struggle. The dogs had licked up the puddle of blood. Rufus wondered who'd taken his rifle from the gun rack.

John peered at Rufus. "I told you, man. They done left your ass! It's just you and these dogs now."

Dread fell upon Rufus. Not commenting, he felt John was right. Rufus's face bore torment. He'd wondered all along how the meat could've contained botulism. It was no accident, he silently concluded.

As John helped him approach the window, he drew the curtain, and stared out at Lynn's house. His heart sank when he saw her front door standing wide open, and a chicken walk inside. His throat ached. He turned around, bumping into John, as if John was invisible. Without saying a word, Rufus went to look inside his bedroom. He couldn't quite explain it, but he felt he was set up to lose.

John followed on his heels. Rufus turned and looked at John. "Pull the bed back for me, will you?" John gave him a peculiar look. He couldn't imagine why he needed him to move the bed, when he could've easily reached under it and gotten whatever it was he needed.

John grabbed the footboard and slid the bed nearly three feet across the floor. They both stared at the small rug on the floor. John watched curiously as Rufus slowly got down on one knee, rolled back the rug, removed the floorboard, and lifted the lid off the churn. Rufus' heart skipped a beat. He nearly tumbled backward. The churn that once protected his valued treasures was nothing more than a sad reminder of what he'd lost. All his money was gone. The letters he'd kept as souvenirs were gone—letters from Jake Junior to Jennifer, and a single letter from Leslie to Maebelle. John watched the blood drain from Rufus' face. He wondered what had been in the churn that had knocked him for a loop. He decided to ask about it.

"Well, what is it, man? What's wrong?" Rufus, still startled, said nothing. Fear and rage shot through his body like firecrackers. He stood slowly—unable to speak.

"You treated them like animals," John remarked. "I'm not at all surprised."

Rufus shot him a razor-sharp glare. Moving slowly, he jabbed John with his right elbow. "Get out of my way with that bullshit talk. What do you know? I never mistreated anybody. You hear me!" he snapped.

John backed out of his way, glaring at Rufus, while shaking his head in disbelief. It galled him that Rufus could stand in front of his face, proclaiming he hadn't abused his family. If he held his tongue any longer, he'd explode.

"Man, quit lying! You stuck your rod in all those girls—from the oldest to the youngest. You've played doctor, and people in town talk about your ass like a dog. You forget I know you like a book. You even prostituted one of them. How you got away with this shit for all these years beats the hell out of me! You must've paid these white folks a whole lot of money for them to sit back and let you do this shit. I mean I know they don't give a shit about us. But this, man—what you've done, man, would make the devil lift his head and take a serious look at you."

Rufus' lips tightened. He swung his shoulder around and glared at John. "Damn you!" he shouted. "That's the way I was raised! The women did it to me! They trained me... So, what if I happen to love what's under women's dresses. I took care of them, didn't I? Now get the hell out of my house! I'll get them back. You'll see. Ain't nobody ever out-smarted me and got away with it."

John's hair stood up on the back of his neck. He looked at Rufus scornfully. "You're one crazy bastard!" Pivoting, John stormed toward the front door.

"Wait!" Rufus called. "Wait."

John stopped abruptly, his face twitching, as he turned around slowly. He could barely look at this demonic man standing before him.

"Help me down the steps. Please. I need to take a look around." He moved toward John.

"Sure!" John replied. "Why not! When you find out all the houses are empty, then what?"

Rufus caught him in the crook of his arm.

"I didn't do one wrong thing to them," he remarked.

John sucked his teeth.

"I'm gon find my family! You hear me!"

John chuckled.

"You really think so? Hmm. I heard two of your girls are geniuses. If that's true, I doubt you'll ever see them again."

Rufus stared at John, wanting to put a hard fist in John's mouth, to shut him up. He didn't need to hear John's doomsday talk.

John continued. "You're lucky one of those geniuses didn't kill your ass. What did the doctor say was wrong with you, anyhow?" Rufus didn't answer.

"Don't answer," John said. "Word is already out on the streets. I just wanted to hear it from you. Somebody made it convenient to give you a dose of botulism. That stuff can be deadly, you know. I bet it was no accident what happened to you." Rufus said nothing. He wished John would shut his big mouth. He needed to think!

They reached the bottom steps, and Rufus' mind was spinning. He was starting to remember. Although his memory was a bit fuzzy, he could swear he'd heard Tara's voice conspiring against him. He heard her swearing at him before he passed out. At first, he thought he'd dreamt it. But now he knew better. He started shaking.

"What's the matter?" John asked, with concern.

"Nothing." Rufus replied, in a low voice. "You--you can go now."

John studied Rufus for a long moment, and then moved away. He walked toward his car shaking his head. He climbed behind the wheel, and reached over and closed the passenger door, and then turned on the engine. He told himself: "That Negro is stone crazy. Shit! I never knew just how crazy he was!" John sped away.

* * *

At dusk Rufus was still checking inside the houses, as though he'd missed some small details that would've given him a lead. He chased the dogs out of the houses and locked the doors. Suddenly, he saw the truck he used to haul the cattle to market was gone—he had missed that piece of evidence earlier—now he knew how they had left. If the police pulled them over for not having a driver's license, he knew he'd hear about it. But that was small comfort, because he wanted his family back immediately. Finally, he stood in the yard screaming, and kicking his weak booted foot into the earth.

"Tara! I know you did this!" he cried. "You took all my money! Ripped apart my dream!" He became overwhelmed with loneliness at the loss of his family. He turned, looking round. "Tara! I should've gone ahead and sired your ass! I'll get you for this! Tara!" His echo went out into the thick woods like a boomerang— "Taararraa...!"

* * *

At eight o'clock Tara crossed the county line into Tildarose, Tennessee, carrying her precious human cargo to freedom. A few yards back, she reached inside her shirt pocket to find the pack of birth control pills and tossed them out the window, severing herself as much as she could, from her ugly past.

She honked the horn to let her family know they had just about reached their destination, with only a few miles to go.

Their jubilant cries of freedom rang out into the night, waking up Maebelle. The boys had untied her earlier, as she was sleeping peacefully. She bolted upward startled, flailing her arms in utter panic. "Oh, God! It's Rufus!" she cried. "It wasn't me! I didn't do it!" She scrambled to her feet and tried to run.

"Y'all grab her!" Yvonne cried. "She gon run out of this truck and kill her foolish self!"

"Oh, shit!" Zeke cried, scrambling to get up. He grabbed Maebelle's arm. "Help me, man!" he said to Elliott.

Elliot grabbed her other arm and helped pull her down on the mattress.

"It's okay, Mama," said Rudi, patting her on the shoulder. "We were just cheering. We're in Tildarose, Tennessee, Mama." Just when they thought they'd gotten through to her, she passed out.

Tara brought out her surprise. "Here, Mama," she said, reaching across Nora. She gave Jennifer the bag of money.

Jennifer took it and put it on her lap, as she would any bag someone had given her to hold.

"I believe there's enough money in there for us to buy the farm, plus pay for college for me and Nora." Tara said.

Nora sat up, with her mouth agape. She was thrilled and taken aback.

Jennifer screamed with excitement. "There's money in here?" she cried incredulously.

"There might be enough money for us to live on for years to come."

Even though Nora couldn't really see Tara's face because it was too dark, she looked at her in stunned surprise. "Where did you...? Why didn't you tell me?"

"I found it by accident," Tara told her. "That low-down dog had cut a hole in the floor under his bed. It was inside a churn. I wanted to surprise you, Mama. There're some letters in there, too."

Jennifer remained puzzled for a long moment. "Letters! From whom?" Then it dawned on her that the letters Tara mentioned had to be from either her father or her brothers, or both. "Jake Junior! They're from Jake Junior!" Tears swelled in her eyes. "He'd sworn up and down that he would always write to me." Her tears fell profusely. "Were they from Jake Junior?" she asked.

"Yes ma'am," Tara replied.

"Who's Jake Junior? Your boy friend?" Nora asked, perplexed.

Jennifer sniffled. "No, honey. He's my brother—mine, Jinni, Lynn, and Jackie. We have two older brothers. We never heard from them after they left to live with Daddy. Us girls thought it was strange, because Jake promised me, especially, that he'd write to find out how we were getting along. He didn't want Mama to marry Rufus. I thought they had abandoned us," she said with a strangled cry. "Oh, my God, my God! I will find my Daddy and my brothers when we get settled. Maybe Jinni will return to being normal once she sees them!"

"Is Leslie Wills Big Momma's sister?" Tara asked, "because there's a letter in there from her to Big Momma." Jennifer sighed throughout momentous silence. She felt too aroused to answer Tara. She thought it was strange the way her present was meeting her past: Leslie had been in Maebelle's life until she got herself into her mess. And here she was again, when mother and family were overcoming their ordeal.

"Well, in any case," Tara said, "this nightmare is over. We're free! Forever!"

"Forever!" Nora said, raising a triumphant fist. But later on she began to wonder if she and her family would ever really and truly be free, given their emotional scars.

With her eyes focused on the road, Tara drove faster, knowing she had assumed control over her destiny. For the first time it felt like her life had meaning. Now she and Nora could pursue their dreams.

A hundred miles back home—in the darkness of the night—Rufus arose out of bed. He wished he were well enough to go looking for his family. He thought by now that the sheriff—or anyone for that matter—would have contacted him with news of their escape, but no one had. The house was as silent as death. He thought that maybe the town had conspired against him. He fantasized getting his family back, without admitting how cruel he had been to his entire Poygoode family—be it Maebelle or Charlotte.

Outside in the yard, he kicked his weak, booted foot into the damp earth, wailing loudly, calling Tara's name. And the rest of his family members: "Nora, Mae-- Maebelle, Adie, Jennifer, Yvonne, Yvette, Elliott, Adam, Rudi, Jinni, Troy, Hattie, Rog-Roger, Jinni. O, Jinni!" His voice became too weak to call the rest of his family members. After awhile, he climbed the steps slowly and went in the house.

Rufus was exhausted and quite lonely when he finally separated his emotional pain from his physical pain. "One day," he told himself, "one day I'll find them.

THE END

Nancy Weaver

About the Author

Nancy Weaver is new on the literary scene. She is a native of Marks, Mississippi and also an alumni of State University New York Empire State College.

Nancy is currently at work on her second and third novel. She resides in New York with her husband.

Nancy Weaver

In Her Presence: A Husband's Dirty Secret
ORDER FORM

Time & Chance Publishing™
P.O. Box 488 NY, NY 10116
www.TimeandChancePublishing.com

Please send me _____ copies of *In Her Presence: A Husband's Dirty Secret*
I am enclosing a Money Order ☐ or Check ☐ totaling $19.95 for each book ($15.95 plus $4 shipping, and $2.00 for each additional copy in the same order). *New York residents (i.e., if we are shipping to a New York address) please include $1.38 sales tax per book.)* **Canada:** Money Order ☐ or Check ☐ total cost $25.50 for each book ($21.50, plus $4 shipping, and $2.00 for each additional copy of the same order)

Please allow two weeks for delivery. Address e-mail inquiries and replies to tandcpublishing@yahoo.com.

Name		
Address		
City	ST	Zip
Phone		
E-Mail		

For a personalized copy, please fill in legibly the person(s) name and who will be receiving *In Her Presence: A Husband's Dirty Secret*.

Autograph to:
Autograph to:
Autograph to:

GIFT ORDERS. If you would like this order or part of it sent to a name and address other than your own, please fill in and check ☐ item to be sent as gifts.

Name_____
Address_____
City_____ST_____ ZIP _____

BM